# Music from Both Sides of the Moon

ROBERT H. GARRETT

Charleston, SC
www.PalmettoPublishing.com

*Music from Both Sides of the Moon*
Copyright © 2021 by Robert H. Garrett

First Edition

ISBN: 978-1-68515-586-5

*for caroline*

# Contents

# Prologue

*While the pockmarked and frigid dark side of the moon portrays wickedness and desolation, even the slightest sliver of a fingernail clipping of the bright side inspires hope, promise and forgiveness for us all. That's what this book is all about.*

*Robert Garrett*

# Chapter 1
## Hap O'Shea
## The Mission

Hap O'Shea turned off the headlights, killed the engine of his Volkswagen van and coasted silently into the parking lot of Pine Elementary School. It was just after midnight and a thick, mushy marine layer had squatted down onto the low-lying coastal areas of Carlsbad, California. Perfect conditions for his mission.

An unexpected speed bump caused the metal tank in the back of the van to slam against the side panel shattering the eerie quiet.

Hap cursed under his breath.

For a moment he thought about scrubbing the mission. This was dumb, really dumb and, not to mention, against the law. He could lose his job and what did he really have to gain? He pressed his forehead the steering wheel, closed his eyes and took a deep breath.

Gradually his resolve returned. The mission was vital. A life was at stake. Maybe more. He vowed to be more careful, and slowly continued through the parking lot. He parked behind a dumpster on the side of the school so that his van could not be seen from the street.

Hap crawled into the back, knelt down and carefully opened the valve on the tank of helium. If there was a leak, in these close quarters, a spark might ignite an explosion or, at the very least, his voice may never be the same.

He reached into his jacket and pulled out a balloon. He slipped it over the nozzle of the tank and bent it slightly. In an instant, the balloon inflated and exploded in Hap's face. The sound was deafening inside the van. Hap was stunned, fully anticipating the arrival of SWAT teams, armored personnel carriers and helicopters with searchlights hovering overhead.

Hap peeked out the open window. A neighborhood dog gave a halfhearted yip but no lights, no sirens and no puka-puka-puka-pukas from hovering helicopter rotor blades.

After several deep breaths, Hap returned to his mission. He filled six balloons, tied them off and attached each one to three-feet of green-colored string. He gathered them up and carefully climbed out of the van.

He was dressed in Navy SEAL black with his face painted combat green. A stocking cap topped off, but barely contained, an ornery riot of red hair screaming to be set free. He grabbed his balloons and crept through the school toward the garden.

**Legal Name:** Hap E. Tim O'Shea
**Profession:** Elementary School Music Teacher, Musician

'Hap' was neither a nickname nor an abbreviated version of a more lengthy or respectable forename. Hap was named by his mother who, incidentally, had never read much of Mark Twain and therefore had no knowledge of Huckleberry Finn's dastardly, drunken, son-of-a-bitch father whom the full-tongued Mr. Clemens had also named Hap. The 'E. Tim' had come from a dear friend of his father's who'd been bitten on the head by a cottonmouth water moccasin as an infant.

Hap's mother had served as a nurse during World War II and was taken prisoner by the Japanese on the island of Corregidor. Just as Allied forces were in the process of retaking the tiny Philippine Island known as 'The Rock', her captors sliced off part of her tongue with a bayonet so, supposedly, she wouldn't be able retell the atrocities she had witnessed as their captive.

4

Multi-syllabic names were impossible to pronounce for a person with the barest stump of a tongue. "Hap" was a name his mother could comfortably coo to her baby in her arms. Later on, "Hap" was a convenient bark she could crack like a whip to freeze a 10-year-old boy and stop him from walking on a just-waxed, linoleum kitchen floor.

Technically, Hap O'Shea wasn't a full-time teacher. Officially, he was an "adjunct" member of the faculty, a part-time music teacher hired out of guilt by the school district after severe budget cuts had eliminated all non-academic curricula. He taught music appreciation to the second through fifth graders at Pine Elementary on Tuesdays and Thursdays.

Hap's status as a part-time teacher of a non-academic subject didn't carry much weight around the school. Complaints from other teachers about the loud noise from the music room disturbing their classes had resulted in several reprimands from the school principal. Plus, his extensive array of brightly colored Hawaiian shirts that he chose to wear, instead of the preferred dress shirt and tie worn by other male teachers, all served to alienate him from other members of the faculty.

More than a statement of protest against conventional dress, Hap's collection of shirts was simply a naive expression of a blatant absence of taste made worse by his Swedish/Irish, ruddy-white complexion. His appearance was topped off by a rooster tail of attention-deficit red hair that made him appear to look like a beach ball fallen errantly into the upper branches of a tropical bouquet.

Although he had not earned any degree of camaraderie or respect from his colleagues at Pine Elementary, Hap had, as he had done when he was a student in elementary school, charmed all the ladies that worked in the cafeteria.

Along with most of his mother's tongue and her ability to speak clearly, the Japanese soldier had removed all of her taste buds along with her accompanying sense of sweet, sour, spicy and salty. As a student in elementary school, while most of young Hap's friends complained about the food, compared to some of the dishes his mom prepared, the food in the cafeteria was gourmet cuisine to Hap. He discovered that a polite greeting and a compliment to the cafeteria ladies usually brought rewards such as an extra helping of spaghetti or a larger slice of cake.

Hap's closest friend at Pine was the school's janitor, Eduardo Machado. Mr. Machado had intimidated the entire administration, all of the teachers, and most of the students so that he could go about his business as he pleased. Although fearsome to most, Eduardo Machado was an icon to the Hispanic kids in the school. A wink or a friendly greeting from the highly respected Mr. Machado brought a needed dose of self-esteem to those kids caught in the barbed wire of the language barriers.

Hap much preferred the janitor's room, which was off-limits to almost everyone, over the teacher's lounge during recess and lunch breaks. Eduardo made dark, thick, 'janitor coffee' and his wife usually sent him off to work with a sack full of homemade baked goods. Hap would have taught for free in exchange for a six-pack of Mrs. Machado's cinnamon rolls. In addition to the rich incense of coffee and pastries, the janitor's room gave off a tangy, sanitary bouquet of just-buffed hallway. A recess period spent in Mr. Machado's room always left Hap with a full stomach and squeaky-clean sinuses.

On a Monday, halfway through the school year, Hap wandered down to Eduardo's room to pass the afternoon recess period and continue their earlier discussion on the San Diego Padres' chances of making the playoffs. The janitor's door was locked so Hap grabbed a copy of Guitar Player Magazine out of his backpack and went to the Teacher's Lounge to spend his 15-minute break between classes.

While studying the tablature of Jimmy Page's famous lead in Led Zeppelin's "Rock and Roll", Hap happened to overhear a telephone conversation between Pine's meanest teacher, Mrs. Hattie Armstrong, and apparently the mother of one of her students. Hap had a teacher much like Mrs. Armstrong in fifth grade—cranky, strict, impatient and the reason school boards created mandatory retirement.

"We've had this conversation about your daughter before, Mrs. Carolina," Armstrong hissed in her well-practiced condescending tone. "Sarah has disturbed the class a number of times in the past and it's painfully obvious, both from her borderline test scores and her disruptive and defiant behavior in the classroom, that she cannot keep up to speed nor stay on track with the rest of the students in her class."

Hap felt the icy fingers of a past memory tighten around his brain. He had heard those same words twenty-two years earlier when he had eavesdropped on a telephone conversation between his fifth-grade teacher, Miss McGlashen, and his mother in which his teacher had determinedly tried to convince Hap's mother to withdraw her son from public school and enroll him in a more disciplined academic situation like military school.

Fortunately, Hap's father was not at home and so his teacher spoke to his mother. Exasperated at not being able to understand what his mother was saying and unaware of her lingual incapacity, Miss McGlashen finally hung up, firmly convinced that Hap was living with a drunk of a mother who was apparently soused in the early afternoon.

Following that phone call, his teacher seemed to ease up on Hap for the rest of the year, more so out of pity rather than any academic or good citizenship turnaround on Hap's part.

Hap O'Shea was begrudgingly promoted to the sixth grade. Miss McGlashen's words to him on the last day of school were delivered on the playground to the effect that with his lack of respect, disobedient behavior, learning disabilities and alcoholic mother, Hap's life was going to be a difficult uphill climb and that he should not aspire to the same goals as the other children in his grade.

Once again, Hap found himself eavesdropping on a student evaluation given by a malicious, broken-down, sour-tempered teacher.

"Perhaps you were aware of our gardening section last week?" Mrs. Armstrong continued.

"No? Well, I asked all my students to bring in a packet of seeds. You know, like carrots, peas, beets, radishes, and that we were going to plant them in the school garden. Do you know what your daughter brought to plant in our garden? She brought a packet of balloons. She said she wanted to grow balloons! Hah! She even told some of the students that she was going to have a balloon farm someday."

Hap snickered behind his magazine and continued to listen to the rest of the one-sided conversation.

"I have been teaching at Pine Elementary School for twenty-seven years and have dealt with hundreds and hundreds of children. However, I don't have the skills nor the patience necessary to deal with a child with, uh, special needs like Sarah. It's my obligation to the school district, my fellow teachers and the other children in my class to emphatically advise you to search for an alternative path for Sarah's educational development. Of course, I have no choice other than to report this incident to my principal, Mr. Bender. He, in turn, may wish to talk to you directly regarding Sarah's behavior but I wanted to speak to you first. I am very sorry but I have to get back to my class. Good day, Mrs. Carolina."

Mrs. Armstrong hung up the phone and stalked out of the lounge fluffing her Brillo Pad coif of tightly permed, blue/gray hair. Even before the door closed behind her, she grabbed the whistle from her lanyard and blew three, sharp warning shots.

"No running!" she yelled at a group of boys playing tag.

The class bell rang but Hap remained in his chair.

Five classes totaling nearly 75 students visited Hap's class twice a week, so remembering every student's name was difficult but Hap found the name, Sarah Carolina, vaguely familiar. Then it came to him. Sarah was the girl who was standing on the keyboard of the piano.

The only thing remotely relating to music in the Music Appreciation Room, prior to Hap's arrival with his own personal collection of percussive and musical instruments, was an old, beat up, badly-tuned, upright piano. The fingerboard cover and top had been removed, apparently to avoid smashed fingers.

The piano was generally ignored by his students after a few rounds of 'Chopsticks' or the 'Black Key Knuckle Sonata in F sharp' in favor of the tambourines, maracas, conga drums, djembe drums, claves, timbales, bongos, tom toms, cowbells, cymbals, kazoos, and other loud and obnoxious musical weaponry that Hap had brought into the classroom.

Hap's lesson plan involved his playing a CD of what he thought was an important piece of music, whether it be classical, blues or rock and roll, and then allowing the children to accompany the music with their instrument of choice.

Hap admitted to himself that his class was more music "depreciation" than "appreciation" but at least the kids had some fun for 50-minutes.

He remembered the day he met Sarah Carolina. His boom box was blasting out the William Tell Overture and Hap was challenging the roomful of fourth graders to grab an instrument and play along with the Philadelphia Philharmonic Orchestra. At first the students were shy and tentative but at Hap's enthusiastic urging, the room was soon filled with a cacophony of percussion, none of which sought to find any syncopation with the famous overture. His students were definitely not captives to Rossini's tempo nor musical structure.

Despite the absence of any musical genius among the students, Hap directed his orchestra with the same unconditional passion that the children played their instruments. Waving his conducting baton wildly in the air, Hap's goal was to whip them into a frenzy similar to a tribal ritual before battle, and then send them off to their math class.

Often swept up in the music himself, minor classroom infractions like drumstick fencing or an occasional tambourine to the back of a student's head, went unnoticed but he remembered Sarah Carolina.

One day after class, Hap noticed one of his students playing a single note on the keyboard over and over and peering intently into the body of the upright piano.

Hap walked over and stuck his head into the piano and spoke in a baritone voice that reverberated in the chamber.

"Helloooo. Whooo are youuuu?"

"Sarah with an H, Twain, like the author, Carolina like the states" she answered, her head still peering down at the sounding board and steadily tapping on an out of tune key.

"What are you dooooing, Sarah with an H, Twain like the author and Carolina like the state?" Hap echoed in return.

"States. There are two of them," she replied curtly.

"Really?"

She gave him a sideways look and a frown.

"Did you know that there's a little wooden thing down there that bangs against a wire when I tap on this? That's what makes the sound?" she asked.

Hap ended up spending five minutes answering a string of question and explaining about the bridges attached to the soundboard and the vibrations in the air that make each note. Every one of his answers fielded a barrage of more questions from Sarah Carolina. Being a guitar player, this curious fifth-grader quickly exposed his limited knowledge of the workings of the piano.

Slumped in a corner chair in the Teacher's Lounge, still choking on the caustic exhaust fumes from Mrs. Armstrong's conversation with Sarah's mother, Hap could see where Sarah's relentless determination and curiosity could challenge and threaten an authoritarian teacher like Armstrong.

And so, it was for all the Sarahs and Haps, whose spirit had been suffocated by teachers like Armstrong and McGlashen, that brought Hap O'Shea to Pine Elementary School's garden just past midnight.

Hap's flashlight illuminated a section of furrows in the garden with 3" x 5" cards stapled to wooden stakes. The cards were labeled with the name of the student and the type of seeds planted. Delicate young sprouts eagerly pushed their way out of the rich, loamy soil.

He spotted a stretch of barren furrow and began to plant his balloons. His plan was to dig holes, tie the loose ends of the balloon string to a rock (which he had brought in his backpack), drop the rock into the hole and then fill in the hole with dirt. He carefully tamped the soil as he filled each hole.

When he was finished, Hap stood back and smiled at the neat row of colorful balloons rising on their green string stems and gently swaying in the vaporous currents of the night air. Careful to make sure he left no sign of his presence, Hap covered his tracks with his hand trowel.

Before he left the garden, Hap turned back and smiled again, this time for himself and Sarah — this time with a mischievous curl at the corner of his mouth.

Hap wasn't fired for the 'Balloon Incident'. Ironically, he was never a suspect in the case. In a haystack of minor offenses, the final straw resulting in his termination may have been the 'Marching Band Incident'.

It was a beautiful spring day and Hap thought that his class should get out of the classroom for some fresh air and a little exercise.

"Grab your instruments and line up outside. We're going to form a marching band!" Hap announced enthusiastically.

He aligned them in formation, counted off the cadence, got them marching in place and yelled, "Forward march!"

The plan was to march quietly through the classroom corridors and onto the playing field where they would strike up their instruments and perform intricate maneuvers as though they were a halftime show at a football game.

As usual, there was just one tiny flaw in Hap's plan. He forgot to tell the students to wait until they got to the field before they began playing their instruments.

With classes in session, the band spontaneously kicked off their show on the one-count following the "Forward march!"

Hap tried desperately to quiet them but his students were having too much fun banging their instruments and counting the cadence out loud.

Students jumped out from their desks and pressed their faces against the classroom windows at the racket outside which, realizing they now had an audience, encouraged the marching band to play even louder. Classroom doors flung open and teachers yelled at the band to be quiet but their voices went unheard above the din.

Hap tried to apologize to the teachers as the band passed by but he had a helpless feeling that this might get him in some real trouble with the principal.

It didn't take the administration very long to figure out a way to get rid of Hap O'Shea. His part-time, adjunct status, along with his non-academic curricula, cut like a razor through the school district's red tape that normally was required to relieve a teacher of their duties. It wasn't in Hap's make-up to protest or threaten the school board with legal action so he resigned quietly.

"Wow, just when I thought I was at the top of my game," Hap muttered to the principal as he signed the required paper work.

"I don't know about anybody else here in this school," Mr. Machado said sadly as he helped Hap load his collection of instruments into boxes. "But I know me and the kids are going to miss you."

Hap and the janitor hugged one another.

"Would it be all right if I stopped by once in a while for your wife's cinnamon rolls?"

Mr. Machado smiled. "Anytime, Hap O'Shea. Anytime."

The instruments filled up six, large boxes. Hap was balancing three of the awkwardly stacked boxes on the way to his van when he noticed Sarah Carolina sitting dejectedly on a bench outside the administration office.

"Hi, Sarah with an H, Twain, like the author, and Carolina like the states. What are you still doing here at school?"

"I'm waiting for my ..."

(To be continued...)

# Chapter 2
## Nathan O'Shea
## Guitar Player

NATHAN O'SHEA WAS BORN IN 1922 IN BALLARD, MISSISSIPPI, a small town near the Pearl River. He was born with congenital scoliosis, an accentuated lateral curvature of the spine which left him with an odd posture and a slight lean to the left. As a child, the condition prevented Nathan from running and roughnecking with other boys his age. When he tried to participate in strenuous activities, his back muscles would spasm and he'd be forced to spend days in his bed, laying on a hot water bottle under his lower back with bags of sand tied to his ankles hanging off the end of the bed. When Nathan was twelve, his father was selected by the Ballard First Baptist Church of God to meet with Mr. Ednus Brooke, General Manager of Hadley's for Music in Jackson to discuss terms for the church's purchase of a new organ. Since it was a Saturday, Nathan was allowed to accompany his father on this prestigious expedition.

Hadley's was the largest music store in the state of Mississippi, one of three Hadley's for Music located in the South. The other Hadley's were located in New Orleans and Atlanta. The Hadley's for Music in Jackson was comprised of two floors in a warehouse-like building across from the state capitol. The store was crammed with everything imaginable that had to do with music from instruments to sheet music to lessons. There were even soundproof booths where customers could listen to 78 rpm records.

Nathan's father was the assistant purchasing manager at the feed mill and had been delegated by the elders of the church to get the very best organ at a rock-bottom price. If word ever got out that the Methodists had out-bargained the Baptists, Nathan's father's status in the church and, very possibly, his chances for a heavenly hereafter, would both be greatly diminished.

While his father waited nervously outside Ednus Brooke's office, perspiring through both his undershirt and his Sunday dress shirt, Nathan wandered through the music store. Not only was each section of the store completely different but each area had its' own unique smell. The band instrument section left a sharp metallic taste in Nathan's nostrils. The sheet music section smelled a lot like the library. The record-listening booths smelled of cigarettes, Black Jack gum, perfume and perspiration.

But it was the intoxicating scent of the guitar department that seduced him.

Nathan walked into a large room where he was surrounded by guitars balanced delicately from hooks attached to carpeted walls. It smelled like a primeval forest filled with the rich, aromatic spices of rosewood tops, maple necks, ash bodies and mahogany bridges. The smells overpowered Nathan's senses and made him slightly dizzy.

The room's tangy fragrances wove a tale of fine craftsmanship, much the same way the scent of a kitchen tells a story about its cook. It was as heady as the vapor from the first rain drops falling on a hot cement sidewalk. Mesmerized, Nathan simply stared at the array of instruments, breathing in their provocative aromas.

In the 1930's, businesses in Jackson, Mississippi ardently enforced the strict codes of racial segregation. However, Ednus Brooke made it very clear to the citizens of Jackson that, although he agreed that it wasn't proper for whites and coloreds to eat in the same restaurant or drink from the same water fountain, there was no color line when it came to music.

14

For years, Hadley's for Music had grown profitable from sales of organs and pianos to the Negro churches throughout the state. Hadley's accepted credit and backed every sale with a five-year guarantee and two free tunings by the state of Mississippi's most highly acclaimed piano tuner, Augustus Magee, an elderly black man who had been blind since the day he was born. Augustus had an ear so fine that he could tell you the note a passing mosquito was humming.

Mr. Hadley himself would occasionally travel up from his home in Baton Rouge and pay a visit to the black preachers whose congregations had purchased an instrument from one of his stores. He wanted to make sure that they were happy with their organ or piano and that they were treated with dignity and respect when they made their purchase. He also made sure that their payments were being made on time.

Nathan was standing hypnotized in the guitar room when a huge black man in overalls and dusty work boots walked into the room. He reached up and pulled down one of the guitars from the wall.

Nathan's first thought was that from the looks of him, this man should not have been in there and he certainly shouldn't be reaching out and grabbing one of those new, shiny guitars off the wall. Nathan looked towards the entrance of the room to see if there was an employee of the store coming to chase the man out. Nathan was worried that he'd get chased out, too, because maybe he wasn't supposed to be there either.

The man sat down, put the guitar in his lap and in an instant the room was filled with the most soothing sounds Nathan had ever heard. The sounds that came out from wherever they were coming out of were unlike any music he had ever heard. The music that man was playing touched something deep inside of Nathan.

Nathan tiptoed out from where he was standing to get a closer look at the man to try and see what he was doing. That same man who, a few seconds earlier, had appeared out of place had been magically transformed in Nathan's eyes. He was no longer poorly dressed, he was no longer a bear of a man, and he was no longer of any skin color. None of that mattered the least bit in the light of the music that was coming out of that guitar.

Nathan thought of the way he himself looked whenever he'd catch a quick glimpse of his reflection in a store window. His body didn't look the same as the other boys. No matter how hard he tried to stand up straight, he was always a little off-kilter.

Nathan wondered to himself that if he could make music like that man, maybe he would be magically transformed in the eyes of other people.

"You play, son?" the man asked in a soft, deep voice that sounded a whole lot like the music he was playing on the guitar.

Startled at being discovered, Nathan answered hesitantly.

"Uh, no, sir, but I'd sure like to know how you do it."

"Ain't much to it. Here, sit down on that chair over there."

The man got up and walked toward Nathan. Nathan backed up without taking his eyes off the guitar, which looked small in the man's huge arms, and stumbled backward into a wooden chair.

The man handed Nathan the guitar. Both the instrument and the man looked much bigger up close.

"Here, set this on your leg like this," the man said gently and placed the guitar in Nathan's lap.

Nathan could feel the cool smoothness of the back of the guitar through his shirt.

"Put your right arm over the body here and your left hand over here on the neck."

The man took Nathan's small fingers in his huge hands and placed them over the strings on top of the fret board. Nathan's right hand could barely reach the strings.

"Now take your pointer finger and put it here, put this finger up here and this finger way up here. Now press down on the strings real hard with the tips of your fingers 'til the strings touch the wood."

Nathan's fingers stung as he squeezed the metal strings downward.

"That's good. Now take this…" the man handed Nathan his guitar pick. "Now let it fall across the strings."

16

Nathan tentatively ran the pick across the strings. With a buzz here and there, he strummed his first E chord.

"Now keep your fingers where they are and rest your ear against the top."

Nathan placed the side of his head against the smooth curvature of the guitar's body as though eavesdropping on what was going on inside.

"Now do it again just a little bit harder."

Nathan strummed the guitar again with his ear pressed against the body of the guitar. He had never heard anything so beautiful and powerful. It sounded like a choir of angels blended in with the rumble of thunder coming from somewhere off in the distance.

Nathan strummed the strings again. He felt the muscles in his back relax. He felt his shoulders unfold and his arms seemed to become more limber and flexible. And he felt ashamed because he could feel tears running down his cheeks and splattering on the guitar.

Nathan handed the guitar back to the man and wiped his face with the sleeve of his shirt.

"What's the matter, son?" the man asked, wiping Nathan's tears off the guitar with his handkerchief.

"Can you teach me to play the guitar, sir?"

The man smiled and ran his hand down his face, squeezing his smile into a frown.

"Well, I'm not sure folks around here would appreciate a colored man teaching a white boy anything. If you really want to learn to play, I'm sure you could find a good, white guitar teacher here at the store."

Nathan looked up at the man's kind face and then down at the guitar cradled in his arms.

"If you'll pardon me sir, I'd like to learn how to play the guitar the way you play it. Just like you. Not somebody else, sir."

"What's your name, son?"

"My name's Nathan, sir. Nathan O'Shea."

"I'm Ben," the man smiled and stuck out his hand. "Ben Williams, although folks mostly call me Big Ben. I'm glad to meet you, Nathan."

"Will you teach me? I get an allowance. I can pay you."

Ben laughed, "Well you do seem to have a way with it. You own a guitar?"

"No, sir. Today's the first time I've ever seen or heard one."

Well, you just might be a natural born guitar player. You sure you want me to teach you? You might have to work real hard."

Nathan stared at Ben and responded with an intensity that surprised himself.

"Sir, I've never wanted to learn anything this much in my whole life!"

"All right then, I do have a little time in the morning on the weekends. You come on over to Darktown on Saturday morning 'round ten or eleven and just ask the first colored person you see where Big Ben's house is. They'll show you the way."

From their first meeting at Hadley's and every Saturday morning thereafter, Nathan pedaled his bike over to Big Ben's house. Although Nathan had not yet been bitten by the venomous prejudice of the South, even in his innocence, he had a sense that it would be best to take the back way into Darktown for his lessons.

Even though Nathan didn't own a guitar, he was a voracious learner. He split a sapling down the middle and sanded it down to resemble the neck of a guitar. He drew six lines in ink pen down the length of the piece of wood, one for each string, and carved twelve notches crossways for the frets. He'd lie in his bed at night and practice fingering chords or playing scales that Ben had taught him with his left hand on his sapling branch.

To help develop calluses on his fingertips, Nathan carried a flat piece of granite in his pocket and would rub his fingertips against the rock.

Nathan's father worked long hours at the feed mill and his mother had all she could do with his five brothers and sisters. His disappearances on Saturday mornings were hardly noticed.

Every Saturday Nathan would pedal his bike at full speed through the woods and back trails eager to feel a real guitar in his arms and anxious to show Ben his progress from practicing all week on his sapling.

A week before Nathan's thirteenth birthday, Ben presented him with a guitar.

"I won it in a craps game Friday night. Had to make a four to get it. Good old little Joe from Kokomo," Ben said proudly. "So, if anybody asks you what kind of guitar you got, you tell 'em it's a 'Made-A-Four' and if they ask what its name is, you tell 'em, 'Little Joe.'"

The guitar was old and scratched up and the neck had a little bow to it but so did Nathan for that matter. He was speechless. It was a Stradivarius in his eyes.

"You mean you're just giving it to me, Ben?"

"It's a birthday present for the both of us. We can tune 'em up, one of us plays rhythm the other can work on his lead chops."

Nathan's exuberance disappeared into a worried expression.

"What's the matter?" Ben asked.

"Can I leave it here at your place?"

"Your momma and daddy still don't know you're coming here?"

Nathan shook his head.

"Probably for the best, Nate."

"But I practice on my sapling all the time!"

"I can tell. Boy, you're the fastest learner I've ever seen. No doubt about that. You keep on doing what you're doing and Little Joe will stay right here waiting for you."

The first year, Ben taught Nathan chord structure.

"Gimme a B flat diminished," Ben would holler out from his kitchen where he'd be making coffee. Nathan would answer with the correct chord.

"How 'bout an A ninth?"

Nathan would strum a chord.

"That ain't no A ninth"

"Sorry. Here it is."

Nathan would play a correct A ninth.

"That's an A ninth."

Ben was knowledgeable in many different styles of guitar. He taught Nathan how to 'cotton pick', a finger picking style used on a song written by Elizabeth Cotton, a left-handed guitar player who played a right-handed guitar and wrote a famous song entitled, 'Freight Train'. Ben taught Nathan how to play to a variety of different beats, tempos and styles.

He learned the complicated chord structure of jazz that was starting to sneak down to the South from New York and Chicago. Ben taught him how to tune the guitar to an open E chord and how to break a pop bottle off at the neck to use as a slide to play "bottle neck" guitar. Ben even taught him how to make flat picks out of snapping turtle shells. And every lesson contained a hearty portion of Mississippi delta blues—a three-chord progression played to a shuffle rhythm. Ben believed that the foundation of all music was the blues.

Nathan would get up early so he could practice on his split sapling before school. In class, he'd run through chord progressions with his left hand on the underside of his desk while strumming with his right hand on the side of his thigh. At night he would lie in bed imagining Ben's rhythm tracks in his head and running out lightning-quick riffs on his make-believe guitar. Nathan's progress was remarkable.

One Saturday following his lesson with Ben, Nathan stopped by Hadley's for Music on his way home and revisited the room with the brand-new guitars hanging on the wall. He inhaled the savory, rich smells and stood mesmerized by the glistening instruments. The necks on the guitars were straight, not bowed like his 'Made-A-Four'. There were no nicks or scratches on the faces and every guitar had bright new strings that glimmered against the shiny fingerboard.

There was no one else in the room so he summoned up his courage and gingerly took one of the guitars off the wall, sat down, and held it in his lap. He ran his hands over the wood, caressing the undulations of the body and running his hand up and down the polished neck. The tuning keys gleamed and turned sure and steady.

Nathan put his arm around the guitar, pressed it against his body and strummed an E chord. The room reverberated with the same rich resonance he had heard Ben create. He began to play as though in a trance. Any number of people could have come in and out of the room without Nathan even noticing. He finally had to quit when his left hand began to cramp.

Nathan's visits to Hadley's after his lesson with Ben became a part of his regular Saturday routine. No one at the store seemed to mind and it wasn't long before the word got out about this talented young guitar player. Occasionally, local musicians would drop by Hadley's on Saturdays pretending to browse through the guitars but with the intention of hearing this kid play.

Nathan hadn't the slightest idea that anyone was listening to him on those Saturdays. He was too young to know the tricks perfume could play on a man's state of mind and just a whiff of the guitar room at Hadley's sent Nathan into a meditative state. He'd carefully pull down a Gibson L-5, sit down on a wooden chair, close his eyes and begin to play. He didn't have to look at his fingers. It seemed to Nathan that all he had to do was put his hand around the neck, close his eyes and the guitar would do the rest.

Nathan's reputation as a prodigy was already well-established in Darktown. As Nathan's abilities became apparent, Ben moved their lessons from the living room to his front porch. Ben was proud of Nathan and he wanted to show off his protégé to the whole neighborhood. The two of them would sit on the steps of the porch and play a 16-barre blues progression over and over, each taking turns playing rhythm or lead. Ben would run off a lead lick and Nathan would watch his fingers intently. When it was Nathan's turn to take a lead, he'd try to duplicate Ben's moves and sometimes even throw in a couple of extra notes. Ben would give him a sideways look and come back with an even more complicated riff. It wasn't long before the line between student and teacher disappeared somewhere between the cracks of that rickety, old porch.

Ben no longer referred to their Saturdays as 'lessons'. He called it 'jammin'.

Their sessions began to attract an appreciative crowd out in front of Ben's house including other musicians. Often there would be a harmonica, spoons and a washboard backing-up Ben and Nathan. The crowd in Ben's front yard would holler out their favorite songs and Nathan would follow Ben's lead until he got a feel for the piece. Every once in a while, this skinny, young girl who always wore tight, flowery dresses and smoked hand-rolled cigarettes, would come up the steps and turn the porch into a night club stage. She could sing so pretty and soulfully that sometimes Nathan would stop playing his guitar and just listen to her.

Occasionally, Ben would take 'sick' on their lesson days. One Saturday Nathan banged on the screen door and Ben called out from his bedroom.

"Is that you, boy?"

"It's me, Nate!"

"Hey, Nate, ol' Ben's a might laid low this morning. Come on back tomorrow after church. I reckon I'll be, uh, feeling better some."

"Yea, he'll be a whole lot better tomorrow," a woman's voice sang out from the room. "A whole lot better!"

Nathan figured that Ben must have been real sick to require the services of a nurse.

Missing a Saturday lesson once or twice every couple of months was fine with Nathan. It meant he could spend a little more time in Hadley's on his way home.

Sunday lessons at Ben's meant Nathan would get to hear the sounds and rhythms that spilled out from the Pentecostal Church of Our Savior at the corner of Ben's block.

*Many years later, Nathan would become a successful studio musician in Los Angeles. He would be sought after by artists breaking out this new sound they called 'rock and roll'. Among all the available session players, Nathan seemed to have a special feel for this newborn style of music.*

*There wasn't too much new about this rock and roll music that Nathan hadn't heard a long time ago on Ben's porch coming out of that little Pentecostal church in Jackson, Mississippi.*

Ben and Nathan would sit on the front porch and play along with the old gospel spirituals that came pouring out of the open windows of the church. They'd both close their eyes, shake their heads and tap their toes to the spicy, syncopated rhythms of the tambourines along with the passionate voices of the choir and church members.

The congregation was made up predominantly of women. When the service was over and the doors flung open, the ladies, many of whom were of substantial girth and all in a highly agitated state of spiritual bliss. The ladies would tumble out of the church and into the sunlight like dyed Easter eggs spilling out of a basket—their dresses in every color and hue imaginable. They staggered down the street like a parade of sleepwalkers, still inebriated from drinking of the blood of Jesus. Some of the ladies had to be helped out of the church. Touched by the hand of the Lord, they had taken to seizures during the service. These women were barely able to walk and their eyes were rolled back into their heads as they were helped down the street chanting, "Praise Jesus! Praise Jesus!"

School was just about out for the summer when Ednus Brooke walked in on Nathan at Hadley's while he was playing one of the guitars.

"Where'd you learn to play like that, boy?" Ednus asked.

Lost in the sounds of the Gibson L-5, Nathan was startled and felt as though he had been caught doing something wrong.

"S..s..s...sorry, sir," Nathan stuttered. "I was just trying out this new Gibson. Here, I'll put it back up on the wall."

"Hold on, boy. I didn't say put it back. I asked you where you learned to play that thing so good."

"Oh...uh," Nathan stopped, aware of the racial attitudes of the town. "Uh, I just kinda picked it up I guess."

Ednus Brooke shook his head in mock amazement, "You know for a while there I thought I was listening to Big Ben Williams."

"Thank you, sir. That'd be a very nice compliment. I've heard that he's one of the best."

"Uh huh, you heard that, too. You're one of Mr. O'Shea's boys ain't you?"

"Yes, sir. My name's Nathan."

"My name's Ednus Brooke. Nice to meet you, Nathan. You know, I've been noticing you playing that Gibson every Saturday and I'm starting to worry that it's gonna turn into a one-master dog."

"A what?" Nathan asked.

"A one-master dog. You know, a dog that won't hunt for nobody but its master. That guitar just may not play as good for somebody else once it's got used to you playing it."

Nathan laughed at the dumb idea of a guitar knowing who was playing it.

"You thinking about buying this L-5?"

"Oh yes, sir. I think about buying this guitar more than a hundred times a day. But thinking about it and doing it are two different things."

"Well, maybe we could look at the price in different terms other'n dollars."

Brooke sat down. His heavy frame made the chair creak and groan as he wiped his brow with a handkerchief.

"I'm gonna need somebody to help around here and take care of local deliveries for me this summer. You know, drop some sheet music over to Mrs. Sherman's School of Music, pick up packages from the post office, maybe sweep up a little here and there, and, oh yea, keep these guitars in here tuned up. Maybe splash a little polish on 'em every once in a while. Wouldn't take more than three or four hours a day. And if you're steady, on time, and polite to the customers, that there Gibson will be all yours when school starts up again in the fall."

Nathan suddenly felt dizzy and nearly fell off the stool. Next to Ben's front porch, Hadley's was Nathan's favorite place in the world.

"Work here and you'll give me this guitar, sir?"

"No, son. I'm not giving it to you. You'll have earned that guitar. It's not a present."

24

There wasn't a single muscle in Nathan's body that wasn't buzzing like a rattlesnake at that moment.

"Mr. Brooke, I'll work here all day and night. I'll deliver a piano to Atlanta on my bike. I'll sweep the floors, walls, even the ceilings if you've got a broom with a long enough handle!"

Ednus Brooke laughed and slowly stood up as the chair moaned in relief.

"No, Nathan, I think the ceilings are fine. When exactly is school out?"

"First week of June, I believe, sir."

"Well then, I'll see you first Saturday morning after school lets out. Nine o'clock sharp. Oh, and by the way, Nathan, you got real good taste in guitars … and music teachers."

During his first summer at Hadley's for Music, Nathan learned everything he could about the guitar. He spent time in the repair department learning how to straighten necks, fine tune tuning pegs, and replace worn-down frets. He learned how to adjust the bridge of the guitar and set the intonation so when a string was played from the 12th fret it was the same note as the string played open. He could tell if the frets weren't laid in level and learned how to adjust the 'action' of a guitar—the distance between the strings and the fingerboard—that could change the way a guitar played. He learned about the different types of tones each different make and model of guitar produced.

And he played that Gibson L-5 guitar with the fancy 'f-holes' in the body instead of the conventional circular sound hole; the genuine elephant ivory nut that resisted being grooved by the strings; the raised pick guard; floating bridge; and the unique sunburst finish that singled that guitar out as the prettiest looking and sweetest sounding guitar in the whole world.

Word of Nathan's expertise and honesty got around and when a customer came to Hadley's to buy a guitar, whether for themselves or their children, they'd often walk right past the salesmen and seek out Nathan. Even the working musicians would come to him for advice. He knew which guitars had tuning pegs that wouldn't hold and always made sure to look down the neck like it was a rifle barrel to make sure it wasn't bowed. And when a customer would ask what kind of a sound they were looking for, Nathan could direct them to the proper guitar. When Nathan recommended a guitar, he would take it down off the wall and play it for a minute or two. Hearing how beautiful it sounded in Nathan's hands, the guitar was as good as sold...except for the Gibson L-5, which was already taken.

On the last day of the summer, Nathan walked out of Hadley's, got on his bike and rode home without his feet ever touching the pedals. In his left hand he carried the Gibson L-5 guitar in a cardboard, imitation alligator case with a tuning fork, 4 picks and two packs of strings inside the case compartment.

Appreciative of Nathan's growing knowledge of guitars, Mr. Brooke offered Nathan a job on weekends and occasionally after school. Nathan worked at Hadley's for almost three years until he was 16, when the mill closed down and his father lost his job. Nathan was faced with a decision to accept an offer for his first paying gig as the guitarist with the Mississippi All Star Dixieland Band out of Biloxi or to move with his family to his uncle's farm in Oregon.

Actually, the decision whether to be a farmer or a musician was an easy one for Nathan. The hard part was whether he should go with the All Stars or stay in Jackson so he consulted with Ben before he made his decision.

"Think I ought to take it, Ben?"

"Well, I sure 'nough run out of things I can teach you. You used me flat up, boy. I don't think there's much headroom left here in Jackson for you."

"You saying I ought to take it?"

"Nathan, you know everything there is to know about the makin's of a guitar and you sure as hell know how to play the damn thing. I think it's time you learned how to be a musician. Ya see, son, sitting around playin' guitar on my front porch is one thing but being a full-time musician is another."

Nathan spent nine months touring the South with the Mississippi All Star Dixieland Band, learning to be a musician. Since most of the "All Stars" viewed the scenery between cities and engagements through the bottom of a thick glass jar filled with home-brewed moonshine, Nathan also learned how to drive. Nathan and the trombone player were the only non-drinkers in the band and the two of them chauffeured the All Stars, instruments and luggage, all crammed into two Model A Fords.

The band fell apart in New Orleans when the leader absconded with two weeks of wages and the drummer's wife. Most of the band members found their way back to their hometowns but Nathan stayed in New Orleans, imprisoned by the magic of the Mississippi River.

Nathan had never seen anything so vast and powerful and yet so subtle and soothing. It was the contradictions of the river that gave it a humanness and personality that transformed it, at least to a young boy alone in a big city, into a friend.

A complicated friend, however. Nathan found the river to be a confusing concoction of opposites. The waters of the Mississippi could be so gracefully hypnotic and yet so stubbornly ungovernable. On the surface, so lazy but quick-tempered and dangerous in its murky depths below and yet so committed and dedicated to its singular purpose of reaching the sea and yet as playful as a dawdling two-year-old in its backwaters and eddies. The river could be a careful and concerned listener at times or it could be cool and unsympathetic as if to say, "Nobody cares about your troubles, boy…"

Just as Nathan was seduced by the smells of the guitar room on his first visit to Hadley's music store, the river carried a rich collection of strange and exotic vapors that tantalized his senses and stirred his imagination.

Nathan also brought the ears of a musician to the banks of the Mississippi. The sounds from the barges, boats, and ferries danced across the surface while the powerful surge of the deep water droned beneath.

Even when he wasn't standing next to it, Nathan could feel the resonance of the river in the distance. It was almost like putting his ear against the body of his guitar, and long after strumming a chord, still being able to hear the reverberations from the strings flowing through the channels of the wooden chambers.

Nathan took a day job with the Hadley's for Music store in New Orleans, thanks to a hearty recommendation from Ednus Brooke. He found a boarding house a couple of blocks from the French Quarter and spent his nights wandering from club to club, listening to the music and trying to sit in with a band whenever he got the opportunity.

Despite his skill on the guitar and a quick ear that enabled him to play all types of music, most of the bands were locked up. He was a kid, had no reputation in the French Quarter and at first glance looked kind of peculiar with his off-kilter posture. His few opportunities to play generally came in the last set when the club was almost empty and the band's guitarist wanted to leave early or to pay a quick visit to his girlfriend before he went home. Most of the time he spent standing outside the entrance to a club, guitar case in hand, listening to the music and watching the fun that was going on inside.

Since the rules of his boarding house were strict against drinking and playing music, the majority of Nathan's practice time came at night under a bridge on the bank of a canal, not far from the Quarter.

The acoustics of the steep slope of the bank, the metal girders of the overhanging bridge and the black, slow-moving water, made his music sound as homesick and lonely as he felt. He missed his family. He missed Ben and their Saturday sessions. He missed the familiarity of Jackson. New Orleans was a big city and every face he saw had a stranger behind it.

He missed playing with the All Stars in front of full dance floors and big crowds,

Late at night on the canal bank, the only crowd he drew was mostly made up of drunks, hobos, and hookers. Occasionally, a musician would wander by on his way home from a club and holler out some encouragement as he crossed over the bridge. Once in a while, a musician might stop and noodle along with Nathan's playing.

That was how Nathan met Wingy Mignon, a one-armed trumpet player. Although tremendously talented, Wingy had a difficult time finding steady work because most of big bands that used horn sections played off sheet music. Wingy could read music all right but with a useless flap of skin for a right arm, he had to stop playing to turn a page. Also, mutes and toilet plungers were popular gadgets used by trumpet and trombone players which produced a sound that sounded like a baby crying, "wah wah", a technique that was a signature riff on many popular songs. Unfortunately, Wingy didn't have a spare arm with which to work a mute.

So, Wingy, like Nathan, would cruise the clubs looking for sit-in work and end up a couple of nights a week on the canal bank under the bridge with Nathan trying to keep up his chops. While Nathan would talk about missing his family and friends back in Jackson, Wingy would talk about missing his right arm, lost to a wheat thrasher when he was 13-years-old. Together they would wrap their music around their lonesomeness and let the silent waters of the canal carry their melancholy out to the Gulf. Wingy was 23-years-old and became Nathan's first friend in New Orleans.

One night, when Nathan was playing all by himself under the bridge, he was startled by the sound of someone sloshing their way towards him wading waist deep in the canal. There wasn't much of a moon and Nathan had trouble making him out.

"Probably a drunk fell in up river," he muttered to himself as he put his guitar away in case there might be some trouble.

"You need some help down there, sir?" Nathan called out.

"Oh, no, I'm just doing a bit of noodlin'," the voice answered. "Are you the guitar player I been listening to every night?"

"Might be," Nathan answered cautiously.

"Well, you damn sure can play that guitar. I can hear your music drifting half a mile down the canal."

"Really, that far?"

"Oh, yea, and when that damn trumpet player joins you there's no peace on the river 'til you reach the delta."

Nathan laughed and realized that he couldn't remember the last time he'd had a good laugh.

"What did you say you were doing down there?"

"I'm noodlin. I'm fishing for catfish."

"I don't see no pole. What are you fishing with?"

"I don't use no pole. No traps, no nets either."

"How do you catch 'em then? You hypnotize them and they just flop out on the bank?"

"Almost. I'm a 'wiggler'. I catch 'em with my hands."

By that point in the conversation, the fisherman had waded his way up the canal and was standing in the water right below where Nathan was sitting. His curiosity peaked, Nathan leaned his guitar case between two rocks and carefully scrambled down the bank to get a closer look at this person who caught catfish with his bare hands.

"How do you catch 'em by hand?" Nathan asked, realizing that the person poised waist deep in the dark waters of the canal was not a man but a boy that looked to be about his same age.

"Here's how," the boy laughed, sticking two fingers up in the air and wiggling them.

"The big, male catfish like to find a hole up alongside of the bank where they can sort of back in and wait to see what comes down the canal. Might be an undercut in the bank, might be in a hollowed-out ball of tree roots. Male catfish take care of their young in these holes, too.

Thinking of quicksand, snakes, leeches, toe-biters, snapping turtles, alligators and other nasty things that lurked below the water line, Nathan's attention was captured.

"You mean you reach in these holes in the side of the bank and pull 'em out with your bare hand?" Nathan asked incredulously. "At night?"

The boy bent over at the waist and his whole body disappeared below the surface except for the top of his head.

A tiny drop of moonlight squeezed through the clouds and splashed against the boy's head. Nathan suddenly noticed that the left side of his skull looked like it was caved in. He didn't want to get caught staring, so he focused his attention back down to the side of the river where the boy seemed to be feeling his way along the bank.

The boy stopped and raised up dripping wet.

"When I find a hole, I put my hand down in it and wiggle these two fingers. I don't know whether old Mr. Whisker fish thinks my fingers are a midnight snack or a prowler trying to steal something from his house, but if he's in there, he can't seem to resist getting himself a little nibble of these."

"You mean he bites your fingers?" Nathan asked. The courage and daring required to reach into a catfish's lair far outweighing his curiosity over the boy's squashed head.

"No, he doesn't exactly bite 'em. He more or less sucks the fingers and most of my hand into his mouth and swallows 'em down his gullet. I wait a few seconds, grab hold of him by the stomach and yank him out."

"They swallow your whole arm? Don't they bite you?"

"Sometimes."

The boy rolled up the sleeve of his shirt and showed Nathan an array of scars up and down his arm.

"I don't know if you can see these but the further up the scar, the bigger the fish," he said proudly.

The boy pointed to a wide and deep pockmark on his bicep, "This one ran about forty pounds."

"You mean they don't know the difference between your fingers and a good meal?"

"Nah, catfish don't see too good. Their whiskers around their mouth help 'em taste their way through the muck on the bottom. They pick up the taste of something good to eat with the whiskers and then the catfish just sucks it in. Sometimes I mix up a little blood and corn meal and rub it into my fingers but that's cheatin' according to the noodler's book of rules."

"What about snakes?"

"Cottonmouth already bit me once when I was a baby," the boy said pointing to the dented side of his head. "Bit me right on the head. I figure if a cottonmouth couldn't kill me when I was a baby, he ain't gonna mess with me now that I'm grown up."

Nathan was startled by how casually the boy referred to his physical deformity.

"This here is a good spot to noodle 'cause the restaurants upstream throw a lot of their garbage in the canal and the catfish grow big off it. You know, there's a promising hole right down here. You want to give it a try?"

"No, thanks," Nathan laughed. "You go ahead and show me how it's done."

"All right, let's see if anybody's in there," he said as he reached under the bank. Almost a minute passed when suddenly the boy's eyes widened and he whispered, 'Uh oh, I think somebody's home."

Suddenly his arm was jerked under the bank and his whole body disappeared below the surface. Nathan's first thought was to jump in and try to save him. His second thought had to do with alligators and cottonmouth water moccasins.

While Nathan was trying to choose which thought to follow, the boy surfaced. Yelling and whooping, he splashed and tumbled in the water. Slowly, the boy approached the side of the bank and pulled his right arm out of the water. Connected to his elbow was the biggest catfish Nathan had ever seen.

"Yee hoo," the boy squealed, struggling to crawl out of the water onto the slippery bank with a 20-pound catfish flopping and twisting on his arm.

"Give me a hand here, will you? This is a big un."

Nathan was flabbergasted. He had never seen anything like that in his life and when asked to help by the boy, he became a flurry of inefficiency. Trying to help the boy out of the water, Nathan slipped on the muddy bank and tumbled head first into the water.

"Here, grab hold of my hand 'fore you drown, guitar player."

With the huge catfish on one arm and Nathan on the other, the boy dragged them both up the side of the bank and the three of them, two young boys and one old catfish, lay exhausted on their backs in the damp grass.

Nathan held out his right hand, "My name's Nathan. Nathan O'Shea."

The other boy lifted his hand with the catfish still attached and held it out to Nathan.

"Nice to make your acquaintance. My name's E. Tim Kelly."

Nathan shook the tail of the catfish attached to E. Tim's arm and the two boys fell on their backs laughing and giggling.

Nathan gathered up pieces of driftwood for a fire while E. Tim gutted the fish. He cut the meat into strips and threaded them through long sticks he had carved to a sharp point. They sat close to the fire, drying their clothes and roasting the fish, turning the sticks over and over until the sweet catfish meat turned golden brown.

They ate and cooked, ate and cooked for over an hour.

"This is the best meal I've had since I've been in New Orleans," Nathan said, thoroughly stuffed.

"Thanks, you oughta taste my pan-fried, Cajun catfish."

"I never knew plain old toasted catfish could taste so good. It must be awful good cooked in a real pan with some fixins."

"I'll tell you what, Nathan, with the right spices and some bacon fat, I can turn a catfish into a T-bone steak. Ain't bragging neither. Speakin' of braggin', you sure can play that guitar. You play in a band?" E. Tim asked, as he pulled off a strip of catfish.

"Nah, not anymore. I was with a band for almost a year but we broke up. I got a day job now working at a music store and I'm trying to catch on with somebody but I'm not having much luck. I get to sit in once in a while with some club bands but this here bridge is about my only steady work as a musician. The pay ain't much and the crowds are slim except for drunks, hobos, a one-armed trumpet player and crazy fools who catch catfish with their bare hands."

"Well, it's hard for me to believe that someone as good as you wouldn't be a helluva catch for some group. From what I've heard, sounds like you can play just about any style."

"I don't know. Maybe I'm just not good enough to cut it in the big city."

"How long you been in town?" E. Tim asked.

"Going on three months."

"Too bad, if you'd got here a couple of months sooner, you'd have seen the river toad orgy. You ever seen the river toad orgy?"

"Nuh uh," Nathan answered. "What's that?"

"Well, near the end of Spring the river toads mate. The males turn into crazy sex maniacs. They'll jump on and hump just about anything. We're talking a piece of bark floating down the river, a leaf, a log, your big toe...hell, they don't care what it is, they got one thing in mind and there's nothing gonna stop 'em."

"The females stay off on the side of the bank just checking out and watching the males. The females can only mate once so they're picky. You know, Nathan, I've watched them toads nearly every year of my life and I still can't tell what's the difference between a male that a female picks and the males that go home alone. I sure can't see what makes one male toad more attractive than another."

"I sure wouldn't know," Nathan shrugged.

"From what I can see, Nathan, just 'cause they don't get picked don't mean the rest of the other male frogs stop trying. You shake one off your big toe and here that same frog comes back trying to hump your ankle."

"That sounds kinda slimy to me."

"Now listen to what I'm saying. The point is, that if you want something real bad and you can't understand why some are getting picked and you ain't, you don't just climb out of the water and go home. You keep humping 'cause who knows what's gonna come floating down the river and out from under the bridge. It might be an old empty beer bottle or it could be the most beautiful girl frog you ever seen in your life with eyes only for you."

"So, the moral of this story is to keep trying and don't go swimming in the river in May, right?" Nathan chuckled.

They both laughed and leaned back against the bank, their bellies so full of catfish even their eyelids were heavy.

"I hear you playing all kinds of music, but I think your blues stuff is really sweet."

"How long you been listening to me play? "Nate asked.

34

"Oh, a couple of weeks. I live down the canal a ways and the wigglin's best at night. To be honest, sometimes I just sit on the bank and listen to you play. I finally worked up the nerve to come down and say hello tonight."

"Do you play a musical instrument?" Nathan asked, a little taken aback thinking that somebody had been eavesdropping on his practice sessions without his knowing.

"Yea, I used to play a little clarinet."

"Licorice stick, eh?"

"Yep, but it's been a while."

"Why don't you bring it down some night and we can play. Clarinet would be a welcome relief over Wingy's brassy old trumpet."

"My stick's in the shop."

"Repair shop?"

"Hock shop."

There was a pause in the conversation as though both boys' thoughts seemed to drift away.

"You miss playing?" Nathan asked.

"Yea, once in a while. This is the first time I've been without a clarinet since I can remember, but I was a little pressed for money."

"What if I, uh, borrow one from the music store I work at and bring it down here, say, tomorrow night?" Nathan asked.

"You can do that? Won't that get you in trouble?"

"Only if I don't bring it back."

Nathan caught a smile on E. Tim's face in the reflection from the fire.

"And I'll bring a fryin' pan, gather up some wild onions and spices and we'll have us a jam session and a catfish feast," E. Tim added happily.

The two boys talked and laughed for another hour or so. They lay sprawled out on their backs and watched for shooting stars, every thread of streaking crystal light weaving a web of friendship between the two strangers.

"Guitar player, it was real nice finally meeting you. I've got an early morning wake up tomorrow so I better get on off."

"Good meeting you, wiggler. Thanks for supper."

The two boys hiked up the bank and walked off in opposite directions. "See you tomorrow night, E. Tim. Same time?"

"Same time. Say, can you borrow a reed or two from your music store?"

"Sure thing," Nathan answered and noticed. as he looked back at E. Tim's silhouette against the lights of the city, that the side of the boy's head was indeed severely dented from the middle of his head down to his ear.

The next evening, just before Nathan got off work at the music store, he went back to the rental room, took a clarinet apart and arranged the pieces around his guitar in his case. It felt a little bit like stealing but he knew he was going to bring it back the next day so he didn't feel too guilty. In all his time working for Hadley's, he'd never even pocketed a guitar pick. He bought a package of three reeds with his employee discount and stuffed them in his shirt pocket.

Nathan halfheartedly made his rounds through the Quarter looking for a sit in. He had it down to hand signals with the band leader. Nathan would walk up to a club and stand near the door. When the band leader happened to look in his direction, Nathan would hold his guitar case up in the air. The band leader would either nod, which meant Nathan might have an opportunity to play or, as was more likely the case, shake his head which meant they wouldn't be needing his services that night. Nathan would return a nod and listen to the band for a little while before leaving and heading for the next club.

As he watched the musicians on stage, Nathan always felt an ache in his stomach. What he missed most was the feeling of playing with other musicians and creating something that was far greater than just their individual talents. When the Mississippi All Stars did a show, or even when it was just him and Ben trading licks on the front porch, there was a bonding, a closeness between the players, that went beyond friendship or even family.

When Nathan was with the Mississippi All Stars, he was the youngest person in the band with little in common with any of the other band members. On the road and in between shows, he often felt left out and isolated from the others. There were factions and cliques within the band and Nathan didn't seem to fit in any of them. There were even two musicians in the band who had gotten into an argument in the past over a hat and they never spoke to one another the entire time Nathan was with the band.

But when they took the stage and broke into their opening number, all personal differences, concerns and conflicts seemed to disappear as though erased by the musical notes that came from their instruments. When they'd all drop into a syncopated rhythm, Nathan would feel as though he were floating over the audience on a magic carpet woven from the notes the band was playing. If his back was aching from driving all day, the pain disappeared. If he was missing his family, he suddenly felt at home. It was a feeling that only came from playing music with other musicians and he missed it dearly.

However, that night Nathan discovered that he wasn't all that driven to find a chance to sit in as he made his nightly rounds of the clubs. Perhaps he was looking forward to another catfish feast with E. Tim later that night, or maybe it was the wear and tear on his spirit. Knowing in his heart that he was a good guitar player and not being able to do what he loved best. Playing guitar was the only thing he was ever very good at in his whole life and not playing music made him feel like he was sinking slowly in quicksand.

As he bumped and snaked his way down the crowded streets, walking past clubs he would normally duck into, Nathan wondered how it was that he always felt the loneliest when he was in a crowd of people.

Nathan found himself at the bridge earlier than usual, a little after midnight. Instead of playing his guitar, Nathan kept it in the case and used it as a back rest. For the first time since the day he walked into Hadley's for Music with his father, Nathan O'Shea didn't feel like playing.

"Hey, how come I don't hear any of that fancy guitar?" E. Tim asked as he suddenly appeared swinging from a girder beneath the bridge.

"Hey, E. Tim," Nathan answered. "Glad you could make it."

E. Tim climbed down from the bridge and scrambled over the rocks and shook Nathan's outstretched hand.

"Permission to enter your studio, maestro."

"Heck, you mean I need permission to enter your catfish restaurant."

"So how come you ain't playing that thing?" E. Tim asked pointing to the guitar case.

"Just wondering that same question myself."

Nathan bent down, opened his guitar case and carefully handed E. Tim the pieces of the clarinet. He watched closely as E. Tim put the pieces together quickly and expertly.

"I rented you that clarinet for tonight. I don't know how good or bad it is. Is a Selmer a good brand?"

E. Tim ran his fingers agilely over the silver valve handles covering the ebony body.

"You can't beat a Selmer. Did you remember to get the reeds?"

"Right here." Nathan pulled the package of reeds out of his pocket and tossed them to E. Tim.

Nathan hadn't really expected too much in the way of musical virtuosity from E. Tim. It seemed to him that just about everybody he'd ever met in his whole life said they played some sort of instrument at some time in their life. His rationale behind the risk involved in sneaking the clarinet out of the store was based more on E. Tim's enjoyable company, payback for the previous night's delicious meal and anticipation of another.

Nathan watched as E. Tim whetted a bamboo reed and clamped it onto the mouthpiece of the clarinet.

"You just gonna sit there or are we gonna play some music?" E. Tim laughed, holding the clarinet up to his lips. "Open up that case and let that beast out of its cage."

Nathan laughed and opened his case. He picked up the guitar and rested it on his thigh.

"You got an E on that thing you could play?" Nathan asked.

Without hesitating, E. Tim played an entire scale ending on an E note. The notes were clear, sharp and strong. The purity of the sound from the clarinet surprised Nathan who was just looking for a starting place to tune his guitar.

Nathan finished tuning and asked, "What do you want to play?"

"Run wherever you want to, Nathan. I'll just try to stay close."

Nathan took off on a twelve-bar blues riff in B flat, a standard clarinet solo key, and waited for E. Tim to join.

E. Tim closed his eyes and let Nathan do a full twelve before playing a single note. As Nathan started a second turn, E. Tim pointed the clarinet up towards the heavens and began to play as though he was giving a private concert to God himself.

Nathan was so taken at E. Tim's playing that he inadvertently dropped his guitar pick somewhere down into the rocks below. Afraid to stop this cascade of notes he never knew could come out of a clarinet, Nathan continued strumming with the back of his fingernail.

The musician's term for a clarinet solo was, ironically referred to as "noodling". "Let's hear the little girl giggle," was the cue for the clarinet player in the band to stand up and take a solo. The clarinet's range was high on the register and cut through the brassy bottom tones of the trombones, trumpets and saxophones. Compared to a solid slide trombone solo that could knock a person off their chair, clarinet solos were more likely to tickle the hairs on the back of the neck. Someone once told Nathan that the clarinet and the tuba were the only musical instruments with a sense of humor.

There was nothing funny about what was coming out of E. Tim's clarinet. The notes spewed out like a meteor shower. After a couple of turns, E. Tim backed down and began to play the root notes of the progression and he nodded over at Nathan, silently giving him a signal to take a run.

Astonished, and a little intimidated by E. Tim's remarkable outpouring, Nathan's fingers stiffened slightly as he started to take the lead but E. Tim was laying down a solid, fertile rhythm bed and Nathan began to relax and drift into the music.

Soon E. Tim was echoing Nathan's leads and throwing in a couple of extra licks more, challenging Nathan to catch him. Nathan would try to match E. Tim's riff and add a few more notes of his own. It was a bit like he and Ben trading musical punches on Ben's front step.

Nathan felt an upwelling of joy as they traded improvisations back and forth.

Suddenly a voice from the bridge interrupted their playing.

"Where the hell is all this music coming from?"

E. Tim stopped playing immediately and set the clarinet on his lap. Nathan looked over at E. Tim, startled at his abrupt halt, and then looked up toward the bridge.

"Hey, Wingy, how you doing?" Nathan called out recognizing the one-armed trumpet player's voice.

Wingy Mignon gingerly sidestepped his way down the side of the steep bank and slid to a halt next to Nathan.

"Jesus Streetcar, who's playing that licorice stick? Sounds like Gabriel himself!"

Nathan smiled and turned proudly towards E. Tim to introduce his new friend to Wingy but stopped when he saw that E. Tim had turned away and was leaning back in the shadows of the bank.

Puzzled at E. Tim's sudden change in demeanor, Nathan stammered through the introductions.

"Wingy Mignon, this is E. Tim Kelly. E. Tim, this is Wingy Mignon."

E. Tim turned shyly towards Wingy and did a subtle double take when he noticed that Wingy was missing his right arm. Wingy reached out with his left arm and E.Tim stepped out of the shadows and grasped Wingy's hand.

"I've seen that same double take many times," Wingy smiled. "Lost it in an accident when I was little. Pleased to meet you, Kelly. If that was you jamming with the boy genius here, you're flat out one helluva clarinet player, son."

E. Tim smiled, "Nice to meet you. Uh, is it Wingy?"

"It was Edwin before I got in a wrestling match with a wheat thresher but I've been going by Wingy ever since the accident. Lost an arm and a first name all in one day. Personally, I miss the arm a lot more than I miss the name, Edwin. Hey, looks like you forgot to duck, too," Wingy smiled pointing towards E. Tim's head.

Nathan held his breath at Wingy's offhand remark but E. Tim laughed it off. "If they call you Wingy maybe ya'll oughta call me Dingy."

They all laughed together.

"Wingy, Dingy and Leany," Nathan giggled. He'd never joked about his scoliosis before and was surprised at how good it felt.

"You boys ready for some catfish cooked bayou style?" E. Tim asked as he scooted down the bank to the water's edge and pulled up a rope with six, pan-sized catfish strung on it. "Build me a hot fire while I clean these here fish."

When the fire burned down to glowing coals, E. Tim reached in his tote bag, pulled out a frying pan and unwrapped a thick slab of bacon. He fried up the catfish in bacon grease and added a couple of handfuls of field greens and wild onions. E. Tim pulled a cloth sack from his bag and took out some dried leaves, crumpled them up in his hands and sprinkled them over the cooking fish.

They ate with their fingers, wrapping the succulent white meat in the tangy, mustard-flavored greens.

They traded stories, laughed, passed around Wingy's flask filled with Tennessee's finest bottom liquor and ate some more until they couldn't eat another bite.

When the last of the fish and greens had been sopped up from the pan, Nathan and Wingy complimented E. Tim on serving up one of the best meals either one of them had ever had.

"So, E. Tim. I told you about me and the wheat thresher. If I may ask, how'd you get that dent in your head? You can tell me it's none of my damn business."

"Bit on the head by a water moccasin when I was a baby."

"You was bit by a snake on the head? I've never heard of something like that. Does it hurt?"

"Naw, don't hurt a bit. Makes buying hats kinda difficult though."

Nate and Wingy looked at one another, wondering if they should laugh at E. Tim's comment.

"What do you boys say to a little after dinner music," Wingy asked, opening his trumpet case. "Y'all don't mind if I sit in with the two of you?"

The three musicians played all night until the first blush of the rising sun began to sting their tired eyes.

The stories go that at times that night their music drew a crowd that packed the bridge to capacity. Neither Wingy, E. Tim nor Nathan ever noticed their audience above them. The music soared out from underneath the bridge as though released from some pent-up corner of their souls, their instruments merely a conduit between them and heaven and completely oblivious to the world in between.

# *Chapter 3*
# E. Tim Kelly
# Struck On The Head By
# A Water Moccasin

E. Tim's father, Boyd Kelly, was born and raised on the bayou backwaters of Lake Fausse, Louisiana and never worked a day in his life that wasn't somehow connected to either hunting or fishing. He ran trap lines year 'round and sold the skins of coon, otter and muskrat. When he wasn't running traps, he'd be hunting, fishing or hired out as a guide.

Without spending one day in school past the sixth grade, Boyd Kelly knew more about the botany, biology, geology, limnology, entomology, ornithology and herpetology of the Lake Fausse region than probably any other person in the world. If it flew, grew, walked or crawled in the swamp, Boyd Kelly could deliver a pretty good lecture on its life history and behavior. He could identify a bird from the sound of its call without ever seeing a feather and then tell you what the weather was going to be like the next day just by sniffing the air.

Knowledge of his surrounding environment was essential to someone who earned their living off the land and out in the water, but Boyd went a step further. He had the curiosity of a baby raccoon and the patience of a Great Blue Heron. He firmly believed that patience could answer a lot more questions than opinions.

Other qualities that enabled Boyd to earn a good living from the place he loved, instead of standing in line waiting for a paycheck, were his ability to improvise and his openness to wonder. A certain amount of improvisation was mandatory just to get by on the bayou, but there was a tendency by most folks on the backwaters to do things the way they'd always been done before. Boyd Kelly was a questioner and a challenger.

By the age of 14, Boyd was full-grown and battle-tested by the swamps and bayous surrounding Lake Fausse. With his knack for innovation, combined with the unceasing energy of his youth, he became one of the most sought-after and respected hunting and fishing guides in all of Southeast Louisiana.

Whenever somebody was reported to be lost in the swamps or if there had been a prison break from nearby Raymond Laborde Correctional Center, Boyd Kelly was the first one called for the manhunt and usually the first to find the dead body since the swamp didn't take kindly to unchaperoned visitors or strangers.

He could read a week-old track in a rainstorm and had the best nose in the bayou next to Len Renaud's bluetick coonhound. Some said it was even better, since it was Boyd Kelly who sniffed out the severed legs and torso of an escaped convict who had been bitten in half by an alligator. If given the opportunity, alligators like their prey to ripen a bit before they eat. Boyd Kelly walked by the spot and smelled something peculiar in the air. Searchers with poles pried out the two halves of the body that had been crammed four-feet under the water beneath a submerged tree limb by the alligator and left to rot for a future feast.

Lying face down off the bow of his flat boat, Boyd gigged for flounder. He fished for largemouth bass, bream, catfish and crappie; ran a drag net for crayfish or mudbugs, as they were called; always kept a razor-sharp ax in his boat in case he spotted an alligator gar, a rare and primitive fish with thick scales like armor plates, some weighing up to five hundred pounds and considered a delicacy when cured and smoked; and he could hamstring and wrestle down a deer by throwing a leather bolo, a feat he learned from an old Indian trapper.

E. Tim Kelly's first breath of air was laced with the steamy, pungent brew of backwater surrounding Lake Fausse.

Five days after he was born, E. Tim Kelly attended his mother's funeral.

Evelyn Carter was 17-years-old and three months pregnant when she married Boyd Kelly. Six months later, the only woman Boyd Kelly would ever love died while delivering their first and only child.

Boyd gave his son his mother's first name, Evelyn. It was the best thing he could do to make sure his son wouldn't forget the mother he never knew. Even though nearly everyone around Lake Fausse knew that Boyd had named his son after the boy's mother, people were careful to make sure that they always called the boy by his first initial and middle name. E. Tim eventually learned that the 'E' stood for his mother, and although he always used the initial instead of her name, he was proud to be named after a person that his father loved so dearly.

E. Tim's first crib was a wooden Barq's Soda case resting on the flat bottom of a Jon boat. With his baby cooing between his boots, Boyd Kelly went about his business as best as he could.

Secure in his soda pop box, swaddled in soft, flannel blankets and sucking on a milk sugar-tit, the bayou filled E. Tim's infant senses, subliminally imprinting an encyclopedia of mysterious smells and sounds from the swamp onto his fertile and eager new brain. Throughout his life, E. Tim would be immediately taken back to his infancy by the smell from the subtle exhale of a lotus blossom.

The bayou was E. Tim's first music teacher. From the insects to the birds, the backwaters produced a symphony of sounds that provided his memory bank with an infinite source of material. Flat on his back, E. Tim learned to listen to entertain himself. When he got older, E. Tim could identify the species of a tree based on the sound the wind made blowing through its branches and leaves.

The cadence of the heavy, dark waters rhythmically slapping at the bottom of the boat, gave him his sense of meter. Against this syncopated back beat, the disharmony of chirps and chatter from the world above the waterline taught him counter rhythms and structural diversity.

E. Tim learned the bayou upside down. Staring upwards through the arthritic knees of bald cypress trees clad in gray-green shawls of Spanish moss, his infant eyes would follow cloudy swarms of winged insects swooping and diving in a perpetual love dance in the morning mist. Then his attention would be stolen by a great blue heron overhead clumsily beating its cumbersome wings against its body enroute to its next fishing hole followed by a formation of brown pelicans gliding effortlessly against the blue sky above him.

Clouds were E. Tim's first stuffed animals.

Whenever he had a guide trip, Boyd would leave E. Tim with Bernice Kynard at Bernice's restaurant in town. Bernice would go about her business, cooking and waiting on tables, while E. Tim gurgled happily in a milk crate on the counter, his nose adding the smells of bacon and chicken fried steak to his growing collection of olfactory input.

Boyd was hired to guide two men from Houston, Texas who were looking to do some largemouth bass fishing. When Boyd brought out his throw net to catch minnows, the men told him to leave the net and the bait bucket on shore.

"No need to bring that, son," one of the men said. "We're gonna plug for bass."

"You gonna what for bass?" Boyd asked.

One of the men opened his tackle box and proudly pulled out a four-inch-long piece of wood, carved and painted to look like a minnow with a three-pronged, hook dangling off the end.

"This old boy down in Galveston hand-carved these for us. If you can put us near some fish, we'll fill up the boat."

Boyd took them down the lake and up a short finger to a quiet bay where he had noticed the largemouth bass starting to nest up.

*Male bass secure a territory and defend it vigorously against all intruders. After breeding, the female swims off, leaving the male to guard the nest and fan the eggs with his pectoral fins to keep them oxygenated and clear of silt. When the eggs hatch, the male will play nursemaid to hundreds of rambunctious, tiny bass fry. During this period, male bass are extremely aggressive and protective of their territory. People inadvertently swimming or wading in waters where these fish were guarding their young have been struck on their legs by male bass protecting their nest.*

Boyd paddled quietly towards the mouth of the bay while his clients, to his consternation, talked and laughed and rattled their tackle boxes against the bottom of the boat. He had learned that next to patience, silence was a mandatory prerequisite to catching fish.

"You boys ought to quiet down, we don't want to spook these fish," Boyd whispered.

"You just relax and keep your eyes on this plug, son," said one of the men standing up in the bow of the boat.

The man cast the plug in the middle of the bay and it landed with a splash that looked like a pelican dive-bombing a school of shad.

Boyd shook his head and stifled a laugh as he watched the man reel the plug toward the boat. The plug scooted along the surface leaving a wake behind it as big as an otter being chased by a gator.

The plug hadn't traveled more than twenty feet when a huge bass flew out of the water and pounced on the lure.

"Eeeee hah, first cast!" the man hollered as he reeled in the fish.

The two fishermen from Texas caught and released over thirty bass that day, many of them much larger than Boyd Kelly had ever caught using live bait. Not only was this new kind of fishing productive, it looked to be more fun than a circus with the fish attacking the plug on the surface and cartwheeling through the air. Boyd was convinced that this was the fishing of the future. No seining for minnows and trying to keep them alive in a bucket. No hooks, sinkers or bobbers, and no waiting for a fish to come along and take the bait.

The men paid him his guide fee and added a handsome tip. They also gave him one of the plugs they were using.

"Mind if I ask what you paid for this plug?"

"Fifth cents apiece, custom made. And you rarely lose one 'cause they float on top of the water."

That evening, Boyd sat on his front porch rocking E. Tim with his foot and turning the plug over and over in his fingers, thinking about making his own line of hand-carved plugs.

Boyd Kelly had been skinning a trap line for seven years and had cleaned or filleted every fish known to the Lake Fausse waters, so he had a pretty good hand with a knife. At fourteen, he'd won a "Ball in Jail" whittling contest where the contestants were each given a four-inch square block of Loblolly Pine and had to carve a free rolling ball inside a "jail" of carved bars. BK finished his "Ball in Jail" in less than two hours and won a new Buck knife as first prize.

First thing Boyd Kelly did the day after the fishermen from Houston left was to strap his son on his back like a papoose and take off into the woods in search of the proper type of wood to start carving his plugs. He gathered up an armful of cedar, pine and basswood.

Over the next couple of weeks, Boyd had carved a tackle box full of plugs. Some looked like a crayfish swimming tail first and were dyed in the same burnt orange color that they take on after a spring molt. He carved plugs that looked like shad, bluegill and baby perch. He'd seen bass attack snakes swimming on the surface so he carved a long, skinny, jointed plug that looked and moved like a small snake in the water.

He had seen plenty of frogs in the bellies of fish he'd cleaned so he carved a plug with a concave front end that would tip forward when he yanked on the line. The plug toppled and jerked through the water like a frog swimming.

Boyd tested out his designs by trolling his different models through the swamp and studying their action in the water. He continued to improve his designs and colors. He'd even figured out a way to cut up a small slice of a tin can lid and mount it behind the eye of the hook so that it spun like a propeller when he reeled it in. The spinning and splashing of the propeller made the plug look like a wounded fish — an easy and attractive meal for a hungry bass.

And boy-oh-boy, did his plugs catch fish!

Within three months, bait shacks and general stores in the area were selling Boyd Kelly's hand carved plugs. When the subject of fishing came up in any conversation, Boyd's phenomenal success fishing with his new artificial baits was the first thing mentioned. Boyd's guiding business nearly doubled with fishermen wanting to get the knack of fishing plugs with the man who made them.

E. Tim was about a year-and-a-half-old and still asleep in the bottom of the jon boat when Boyd Kelly took off an hour before sunup to test a radical new design of a plug he was working on. The plug had a flattened and extended nose in front of the hook that made the plug dive downward when the line was reeled in and then floated back up to the surface when the line went slack. He was trying to find a way to get down to the bottom in deeper water where the larger fish were located.

On his third cast of the morning, something struck his plug and bent his pole nearly in half. Whatever it was that inhaled his piece of whittling was huge. At first, Boyd thought he had snagged an alligator gar. Despite pulling as hard as he could, Boyd couldn't gain an inch on the fish. Slowly and steadily his boat was being towed towards the middle of the lake. Boyd leaned back and put his full weight against the fish trying to turn it towards him. Suddenly the biggest largemouth bass Boyd Kelly had ever seen broke water thirty feet off his bow. It was a record-breaking, money making, monster bass.

"By God, Evelyn," Boyd whispered both to his sleeping son and his deceased wife. "This fish is so big the level of the lake dropped two inches when he came out of the water!"

As soon as Boyd realized the potential business that a fish of this extraordinary size could bring to his plug sales and guide service, the battle took on a more serious nature.

He carefully fought the fish with all the expertise and finesse he'd learned over the years while all the time speaking softly to E. Tim.

"You gotta let these big ones have their head, son. When they want to run, give 'em plenty of line but keep it snug or they can snap your line like it was a spider's web." "That's right, just like that...come on you swamp donkey, you're gonna make us some money."

The battle lasted about twenty minutes until the giant fish, exhausted and beaten, finally floated on its side next to the boat. The fish was so heavy, Boyd had to use two hands to get it in the boat. Boyd leaned over the low rail, grabbed the huge fish by the gills and slung him over the side nearly tipping over the boat.

The fish lived up to its "bucket mouth" nickname. Boyd could have stuck his whole head inside the fish's mouth. The giant bass had swallowed the plug and it was deep in the gullet of the fish. As he peered into the fish's mouth in the pre-dawn darkness, a flash of white suddenly shot out of the fish's mouth and struck Boyd on the neck.

In an instant, Boyd realized that he had been bitten by a cottonmouth water moccasin. Big bass were known to eat snakes that had dropped out of a tree or were out for a swim, especially when they were guarding a nest of eggs or fry. Apparently, prior to striking his plug, the giant bass had attacked the swimming snake from the rear. The fish was still in the process of swallowing the snake whole when Boyd's plug came splashing through the fish's territory. Aggressively defending its' young, the fish struck the plug.

Boyd grabbed the snake and pulled its' fangs out of his neck. Almost immediately, he felt a numbness in his face. He'd been bitten once before by a young water moccasin but the snake had hit him on the lower leg. It was painful and it took three weeks before he could get his foot in his boot, but it wasn't deadly.

This was a bigger snake and the fangs had penetrated his carotid artery which provides blood to the brain. He began to feel the effects of the snake's potent toxin almost right away. He fell forward off the rear seat, his knees straddling his baby son. He panicked at the thought of his infant son in the boat with the wild and frightened water moccasin.

He spotted the snake as it crawled out of the soda case. Fighting to stay conscious, Boyd grabbed his ax and cut off its' head.

However, before Boyd could kill the snake, the water moccasin had fallen into E. Tim's soda box and struck the sleeping child, injecting the last drops of its supply of venom into the baby's skull.

The next morning a trapper discovered the boat near shore, drifting in a bed of duckweed with the lifeless body of Boyd Kelly and his comatose infant son. Alongside the two bodies in the boat were two halves of cottonmouth water moccasin; and the biggest largemouth bass anybody had ever seen—all laying in the bottom of the boat.

The trapper got E. Tim to Thibodaux County Hospital. Cold, dehydrated and snake bit, the baby was listed in critical condition. While the doctors tried to save Boyd Kelly's infant son, the rest of the community of Lake Fausse tried to figure out what must have happened out on the swamp. Members of the sheriff's department, the customers at Bernice's Restaurant, and the clientele at Big Ed's Taxidermy all arrived at the same conclusion based on the evidence that:

1. The plug was still in the bass' mouth.
2. The snake's fang marks were on Boyd's throat and the baby's head.
3. There were fresh bite marks from the fish on the snake's body.

The story about the guide who was killed by a water moccasin in the mouth of a largemouth bass was so bizarre that it needed no embellishment from its tellers. It was said that 10 years after the incident you could get the same identical version of the story from five different storytellers. The story was so bizarre it was unstretchable.

E. Tim survived the bite mainly because the snake had released most of its poison into his father's neck prior to striking him on the side of the head.

The doctors' prognoses for E. Tim ranged from paralysis, severe and permanent brain damage to the possibility of death.

Despite the dire predictions of the Lake Fausse medical community, Evelyn Tim Kelly would grow up to become an intelligent, healthy and perfectly normal young man…almost.

An infant's skull plates are not fused together at birth. This allows the head to fit through the narrow birth canal and provide room for the head and brain to grow. What was left of the snake's venom after striking his father, damaged the bone cells responsible for growth of the skull.

In the coming years as his body grew, including his skull, the left side of E. Tim's head grew normally while the right side remained atrophied, leaving an indentation that looked as though he had been smacked on the side of the head with a baseball bat.

Ten days after the incident, E. Tim was released from Thibodaux General Hospital in the care of his mother's sister, Ethel. He spent three years in Memphis, Tennessee with Ethel, her husband, Jarvis, and their three children until the early signs of E. Tim's physical defect became apparent and the stares in the grocery store became too painful. It also seemed to Ethel and Jarvis that the boy's speech development was not progressing as it should.

"The side of his head keeps sagging and he don't talk good," Ethyl told the doctors at Thibodaux General when she brought him back for further testing.

"The poor thing gets pointed at and teased so much it just breaks my heart and to tell you the truth, I don't think I can give him the attention he needs what with three kids of my own and a husband who ain't worth a damn. He just sits there. I'm talking about the baby, although I guess I could be talking about Jarvis as well. Doctor, can you tell me if he's a normal child or is he damaged?"

The doctor who looked at E. Tim was not encouraging. He explained to Ethyl that the brain, although only three-percent of a human's body weight, used twenty percent of all the oxygen consumed by the body. With only one-half of a skull, there would never be sufficient space to accommodate the circulatory system required to supply sufficient blood to E. Tim's brain.

"My best guess, ma'am, is that he will suffer from severe mental and motor retardation and I wouldn't expect him to live much past his fifth birthday," the doctor told Ethel.

"Merciful Jesus, you poor thing!" Ethyl cried and ran her fingers through E. Tim's hair on the normal side of his head. "What am I gonna do with this child?"

Thibodaux General accepted the return of E. Tim from his aunt and forwarded him to the Atchafalaya County Home for Orphans and Handicapped Children, ironically located on the shores of Lake Fausse where E. Tim was born and nearly died.

Despite E. Tim's prognosis by the doctors, he lived well beyond his fifth birthday. Other than an occasional migraine headache that felt as though someone had poured turpentine in his ears and dropped a match right after it and a skull that collected rainwater in a downpour, E. Tim grew into a lively, healthy and normal boy. He had inherited his legendary father's passion for hunting and fishing the backwaters of Lake Fausse. When he was old enough to paddle a jon boat and run a few traps, E. Tim helped supply the County Home's dinner table with fresh fish and game.

E. Tim was an official resident of the Atchafalaya County Home for thirteen years until he was legally adopted by Bill and Bernice Crady for a small monetary contribution to the Director of the home.

Bill Crady was owner and manager of 'The Strangest Show On Earth—Professor Crady's Traveling Show of Oddities and Prodigies' that toured the South from Louisiana to Georgia and as far north as Tennessee and Kentucky.

Victor Hugo, in his book, *'The Man Who Laughs'*, tells of 'The Comprachicos', a hideous band of wanderers, famous in the seventeenth century. 'Comprachicos' comes from the Spanish word signifying "child buyers". These people purchased young children and deformed them, stunted their growth and distorted their features and then sold these human toys to royalty or used them for street shows.

> *"The Comprachicos worked on a child as the Chinese work on trees. They had their secrets, as we have said; they had tricks which are now lost arts. A sort of fantastic stunted thing left their hands; it was ridiculous and wonderful. They could touch up a little being with such skill that its father would not have recognized it. Sometimes they left the spine straight and remade the face. Children destined for tumblers had their joints dislocated in a masterly manner; you would have said they had been boned. Thus, gymnasts were made."*

Hugo told of Chinese dealers who took children of two or three years of age and put them in grotesquely shaped porcelain vases that were made without a top or bottom, that allowed the head and feet to protrude. At night they laid the vase on its side so the child could sleep and, in the morning, set the vase upright.

> *"Thus, the child thickens without growing taller, filling up with his compressed flesh and distorted bones, the depressions in the vase. This development in a bottle continues many years. After a certain time, it becomes irreparable. When they consider that this is accomplished, and the monster made, they break the vase. The child comes out and, behold, there is a man in the shape of a mug!"*

While certainly not one of Hugo's Comprachicos or a Chinese torturer, Professor Crady's talent-scouting tactics involved scouring the asylums, hospitals and county homes in search of the odd and abnormal to use as performers in his traveling side show.

In fact, Bill Crady was a kindhearted man and considered all his performers as members of his own family. There was a rumor among the members of the show's cast that Professor Crady and his wife had a son that died young from a terrible disease that made a five-year-old look like an eighty-year-old. Although the Professor did use words such as 'freaks', 'mutations', 'anomalies' and 'oddities' as the barker outside the tent, his overall message dealt with compassion for those whom God had made different from the rest of us.

"Some sights that wait inside this tent may not be for those with weak constitutions. Let me remind you that any woman who suspects that she may be with child is not allowed in, for there are some opinions among the medical community that a pregnant woman, upon seeing sights as haunting and shocking as those inside this tent, could possible leave a lasting mark on her unborn baby."

After a lengthy pause, in which he stared intently at each of the faces in the crowd as though seeking to weed out the weak, Professor Crady would add, "If you walk in this tent in search of freaks you will, indeed, see freaks of frightening proportions. But if you enter in search of finding inspiration from human beings subjected to the cruelest acts of nature and who are able to overcome the most incredible and seemingly insurmountable obstacles, you will see the most startling display of human courage and spirit you will ever lay your eyes upon."

Professor Crady taught E. Tim him how to multiply two and three-digit numbers in his head and to memorize the capitals of every state in the union. He was billed as "The Boy with Half A Brain". When the crowd entered the tent, E. Tim was on a stool in a roped off area wearing a baseball cap and looking like a normal boy. Crady would herd the crowd over to where E. Tim was sitting and ask them to gather around.

"Our first exhibit, ladies, gentlemen, boys and girls, is this handsome young man..."

At this point, Bill would dramatically take the hat off E. Tim's head. As the crowd gasped at E. Tim's caved-in skull, Bill would continue.

"...born with only half a brain and yet he has an IQ of genius proportions. Is there a member of this group handy with mathematics?"

The Professor would find a volunteer who claimed to be skilled with numbers and give them a pad of paper and a pencil. He'd then ask someone in the audience to give E. Tim a multiplication problem using two- or three-digit numbers.

"What's 94 times 63, boy?" came from a voice in the crowd.

In less than thirty seconds, E. Tim would turn to Uncle Bill and ask, "Is the answer five thousand, nine hundred and twenty-two?"

While E. Tim was in training, the Professor explained to him that if he posed his answer in the form of a question, the audience would take kindlier to him a lot more than if he acted like he was a smart-ass, know-it-all who was a whole lot more intelligent than everyone else.

It usually took the volunteer mathematician in the crowd a lot more than 30-seconds to work out the answer with pencil and paper. While waiting for confirmation of E. Tim's answer, the professor would bellow out, "What's the capital of New York?"

After a volley of smart-alecky comments from the would-be comedians in the audience such as, "Who the hell cares..." and "I believe the N and the Y are the capitals of New York...", E. Tim would answer softly, "Albany, I believe."

Half of the rationale for Bill Crady's advice to E. Tim about adding an air of indecisiveness to his answers was based on sound psychological theory and certainly had a positive effect on the audience.

The other half of his rationale for teaching E. Tim to answer the questions with some degree of uncertainty was that the merest hint of self-doubt in his response could open the door to a dispute which would occasionally lead to an opportunity for a small side bet between a customer and Professor Crady.

The capital of the state of Washington always brought out a someone who was convinced that the correct answer was Seattle. Bill would bring out his Rand McNally Atlas, point out the star over Olympia and collect the money.

"Olympia! Who ever heard of Olympia? "

Initially, the customer's stares were directed toward E. Tim's lopsided skull which was nothing new for E. Tim. People had been doing that his whole life. But when he'd come up with the answer to a difficult problem, the audience would hoot and holler and clap their hands. When his act was over and he was finished demonstrating his mathematical and geographical skills, he could tell from the smiles and nods from the people that most of them appreciated and respected what he could do despite his physical misfortune.

When the crowd eventually moved on and followed Bill to see 'The Incredible Rubber Man', E. Tim usually felt fairly good about himself.

'The Incredible Rubber Man' was 25-year-old Harold Basker who was born with a genetic condition known as hyperelastica, a failing of the formation of the skin fibers. Although he looked quite normal at first glance, Harold could pull the skin on his cheek more than eight inches away from his face, let it go and it would snap back into place. He could pull the skin of his chest over his head and cover one leg with the skin from the other.

'Pint-Sized Heintz' was the show's dwarf and was the next stop on the tour after 'The Incredible Rubber Man'. While Professor Crady lectured the crowd on the medical differences between a dwarf and a midget—a midget having all his body features of normal proportions, only smaller, while a dwarf's head and torso were in disproportion to his arms and legs—Heintz would perform gymnastic acrobatics and lift a bale of hay over his head, all the time smiling happily to the crowd.

Heintz was, indeed, the happiest member of the cast. Heintz (no one knew his last name) had escaped a year earlier from Germany where, in 1936, Hitler and his Nazi party had begun cleansing their race by eliminating anyone who was physically abnormal. During their reign of terror, the Nazis would exterminate over 10,000 midgets, dwarfs and exceptionally short people. Following the war, circus owners in Europe had a difficult time finding dwarfs and midgets for their clown troupes because of the mass killings.

Heintz escaped to France with a young couple by posing as their baby even though he was 24 years old. He took a job as a clown on a cruise ship and ended up in New Orleans, where Uncle Bill discovered him in a hospital suffering from pneumonia.

Heintz recovered, Uncle Bill paid his hospital bill and added a 49-inch tall, 61-pound dwarf to his ensemble.

Lucy McAllister was the show's perfunctory fat lady. She was a cheery, 454 pounds according to an official document signed by the State of Alabama's Weights and Measures inspector, Thomas L. Bunsinger, who verified Lucy's weight at a hog inspection station in Birmingham.

After displaying the framed official document to the crowd, the Professor would add, "This here official weigh-in was back in April and I do believe Miss Lucy may have added a few pounds to her already voluptuous figure. Is that correct Miss Lucy?"

Reclining regally in a red velvet upholstered love seat that had been reinforced with steel bars, and resplendent in a flowing gown of purple satin, the smiling, rosy-cheeked Lucy would giggle, glance coyly towards her mountainous breasts and admit, "Well, I may have added a little here... and a little there."

There was a sensuousness and confidence about Lucy, as though she felt that the stares from the men in the audience were not directed at the rolls of fat that dripped like candle wax down her body, but instead were longing glances from men desirous of a woman of her erogenous excesses. In some cases, she was right. On several occasions, Professor Bill was forced to remove a patron who ventured an over-amorous proposition from the other side of the ropes.

Ironically, Lucy's feet were tiny. She wore a size five shoe and her feet were always giving her great pain. One night after a show, she invited E. Tim to her trailer.

"I'll show you my boobies if you rub my feet, E. Tim."

Having been brought up by the staff at the county home to be respectful to women and a gentleman at all times, behavior that greatly increased an orphan's chances for being adopted plus, having no desire whatsoever to see anymore of Lucy than he had already seen, E. Tim politely declined.

"I'd like to, Miss Lucy, but I've got some tent mending to do. Thank you anyway".

Professor Crady happened to be passing by Lucy's trailer and over-heard their conversation. As E. Tim was escaping from the trailer and running down the stairs, Bill grabbed him by the back of the shirt and threw his arm around E. Tim. "I certainly appreciate your manners son and your gentlemanly declination of Miss Lucy's prurient offering but I must remind you, E. Tim, that although we are a family here, each of us has our own individual needs. Miss Lucy needs to feel desired, possibly a bit more than most ladies, as I'm certain you will find out later in your life. If she feels unwanted, it could change her whole disposition and possibly break her gregarious spirit".

"Now I want you to go back in Miss Lucy's trailer. I want you to go inside and tell her that you'd got someone else to do your chores because you'd just love to get a peek at her big, beautiful boobies. You "ooh" and "aah" and make a fuss out of 'em when she shows them to you and then you rub her feet 'til she tells you to go on off. Then you thank her, pay her boobies one more compliment and then get back to the tent and finish your work."

One year after E. Tim had joined the show, the whole cast contracted food poisoning from a batch of tainted oysters. Lucy had consumed many more oysters than anyone else in the cast and after feeling "a little peaked" the following day, had gone to bed that night extremely ill. She collapsed in her bed and fell asleep on her back. Unable to roll over, Lucy became sick and drowned in her own vomit. She was found dead in her trailer the next morning.

It took six strong men to load her casket onto a railroad freight car and cost Bill Crady $40 to send Lucy McAllister back home to her mother and father who lived in Gifford, South Carolina. On the outside of the casket, Bill Crady taped an envelope containing a note that read:

*Dear Mr. and Mrs. McAllister,*

*It grieves me to return your daughter to you in this condition. She fell victim to a plate of bad oysters and expired in her sleep. Lucy was loved and greatly admired by everyone in our troupe. She never missed a show and was one of our most popular performers.*

*Sincerely,*

*Professor Bill Crady*

Bill painted over the billboard on the side of her trailer advertising "Miss Lucy McAllister, ¼-ton of Amorous Femininity" and never looked for another fat lady for the show again.

The only other female member of the cast was Carmen Ramirez, the bearded lady. She was a full-blossomed girl in her late twenties of Spanish descent with long, dark hair on her head and silky, dark brown whiskers approximately four inches in length covering her cheeks, chin and upper lip. In addition to her face, her arms and legs were covered with hair of a shorter length.

Her beard was soft and downy and appeared early in her life. The doctors who diagnosed her condition as hypertrichosis warned her that if she tried to shave the hair it would grow back even thicker and longer, so Carmen had never harmed a hair on her body in her whole life.

Throughout her childhood, Carmen had tried to hide her hair from others by wearing veils but when she reached an age where she realized that she could earn a living from her rare condition, she treated her furry covering with great pride and rinsed it in warm milk nightly.

It was rumored that Carmen had a patch of hair on her upper back, almost like a horse's mane, that exceeded 12 inches in length. The hair reportedly grew from a large mole located between her shoulders.

Carmen was also the subject of a controversial court case choreographed by Professor Crady.

After a slow weekend in Birmingham, Alabama, Bill Crady paid a distant cousin of his to file a complaint with the police claiming that he was convinced that the bearded lady in the show was actually a male dressed as a female, for no woman could possibly grow hair such as covered Carmen. He demanded that the show be closed down for falsely advertising and trying to pull a con on the members of the community. He also wanted a refund on his price of admission as well as bus fare to and from the show.

The complaint was highly publicized in the local newspaper. Professor Crady and Carmen were brought to trial by the end of the week.

Dressed in a green, taffeta tea gown cut off her shoulders and her face, legs and arms covered with milk-soaked and well-brushed hair, Carmen took the stand.

After swearing on a bible to tell nothing but the whole truth, Carmen testified, in front of an overflowed courtroom, that she was indeed a woman, had always been a woman and that the hair that covered her face and body was real and her own, as well.

The judge called a recess after Carmen's short testimony and walked across the street to the Full Cup Cafe. He came back several minutes later with Clara Marywood, a waitress who had worked at the Full Cup Café for twenty years.

For most of those same twenty years, the judge had eaten lunch at the Full Cup Cafe and had been waited on by Clara Marywood.

Their normal lunch routine was the judge would look over the menu and ask Clara for her opinions on the daily fare.

"How's the chicken pot pie today, Clara?"

I don't think it's up to snuff, your honor."

"How about the chicken fried steak?

"Cream gravy's a little runny."

"What's the soup today?"

"Don't ask."

"Guess I'll have a tuna sandwich then."

"Good choice, sir."

Based on her honesty on the Full Cup Cafe's menu, the judge regarded Clara Marywood's testimony to be reliable. He knew that whatever she found under the bearded lady's clothes, no matter how traumatic, Clara would tell the truth.

When the trial was reconvened, the judge deputized Clara in front of all in the courtroom and directed her to take Miss Ramirez back to his chambers and give her a full inspection.

There was an eerie silence in the courtroom as all eyes turned towards the judge's chambers and every imagination clamored to slip under the door.

After a few minutes, Carmen, the bearded lady, and Clara, the deputized waitress, both entered the courtroom from the judge's chambers in a serious, official and dignified manner.

After swearing to tell the truth on the witness stand, Deputy Clara Marywood, soon to be retired as an officer of the court but on her way to becoming the most requested waitress in the most crowded cafe in Birmingham, Alabama, testified that Carmen was definitely a female and that the hair that covered her body did, indeed, belong to her.

The judge dismissed the case and chastised the plaintiff for wasting the time of the court and doubting the integrity of an upstanding entrepreneur such as Professor Crady.

Professor Crady's Traveling Show of Oddities and Prodigies set a box office record that weekend and enjoyed a two-week extended run in Birmingham.

Perhaps the most remarkable character in the show was Ignacio Pernaud, 'The Man with No Arms'. Born without any semblance of upper limbs, Ignacio was a marvel and a great source of inspiration to E. Tim.

Using only his dexterous feet and toes, Ignacio could sign his name in an elegant script (at five cents per autograph); shave with a scalpel-sharp straight razor; shuffle and deal a hand of cards; shine a shoe; light a cigar; and pull a cork out of wooden keg that had been lodged so tightly that no one in the audience could pull it out.

Ignacio varied his act from show to show because just about everything he did was remarkable and left a great impression on the crowd but he always closed his portion of the show by playing a lively tune on the xylophone with his feet. The crowd would roar their approval and Ignacio would take a long, deep bow, smile and exit the stage.

Professor Crady demanded that the troupe keep their own company. Part of the reason for sequestering his performers was for their own protection from the cruelties of the world outside. He was also concerned that the novelty of his oddities might wear off if the people of the town saw them coming and going and that it might affect his business.

So, the members of 'Professor Bill Crady's Collection of Oddities and Prodigies' kept to themselves like a band of gypsies, camping in the surrounding countryside and avoiding strangers. Like a large family, they took care of one another. Carmen, the bearded lady, had a fine hand with a needle and thread and could sew on a loose button or mend a pair of ripped trousers. She also had a way of soothing E. Tim's headaches by gently massaging his neck and temple.

Heintz, the dwarf, was a ball of energy and extremely strong. If there was anything to be done during set-up or take-down, Heintz cheerfully took on the task with enthusiasm. E. Tim taught Heinz to fish and when the dwarf landed a catfish that weighed nearly as much as he did, Heintz exclaimed in his broken English that it was the happiest and proudest day of his life.

E. Tim learned to play cribbage at a table with a bearded lady, a rubber man who nervously pulled the skin from his neck and snapped it back into place whenever he had a hand requiring a difficult decision, and the remarkable Ignacio, who could not only shuffle and deal the cards, but was able to move the tiny wooden pegs of the cribbage board with his toes.

It was Ignacio who taught E. Tim the most valuable lessons. Quiet and uncomplaining, Ignacio was living proof that any task, no matter how daunting or difficult, was achievable despite whatever handicaps one may be faced with.

With one exception: the clarinet. Ignacio loved the happy sound of the instrument and had bought one hoping to include it in his act. He taught himself how to lip it correctly, how to change reeds and the proper fingering — or toeing in his case. But he could never quite play it the way he heard it played on the radio. The clarinet was one of the few challenges that Ignacio had not met with success, although he did succeed in convincing E. Tim to take up the instrument.

Ignacio begged and badgered E. Tim to not only learn the clarinet but master it. Every day, Ignacio pestered E. Tim into practicing for hours, sometimes accompanying him on his xylophone.

With the same determination it took for a man with no arms to learn to shave with a deadly sharp straight razor, Ignacio implanted his unconquerable will into E. Tim's education at mastering the clarinet.

Unlike other owners of similar shows, Professor Bill Crady benevolently shared the profits from his show with each of the members of his troupe. During this period of the late 1930's and the early 1940's, the United States was in the final grips of the Great Depression and, in comparison to the income earned by most folks in the audience, the members of the troupe felt as though they were pretty well-off.

E. Tim's first months with the show were difficult and he thought about running away. However, he had never been out in the real world. Throughout his whole life he'd been put away with either orphans or freaks. And with a dent in his head, the outside world seemed a little scary. Besides, E. Tim wasn't quite sure where he'd runaway to.

Gradually, he began to lose his sense of self-consciousness along with the shame and embarrassment of being associated with the other strange-looking members of the show. He was getting pretty good money for a boy his age and the other performers in the show were friendly and kind to him.

At the county home, E. Tim never got too close to any of the other children. His peculiar-shaped head kept a lot of the other kids away but it seemed like every time he'd finally find someone with something in common and a friendship would start to grow, they'd get adopted and be gone from his life. Sometimes they'd be brought back to the home, but they never seemed to be the same and the friendship never picked back up again. So, E. Tim stayed to himself and the backwaters of Lake Fausse.

Members of the troupe genuinely cared for one another and couldn't help but overlook any physical deformities in one another. For a young boy with the side of his head caved in, E. Tim could not have possibly fallen in with a more loving and understanding group of people. Although he missed the bayou, compared with his years at the Atchafalaya Country Home for Orphans and Handicapped Children, his time with Professor Crady's Strangest Show on Earth was E. Tim's only recollection of feeling as though he was part of a real family.

E. Tim stayed with the show until he was 18, when an unfortunate incident occurred in Covington, Louisiana, across Lake Pontchartrain from New Orleans.

In an effort to stimulate dwindling crowds, Bill Crady had brought in a recent addition to the show, a hulking, brooding Russian whom the professor billed as 'Alexander the Geek'.

After Ignacio had shown off his skills and played his xylophone finale, Professor Crady would get up on the main stage and speak in his most dramatic manner to the crowd while Ignacio played a long drum roll on a kettle drum.

"Ladies and gentlemen, many of you are thinking right now that you've seen it all. Well, not quite. There is more...for some of you, that is. I am required by the Louisiana State Board of Psychopathic Behavior to warn you that what you are about to experience could have some serious psychological consequences. If you are now, or have been within the past ten years, suffering from any type of psychological malady or, for that matter, any weakness of the heart, stomach or digestive system, I must ask you to leave the premises immediately."

The Professor would wait for a moment while a few parents dragged their children, screaming and begging to stay and see what was going to happen, out of the tent. He'd give Ignacio a signal to stop his drum roll and a deafening silence would fall over the crowd. Beads of sweat would appear on the faces of the audience and glisten like nuggets in the golden light thrown by the lanterns hanging inside the tent.

"Anyone else among you favoring discretion over valor? Mind you, there's no shame in turning away. If you decide to stay and should suddenly feel nauseated during the performance, please make sure that it's your own shoes you ruin and not the person's next to you. Lastly, I suggest that you give yourself some space between one another and let the air circulate around you."

The Professor would wipe his brow with his handkerchief and draw in a long, deep breath before he continued.

"Professor Bill Crady's Collection of Oddities and Prodigies presents the most bizarre and grotesque act you will ever witness in person. Ladies and gentlemen, from the frozen, primitive, barbarian lands of Russia, I bring you, Alexander Von Romanoff."

The Geek would appear from behind a black curtain and the audience would gasp. He was six and a half feet tall and weighed nearly 300 pounds. The stage was a good two feet off the ground so the Geek looked even bigger as he towered over the crowd. His thick, black, curly hair was long and frazzled. He wore only black bathing trunks and shin-high dough-boy boots. He dragged a heavy chain, one end bolted to the back of the stage, the other attached to a thick, metal collar around his neck.

Like a chained wild animal, the Geek would stalk around the stage, snarling at the audience. His eyes were bloodshot (from a drop of lemon juice just before he went on) and a trickle of drool spilled out from the corner of his mouth.

After a few minutes of intimidating the crowd, the Geek would go back behind the curtain and then reappear seconds later. In one hand he held a live chicken, squawking and beating its wings against the Geek's bare thigh. Before the audience had a chance to figure out what was going to happen next, the Geek bit off the head of the live chicken.

It was a hell of a show closer.

For whatever reason (E. Tim always suspected that it must have been due to Alexander's amorous advances being thwarted by Carmen or perhaps he was totally consumed by his character as actors are known to do), one evening, after a particularly savage beheading, Alexander the Geek, blood covering his face and chest, pointed the headless, feathered torso toward the stunned and repulsed audience and began squeezing the body of the chicken, dousing them with a stream of warm, fresh blood.

A man in the front row who had taken the brunt of the spraying, charged the stage. Alexander, part psychotic, part lovesick, part homesick and part still in character, picked up the man, lifted him over his head and threw him back into the audience.

Thinking that the mammoth Russian had gone mad, the crowd panicked and stampeded for the exit, accidentally knocking over several lanterns and setting fire to the tent.

The charred body of an elderly man, evidently trampled in the panic and burned to death in the ensuing fire, was found the next morning among the ashes.

Alexander was charged with second-degree murder and Uncle Bill was arrested for inciting a riot and an accessory to murder.

By the following evening, the little troupe of oddities and prodigies from "Professor Crady's Collection of Oddities and Prodigies" wandered off and disappeared into the cracks and crevices of the South.

E. Tim canted his cap over the side of his head to hide his deformity and hopped a bus to New Orleans where he found a job the next day working on a shrimp trawler. He'd had his fill of show business and vowed never to stand in front of an audience again.

E. Tim had kept that promise until the night he, Wingy and Nathan played together under the bridge of the canal.

# Chapter 4
## Joleen Salveson
## The Coach's Daughter

*J*OLEEN WAS THE COMBINED NAMESAKE AND ONLY CHILD BORN of Joe and Eileen Salveson. Joe taught geometry and coached the varsity football team at Thief River Falls High School. Eileen was a piano teacher.

Eileen McKensie married the boy she had fallen in love with in the fourth grade after watching Joe Salveson break up a fist fight on the playground between Stuart Boreen and a new kid in school, Buzzy Duber. Thief River Falls was a small town in northern Minnesota and a new boy, if he didn't play hockey, hunt or fish, normally had a difficult time finding acceptance among the other boys.

Buzzy and his parents had moved to Thief River Falls from New York City just before school started. He didn't play hockey and he didn't hunt or fish. None of the members of the Duber family looked or spoke like the majority of Scandinavians in town. Nor had they made a single appearance at any of the fourteen Lutheran churches since they arrived.

Another factor that made it difficult for Buzzy to fit in with the rest of his classmates was that he was a little… odd. He had an assortment of nervous tics and twitches and would occasionally talk to an imaginary friend.

The self-imposed code of proper social behavior for a fourth grader in Thief River Falls was fairly rigid and by the end of his third week of school, Buzzy had broken just about every single rule.

Tolerance thresholds had already been worn thin when Buzzy walked into the classroom one morning and invented a new rule to break. He was wearing shoes with deep, corrugated rubber soles. The gaps in the waffled bottom of his shoes were packed solidly with dog feces.

Stuart Boreen, the biggest kid in the class, happened to sit directly in front of Buzzy and had noticed the foul odor but initially thought that it had emanated from Myrtle Gabrielson, whose desk was in front of Stuart's.

Myrtle was the daughter of a dairy farmer and, unfortunately, severely lactose-intolerant, thus bestowing upon poor Myrtle with the reputation as the most prolific farter in school. A boy with a reputation like that could gain some prestige from his peers but Myrtle's particular talent was not a becoming feature for a fourth-grade girl.

On more than one occasion, Stuart was made to sit on a stool in the corner of the room for groaning aloud, "Jeez, Myrtle cut another one!"

The foul odor from Buzzy's shoes began to envelope the whole classroom. The teacher, Mrs. Anderson, faced a classroom of students pinching their noses with all heads turned toward the hapless and wrongly accused, Myrtle Gabrielson.

It didn't take Mrs. Anderson long to discover the source of the stench. She walked over and stood beside Buzzy's desk.

"Buzzy, you go outside and take those shoes off right now!"

Still believing that the smell was coming from Myrtle and her lactose intolerance, Stuart innocently turned around and looked under the desk behind him. Poor Stuart got a full whiff from both of Buzzy's shoes. Not only was the smell repulsive, but the sight of the clumps of feces, mud and grass clippings dangling off Buzzy's twitching feet was nauseating.

Stuart had been spinning on the swings before the bell rang and was still feeling a little queasy. The sickening sight of Buzzy's shoes was more than Stuart's already unsettled stomach could take. Without warning, Stuart vomited all over his teacher's shoes.

Mrs. Anderson ordered Stuart to go to the nurse's office where he had his temperature taken and was ordered to lie down for 15-minutes.

A big-for-his-age farm boy, Stuart wasn't the sharpest student in the class but he was savvy enough to foresee the embarrassment and disgrace he was going to suffer for not only throwing up in class but doing it all over the teacher's shoes as well. He knew he was going to be a target for teasing by the rest of the whole school and it would all be the fault of that weirdo, new kid, Buzzy Duber. He also knew that there was only one way he could possibly salvage his reputation.

The nurse diagnosed Stuart's sudden illness as simply an upset stomach and asked him if he'd like her to call his mother.

Stuart thought about the offer. It was tempting. Maybe he could fake it and stay out of school for a couple of weeks until the whole episode was forgotten. On second thought, he realized that throwing up on the teacher's shoes was not something his classmates would easily forget. Then he heard the recess bell and the sound of the schoolyard filled with screaming and yelling children.

"No, ma'am, I'm feeling a whole lot better now," Stuart said politely. "I think I'm all right."

Stuart flew out of the nurse's office and onto the playground where he found Buzzy Duber walking along the edge of the chain link fence cheerfully talking to himself.

Stuart tackled Buzzy and had him on his back in seconds. With his knees holding Buzzy's arms down, Stuart pounded his fists into Buzzy's face. In no time, most of the students on the playground had circled around the two boys, most of the onlookers imploring Stuart to beat the snot out of the weirdo new kid.

Eileen McKensie and her friends abandoned their game of four square and ran over to see what was happening. Eileen's first glimpse of the fight was of Buzzy's bloody face. Her heart sank. Buzzy was pleading for Stuart to stop but the crowd's lust for blood and Stuart's rage at being humiliated prolonged the beating beyond a normal playground fight's conclusion.

Eileen remembered desperately looking around, hoping to see a teacher coming to break it up. When she turned back towards the fight, she saw another fourth grader, Joe Salveson, break through the crowd, grab Stuart by the back of his shirt and throw him off the bleeding and sobbing Buzzy Duber.

"He's a weirdo, Joe!" Stuart panted almost apologetically. "He deserved a licking. He made me throw up on Mrs. Anderson's shoes!"

The bell ending recess rang and the crowd began to return to their classrooms but Eileen stayed and watched as Joe took out his handkerchief and wiped the blood off Buzzy's face.

"Now you go on to the nurse, tell her you fell off the swings," Joe told him. "Don't say nothing about Stuart or the fight. You'll be all right. Go on now."

Buzzy didn't return to class after recess. However, as the children filed into the cafeteria for lunch, Buzzy, with cuts all over his face, a swollen eye and a puffy, purple lip, was sitting by himself at one of the tables staring down at his plate. News of the dog poop incident and the subsequent fight had spread throughout the school and the students carefully avoided sitting at Buzzy's table.

The roar of lunchtime chatter suddenly hushed when Joe Salveson came through the cafeteria line and sat down next to Buzzy. Eileen watched the heads turn and she could hear the whispers around her.

"What's Joe Salveson doing sitting next to that creep?"

"That's the guy who stepped in the dog shit. Who'd want to sit next to him?"

From the time it took nine-year-old Eileen McKensie to pick up her tray and sit down at the table next to Joe and Buzzy, she had made up her mind that someday she was going to marry Joe Salveson.

"Would you mind if I sat down and ate lunch with you?" she asked them both.

71

When Joe nodded and smiled the kindest, warmest and most understanding smile Eileen had ever seen or felt in her life, they became best friends from that day forward.

Joe and Eileen remained best friends all the way through high school and into college where they both attended the University of Minnesota. Joe on a football scholarship, Eileen on a music scholarship.

In college, Joe enjoyed Eileen's company more than his roommates or teammates. He preferred sitting on one of the sofas in the reception room at Eileen's dormitory where they would talk, mostly about football. Near the end of their evenings together, Joe would always ask 'Leen', as he called her, to "tickle those eighty-eight".

Girls from the dorm would wander down from their rooms and gather around the piano as Eileen played the popular songs of the day while the rest of the girls sang along. Joe would lean back in the sofa, smiling and tapping his toe. When Eileen would accidentally hit a wrong note or chord, she'd glance over at Joe and flash him a wide-eyed and innocent 'whoopsie daisy' smile. Joe would give her that same kind, warm smile he gave her in the cafeteria back in fourth grade and Eileen would have to look away and take a couple of deep breaths because that smile always made her a little dizzy.

Eileen's ability to read a complicated sheet of music and perform a classical piece by Mozart or play 'Ragtime Cowboy Joe' with equal proficiency was extraordinary to Joe.

In addition to music theory, Eileen knew football. She had seen every football game Joe had played from junior high school through college. She observed the game in much the same way she studied music. She appreciated the fundamentals of the game and had respect for the strategies and nuances as well as the physical and athletic skills required of each player and position. She could even perceive subtle changes in tempo during a game, much like the works of the great composers. But what touched her deepest and related closest to her love for music was the element of passion and inspiration in the game and how those emotions could motivate a player or a whole team to seemingly play over and above their inherent capabilities.

There wasn't a couple on the campus that enjoyed each other's company more than Joe and Eileen.

At the end of his senior year in college, Joe received an offer to be the head coach at his alma mater, Thief River Falls High School. The retiring coach, after 35 years at the school, had suggested only one name to be his successor even though Joe had no previous coaching experience.

Around the same time Joe received his offer to coach in Thief River Falls, Eileen received offers to teach music from three schools in the southern part of the state. Thief River Falls was located near the Canadian border in the northernmost part of the state which meant Joe and Eileen were faced with the possibility of being separated by more than a few blocks for the first time since kindergarten.

Their dilemma was solved the week before finals at an ice cream parlor, not far from the university campus, where Joe asked Eileen to marry him. A unanimous decision was reached after the first sip of their chocolate malted milks.

The following weekend, Joe and Eileen were married in the Minneapolis County Courthouse. There was no maid of honor or a best man. The ceremony was held with just the two of them along with the judge's secretary who served as a witness. They packed their clothes, got in Joe's car and drove back home to Thief River Falls.

Coach Salveson was the first coach to ever have his wife travel on the bus with the Thief River Falls High School football team. Not only did Mrs. Salveson travel with the team but Joe was known to, at critical times during a game, walk over to the front row of the stands and consult with his wife—often without first consulting with his assistant coaches.

Following each game, Joe and Eileen would come home and discuss the game over a late supper. After dinner they'd take their coffee and dessert into the living room where they would continue their analysis of the game. They shared the joy of each victory and the disappointments of every loss and like all good football minds, they could always find improvements to make in a win, as well as promise for the future in a loss.

What was uncanny about their conversations was that they spoke in partial sentences, each one anticipating and finishing the others thought as though only one person was speaking.

Joe might open the dialogue with, "Jeez, if only Jensen had held onto the football..."

"...we'd have been first and ten on their 28-yard line..." Eileen would add.

"...with still a minute, forty-six left to play." Joe would finish.

"Yep," they'd both agree.

"If O'Brian doesn't miss that tackle..."

"..what was it, third and eight...?"

"...they'd of had to punt."

"Yea, sure," they'd both agree.

It was a most remarkable relationship.

Eileen gave private piano lessons and baked cakes, pies, cinnamon rolls and coffeecakes that were legendary throughout the northern part of Minnesota. In the wake of any sort of celebratory event or misfortune, residents of the town could be assured of a visit by the coach's wife and a plateful of something just out of the oven. There was a rumor in town that a local, unmarried farmer with a voracious sweet tooth once faked a serious back injury in order to get a pan of Eileen Salveson's cinnamon rolls.

Those same renowned cinnamon rolls were also the marketing secret behind Eileen's thriving piano lesson business. She always had a waiting list for her lessons and her students seemed to continue their studies much longer than most beginning piano students. Many of whom would admit to enduring the painful agony of weekly piano lessons and daily practice in exchange for a glass of milk and a cinnamon roll that came as a reward at the end of their 30-minute lesson.

In Joe's second year as head coach and in the midst of a six-game winning streak, Joleen Francis Salveson was born. As she lay nestled against her mother's breast in the hospital, Joleen's first bedtime story she heard was her father's account of Thief River Falls' 28-14, fourth quarter, come-from-behind victory over Crookston that afternoon.

By birth, Joleen was officially initiated into an extremely exclusive club with a very close-knit and limited membership. Despite sharing both members' first and last names as well as their combined gene pools, she was, at best, an honorary member.

Joleen was always envious of her parent's relationship.

Not that she ever lacked for love or was in any way neglected growing up. It was more as though she felt like a third person tagging along with two best friends. It was difficult to find a place to fit in between two people who were so close. Even more annoying to a young girl trying to establish her own identity, Joleen grew up in a town where her father was revered and her mother perceived as a saint. Joleen was always referred to as "Joe's kid" or "Eileen's little girl". The references were always made lovingly and she was always treated with kindness and respect by the people in town, but she couldn't help wondering if the way she was regarded by others had more to do with who her parents were, rather than the person she was.

Joleen tried rebellion in her early teens but no one took her seriously. She even ran away once but came back home when she started to worry that no one would notice that she was gone. She was like a boxer trying to find an opening so she could land at least one punch. Eventually, Joleen stopped fighting and began to appreciate her parent's relationship with one another and with the people of the town.

Joleen's senior year in high school, the class of 1940, was a year that was clouded over by the ominous rumors of war overseas. The newspapers and radio broadcasts in the early stages of the Nazi regime referred to the rumors as "the phony war in Europe". However, in largely Scandinavian Minnesota, reports of Adolf Hitler's army overrunning Denmark and Norway were taken very seriously.

That same year was also Joe's 19th year as head football coach at Thief River Falls High School. No other high school coach in the state came close to Joe's winning record even though he competed against towns and cities much larger than Thief River Falls.

During his tenure as a head coach, Joe had numerous opportunities to coach at a higher level with promises of a salary increase as well.

Every year, two or three universities would send a couple of alumni up to Thief River to try and convince Joe to bring his talents to the collegiate ranks. But each year he would politely turn them down and send them back home…with a plate of Eileen's cinnamon rolls, of course.

Joe was right where he wanted to be. He enjoyed coaching players from the same town where he was raised. He had grown up with many of the parents of the players and looked at his players as members of his own family. His former players still came to Joe to seek advice on major decisions in their lives or to talk over problems. Joe felt that leaving Thief River Falls would be like abandoning his family.

There was one negative aspect to Joe's position of respect and admiration in the eyes of the community. His daughter, Joleen, was the only member of the Thief River Falls High School cheerleading squad who had never been out on a real date. Although she was friendly, pretty and popular with the kids, there were very few boys brave enough to date Coach Salveson's daughter. Those few with the initiative and daring to consider asking her out on a date also happened to look up to Coach Salveson as a father figure which, after thinking about it for a moment, realized that dating Joleen would be the equivalent of dating their sister. So, they never asked.

For 18 years, since little Joleen had been old enough to be watched by a baby sitter, Eileen Salveson had traveled on the school bus along with her husband, coaches, players and cheerleaders, to every one of Thief River Falls' away games. Mrs. Salveson always sat in the stands and was always close to the field in case Joe needed to run an idea by her. In the Fall of 1940, the school district's insurance company sent a letter to the principal of warning that the school's transportation coverage could be canceled because the coach's wife was not covered under the school travel policy.

It was rumored that a disgruntled ex-assistant-coach-turned-insurance salesman, who still carried some resentment of Joe's policy of consulting his wife before his coaches, was the person behind the threat.

At the risk of having the school's insurance canceled, Joe elected to drive to games in his own car with his wife.

A light snow had dusted the countryside as the school bus, carrying the team and the cheerleaders, followed by Coach Salveson and his wife in their car and several dozen or so cars filled with Thief River Falls supporters, made the 28-mile trip through the mountains up to Strandquist on a cold, gray October afternoon.

Joleen was sitting in the back of the bus with the rest of the pep squad. In the middle of the whirlwind of laughing and gossiping, Joleen had an eerie feeling come over her and turned around to look out the back window.

She wiped off the condensation with her hand and pressed her face against the back window. She screamed as she saw her parent's car swerving out of control on the slippery road. As if in slow motion, the car spun around in a circle and disappeared off the side of the road and down a steep embankment.

A fiery explosion followed by a plume of thick, black smoke bellowed up from the canyon below as the bus and its entourage pulled over to the side of the road.

Joe and Eileen were both killed in the crash.

Joleen's parents were essentially her whole family. Both Joe and Eileen were only children. Eileen's parents had died before Joleen was born. Joe's mother and father were killed in a fire when Joleen was nine. No grandparents, no aunts, no uncles, no cousins. Joleen was suddenly an orphan without any family.

The funeral for Joe and Eileen Salveson was the largest gathering anyone in town could remember. It was attended by almost every person who lived in Thief River Falls plus those whose lives had been touched by Joe and Eileen but had moved away. Former players, coaches and sportswriters came from all over Minnesota and neighboring states as well. The governor even sent a representative.

Dr. and Mrs. Lars Lindqvist, along with their two daughters, sat with Joleen in the front row at the service. With an overflowing crowd in attendance, Pastor Blough took the opportunity to try and impress a few of the out-of-town souls with some of his best Lutheran preaching. Had he known that he was speaking to sportswriters, he probably wouldn't have even tried.

The church was filled to capacity and many more people stood outside but Joleen had never felt more alone. Pastor Blough went on and on but Joleen never heard a word. She sat with her hands folded in her lap, fighting for each breath and trying not to suffocate beneath the staggering grief and rising tide of panic whenever she started to think about the future without her parents.

She stared at the two identical closed coffins and wondered who was inside each. She wondered what the bodies must look like. Were they burned corpses or a pile of ashes? She tried not to get sick to her stomach. She focused all of her attention on keeping her hands knitted together. She was certain that if her fingers came apart, so would she.

In the three days since their deaths, she missed her mom and dad dreadfully and although she had always considered herself an independent sort, Joleen found that thoughts as simple as wondering what to do tomorrow left her anxious and frightened.

She had been staying with Dr. and Mrs. Lindqvist and their two daughters since the accident. The two Lindqvist girls had moved into one bedroom giving Joleen her own room.

After the funeral, Dr. Lindqvist told Joleen that his family would be honored if she were to move in with them. Familiar with the same Scandinavian pride and stubbornness that helped carve farms out of plains scraped bare of soil by glaciers and provided the fortitude to endure the long, bitter-cold winters of the far north, Dr. Lindqvist offered Joleen the opportunity to work in his office after school to help earn her room and board.

Joleen accepted the offer. In the months that followed she discovered that not only had the Lindqvist's opened their hearts to her, but the whole town had suddenly adopted her as their own child.

When Joleen was asked to do some errands in town for the doctor, the druggist would box up a number of personal items and hand them to Joleen as a gift from his wife. Mr. Stevenson at the mercantile would call her over from across the street and invite her into his store to see if a new pair of boots he had just got in happened to fit. He always seemed to have a sweater or coat or a pair of wool socks for Joleen.

Whenever Mr. Andersen saw Joleen, he'd invite her into his bakery for a slice of pie, coffeecake or other fresh baked goods out of his ovens.

"Now I know it's nowhere as good as your momma used to make, God rest her soul, but I've got a slice of pound cake here and I'd sure appreciate it if you'd try a sample and be good enough to tell me just where I went wrong with it."

Joleen found herself growing up very quickly. Along with her parents, the accident also took away the remainder of Joleen's adolescence. Although she realized that there really wasn't too much left of her high school and teenage years, she had suspicions that she had probably just skipped over one of the best parts.

Joleen's life had changed drastically. She had gone from being Joe and Eileen's daughter to the communal child of the entire town.

As she wrestled with the process of grieving over the loss of her parents, Joleen found herself feeling angry and resentful of the town's generosity. She saw it as a form of pity.

It was Helen Lindqvist, the doctor's wife, who recognized Joleen's struggle and spoke to her one night before bed.

Joleen was sitting down in front of her dressing table brushing her hair when Mrs. Lindqvist came into her room.

"Here, let me do that, honey," Helen said, taking the brush from Joleen's hand.

At first, Helen was silent as she brushed Joleen's long, golden hair. Joleen's shoulders gradually relaxed and she closed her eyes.

"You know the people in this town miss your parents almost as much as you do. They're grieving, too, and when they see you, they're reminded of how wonderful your mom and dad were to us all."

Helen continued brushing Joleen's hair.

"I know it probably doesn't seem to you as though your parents left you much but they invested their lives in this town and in the people who live here."

Helen could see Joleen's tears in the reflection of the mirror.

"Everything all of us are trying to do for you is really a way to thank your mother and father for all the things they did for us. And since they left us so…so… suddenly, we feel that we didn't get the opportunity to properly thank them for how much better they made our lives."

Helen stopped brushing and placed her hands on Joleen's shoulders.

"It's you, child. You are what they have left us with and it is through you that we can repay your parents. They've gone to a wonderful place and left you and all of us behind but their love is still here. Their love for you is living in the people of Thief River. That love is still looking out and caring for you."

"Your inheritance is a whole town, Joleen Salveson. Money gets spent but your mother and father left you a lot more. I know how hard it is to feel love through all your pain but try and let them all love you, honey. Let the gifts your parents gave keep changing hands."

Helen handed her a tissue.

"Now get into bed. I'll bet you've got a busy day at school tomorrow."

That night, Joleen cried herself to sleep.

Her tears and Helen Lindqvist's thoughtful words dampened her anger and resentment. It was difficult at first but eventually she realized that the town's generosity was genuine and she learned to accept their kindness as a form of tribute and respect for her mother and father.

Working three days a week in Dr. Lindqvist's office, Joleen found that she could return some of that kindness with compassion towards those in Thief River Falls who were sick or recovering from an injury or illness. In a way, that's what her mother and her cinnamon rolls did for the people in town. She discovered that as she gave of herself to others, the closer she felt to her parents.

For one of her last high school assignments, Joleen wrote a book report in English class on Clara Barton's autobiography, *The Story of My Childhood*. Joleen was moved by Barton's humanitarian efforts including her formation of the American Red Cross; relief work with yellow fever in Florida; the Johnstown flood; the Russian famine; and the Spanish-American War. The last question on the book report form was, 'How did this book affect you?'

"It made me want to become a nurse someday," was Joleen's answer.

Three days after her high school graduation, Joleen turned 18 and enlisted in the Navy Nursing Corps. She waved goodbye to nearly half the town who had gathered to see her off as she boarded the bus for Chicago and the Great Lakes Naval Training Center.

# Chapter 5
## Bobby Carolina
## Tamper/Farmer

B OBBY CAROLINA GREW UP ON HIS PARENTS' FARM IN GREEN Valley and attended the University of Arizona in Tucson on a basketball scholarship. His senior year he averaged fourteen points and eight rebounds per game and graduated with honors from the College of Agriculture with a major in Soils, Water and Engineering.

After graduating from college, Bobby went to work in the copper mines north of Tucson. The mines didn't ask for a diploma or care about honors or grade point averages but they did pay well, much more than any college graduate could expect to make right out of school.

Bobby worked as a 'tamper', one of the highest paying and most dangerous jobs in the mine. To open a new tunnel or extend a current one, the miners drill holes, three to four inches in diameter and up to forty-feet long, into the rock wall.

After the holes have been drilled, the tamper mixes a concoction called ANFO, a highly explosive combination of diesel fuel and ammonium nitrate, and then carefully tamps the slurry to the far end of the drilled hole with a long rod. Once the proper amount of ANFO has been planted, the tamper inserts a blasting cap and a priming cord which is connected to a detonator. Although the whole process is extremely dangerous, the most hazardous portion of the job comes when the tamper has to seal the hole with filler so that the impending blast will shatter the surrounding rock and not back fire out of the hole. The job requires towering amounts of concentration and composure as well as an intuitive ability to "feel" through 35-feet of solid rock. Every time Bobby hollered, "Fire in the hole!" before setting off the detonator, he knew there was a chance he would never taste another breath of fresh air.

Bobby's intention in working at the mine was to earn enough money to buy his parent's land. They were ready to retire and were having trouble keeping up with the costs and demands of running a farm. The mines were the fastest way to earn money but it was hard-earned money. The shafts were filled with bad air, dust and particulate matter and were always wet, cold and claustrophobic. Plus, there was always a chance of a cave in. Bobby's normal shift was four, ten-hour days on and four days off unless the price of copper went up in which case it meant the miners could work as many hours as they wanted.

After two years in the mines, Bobby returned to Green Valley with a substantial down payment on the farm. Bobby and his father signed the papers at the bank on a Thursday and by Friday morning his parents had loaded up their motor home and were on their way to San Diego.

The hours Bobby put into the farm made his mining days look like a part-time job but he found no greater joy than working his land and watching his crops flourish. He took a scientific approach to farming and tested fertilizers, pesticides, soil development techniques and kept up with the latest in genetic engineering to increase his crops production. After two harvests, Bobby was growing the thickest cotton and the tallest corn in the valley on his 450 acres of rich Santa Cruz River bottom land.

Nearly every backyard in Green Valley had a truck garden of some sort growing a variety of fruits and vegetables such as tomatoes, carrots, cantaloupes, squash, chili peppers and peas for the dinner table.

Bobby Carolina's garden was legendary for its exotic crops including white asparagus; pink celery that tasted a bit like a radish; lemon cucumbers; eggplant the size of watermelons; strange varieties of lettuce; peanuts with four or five nuts per shell; strawberries as big as a child's fist; honey lope melons (a cross between a honeydew and a cantaloupe) and four, blood orange trees sent from Israel by an old friend from college.

Bobby linked his garden and part of his corn field to a small aquaculture project he built himself comprised of four, thousand-gallon tanks each filled with about five hundred catfish. Starting with fingerlings, Bobby could get two to three harvests a year which he sold to a fish processor. His well water was warm and of good quality which contributed to the fast growth of the catfish. The fish were fed on fresh-ground corn from Bobby's fields so the meat was sweet and tasty. The nitrogen-rich effluent that drained out of the fish tanks fed directly back into the corn field as well as the garden.

Some people claimed, "You could plant a rock in Bobby Carolina's garden and a statue would sprout up".

The farm provided a good enough living for Bobby to marry his high school sweetheart, Eleanor Wheatley. Bobby and Eleanor had two children; their firstborn, Molly, and their second, five years later, a son, Ethan.

# Chapter 6
## Molly Carolina
## Secret Keeper

T HE EASTERN SKY WAS BRUISED WITH THE COLORS OF THE COM-
ing dawn as Molly Carolina stomped through the recently
planted field. The land steamed with the heady morning breath
of the rich, newly fertilized earth.

Driven by a blinding rage so overwhelming and alien that she
could never have imagined that it had been lurking within her
emotional make-up, Molly stumbled towards the far end of the
field and a thick stand of salt cedars bordering the Santa Cruz
River. The steeply angled furrows and crumbly, just-turned soil
in the field buckled her knees and twisted her ankles. Molly stumbled and reeled as though she were at sea on the deck of a ship
being pounded by storm-driven swells. Maintaining her balance
was made even more difficult by a heavy, leather-bound scrapbook
she clutched tightly across her chest.

The first rays of the sun to cut across the field stung Molly's swollen
and bloodshot eyes. She couldn't stop crying and when she would try
to wipe the tears from her face, she inadvertently rubbed dirt in her
eyes which made them burn even more. At times it seemed to her as
though the trees and the river kept running away from her as if this
was part of a dream.

But this wasn't a dream. Dreams are often forgotten at the mere opening of an eye. Even the worst nightmares can be washed away with a splash of cold water and a couple of deep breaths.

At that moment, Molly Carolina was breathing deeply and the tears had washed her face a hundred times over but this nightmare wasn't going to go away…ever.

She had never been this angry in her life and wondered how such fury could be born out of desperate sadness. But it was a stupid, meaningless, academic question. She was sick of asking questions and sick of searching for answers. She was sick of herself because she knew she should have helped. She knew she could have saved her family from this terrible tragedy. But she didn't.

After all, that's what Molly Carolina did. She was a helper. She was a listener. She was the one person in Green Valley, Arizona to whom anyone could confess the most condemning of sins or reveal the most shameful of dreams or desires and then walk away with the unweighted bliss of confession, confident in the security of their secrets and totally assured that their admission was received by Molly without a squinted eye or speck of judgment. Molly was a note taker, a caretaker, a secret keeper, a carpet sweeper and a birthday rememberer. That was her nature.

As a child, Molly Carolina had a remarkable ability to reach out and pull the plug out of a person. Sometimes things would pour out that had been stored away for years and years.

"Well, what do you do Mr. McMillan?" was the first question Molly asked Hal McMillan the day he and his family moved in next to the Carolina's farm.

"I'm in the insurance business," Molly's new neighbor answered.

Molly's next question was a bit more penetrating.

"Did you grow up to be what you wanted to be, Mr. McMillan?"

Molly was two months short of being five-years-old when she first met Hal McMillan. Their initial conversation went on for over two hours. Their friendship lasted for 18 years.

Hal McMillan was in his late forties when he first discovered Molly. She watched him quit the insurance business, become one of Arizona's most celebrated sculptors; publish three books on indigenous Arizona Indian tribes; and solo kayak the Colorado River every summer from Lee's Ferry to Diamond Creek with some of the most treacherous Class V water in North America. On his 7th trip, he misjudged the entrance to Lava Falls and dropped into the rapid's treacherous hydraulic. The kayak was spit out by the 20-foot mountain of churning water but Hal was trapped in the back flow.

According to onlookers, McMillan was being thrashed by the giant wave and after several minutes of struggling in the hypothermic, thirty-eight-degree water, he began to lose his strength. As a last resort, the experienced river boatman took off his life jacket and tried to force his body toward the bottom of the hydraulic hoping to catch an undercurrent. His body was never found.

At the reading of Hal McMillan's will, he left his wealth and worldly goods to his wife and children but specified in writing, and read aloud by his attorney, that he bequeathed his passion for life to Molly Carolina.

When other kids in Green Valley rattled through the neighborhood on noisy, plastic big wheels or wobbled on new bikes, Molly preferred long walks with her father.

A walk with Molly rarely lasted less than an hour yet could only cover 100 feet in either direction of her front gate. Molly was fascinated by everything. Weeds sprouting out of cracks in the sidewalk were a celebration to Molly. A column of ants marching single file was mesmerizing. A fallen leaf, a dead bug, a sparkly rock, chirps from invisible birds, or the smell of a curious flower peeking over a garden fence were enough to provide Molly with wonder and amazement.

Molly's father, Bobby Carolina, had learned about patience from earning his living from the earth so he was comfortable with her endless series of questions. He found, "Well, what do you think, Molly?" to be the best response.

"Where do you think all these ants are going? Are they all the same age? Are there some ants that are best friends? Are there families and do they march together?" Molly would ask.

"Well, what do you think, Molly?"

After a minute or two of serious concentration, Molly could usually come up with an answer that satisfied her curiosity.

On one of their walks, Molly's ever-attentive eyes spotted a peculiar shadow on the sidewalk. She studied it carefully while her father absentmindedly flirted with a plan to trim the overgrown oleander hedge that surrounded his yard.

"Daddy, quick!" she screamed, pointing up into the limbs of a majestic cottonwood tree above them. "We have to save him!"

Molly had spotted the shadow cast by a flailing cabbage butterfly trapped in a spider web high among the branches of the tree.

Bobby Carolina looked up, shading his eyes from the sun, and finally located the butterfly.

"We have to save it, Daddy! We have to save the butterfly! Please, Daddy! Please!"

The rescue necessitated a balancing act by Bobby on the very top step of a twelve-foot ladder plus an eight-foot fly rod extended at full arm's length.

Bobby was aware that there were about 8 billion cabbage butterflies flapping their herky-jerky wings through the valley this time of year and that this particular one was probably not going to be missed.

He was also sensitive enough to realize that the 'National Geographic approach', "The spider needs to eat, too, Honey..." was never going to find accord with Molly.

After freeing the butterfly from the web, Bobby carefully unwrapped the spider's silky threads from the wings of the butterfly while his daughter held her breath in anxious concern.

Remarkably, the butterfly survived and was able to fly away. Molly watched it's wings flicker for as far as she could see.

Neither Molly nor her father spoke a word after the butterfly had disappeared but Molly would always remember being filled to the brim with love and admiration as she held her father's rough and callused hand on their walk back home.

It was a sacred moment between father and daughter that would be remembered every spring when the cabbage butterflies returned in the valley.

"Those darn butterflies are back," Molly's mother, Eleanor, would complain over dinner.

And while she would go on and on about them flying in her hair, clogging people's radiators and clouds of them so thick at night outside the 7-Eleven that you can't even stop to get a Slurpee, Molly and her father would exchange a secret wink and a wrinkle of a smile.

At some point during every vacation the Carolinas took when Molly and her younger brother, Ethan, were growing up, a search party would have to be organized to find Molly. Whether the family was camping up in the White Mountains or on the beach in San Diego, "Has anyone seen Molly?" was always the most frequently asked question.

She could be found sitting inside a camper listening to the life story of a retired truck driver. She loved the "Well, when I was a kid..." stories and could listen for hours to people talk about their lives. Her patience and inquisitiveness always seemed to form a bond between Molly and her latest, new-found friend.

For the cost of a missed lunch and a mild scolding from her parents, Molly had a new entry for her journal that she wrote in almost every night.

On one of her excursions during a family camping trip, six-year-old Molly met 'Tripod', a rambunctious and fully functional four-year-old Labrador retriever with an amputated left foreleg. After spending the afternoon throwing sticks, wrestling and running with 'Tripod', Molly returned to camp and announced to the whole family that she was going to be a vegetarian when she grew up.

"A vegetarian?" her dad asked. "Good idea, I think the world could use more vegetarians."

Bobby bent down and asked in a whisper, "By the way, what exactly does a vegetarian do, Molly?"

Not wanting to embarrass her father, she whispered in a slightly condescending tone, "Daddy, a vegetarian is a doctor that takes care of sick and injured animals."

# Chapter 7
## Ethan Carolina
## The Desperate Son

MOLLY CAROLINA INHERITED HER FATHER'S HEIGHT and his athletic ability. She was five-feet, ten-inches tall her freshman year in high school and bigger than most boys in her class. Had Molly been raised in Paris or New York, her classic facial structure, height and slender figure would have captured the interest and attention of the modeling world.

However, in Green Valley, Arizona, Molly was considered to be just tall and skinny. She was an excellent athlete which added "tomboy" to her resume. Her height and athleticism kept Molly out of the high school dating frenzy which was perfectly fine with her. She was more interested in friendship. Not guilty of being an old flame or a possible threat, Molly Carolina was a barrel overflowing with the poured-out passions of her heartbroken girlfriends.

To the boys in school, Molly was not a girl they had to show off for, or play it cool with or engage in any of the other strategies used by high school boys to impress girls. She was just… Molly. Plus, she could throw a football 50 yards which brought her even more respect.

Molly's brother, Ethan, was five years younger and the complete opposite of Molly in almost every way. Physically, he was one of those boys who seemed to miss their appointment with puberty. His skin was creamy white and he was never able to shed the baby fat that padded his pear-shaped build.

Junior high school was painful for Ethan. He was the boy, and there was one in almost every junior high school in America, that put his jock strap on backwards the first day of gym class. There were no diagrams or directions on the small cardboard box and taking it out, too shy of his own nakedness to look at the other boys dressing for P.E., Ethan slipped it out of the carton and pulled the tight elastic band up to his waist. He looked down, reached back and felt the bulging pouch behind him. Just as he realized that he had put it on backward, the other boys had spotted his blunder and began to make fun of him.

"Maybe he thinks it's a turd catcher!"

One of the boys taunting Ethan put his own supporter over his face, "Hey, Carolina, if you get a cold, you can wear it like this to stop your nose from dripping!"

The terror of taking off his clothes with other boys around, his self-consciousness of his pudgy breasts and soft folds of belly compared to the sun-browned, lean and sinewy bodies of the other boys, was now compounded by their teasing. Ethan stared at the concrete floor as he put his supporter on correctly and wished that he could instantly disappear or suddenly be struck dead of a heart attack.

"That would teach them," he thought to himself.

Just as the repercussions from his jock strap blunder had finally begun to die down, the P.E. teacher, who was also the football coach with a reputation for bullying unathletic students, challenged Ethan's class to a mile run.

"You've got 12 minutes to do 4 laps around the track. If any one of you doesn't finish in that time the whole class is going to have to run it again!"

While the rest of the runners had finished under the time limit, Ethan was panting and stumbling, still more than 100 yards behind the last runner.

Exhausted, Ethan staggered to the finish line to the taunts and jeers of the other boys.

The coach stood over Ethan who was bent over, panting and wheezing.

"Carolina, you've cost the class another mile! Line up, boys. Let's do it again!"

Ethan collapsed on the grass infield while the rest of the class ran another mile under the hot Arizona sun.

Standing under the cold spray of the shower in the locker room, the first gym towel snap struck Ethan on the back of his thigh. The next one got him in the buttocks. Ethan cringed in the corner of the showroom, weeping uncontrollably, while the other boys attacked with well-practiced and expert towel snapping marksmanship creating jagged red welts on Ethan's back, buttocks and legs.

Bowing to an angry ultimatum from his mother, the administration reluctantly excused Ethan from P.E. He spent his physical education period sorting books in the library along with other students who were unable to participate in P.E. Ethan spent the rest of the school day, including lunches and recesses, alone.

While Ethan's spirit was slowly decomposing in junior high, Molly's social life was blossoming in high school. She played volleyball and basketball for the girls' teams, although she could have started for the boys' team, and wrote for and eventually became editor of the school newspaper, *'The Green Sheet'*. Every annual edition of the *"Green Valley High School Anthology"* always contained at least four or five of Molly's poems.

Each year Molly served in some different capacity on the Student Council and was Chairman of the Decorating Committee mainly because she could string crepe paper garlands higher than anyone for the school dances in the gym. Although often without a date, Molly was always a welcome addition and could be counted upon to cheerfully announce the King and Queen of the dance.

Molly graduated at the top her class and was accepted to the University of Arizona, thirty miles north of Green Valley. Her major, as declared after playing with the three-legged dog named 'Tripod', was Pre-Veterinary Science (since there wasn't a Pre-Vegetarian major listed in the school's catalog).

The competition among pre-vets and pre-meds for top grades was far fiercer than the annual football rivalry between the U of A and its' enemy to the north, Arizona State University.

Molly's undergraduate classes included: Microbiology, Biochemistry, Physics, Inorganic Chemistry, Organic Chemistry, Molecular Biology, Anatomy and Physiology, Animal Science, Genetics, Calculus, Statistics and Behavioral Science as well as the dreaded Freshman English, Humanities and other required core classes. And this was just scholastic boot camp for these med-school hopefuls.

Undergraduate degrees were a mere bump in the road and of little use to these overachievers. M-CATS, veterinary school, medical school, internships, residencies, post-doctoral fellowships and specialty board certifications were all a part of their future and only achievable with an outstanding undergraduate academic performance.

While Molly Carolina was being swallowed up by the formidable currents of her sophomore year at the U of A, Ethan had found some solace in the high school drama department playing characters safely outside the rigid and intolerant realm of high school social structure. Ethan had discovered a place where he was accepted more for who he could be than for what he was or what he wasn't. In his sophomore year, Ethan won the "Outstanding Performance" award at the Arizona State High School Shakespearean Festival for his performance of Brutus' monologue prior to his suicide in *Julius Caesar*.

Ethan was befriended by another drama student named Sherman Belyard. They would share their lunches on the steps of the school theater and make fun of the jocks and other cliques and talk about their favorite movies and music.

Ethan and Sherman had decided to team up together for the Spring Shakespeare Festival and do a scene from *Romeo and Juliet* between Tybalt, Juliet's cousin, and a member of the Capulet family, Mercutio, Romeo's best friend.

As auditions for the festival neared, Sherman invited Ethan over to his house to rehearse. Sherman had his driver's license and Ethan promised his mother that Sherman would give him a ride home after their rehearsal.

Sherman lived in a tract of newly constructed homes. Freshly paved roads and neighbors so close they could see into one another's windows were a strange sight to Ethan who had grown up around dirt roads and neighbors that were just a light in the distance. Sherman lived with his mother, who worked for a real estate company during the day, so the two boys raided the refrigerator and went upstairs to Sherman's room to work on their scene.

After rehearsing the sword-fight scene using yardsticks as weapons, Sherman jumped on his bed and lay back on his pillow with his hands behind his head.

"Ethan, do you jerk off?"

A little winded from the exertion of the sword fight and wheezing slightly, Ethan was startled by Sherman's question.

"Do I what?"

"I asked if you ever masturbated."

Ethan winced at the question, anticipating that Sherman was going to make fun of him.

"What do you mean?"

"Don't play dumb, you know what I mean. Everybody does it. They just don't talk about it. Hell, I do it all the time."

Ethan's first instinct was to look for hidden microphones or to check under the bed for those same boys from the shower. He thought carefully about the consequences of his reply.

"You do it all the time?" Ethan asked, stalling to find out where this line of questioning was leading.

"I've even done it at school."

Ethan's eyes widened, "You did it at school?"

"Yea, in the bathroom between classes. It kinda eases the tension, you know what I mean?"

Sherman had never made fun of him so Ethan took a chance.

"Sure," Ethan admitted timidly. "I do it every once in a while, I guess, but never in school."

Sherman sat up in bed, "How do you do it?"

"I guess, uh, I do it like everybody else does."

"How?" Sherman prodded.

"Why do you want to know?"

"I'm just curious. What's your technique?" Sherman laughed.

"Well, I don't know. I just twist the end around with my fingertips," Ethan blushed. "How do you do it, Sherman?"

"Here, I'll show you."

Sherman unbuckled his belt, pulled down his pants and underwear to his knees and grabbed on to his penis.

Ethan looked away and out the window.

"What about your mom? Aren't you afraid of her catching you?"

"Aw, she's caught me a bunch of times. She says I'm gonna make myself go blind. That's why I always keep one eye closed," Sherman laughed.

"That's a joke, Ethan. "Besides, we're safe. She won't be home until six-thirty. Here's how I like to do it."

Ethan felt a wave of excitement surge through his body as he looked down at his friend laying on the bed with his now fully-erect penis in hand and smiling up at him. Ethan felt his face flush and he began to perspire. He felt his own penis begin to enlarge.

Sherman stopped, scooted over on the bed and motioned for Ethan to sit down next to him.

"Show me how you do it," Sherman spoke softly. "Do it to me."

"You want me to do it to you?" Ethan stammered.

"Sure."

Sherman reached out and grabbed Ethan's hand.

"Do what you do to yourself except do it to me."

Ethan felt the rough mat of pubic hair and felt Sherman's penis against his hand.

"Go ahead, E. Grab hold of the old steel blue throbber."

Ethan knew they were doing something wrong but it made him all the more excited. He took Sherman's penis in his hand and felt it swell at his touch. Sherman lay back down on the bed and closed his eyes.

"Keep going, Ethan."

96

Ethan had never felt like this in his life. He felt a sudden sense of power. His own erection pressed painfully against his pants as he became aroused.

Within seconds Sherman's body stiffened and he collapsed into the bed.

"Whew, fourth time today," Sherman said and let out a groan of satisfaction. "OK, let's go over the part where I stab you. What's your line?"

"A...a...a plague o' both your houses," Ethan stammered.

Neither boy spoke as Sherman drove through town and out to the Carolina farm. Ethan struggled in silence with the wonder of his new found sexuality versus an encroaching paranoia warning him to anticipate that something bad was going to happen.

Sherman pulled up in front of Ethan's house. Ethan gathered his books from the center of the seat.

"See you tomorrow at school?" Ethan asked as he opened the door.

"Sure, see you tomorrow, E."

Ethan felt a warm glow as Sherman drove off.

The two boys would spend several days a week after school at Sherman's house, rehearsing their scene.

Ethan felt a change come over himself. Others noticed it, too. His parents thought he might have a girlfriend. They were partially right.

For Ethan, classes seemed to drag on forever. He couldn't wait for the school day to end. The omnipresent feeling of self-consciousness, that someone was making fun of him while he walked between classes or to the snack bar seemed to disappear. Just the sight of Sherman walking into drama class would make his cheeks flush and his breathing rapid and shallow. He felt his first pangs of jealousy when he saw Sherman cutting up with some of his other friends.

One day during drama class, Sherman passed him a note asking him if he could get out of his house that night? Ethan followed Sherman as they were leaving class.

"Why?" he asked.

Sherman winked at him, "It's a surprise," he grinned. "You're gonna love it. I'll pick you up around seven o'clock."

Ethan tried to do his homework after school but he couldn't concentrate. He kept thinking about Sherman and his surprise. He was so excited he couldn't finish his supper.

"You all right, son?" Bobby asked when Ethan excused himself from the table with half a plateful of food left untouched.

"Oh sure, Dad, I'm great. Just a little hyper about the festival auditions. You know how that goes."

Bobby didn't but pretended like he did.

"Oh, yea, they can be very stressful."

Ethan had told his parents during dinner that he was going to the library with Sherman to do some background work on their scene. When Sherman pulled up in front of the house and honked, Ethan jumped up from the table.

"I might be home a little late," Ethan yelled as he ran out the door.

"School night, hon," his mother shouted. "Be home by ten."

Bobby's and Eleanor's eyes met from across the room and then shifted their stares towards the front door and the sound of Sherman's tires spinning in the gravel in front of their house.

"There must be something about acting that I don't quite get," Bobby mused.

Eleanor shook her head and smiled, "No, Bobby, I don't think that drama was your strongest subject."

"He's been acting kind of strange lately, Eleanor. I mean, stranger than normal."

"I've noticed it, too. Maybe it's the festival auditions."

"Oh, yea," Bobby laughed back at his wife who had known him practically his whole life. "I know how nerve-wracking those Shakespearean festivals can be."

"Where are we going?" Ethan asked excitedly as Sherman peeled away on the dirt road.

"You know who Leslie Graham is? She's that girl in the choir with the white, white skin and gigantic boobs. I talked her into giving us hand jobs tonight. She gives 'em out of her house through her bedroom window!"

Ethan felt his stomach turn sour.

"You mean we're not going to your house?"

"Nah, this is going to be a hoot. Jack Reilly and Jim Moore told me she did them two nights ago. She charged 'em a buck apiece and well worth the money they said."

They listened to country music on the radio as Sherman drove back towards town and then turned off on a side street, following directions written on the palm of his hand.

"Hell, I'm so excited I've almost sweat off her address! This must be it, seventy-three sixty-two La Cholla Lane."

Sherman parked on the opposite side of the street.

"Be quiet and stay close to me. We don't want her parents to spot us."

They could see the light from a television through the window in the front room. A dog barked several houses away.

"This way," Sherman whispered as they crouched down below the window, crept along the side of the house, through an open gate and into the backyard. The boys tiptoed across the patio to the far end of the house where a bedroom window was wedged open by an upright World Book encyclopedia.

Sherman peered through the open window. The room was pitch dark.

"Maybe she's not home or maybe she's asleep," Ethan whispered.

They could hear someone washing dishes in the kitchen not more than twenty-feet away from them.

"Pssst, Leslie. It's me, Sherman, and my buddy, Ethan. You in there?"

Both boys took a step back as a large, white arm snaked out of the window. The short, pudgy fingers of a right hand brushed against the thumb and then opened with the hand out, palm facing upward. Sherman pulled two dollar bills out of his pocket and placed them in the hand. The hand grabbed the money and disappeared back into the dark room.

"Sherman, I don't think ..."

"Shhh, Ethan. Here come the magic fingers."

The hand reached out of the window and pointed towards a plastic milk crate near where the boys were standing.

Sherman grabbed the crate and set it against the side of the house under the window. The hand waggled its index finger.

Sherman cast an excited grin at Ethan and climbed up on the box. He unbuckled his pants and let them fall to his feet.

The hand appeared again wearing a yellow rubber glove, the kind Ethan's' mom used to wash the dishes. The palm of the glove was covered with a greasy substance as it reached out and took Sherman's penis in its grasp. The hand squeezed, pulled and yanked on Sherman's organ.

Suddenly Sherman's expression changed. His smile disappeared, his eyes pinched shut and his front teeth bit down upon his lower lip. It was a familiar look that had brought great satisfaction to Ethan over the past weeks when he'd seen it in Sherman's bedroom. But tonight, it made him feel as though he was going to throw up.

Sherman swaggered off the crate, pulled up his pants and zipped up his fly.

"Your turn big guy," Sherman whispered.

Ethan was numb and nauseous, not the slightest bit aroused. But he reasoned that if he did what Sherman wanted him to do, they could get this over with and go back to their own relationship.

Ethan climbed up on the crate, fumbled with his pants and let them drop. The hand reached out and grabbed his penis. He felt the cold sting of the lubricant as the hand went to work. It pulled, massaged, jerked, changed speeds and even re-lubed but nothing it did could produce a response. More determined, the hand pulled harder and faster.

Ethan began to feel the familiar ache of embarrassment. He looked over towards Sherman for a moment and then down at the yellow-gloved hand.

Apparently frustrated by Ethan's lack of arousal, the hand pushed him in the stomach and knocked him off the crate. He fell backward and landed in the damp grass; his pants twisted around his ankles.

Sherman was on his knees with both hands covering his mouth trying to suppress his laughter. Ethan struggled to get to his feet and pull up his pants. He ran past Sherman, through the backyard and across the street where he climbed into the truck, completely humiliated.

"What's the matter, Ethan? Did she pull your pecker too hard?" Sherman laughed when he got into the truck.

Ethan looked away and rolled down the window so Sherman couldn't tell he was crying.

"You need to go to the hospital or something?" Sherman asked, still giggling as he started the engine and drove away.

Ethan stuck his head out the window and the cool night air stung his cheeks. The wind in his ears covered up the taunting voices in his head.

Sherman turned on a country music radio station and sang along with the music as he drove towards Ethan's house.

After about ten few minutes, Ethan turned to Sherman.

"I thought it was just going to be you and me."

"What? "What do you mean...you and me?" Sherman asked with an angry edge to his voice.

"I thought...I thought..." Ethan stammered. "I love being with you. I've never felt like this with anyone. I guess I thought you felt the same."

"Love! What the fuck are you talking about? You're talking like we're a couple of fairies for God sakes! You think I'm a...!

Sherman slammed on the brakes and the truck skidded to a halt. By now they were out in the country, about a mile from the Carolina farm. Ethan tried to disappear into the corner of the truck cab.

Sherman got out of the truck and stomped over to the passenger side.

"Get out of my fuckin' truck!"

Sherman yanked the door open and pulled Ethan out onto the gravel shoulder of the road. When he tried to get to his feet, he felt a solid blow to the side of his face. Everything turned dark except for a cloud of tiny gold flecks floating in front of his eyes. Blood began to pour out of his mouth and he could smell its' metallic odor. Another jolt of pain exploded from his side as Sherman delivered a vicious kick to his ribs.

"If you ever say anything about you and me doing anything...anything, I'll get my shotgun and shove it half up your ass before I pull the trigger so you can watch your guts fly out of your mouth!"

101

Sherman rolled Ethan over on his back with the toe of his boot. Ethan cringed and covered his face anticipating another blow.

"Look at you," Sherman spat. "You're fuckin' pathetic. I don't want you hanging around me anymore at school!"

Ethan heard Sherman get back in the truck and start the engine. He prayed that Sherman would run him over but all he got was the sting of flying gravel against his face as Sherman screeched away. Ethan lay on the side of the road and listened to the sound of the truck driving away until it was drowned out by the noises of the night.

By eleven o'clock, Ethan still wasn't home and Bobby and Eleanor began to worry. Bobby found Sherman's number in the phone book and spoke with his mother.

"Hello, Mrs. Belyard, my name is Bob Carolina and I'm very sorry about calling you this late at night but my son, Ethan, went out with your son tonight and he's not home yet. It's a school night and we're a little worried. Is he still at your house?"

"Oh hello, Mr. Carolina. Well, Sherman's home. In fact, he's upstairs in the bath tub right now. I haven't seen your son all night

"Your son's there?"

"Yep, he's been home for a little while."

"Would you mind asking him if he knows where Ethan might be?"

"Well, I gotta go up the stairs and all. You sure he's not just out being a boy?"

"That may be but they left the house here together and I'd figure they'd come back home together."

"Oh, all right. I'll go on up and ask him."

Bobby waited for what seemed like a long time before Mrs. Belyard returned to the phone.

"Mr. Carolina, Sherman says he dropped him off somewhere on the road just up from your house. Evidently your son told Sherman he wanted to walk and get some fresh air."

"What time was that, Mrs. Belyard?"

"Oh, hell…"

Bobby heard her drop the phone again.

"Sherman, what the hell time was it you dropped that boy off? What time did you say, honey?"

Mrs. Belyard picked up the phone.

"Sherman says he's not exactly sure what time it was but he thinks it was about an hour ago."

"Okay, thank you for your help, Mrs. Belyard. I'm sorry for bothering you."

Bobby repeated his conversation with Sherman's mother to Eleanor and they both agreed that he was probably walking down the road and would be coming through the front door any minute.

Responding to a disconcerting surge of nervous energy, Eleanor gathered up a basket of laundry and carried it out to the garage. As she dumped the clothes on the cement floor in front of the washer, something brushed against her shoulder in the darkness. She turned around, fumbled for the switch and turned on the light.

"Oh my God! No!" she screamed. "No...no...no!" her words welling up from deep inside her.

The light revealed the body of her son hanging from a rafter with a rope around his neck. His clothes were dirty. His face was bloody and swollen. A trail of vomit spilled from his mouth down into a puddle on the garage floor.

Eleanor tried to lift Ethan up by his legs but the body sagged limply against her and swung around throwing her off balance. She slipped in the pool of vomit and fell to the floor holding one of her son's shoes in her hand.

"Bobby! Bobby! Come help him! Help him!" she screamed. "Oh, God, please come and help him!

During questioning by detectives, 17-year-old Sherman Belyard admitted to getting in a fist fight with Ethan on the night of his death. He claimed that Ethan had made homosexual advances towards him while they were driving and that he was only trying to protect himself. No charges were ever filed.

Sherman and his mother moved to Phoenix six weeks later.

The cuts on Ethan's face, along with the bruises on his rib cage, were commensurate with superficial injuries that could have been sustained in a fight. Sherman's account of the fight corroborated the coroner's finding that the cause of death was due to asphyxiation by strangulation.

Dr. Luke Knudsen, Green Valley's only board-certified general practitioner, served as the county coroner and was regarded as a noted forensic expert. Luke and Bobby had been friends since Little League and after it became clearly evident that the cause of death was not a result of the fight but was a case of suicide, Dr. Knudsen requested that the Sheriff's Department seal his report since some of his findings, if revealed, would only bring more pain to the family.

One piece of information that the Carolinas would never know about was, based on the temperature of the body, was that their son had only been dead no more than 10 minutes when Eleanor found him. Another detail kept secret from the family and possibly even more devastating than the time of death, was that there were two sets of bruises on the boy's neck and that the rope showed evidence of two separate knots being tied. Apparently, Ethan was unsuccessful in his first attempt at hanging himself. It appeared that the first knot came untied. However, on his second try, the knot held and supported his body as he strangled to death.

Molly Carolina was asleep in her dormitory room at the University of Arizona when her father called from the hospital.

"You need to come home, honey."

"What's wrong, daddy?"

"You just need to come home, now. Drive carefully. There's… there's no hurry."

It took Molly thirty-minutes to drive from Tucson to Green Valley. As she turned onto the road leading to the house, she saw a sheriff's car parked out front. The sheriff's flasher lights were on and Molly realized that she had been conscious of the lights for the past 15 minutes. The land of the flood basin was so flat and the night so clear, it was as though Molly had been drawn to the red flashing beacon. Her simple curiosity turned into a sickening fear as she approached the farm and realized that the distant signal of warning and danger was being broadcast from her house.

As Molly got out of her car, she saw her father walking towards her.

"Daddy, what's wrong? What happened?"

Her father took her in his arms and held her tightly. She could feel his body heaving as he wept.

"Ethan is dead, honey."

"Dead? How? When?"

"He took his life tonight," Bobby whispered.

Molly regained consciousness on the couch to the acrid smell of ammonia and the voice of Dr. Knudsen.

"Molly, Molly, are you back with us?"

She opened her eyes to the faces of Dr. Knudsen and her parents. It was immediately apparent from the sadness in their eyes that she had not awakened from a bad dream.

Molly spent the rest of the night with her parents in the living room of a house that seemed to have suddenly changed. The same house that was once warm and comfortable had abruptly become as curiously cold and distant as an old friend who had mysteriously turned against you.

Ethan had taken all the answers with him, leaving those who loved him with only questions — unfathomable and unanswerable questions.

The doctor had given Eleanor a strong sedative with the intention of allowing her to sleep but instead the medication seemed to put her into a daze.

She came out of the den, her slippers scuffling along the carpet and carrying an armful of family photo albums.

"Oh, no, Eleanor," Bobby moaned. "Please not now."

"I have to see him alive, Bobby. I have to see him somewhere other than hanging in the garage."

Bobby stomped out the front door but Molly sat down next to her mother on the couch and they slowly went through the album.

The two of them watched Ethan grow up through family trips, birthdays and Christmas mornings. Though it had been several years since Molly had looked at the pictures, her brother looked different to her now. Real or imagined, when she looked closely at the photos of her brother there seemed to be the slightest hint of sadness behind Ethan's smiles and expressions that she had never noticed before.

Molly felt a surge of outrage beginning to replace her sadness. She was angry at her brother but felt the anger turning around and pointing its' finger at her. Looking through the albums, she wanted to go get some scissors and cut herself out of every picture of the two of them together. She felt that she didn't deserve to be standing next to him. A real sister would have been there for him. A real sister could have saved him.

As the sun began come up over the valley, Eleanor was still restless and went into the kitchen to fix a breakfast that no one would eat. Bobby Carolina lay exhausted on the couch and fell into a fitful sleep.

Molly began to feel claustrophobic. The house seemed to be shrinking and closing in on her. Anger and bitterness washed over her like giant rogue waves and guilt stalked her wherever she went in the house.

Molly walked into her room, still not yet converted into a sewing room as planned by her mother and looking much the same as when she left for college.

Ever since she was a little girl, Molly would periodically make lists of the things she would grab if the house was on fire and she could only make one trip. The list established a hierarchy of what was most important to her at that stage of her life. The one item that always remained at the top of her list was her journal.

'Molly's Journal', as it was titled, was more than four inches thick and contained all her notes, thoughts and feelings about old friends, people she had met, places she had visited, dreams, disappointments, wishes, promises and secrets. It held her poetry, short stories and was scattered with newspaper clippings touting her athletic, 4-H and literary accomplishments. The journal was the fairy-tale of her life and still occupied the room's most privileged position on the night table next to her bed.

Molly looked down at her journal. It was all a fake, a counterfeit, a forgery, a book of lies. She grabbed the journal and ran out of the house in the predawn light towards the river.

Molly finally made it across the field and fought her way through the dense thicket of salt cedars, their brittle branches raking and clawing at her. Her dirty face streaked with tears and her arms cut and bleeding, Molly finally reached the shallow, narrow river, now barely more than a creek. She slid down the bank and walked down the stony river bed. She crossed at a bend and stopped at the edge of a curtain of roots dangling from the base of a huge cottonwood tree that had been undercut by a 100-year flood that had struck the valley years before Molly was born.

The flood had carved out a cave in the bank. The tree's bared roots provided a trellis for the wild vines, moss, multicolored lichens and other vegetation to grow and provide a perfect blind to Molly's childhood secret hiding place.

Ethan had discovered the cave when they were young. He sold his find to his sister as an office for her literary career in exchange for one month of her desserts.

Molly slipped between the roots and ducked into the cool, damp and yeasty darkness. The cave was semi-circular; ten feet across the front, six feet deep and about five feet high. The ceiling was the underside of a mosaic of boulders, rocks, clay and dirt, knitted together by the roots of the giant tree.

Although littered with the scat of animals and draped in cobwebs, her office was just as she had left it years ago. Her table and chair were still in the same place on the sandy, riverbed floor.

Molly set her heavy scrapbook down on the table.

A rusted Coleman lantern hung from an exposed root. Molly shook the lantern and was surprised to find there was still some fuel remaining. She pumped up the lantern and then grabbed a cigar box resting on a rock wedged in the side of the cave. Molly pulled out a jar of matches, kept dry from the moisture by the tightly sealed lid, struck a match against a rock, and held it beneath the paper-thin mantle.

Remarkably, the lantern worked, casting an eerie light through smoke-stained glass lens.

Molly sat down in the chair. She opened the cover of her scrapbook and turned through the pages containing all her life's accomplishments. She skimmed through poetry written in perfect iambic pentameter, haiku with carefully counted syllables, and stories written all with a "...happily ever after" ending.

Carefully and deliberately, Molly removed each sheet and tore it down the middle. She tossed the pieces into a small fire ring she had built years before. When the papers began to pile up, she struck another match and tossed it into the pile. The papers eagerly burst into flame.

The fire blazed and threw shadows of smoky, dancing ghosts against the wall of the cave as she continued to feed it with her life's work. Destroying her paper achievements seemed apt punishment for her brother's death and, for the moment, seemed to quiet the angry demons that raged inside her head.

# Chapter 8
# The Night Bloomin' Jazzmen

I T WASN'T LONG BEFORE THE CANAL STREET BRIDGE BECAME one of the most popular after-hours spots in the French Quarter. Nathan, Wingy and E. Tim were joined by some of the finest musicians in the city wanting to sit in and play the sun up. Drummers would bring their sticks and play on the bridge railing, on bottles, cans or pieces of driftwood. Many of the musicians would just sit and listen after playing their gigs, passing around a bottle of hooch or smoking 'tea', or marijuana as it was called.

"What do you boys call yourselves?" a voice called out from the bridge between songs one night.

Nathan, E. Tim and Wingy looked at each other and shrugged their shoulders. It was a warm, humid night and the heavy perfume of jasmine hung over the canal.

"We're The Night Bloomin' Jazzmen," E. Tim yelled back.

The following week, Harlan H. Howard stood on the bridge among the growing crowd and listened to the magical music coming from the canal below.

"Who are these boys?" he asked a man holding a trombone case standing next to him.

The musician smiled, "I heard they call themselves the 'Night Bloomin' Jazzmen'. They can sure play up a storm, huh?"

"Where do they play? I don't think I've ever heard of them."

"This is where they play, under the bridge every couple nights a week or whenever they feel like it."

Howard muscled his way to the front of the crowd. He leaned over the bridge railing and peered down into the darkness of the canal below.

"You boys looking for a place to play?" Howard asked.

"Got one," E. Tim answered.

"I'll give you $10 a week and a piece of the cover if you draw well."

"How many nights?"

"How many nights you want? Four, five, six?"

"What's the name of your place?"

"Uh, the Redfish Club."

"Never heard of it."

"Used to be called 'The Flaming Rose'."

"That's a whorehouse ain't it?"

"Not anymore. It's legit now. I'd sure appreciate it if you boys could start this Thursday night."

"Give us an advance?"

"I'll pay you the whole week up front if you can start Thursday night."

"What are the hours?"

"How 'bout nine to one? We gotta deal, boys?"

E. Tim looked over at Nathan and Wingy and hunched his shoulders up towards his ears. Nathan and Wingy looked at each other and then nodded their approval at E. Tim.

"Deal. We'll be there," E. Tim answered.

"Tell me your name again so I can put it on the marquee."

"We're the 'Night Bloomin' Jazzmen', spelled like jazz and men stuck together," E. Tim hollered back.

The Flaming Rose was a combination strip club and bordello in the French Quarter owned by Harlan Howard. After paying off the police and other city officials, Howard made a fine living off the shady side of New Orleans' night life.

However, Howard fell madly in love with one of his dancers named Darlene Monet. Following four weeks of making his feelings for her perfectly clear, Harlan and Darlene were married at the First Presbyterian Church of New Orleans.

After saying their vows at the altar, the couple strolled up the aisle arm-in-arm, Harlan proudly beaming with joy and smiling to all of his friends—most of whom had never been inside a church before.

Halfway up the aisle, Darlene elbowed Harlan in the ribs nearly knocking the wind out of him.

She leaned towards him with a loving expression on her face and whispered softly, "I hope you realize, Harlan Howard, that I ain't gonna be the wife of no man who runs a strip club and a whorehouse."

Six days later, 'The Flaming Rose' changed its name to 'The Redfish Club'. It also changed its ownership papers to Mr. and Mrs. Harlan Howard and repainted its marquee to read, 'Fine Dining and Live Music'.

Now that they had a job, the Night Bloomin' Jazzmen' had to fill out the members of their band. Wingy got his old friend Tubby Dixon to play drums. While other musicians were known to drink hooch, shoot dope, smoke tea, roll dice and run women, Tubby, who weighed somewhere near 250-pounds, had only one vice.

"Sure, I'll play with you guys. Long as they serve good food in this joint."

Tubby liked to set up his drum kit close to the kitchen doors so that he could reach out and grab a dinner roll or a couple of fried shrimps off the waiters' trays when they weren't looking. Tubby could polish off a whole chicken leg without using his hands while playing a drum solo at the same time.

Tubby got his best friend, Troy Arlington, to play stand-up bass. Bass, drums and Nathan on guitar provided the rhythm track or the foundation of the music. Tubby and Troy's friendship and their ability to anticipate each other moves brought a much-needed tightness to a band that didn't have much experience playing together.

They were a curious looking pair standing next to one another on stage —a drummer with the body of a bass fiddle and a bass fiddle player with the body of a drumstick. Despite their physical differences, together they provided a rock solid under current to the music that allowed the soloists to venture wherever they felt like exploring.

Bobby Lee Cunningham worked with Nathan at Hadleys for Music. Bobby Lee could play every instrument in the store from an accordion to a zither. He had abandoned the life of a working musician when his second child was born and he was forced to take on a regular job as a sales clerk and music teacher at Hadley's

Nathan asked Bobby Lee if he'd fill in on saxophone for the Night Bloomin' Jazzmen until they could find a regular sax player and was surprised by Bobby's enthusiastic acceptance of the offer.

"Fill in? Hell, Nathan, you got yourself a full-time sax player! Tenor, alto, soprano, baritone…which ones you want?"

Bobby later admitted to Nathan that his mother-in-law had moved in with his family. She was helping his wife who had just given birth to their third child and that he would have played for nothing just to get out of the house.

On opening night, the 'Jazzmen' arrived at the Redfish early. As they loaded in their equipment and set-up on stage, it was the first time Harlan Howard would actually have a chance to get a look at the musicians he'd hired from under a bridge in the middle of the night out of desperation.

Business had not been good during the first weeks of the transition from the Flaming Rose to a legitimate night club and restaurant. Harlan had taken an earful from his former patrons who came to the club expecting the usual array of entertainment and were vociferously unhappy with his decision to go straight.

So, part of his potential customers wouldn't come to his restaurant because it wasn't a brothel and the other part of his potential customers wouldn't come because they thought it was. Harlan was facing a daunting marketing problem.

The costs and headaches of renovating his club, the constant stream of complaints from angry past customers and several nights of staring at empty tables and the bottom of an empty cash register had driven

Harlan Howard precariously close to the brink of depression. His business worries had also affected his ability to perform his husbandly duties with his new bride. Poor Harlan had a new business and a new wife and wasn't getting anything from either one.

However, he had found a band that sounded pretty good and the vision of live music and a full house began to rekindle his spirits.

When Thursday night arrived, Harlan was back to his cheerful self as he rinsed glasses behind the bar.

"What the hell is this?" Darlene asked, pointing towards the band setting up on the stage and poking Harlan with a now familiar jab to his already bruised rib cage.

"Did you hire a band or a God dammed carnival side show?" she hissed between clenched teeth.

Harlan straightened up painfully and took his first look, in the light, at the Night Bloomin' Jazzmen on stage. Nathan sat on a stool tuning his guitar, his body shaped like a question mark. Wingy was warming up on trumpet, his flipper of an arm dangling against the sides of his pinned-up, short sleeved shirt. E. Tim was putting together his clarinet while sucking on a reed. He was wearing a black beret that, after a brief rain shower earlier in the evening, did little to hide the vacancy that lay beneath one side of it. Troy Arlington looked like a loose string dangling alongside of the bass fiddle who was standing next to a corpulent drummer. Even the sax player had the haggard look of a man who hadn't slept in weeks.

Harlan looked at the members of his band from behind the bar and the embers of his recently rekindled spirit were immediately extinguished.

He dropped his head onto the bar and spoke quietly to himself.

"Look what I've done. I blindly hired a band made up of misshapen trolls, condemned to play their music from underneath a bridge. I've also married a woman who behaves much different on stage than off and to top it all off, I'm just about to go bankrupt".

When Wingy asked Harlan for their advance before they began playing, Harlan seriously thought about giving them the money and

*Music from Both Sides of the Moon*

asking them not to play. He was convinced he was going to be the laughingstock of New Orleans and that this was the final step in the ruination of his life.

Harlan handed Wingy a ten-dollar bill without saying a word. Saving face didn't matter. Nothing mattered any more.

The Night Bloomin' Jazzmen played their first set at the Redfish on a Thursday night. Word of mouth about this new band spread quickly. By the following Saturday night, the club had become one of the hottest spots in the French Quarter. At ten o'clock on that Saturday night, club proprietor, Mrs. Darlene Howard, sashayed her way through the crowd and proudly hung up a handmade "Standing Room Only" sign on the front door. Harlan was too busy smiling at his register and pouring drinks behind the bar to notice. Later that evening, Harlan, despite his bruised ribs, would make passionate love to his wife for the first time in weeks.

Nathan generally opened each set with several ensemble cover pieces of popular songs with minor signature licks played perfectly, if not passionately, by the band. His intention was to allow the boys a chance to warm up and also to lull the audience into thinking, "They're good, but what's so special about this band?"

By the third or fourth song in the set, Nathan would call out one of their originals composed during their sessions from under the bridge. Suddenly, the room would bristle with energy. Conversations and drink orders would stop in mid-sentence. Heads would turn towards the stage as the band began to lift off the lid on their music.

There were moments where it seemed as though the air had suddenly vanished from the room when Wingy and E. Tim would turn towards the audience, both soaring into riffs like fireworks displays, showering the house with sparks of notes, countering and challenging each other, displaying their incredible mastery and power while at the same time revealing their physical vulnerabilities and flaws.

The Redfish was the buzz of the city. The band was hot, Harlan was happy and Darlene, hearing the call of the stage once again, had

114

taken on emcee duties. Several of Harlan's strippers from the old Flaming Rose waited tables which made the old patrons happy. Two girls, former employees from the now closed bordello, turned out to be gourmet chefs and had taken over the kitchen putting together a mouth-watering menu made-up of hot and spicy Cajun dishes.

Several times a week after their show, E. Tim and Nathan would get a tub of boiled shrimp and a bucket of iced beer from Harlan and sit on the bank of the canal where they first met.

E. Tim told Nathan all about his experiences growing up in the swamps of Lake Fausse, his life at the county home and his years with Professor Crady's Strangest Show on Earth. Nathan talked about Ben, their concerts in Darktown and his travels with the Dixieland All Stars.

They'd play a little music, work on a troublesome transition and trade ideas for a new tune one of them had come up with but mostly they sat on the bank of the canal and became best friends.

Sometimes they talked about what they were going to do next.

"I'd like to see what's on the other side of the country, Nathan."

"Me, too, E. Tim, but the South is where our music comes from."

"I don't know, they're still paying twenty-five cents to see a man bite the head off of a chicken down here.

Both boys laughed.

"How do you think we'd do in Chicago or even New York, E. Tim?"

"I reckon we'd do all right but I'll tell you where I think we oughta go."

"Where?"

"California," E. Tim grinned.

"You mean Hollywood's California?" Nathan asked.

"Yeah, over that way," E. Tim said pointing towards the west with his thumb like a hitchhiker. "I think California is a hot frying pan just waiting for a big old helping of red beans and rice."

"You think we could do all right out west, E. Tim?"

"I do. You know they say the Pacific Ocean is blue, Nathan. I've been on the water all my life and I've never seen blue water. I'd love to see water the color of something other than mud."

115

"Well, maybe we'll just play the Redfish a mite longer, get a little more famous and then head out for Hollywood," Nathan answered.

"Yeah, and maybe we'd get discovered and be in the movies," E. Tim laughed.

"Hey, you never know what's going to happen to a couple of handsome guys like you and me."

Their laughter echoed under the bridge as the sun began to turn the night sky into a dusty gray.

There were a number of things that Nathan loved about playing with the 'Night Bloomin' Jazzmen'. Although he knew he would never stop learning how to play the guitar, he liked being good at something. He felt completely different about himself when he was playing than when he was working at Hadleys, or doing errands or just walking around the city. He also liked actually belonging to something. He always felt like an outsider with the Mississippi All Stars. His scoliosis had always prevented him from being fully accepted by the other boys in school but now he was part a bunch of guys he could joke around with and talk to.

Up until he met E. Tim, Nathan's best friend had always been Mr. Gibson, his guitar. Mr. Gibson was a good listener and always seemed to know how Nathan was feeling. When Nathan felt lonely and picked up his guitar, there was nobody better at commiserating with than Mr. Gibson.

But the very best part of playing in the band for Nathan was when E. Tim would take off on one of his meteoric leads. Then it was time to lay his guitar in his lap, watch the expressions on the faces of the audience and just listen.

E. Tim could make the clarinet sound like a full orchestra. Even when he was suffering from one of his headaches, he could pack a 4-beat measure with more notes than you could find space on the sheet music to write them.

Occasionally, an aspiring clarinet player would come in to the Redfish to hear E. Tim play. They were easy to spot. Only a musician could nurse one beer through three sets. They'd heard about E. Tim and had come to listen and learn. After hearing E. Tim, many of them went home dejected and never took their instrument out of its' case again.

Nathan would peek through the valley of his guitar and watch these would-be musicians after E. Tim would play a lead. The expressions on their faces read, "How the hell did he do that?"

If E. Tim had been out wiggling the night before they played and a big catfish happened to have taken a bite or two out of E. Tim's arm, his right arm would sometimes start to bleed on stage from rubbing against his long-sleeved, white shirt. The sleeve would start to turn pink and then redden. E. Tim would often close the set with actual drops of blood dripping from his cuff onto the stage.

"Jesus, he plays so fast his arm bleeds!" one musician exclaimed and another bit of lore was added to the legend of E. Tim Kelly and the Night Bloomin' Jazzmen.

Two months after their opening at the Redfish, on a rainy Wednesday night, E. Tim Kelly collapsed on stage in the middle of a solo and was dead of a cerebral hemorrhage before his clarinet shattered on the floor. It was the night before Thanksgiving, November 26, 1941.

Nathan arranged to have E. Tim's body buried in a cemetery on a grassy knoll overlooking Lake Fausse. It was the same cemetery where his father and mother were buried. The burial was attended by three grave diggers and five musicians but there wasn't a single musical note played. On that cold, damp afternoon, not even a word was spoken as E. Tim's body was lowered into the rich, damp, Louisiana bayou soil. Inside the coffin, nestled between E. Tim's folded hands, was a brand-new clarinet and a packet of reeds.

Harlan Howard was not without compassion. He gave the band a week off to grieve for their friend. Besides, it was fairly easy for him to find a temporary band for less money than he was paying the Jazzmen since every musician wanted a chance to play the hottest club in the Quarter.

The terrible vision of E. Tim suddenly falling off the stage and crashing to the floor would haunt Nathan for the rest of his life.

Nathan grew bitter over the loss of his best friend. It was the first time he had ever lost someone that close. He was angered at the realization that he hadn't really felt the depth or value of his friendship with E. until it had been taken from him. He vowed not to ever let it happen again with any relationship and that he would work hard at appreciating those precious threads that weave strangers into friends.

Even in his later life, watching a friend or loved one walk away, or his child leave for school, was difficult for Nathan. He would get a twinge in his heart and have to call out, even after all the "goodbyes" had already been said, to catch their attention, to get one more look at their face. With a hesitant post script ranging anywhere from a simple, "See ya" to, "I love you very much," Nathan would reassure himself that he truly appreciated his feelings for that person.

Without E. Tim around, New Orleans lost its familiarity to Nathan. Walking though the damp streets, the once familiar smells of the French Quarter seemed foreign. The people in the crowds, both visitors and locals, seemed strange. He avoided going anywhere near the canal where he and E. Tim first met. Every time Nathan would see the murky dark waters of the Mississippi or any of its waterways, Nathan would feel sad for his friend who never got to see the blue waters of California's Pacific Ocean.

By the end of the seven days following E. Tim's death, despite Harlan's efforts to provide the best replacement entertainment he could find, the crowds who had swamped the Redfish to hear the Night Blooming Jazzmen, began to turn elsewhere.

In a desperate effort to try and get his customers back and after a great deal of cajoling with each member of the band, Harlan convinced Tubby, Troy, Bobby Lee, Wingy and Nathan to make a special appearance at the club as a tribute to E. Tim. Harlan had even printed up a stack of handbills that read:

**The Redfish Club proudly announces the return of the
Night Bloomin' Jazzmen in a tribute to their deceased comrade,
E. Tim Kelly**

—

**Saturday Night, Dec. 6
Showtime: 9 p.m.**

"Come on, boys, just give it a try," Harlan pleaded. "The club is starting to turn poorly since you've been gone and I've invested money in all these hand bills and such. Hell, between you and me, I'd think E. Tim would want you boys to keep playing music instead of moping around waiting for a bug to fly up your nose."

After passing expressionless stares to one another, the boys reluctantly nodded in agreement and told Harlan that they'd do the show.

By eight o'clock on Saturday night, it was standing room only in the Redfish. People were three-deep on the sidewalk, pressed against one another just to look through the front window of the club.

Thirty-minutes before show time, the band arrived. The loud roar of laughter and spirited conversations quieted into silence as the boys walked through the door. The whole city had heard about this remarkable band with an incredible clarinet player who died a tragic death on stage. All eyes turned towards the musicians as they slowly made their way through the crowd and towards the stage.

The room remained silent as they tuned and warmed up their instruments. When they were ready to play, they looked toward Nathan for the downbeat but Nathan's eyes were transfixed on the empty part of the stage where he was used to seeing E. Tim.

Twice, Nathan turned back around towards Tubby as though to call out a song but both times he balked and returned his stare to the empty side of the stage.

With tears flowing down his face, Nathan finally got up from his chair and put his guitar back in its case. He snapped the latches closed, looked out into the crowd, he shrugged his shoulders and mouthed the words, "I'm sorry".

His bent body leaning against the weight of the guitar, Nathan walked through the crowd and out the door. Remarkably, no one in the audience uttered a word as the rest of the band packed up their instruments and followed Nathan.

The next day, Sunday, December 7, 1941. New Orleans, along with the rest of the United States and the world, were shocked to hear the news that Japanese airplanes had attacked Pearl Harbor

The following Tuesday, Nathan was on a train pulling out of New Orleans heading westbound for the Pacific Ocean.

# *Chapter 9*
# MGM Night at the Hollywood Canteen

O N FRIDAY, DECEMBER 5, 1941, LIEUTENANT JOLEEN SALVESON
concluded her training at the Great Lakes Naval Training
Center on the shores of Lake Michigan, 15 miles south of
the Wisconsin/Illinois state line. She had completed her basic training,
officer's training and nursing training. She had finished every course
either at, or near, the top of her class.

She also received significantly more mail than any of the
other nursing candidates. Not surprising when you considered
that she was the adopted child of the entire town of Thief River
Falls, Minnesota. Not only did she receive bundles of letters that
kept her up into the late hours of the night trying to read, but she
also received bales of packages filled with tins of smoked meats,
homemade candies, cookies, pies and other baked goods. Joleen's
class was the only basic training class in the history of the Naval
Training Center in which the candidates gained weight over their
twelve weeks of training.

Every night Joleen would write a letter to the whole town simply
addressed to: Thief River Falls. Irv Scanlon, postmaster and town barber, would post her letters on a bulletin board in the window of his

barber shop and over the next couple of days, the whole town would pass by and catch up on Joleen's progress in the Navy.

If someone had missed a day or two due to work or illness, Irv had a neat file of all of her letters. By December, the file contained almost a hundred worn and dog-eared letters that had been read over and over.

The whole town shared in her accomplishments during Joleen's training. Her graduation and promotion to lieutenant was a huge source of celebration and pride for every citizen of Thief River Falls.

On Graduation Day, Saturday, Dec 6, 1941, Joleen received her lieutenant bars and her navy nursing insignia along with a three-week pass to go home for Christmas. In her stow bag were orders to report to the Naval Hospital in San Diego and from there to ship out for Sternberg General Hospital in Manila in the Philippine Islands. Joleen's hard work and high marks had earned her an envious assignment in what the Training Center cadre called "The Pearl of the Orient".

The following afternoon, Sunday, December 7, Joleen was waiting in the Chicago train station for the 3:45 train to Minneapolis/St. Paul when she heard an announcement over the public address system requesting all military personnel to report immediately to their bases. Word of the bombing of Pearl Harbor spread through the stunned crowd like an epidemic. Joleen stuffed her ticket home in her coat pocket and rushed to catch the next bus back to the Great Lakes Naval Training Center.

Three days later, Joleen was back in the Chicago train station, this time shivering in the icy cold without the comforting thoughts of going home for Christmas to keep her warm. Instead, she held a ticket to California and temporary duty orders assigned to the Veterans Hospital in Los Angeles.

Nothing in her training had prepared Joleen for what she was exposed to at the Veterans Hospital. Casualties from the Pearl Harbor attack had begun to arrive at military hospitals up and down the California coast from San Diego to San Francisco. The wards were filled with soldiers suffering from burns, re-constructive surgeries, amputations, spinal cord trauma, fractures and head injuries. They were just boys, cut down in the prime of their lives and destined to live the rest of their days as shattered reminders of an attack that lasted less than two hours.

Joleen's shifts initially were twelve-hours on and twelve-hours off. But as the wounded continued to arrive at the hospital, the hours on duty grew longer while the off-duty hours grew shorter. Although she had never spent a December without snow in her life, she barely noticed the warm California weather as she trudged wearily back and forth between the hospital and the nurses' quarters. Christmas was two days past when she came to realize that she had forgotten it completely.

Joleen had lost nearly 10 pounds in her first three weeks at the Veterans Hospital. Her sleep was torn into broken pieces by dreams of wounded patients crying out in pain. She would wake up, her heart racing, realize that she had been dreaming, and then try and fall back to sleep.

On New Year's Eve, while assisting a skin graft surgery on a burn victim, Joleen collapsed from exhaustion and was ordered on 72-hour mandatory leave.

The first twenty-four hours of her leave were spent sleeping in a near comatose state with the aid of a sedative. The first thing she did, after finally waking up and fighting off the grogginess, was to sneak back over to the hospital, an act which was against orders, and unobtrusively check on several of her patients. Her second act was to write a letter to her Thief River Falls family.

The previous letter from Joleen posted on the barber shop window was postmarked Great Lakes Naval Training Center. It was cryptic and stated that she would not be coming home for Christmas and, because of security precautions, she was not allowed by naval regulations to say where her next duty station was located.

Her next letter, written from the V.A. Hospital in California, was also brief.

*My dear friends,*

*I'm sure your world has been turned upside down by the bombing of Pearl Harbor, as has mine. I am working at a hospital and have seen first-hand the damage done to our unsuspecting servicemen.*

*I know that the bravest and strongest of Thief River Falls sons will soon answer the call of our country. May God watch over them and protect them from the ravages of war.*

*I miss you all so much right now but I must go.*

Recalling that almost every conversation between the townspeople of Thief River started with a comment about the weather, Joleen added a post script to her letter: *p.s. It was 72 degrees and sunny out here today!*

On the last day of her leave, Joleen put on her dress blue uniform, took a bus down Wilshire Boulevard and a streetcar up La Cienega to the famous Hollywood Boulevard. Although it was early January, the sun was bright and it felt warm and soothing on her face. Joleen strolled up Hollywood Boulevard, looking in the shops and past the famous Grauman's Chinese Theater with all the hand prints of the stars in the sidewalk cement. The exercise felt good so she walked up to Sunset Boulevard and eventually found herself outside the USO's 'Hollywood Canteen'.

It was Friday afternoon and a full orchestra was playing inside the USO. There was a lovely couple standing outside the door and Joleen thought that they bore a strong resemblance to James Stewart and Linda Darnell. The man handed her a cup of coffee and opened the door for her.

"Thank you, sir," Joleen said politely.

"My pleasure ma'am," the man answered in an unmistakable drawl.

"Oh, my goodness," Joleen stammered. "You are James Stewart!"

"And you are?" Stewart asked.

"Me? Oh, my name is…" Joleen paused for a second. She had never felt her mind go blank like that before. There she was standing in front of two of her favorite movie stars and she couldn't think of her own name.

"Joleen... Joleen Salveson!" she blurted out.

"Nice to meet you, Joleen," Linda Darnell smiled. "Have a nice time."

"Thank you," she swooned.

Joleen bounced into the USO feeling almost giddy. She looked around the room and took a deep breath trying to calm herself.

The orchestra was playing "Chattanooga Choo Choo" and the dance floor was alive with young, handsome soldiers in various military uniforms dancing with pretty girls, each of whom looked like a Hollywood star. The soldiers were even dancing with one another out on the huge floor.

"If they could only see me now," Joleen giggled to herself, hiding her grin behind her paper cup of coffee and re-connecting with her past for a moment. She made a mental note to save the cup and mail it back to Thief River Falls with a note that read, "Oh, by the way, James Stewart handed me this cup of coffee when I was in Hollywood."

She laughed out loud when she imagined the cup pinned to the bulletin board in the window of Irv's barber shop.

A freckle-faced boy with a thick southern drawl tapped her on the shoulder.

"Would you care to dance, Lieutenant?"

"Oh, I'm sorry, what did you say?" Joleen asked, her imagination still standing outside of Irv's barber shop back in Thief River Falls.

"Would you care to dance with me, Lieutenant?"

The boy was wearing an olive-green Army uniform and his accent made his words sound like they were made out of rubber.

She blushed in surprise.

"Oh, thank you, but I'm really not much of a dancer."

"You sure look like you're a good dancer, if you don't mind me saying so."

She stared at the soldier. He was about her age. In his face she saw the faces of her patients superimposed upon his lean, strong and perfectly intact body. A wave of sadness staggered her and she brushed a tear from her cheek.

"Is everything all right ma'am? I didn't mean to offend you."

"No, I'm sorry, I just..." she heard the band playing 'I Don't Want to Set the World on Fire'. "Sure, I'd love to dance with you but I'm really not very good."

"Lieutenant, you just stay close to me and I'll do all the work. You happen to be in the capable hands of Private First Class, Henry Monroe, Waynesboro, Georgia's finest ballroom dancer, rather, its former finest ballroom dancer who is currently soon to be Waynesboro's finest infantryman."

As they walked towards the dance floor, Joleen turned back towards the door, "That really was James Stewart and..."

"And Linda Darnell at the front door, ma'am? Sure was. Every Friday night is MGM Night at the Canteen. All the big stars come in. More than you know. A lot of them just work back there in the kitchen making coffee and sandwiches."

As Joleen circled the dance floor in the capable arms of Waynesboro, Georgia's finest ballroom dancer, she spotted Hedy Lamarr and Mickey Rooney. When she stopped dancing to catch her breath, Clark Gable served her a sandwich and a cup of punch. She felt it was simply the most incredible day of her young life.

Joleen left the USO after spending the afternoon learning the foxtrot, the big apple and, the most popular dance of the day, the jitterbug. When she wasn't dancing, she was stargazing. On her walk to the bus stop her feet barely touched the ground.

When the bus pulled into the Veterans Hospital grounds, Joleen returned to the grim reality of the attack on Pearl Harbor and the long, grueling hours, but fully committed to making the arrangements necessary to take some of her patients to MGM Night at the Hollywood Canteen the following Friday night.

# Chapter 10
## 12 Million Drafted for the Duration

*The Selective Service and Training Act of 1940 began with a mandate to induct 900,000 men into the armed forces, initially for a 12-month period. It was the first peacetime draft in United States' history. The Act was extended to 18-months as the "phony war in Europe" turned real when Hitler's armies overran Denmark, Norway, Belgium and Luxembourg. Eventually, the Selective Service would induct 12 million men for a period specified as "the duration of the war".*

*Thirty-percent of all registrants were rejected for physical defects. The 4-F classification was given primarily for muscular and bone malformation, hearing or circulatory ailments, mental deficiency or disease, hernias and syphilis.*

Nathan had registered for the draft and received his notice for a physical from the Selective Service Board while he was in New Orleans.

His scoliosis was quickly diagnosed by the examiners and Nathan was declared 4-F. Although he understood that it would be painful for him to carry a pack and a rifle across Europe, Nathan was ashamed and felt like a traitor, unable to fight with his countrymen.

# Chapter 11
## Nathan O'Shea
## Los Angeles, 1941

T HE FIRST THING NATHAN DID WHEN HE ARRIVED IN LOS Angeles was to take a bus from the train station to Santa Monica and walk out on the Santa Monica Pier. He stood on the end of the pier and stared out at the clear, blue water of the Pacific Ocean. Nathan had never seen a body of water so transparent. It was in stark contrast to the muddy and rusty waters of the Mississippi and the Gulf Coast.

"You were right, E. Tim. It's hard to believe how beautiful this is. I sure wish you were here standing beside me."

Nathan found a place to rent in Santa Monica, two blocks from the ocean. He felt a closeness between the ocean and his memories of New Orleans, E. Tim and the Night Bloomin' Jazzmen.

Nathan found a Help Wanted ad in the newspaper that read, "Serve Your Country—Drivers Wanted", and took a job with Signal Oil, driving a gasoline truck between Long Beach and the San Diego Naval Bases.

The trucks carried 5,000 gallons of gasoline and with the wartime rubber shortage, the tires on most of the gasoline trucks were so bald that the drivers had to use what was called a 'retreader', a tool that could squeeze a few extra miles out of a tire by melting grooves in the smooth, thin rubber to try and provide some traction.

In addition to hauling two-and-a-half tons of gasoline on tires as thin as a bass drum head, there was also a blackout in effect along the California coast which meant that the truck drivers could not turn on their headlights at night. It was believed that the Japanese had submarines lurking off the coast with their primary mission to stop the flow of fuel for the fleet in San Diego, so all deliveries had to be made at night.

The trucks were equipped with 'dim-out lights', small lights that shone weakly on the pavement to avoid detection by the suspected offshore enemy. The lights were of little help to drivers trying to see what was ahead of them and equally difficult as to be seen by oncoming vehicles.

Bad tires, no lights, the possibility of being blown up by a Japanese submarine, and patches of fog that were thick as the marshmallow in a Moon Pie, all combined to make Nathan feel as though he was putting his life on the line for the war effort.

Sometimes he would fantasize, bouncing along in the dark and unable to see further than 10-feet ahead of him, that he was driving arms and ammunition to the front lines to save a unit which had been pinned down.

By the end of his second month on the job, Nathan began to suffer from severe headaches and discovered that he had completely lost his sense of taste and smell from the powerful gasoline fumes seeping out of his tanker. Sometimes the headaches were so severe that he was forced to stay home all day with the curtains closed and cold, wet washcloths over his eyes and forehead.

Nathan's complex was made up of five bungalows arranged in a U-shape, all facing a common courtyard with a cement walkway down the center. His neighbors included an elderly couple who seldom went outside and whom Nathan had only seen once or twice. Their cottage was always dark, with the blinds pulled shut. A small banner of white satin with a gold star in the center was hung against the living room window, the only sign of communication from the occupants to the world outside.

Nathan learned that a banner with a blue star meant that a member of the family had gone off to fight. A banner with a gold star sewn over the blue meant that someone from the household had been killed in the war.

A writer lived in one of the other units. He was a scriptwriter who worked at Metro Goldwyn Mayer Studios in Culver City and seemed to spend every waking moment hammering at his typewriter.

The wife of a serviceman lived in the rear unit. She had two young children whose toys, shoes, balls, tricycles and clothes were always strewn around the courtyard as though a giant had picked up one side of their bungalow and emptied out everything through the front door.

The unit next to Nathan was occupied by a young woman who worked the swing shift at Hughes Aircraft Company. When she was home, she played hit records of the day on her phonograph. When it was a warm day and she opened her windows, Nathan could hear her singing along with the music.

Nathan had driven a Long Beach to San Diego turnaround and went to bed about four in the morning with a throbbing headache. He had finally fallen asleep when he was awakened by pounding on his front door. Nathan put on his robe, stumbled through the dark living room and opened the door. The bright morning sun stung his blood-shot eyes and for a moment he was blinded. Although he couldn't see, he could hear the voice of a woman who seemed to be highly agitated.

"Mr. O'Shea? Mr. O'Shea? That's your name, isn't it? That's what it says on your mailbox, right?" came a voice out of the searing sunlight.

Nathan's vision began to slowly return but all he could make out was the silhouette of a girl's head against the sun. The voice seemed to belong to his next-door neighbor.

"Would you like to come in?" he asked.

The screen door slammed noisily behind her as she breezed by Nathan and stood nervously in the center of the room. After staring into the sun at the front door, Nathan still had trouble seeing in the darkness of the living room. He partially opened the curtains.

"Yes, I'm Mr. O'Shea. How can I help you, miss? Uh, would you care to sit down?"

"Oh, I can't sit down," she sighed, pacing back and forth, her high heels tapping sharply on his hardwood floor.

"Now, I don't want you to think that I'm nosy or anything but I happened to notice that when you moved in you were carrying a guitar case. I just happened to be looking out my window, and, my being a musician as well, it kind of caught my eye."

She stared at Nathan as though she was expecting an answer from him. He stared back at her trying to remember if there was a question he was supposed to answer.

She squinted at Nathan, "Well, do you?"

"Do I... oh, do I play the guitar?" he stammered, struggling to get focused. "Yes, I play some."

Nathan looked towards the hall closet where he had imprisoned his guitar since arriving in California. "I used to play a little guitar."

"A little guitar? You mean like a ukulele or something?"

Nathan smiled, "No, I play the guitar... a regular-sized guitar."

"Thank goodness! All of a sudden I began to think that maybe it could have been a machine gun in that case and not a guitar and that you were going to have to kill me because I discovered you were a killer and the audition wouldn't matter anyway."

Nathan rubbed his temples and shook his head, completely lost in the conversation.

"Are you good? Can I hear you play? Oh, God, please be good. Creepers, look at me, I just barge right in here without introducing myself. I'm so sorry. My name's Helen and I live next door and, oh, my God, I've got about the biggest break in the world and I need an accompanist for an audition to sing with the Freddie Martin Band. The Freddie Martin Band as in Freddie Martin from the Coconut Grove Freddie Martin Band, and I don't know anybody I can get to accompany me so here I am, begging a guy in his bathrobe who I've never spoken to before. Jeepers, can you play, 'How High the Moon'? Do you have any tea? My throat gets rough from the dust and stuff flying around at the aircraft plant."

Nathan smiled. He had never been around anyone quite so wound up.

"What key do you sing it in?" he asked wearily.

"What key?"

"Yea, you know, one of those letter things like A, B flat, C...."

"Gosh, I don't know, the same as it is on the record, I guess. Whatever key that is. I can bring you the record, will that help?"

"Let me put on some pants and some coffee. Sorry, I don't have any tea. Why don't you go back to your place and put on the record. I don't have anything to play a record on here. Open your window and turn it up loud so I can hear it and I'll figure out the key. Then we'll see if I can play it to your satisfaction."

Helen sprinted out of the house, slamming the screen door behind her. Nathan put on a pair of pants and his house shoes and started to make coffee. He could hear the Benny Goodman Orchestra playing "How High the Moon" coming from next door.

He walked to the closet and opened the door. He stared at the case leaning in the corner. Nathan had not played a note on his guitar since he arrived in California. As much as he loved the guitar, he'd been afraid of all the painful memories that would come pouring out if he opened the case.

But the poor girl seemed desperate so Nathan opened the case, tuned up his Gibson with a tuning fork and caught up with the song at the last verse. It was in B flat, the same key that the Jazzmen used to play 'How High the Moon'. For a moment he could hear the sweet notes from E. Tim's clarinet, hopscotching back and forth while Nathan strummed chords around the melody.

Before Nathan had a chance to begin to get too melancholy, the screen door slammed again and his neighbor was back like a whirlwind in his living room.

"Could you hear it from my place? Did you..."

She froze, mouth agape, eyes wide open as she listened to Nathan playing 'How High the Moon' easily and perfectly.

"You can play! You can play good, too! I've got an accompanist!"

She dropped to her knees in front of Nathan and pleaded, "You can make it can't you? You know, play for my audition. It's at one o'clock today at the Coconut Grove. Please say you can make it!"

It was Nathan's day off and he thought it might be fun to see the famous Coconut Grove.

"Sure, I can make it, Helen. I'd be happy to accompany you for your audition. You want to run through the song a couple of times here first?"

"Like a rehearsal? That would be terrific! Creepers, my hair, my hair! Can you come over to my place so we can practice while I do my hair? Whoops, I have to change my name, too!"

"What's wrong with Helen?" Nathan called out as she ran towards the door.

"Schlosky! My last name's Schlosky. I can't audition as Helen Schlosky!"

Nathan looked down his guitar, "How about Gibson?"

The screen door slammed again.

"Gibson? Helen Gibson! It's perfect! Oh my god, I sound like a movie star. Helen Gibson!"

Helen didn't get the job with the Freddie Martin Band. However, there were two other singers auditioning whose accompanists never showed up, so the band leader, Freddie Martin, asked Nathan if he'd mind accompanying the other singers.

Nathan had never learned to read music very well and as the singers walked up on the stage to audition, they handed him their sheet music. Fortunately, he had either played the song before or was familiar enough to fake his way through so he just figured out what key the song was in and played it by ear while pretending to read the charts.

None of the singers auditioning were hired. Ironically, Nathan O'Shea, the accompanist, was the only person at the audition who received an offer to play with the Freddie Martin Band that day.

The band had recently lost their guitarist to the draft and planned to find a replacement through the Hollywood Musician's Union Local 47 until Martin heard Nathan play.

"It's four nights a week, Thursday through Sunday, here at the Grove, plus, we play an early show every Friday night at the Canteen."

"The Canteen?" Nathan asked.

"Yea, the USO, the Hollywood Canteen over on Cahuenga just off Sunset. We play for the boys in uniform every Friday night before our ten o'clock show here at the Grove. You start at $20 a week plus we buy you a tuxedo. You want the job?"

Just as Nathan began to try and sort through the sudden and surprising circumstances that had happened that day, as well as his feeling a need to reflect on whether or not he was ready to play music again, the deliberations ended abruptly when a voice from somewhere within him answered, "Yes, sir, I sure do!"

"What's your name, son?"

"Nathan O'Shea, Mr. Martin."

"You're a pretty good guitar player, Nathan O'Shea. Who have you been playing with around here? I don't believe I've heard of you."

"No one, sir, I'm just in from New Orleans. I played with a band in the French Quarter."

"Bourbon Street, eh?" Martin smiled. "Best food on the continent."

"Yes, sir. Pretty good musicians, too," Nathan smiled.

Freddie Martin opened his briefcase and handed Nathan a stack of sheet music.

"Here are the charts for the show if you want to go over them before rehearsal tomorrow. Looks like you're a pretty good reader so you shouldn't have much trouble. As we go along, we'll work in a couple of solos for you."

Nathan nonchalantly thumbed through what looked like forty or fifty songs, knowing he had some serious homework to do.

"There's a Jim Clinton's Men's store down the street. They'll fit you for a tux, shirt and shoes. Just tell them to put it on my account. Rehearsal's tomorrow afternoon at three, right here and right on time. I'll see you then, O'Shea. Welcome to the band."

Helen would not speak to nor look at Nathan during their trip home. She stared straight ahead with her chin stuck out and her mouth puckered through two bus transfers, a trolley car ride and for most of their walk back to their bungalows.

134

Not knowing exactly what to say, Nathan didn't say anything until they were a block from home.

"Listen, Helen, you sang great," Nathan said, acting like he knew something about auditions and trying to console her. "You never know what bands like that are looking for. Sometimes it's not the best singer that gets the job. Maybe they're looking for a brunette or a redhead. Maybe you were too tall or not tall enough. Was this your first audition?"

"Yes," she answered curtly.

"Well, there you go. Nobody ever gets a job on their first audition. Some people say you gotta do a hundred auditions before you get a job, particularly out here in L.A. where it seems everyone wants to be a star."

"I didn't notice you going out to 99 auditions before today," she snipped.

"You know, Helen, you just sang on stage at the Coconut Grove. How many singers in this town can say that?"

Helen wiped her eyes with her hanky. "I did, didn't I. I sang on stage at the Coconut Grove in front of Freddie Martin."

"And you sang terrific."

"That's pretty good for a Midwest girl from Milwaukee, huh?"

"Heck, yes," Nathan answered. "That's pretty good for a girl from anywhere."

Helen forced a smile and put her arm in Nathan's as they walked up the sidewalk to their bungalows.

"Thank you for accompanying me, Nathan. You were pretty terrific yourself. And on such short notice, too. I probably wouldn't have even gotten to sing at the Coconut Grove if it weren't for you. Thank you and congratulations on getting a job with the band."

"No, Helen, it's me who should be thanking you. I just went from driving a smelly gasoline truck to the bandstand of the one of the most famous orchestras in America because some very talented singer woke me up this morning and asked me to accompany her. It's me who should be doing all the thanking here and I promise I'll pay you back."

"Ah, forget it, kid. It was nothing," Helen said doing her best James Cagney imitation.

"No, I won't forget it. Not too long ago, I learned an important lesson about appreciating people. I promise to find a way to pay you back for the break you got for me."

Helen gave him a kiss on the cheek as they neared her walkway.

"Jeepers, I gotta get to work! See you later Nathan."

Nathan was a musician again and performing with some of the finest players in the world. The Coconut Grove was one of the top clubs on the West Coast and was always crowded with bigwigs, celebrities and movie stars. Nathan couldn't believe his good fortune. It seemed like one day he was in overalls worrying about Japanese submarines and flat tires, and the next he was wearing a tuxedo and worrying about hitting a flat seventh.

Playing at the Grove was wonderful, but he was happiest entertaining the soldiers at the USO in Hollywood. On Friday nights, Nathan would arrive a couple of hours before the rest of the band, find a chair or sofa in the club, and take out his guitar. Within minutes he'd be surrounded by soldiers calling out requests for their favorite songs.

Occasionally, some of the stars visiting the USO like Dinah Shore, Bing Crosby or Martha Raye would join in singing with Nathan and the soldiers.

"I'll play it if you sing it," was always Nathan's cheery reply to a request.

Nathan would start playing and the group of soldiers would break into the song, sometimes harmonizing in three or four parts. Nathan would play until the rest of the band arrived and he had to set up on stage.

Sometimes on his off nights, Nathan would make the trip from Santa Monica to the Hollywood USO and play all night if there wasn't any other entertainment. He enjoyed mingling with the men and would listen attentively to their stories about where they came from, what they did, and what they'd heard about the war.

136

The musicians didn't get paid for playing at the USO but no one grumbled. Friday night was MGM Night at the Hollywood Canteen and you couldn't look anywhere without seeing somebody famous. Stars like Hedy Lamarr, Clark Gable, Spencer Tracy, Judy Garland, Ray Bolger, Mickey Rooney, Ann Southern, Linda Darnell and many others all showed up to serve sandwiches, coffee and doughnuts, or sew on an insignia or button or dance with the soldiers. Orsen Welles would get up on stage and do magic tricks. One night for a grand finale, he sawed Marlena Deitrich in half.

Dinah Shore and Red Skelton would spend the whole night in the back, helping with the cooking and cleaning in the kitchen. There were priests, rabbis and preachers from every denomination imaginable willing to sit and talk to the men. There were books and quiet places to read. There were nooks and crannies to steal a last kiss from a girl you just met before being shipped overseas. The USO was a place where a soldier who'd spent more time in a cotton field than in a classroom could get help writing a letter to the folks back home.

From his place in the center of the bandstand, Nathan would peer over his music stand, that held sheet music he couldn't read, and look out onto the crowded dance floor.

The soldiers were young, brash and cocky. They came from every state in the union. They were from the country and the city. They left farms and factories to go across the ocean and fight. It didn't seem to matter to them that they didn't know much about the war on the other side of the world. Their attitude seemed to be, "Tomorrow we'll kick the crap out of the Krauts and the Japs but tonight, what the hell, let's dance!"

Lt. Joleen Salveson pulled every string she could to secure a bus and a driver from the Veterans Hospital motor pool. Surprisingly, she had an almost equally difficult time convincing her patients that they needed to get away from the hospital for a while. She promised them that they were going out for a night on the town and that it would be a huge surprise. She was still buzzing over meeting James Stewart and Linda Darnell and was convinced that a visit to the Hollywood Canteen would revitalize the men's spirits.

On that Friday night, four burn patients, three amputees, two facial reconstructions, and a young private who showed no physical wounds but refused to speak, all loaded into a hospital bus parked outside their ward. Each of the young soldiers had been wounded in the attack on Pearl Harbor and although their wounds seemed to be healing normally, none of them were responding to the hospital staff's rehabilitative efforts. Joleen had witnessed first-hand, at the side of the surgeons, the terrible damage war could do to the bodies of these young men. She was still in the process of trying to understand what it had done to their spirit.

When the bus arrived at the Hollywood Canteen, the sidewalk in front of the USO was crowded with soldiers in uniform and young girls dressed in all the current fashions of the day.

"Here we are, men," Joleen announced proudly. "It's the Hollywood Canteen. There's a great band and a bunch of movie stars inside. There's food and drinks and cookies and cake. You're going to love this place and it's just for soldiers. Come on, let's go!"

None of the soldiers moved. They stared out of the windows of the bus and sat frozen in their seats.

"What's the matter, don't you fellows want to go inside?" she asked.

The men turned away from the windows and looked at one another. They saw faces covered with bandages, arms and legs in casts, empty sleeves and pant legs dangling where strong limbs used to be.

"Lieutenant, we… we can't go in there," one of the men said.

Suddenly the realization of how the men must have felt struck Joleen like a fist in her stomach. Outside of the bus were the men who were going to win the war and save the world. Inside the bus, in the minds of her patients, were the men who had lost the battle of Pearl Harbor.

Her face flushed and she felt as though her tears were going to burst from her eyes. Joleen spun around and ran blindly down the steps of the bus, flinging open the doors with her shoulder. She leaped onto the sidewalk and, running at full speed, collided squarely with an unsuspecting, young man carrying a guitar case.

Nathan's guitar went sailing across the sidewalk and he landed flat on his back with Joleen sprawled on top of him.

Joleen rolled over and lay face down on the sidewalk sobbing.

Nathan never saw what hit him. One minute he was walking down the street whistling a tune and the next he'd been blindsided by a runaway bull busting out of a freight car.

Nathan got up on his hands and knees and wiggled around to see if anything was broken. His shoulder ached and his tuxedo was roughed up a bit but there didn't seem to be any serious damage.

He stood up slowly and discovered Joleen lying on the sidewalk next to him. Nathan saw that she was crying and put his hand on her back.

"Are you hurt?"

Joleen turned her head and looked up into Nathan's face.

"Oh, I am so sorry. I just ran right into you. I'm so sorry. Did I hurt you?"

"No, ma'am, I'm OK. Are you okay?"

Joleen sat up and wiped her eyes with the back of her hand.

"Yes, I think I'm OK. Just feeling pretty stupid right now."

"Look, your hands are cut," Nathan said.

He took her hands in his and gently turned them. The palms of her hands were scraped and bleeding.

"Let me take you inside. They have a doctor in the USO."

"No, I'm all right, I'm a nurse. I have to go. I have these men..."

Tears rained from her eyes again when she saw some of her patients hobbling down the steps of the bus to help her.

Nathan followed her eyes to the bus and read "Veterans Hospital" on the side. He saw two young men getting off the bus, one whose head was covered with bandages, and another who was missing an arm. They were both wearing Class A Army dress uniforms.

"You hurt, lieutenant?" one of the soldiers asked.

"No, I'm fine, I'm fine," Joleen answered, wiping her tears from her cheek.

Nathan reached out, put his hands on her shoulders, and opened his mouth to speak. At that very moment when she looked up at him, Nathan felt as though he'd just been knocked off his feet again. He couldn't speak and couldn't breathe. He felt like his heart had stopped. It was the strangest feeling he had ever felt in his life.

Suddenly he realized that he was sitting in the middle of the sidewalk and was about to say something but he had completely forgotten whatever it was he was going to say.

Joleen looked up at Nathan expectantly waiting for him to speak. She noticed that his eyes were glazed over and he seemed dazed. She wasn't sure if he was going to speak or faint, so instinctively, she took his hand and checked his pulse. It seemed a little high.

Nathan stared down at her hand on his wrist. Her touch was soft and gentle and he could feel the warmth from her fingers all the way up his arm.

After a few moments, Nathan finally cleared the fog from his head, the frog from his throat and handed Joleen his handkerchief.

"Why don't you go inside to the ladies' room. Rinse your face and run some water over your hands. You don't want to get blood all over your uniform, lieutenant... lieutenant...?"

"Salveson. Joleen Salveson."

She looked back towards the bus. "I can't, I've got to..."

"I'll take care of these guys," Nathan interrupted.

"You go on inside Lieutenant Salveson. Me and the boys will be just fine. By the way, my name's Nathan..."

"...and, by the way, you happen to be the most beautiful woman I've ever met," he thought to himself.

Joleen looked down at her bloody hands and nodded at Nathan.

"OK, I'll be out in a second."

Nathan picked his guitar case off the sidewalk and walked onto the bus.

"Mind if I come aboard?"

He didn't wait for an invitation. The two soldiers and Nathan climbed into the bus.

"Hey, guys, what's cookin'?" he smiled. "Does the lieutenant do that all the time or does she just wait for short musicians to run into?"

Several of the men laughed.

"You coming in the club tonight?"

The laughter stopped abruptly and Nathan looked around at the men.

"It's just as well. I hear the band's lousy."

"You the guitar player?" asked a soldier missing an arm.

"Yea," Nathan answered. "How'd you guess?"

"I used to play a little guitar," said the soldier. "Your case wasn't the right shape for a trombone. What kind of axe you got?"

Nathan laughed and took out his guitar.

"A Gibson L-5, huh?" the soldier said. "That's a sweet guitar."

"Want to play it?" Nathan asked, nonchalantly tuning up the guitar.

"Just in case you hadn't noticed, I'm a little short-handed at the moment," the soldier said, motioning his head toward the empty left sleeve of his uniform.

Nathan stepped around and sat on the seat to the left of the soldier and nudged him over toward the window. He placed the body of the guitar on the soldier's left thigh.

"That doesn't matter. Here, I'll be left hand, you play right." Nathan said in a casual tone as he handed the soldier a pick.

The soldier looked numbly over at Nathan who was fingering chords along the neck of the guitar with his left hand.

"What do you guys want to hear?" Nathan asked the men.

The soldier ran the pick across the strings with his right hand as Nathan made an E chord with his left. The rich, deep resonance from the guitar filled the bus. The soldier smiled at the sound and strummed the strings again.

"How about a little 12-barre blues to warm up with?" Nathan asked.

"Count it out" the soldier answered.

The rest of the men on the bus began to whistle and applaud as Nathan and the soldier played, Nathan fingering the chords with his left hand, while the soldier strummed the strings with his right.

"What's your name?" Nathan asked while they were playing.

"Ken Petersen," the soldier answered.

"Nathan O'Shea. Nice to meet you. How'd it happen?"

"Pearl."

They finished playing and Nathan announced, "How about a hand for the guitar duo of Petersen and O'Shea?"

The other men whistled and cheered.

"How about an arm, too?" Petersen whispered.

Nathan caught his breath realizing his thoughtless remark. His mind must have still been on the beautiful Lieutenant. Petersen just laughed and kneed Nathan in the side of the leg.

Nathan let out a relieved chuckle.

"Hey, let's play stump the band," Petersen smiled. "Get it? Stump the band?"

"You guys know "Pennies From Heaven?" someone called out from the back of the bus.

"Sure, we do," Nathan answered.

"You sing it, we'll play it. Count it out, Petersen."

The very last thing Joleen expected to find when she returned from the USO club was a busload of her patients singing, 'You Must Have Been a Beautiful Baby' with Sgt. Petersen and the man she knocked over on the sidewalk— both playing the same guitar. Her intention was to apologize deeply to the men for being so insensitive, get them back to the hospital as soon as possible, and request an immediate transfer.

When she climbed back on the bus, rehearsing to herself the apology she would deliver to the men, she was thoroughly startled at the serenade from the group and stood dumbstruck at the front of the bus. Out of nowhere, she began to cry again.

"Gosh, lieutenant, were we that bad?" one of the soldiers asked as they stopped the song.

"No, you all sounded wonderful. I just didn't... maybe I'm a little emotional tonight. Sergeant Petersen, I didn't know you played guitar."

Peterson laughed. "I'm not half as good as I used to be. This guy O'Shea slows me down quite a bit though."

Nathan's ears plugged up. Petersen's words sounded garbled and distant and everything seemed to be in slow motion when he looked at her standing in the aisle of the bus.

Joleen sat down in one of the seats and turned back at the smiling, laughing faces of her patients. She was both moved and bewildered at the drastic change in the men's morale.

O'Shea and Petersen played guitar while the men and Joleen sang on the Veterans Hospital bus parked in front of the Hollywood Canteen for over an hour.

In the midst of their curbside performance, Nathan O'Shea fell desperately and helplessly in love for the first time in his life. Whenever Joleen's eyes would meet his, Nathan could feel his face flush and he'd miss a chord change. In one-hour of playing in front of Lieutenant Joleen Salveson, Nathan made more mistakes than he'd made in a month playing with Freddie Martin's band.

Nathan decided he'd better pay more attention to what his left hand was doing when he noticed the time on his watch. He was supposed to have been on stage five minutes ago. It seemed to him as though he'd been playing on the bus for no more than ten minutes.

Nathan stood up. "Hey, I gotta go. Petersen, it was great jamming with you, man. I used to play in a band with a one-armed trumpet player down in New Orleans. Lost his left hand on a piece of farm machinery when he was a kid. He could play that bugle."

Nathan turned to the rest of the soldiers, "Great playing with all of you guys. If you decide to come in, I'll buy you a cup of coffee and a doughnut."

As Nathan walked towards the front of the bus, he stopped in front of Joleen.

"It was real nice running into you, Lieutenant, or was it real nice being run into by you?" Nathan said with a smile. "Either way, I'd like to do this again sometime if that would be all right with you, ma'am."

Joleen blushed as her mind raced from an apology, to a thank you, to some other feelings she couldn't quite put her finger on. The end product of her whirlwind of thoughts was a simple, genuine smile, a smile that Nathan felt all the way from the end of his cowlick to the tips of his toenails; a smile that would stay with Nathan through all the long years of the war and take him halfway around the world.

Nathan was waving to the men on the bus from the sidewalk when Joleen stuck her head out of the door.

"Maybe we could have lunch tomorrow," she said as the driver started the engine. "At the Veterans Hospital on Wilshire."

Nathan smiled so wide his lips disappeared.

"That would be swell," he yelled back. "That would be swell!"

The bus pulled away and Nathan floated into the USO Canteen.

Inside the USO, Nathan felt feverish and wondered if he might be coming down with something.

The following morning, Lieutenant Joleen Salveson, along with twelve other nurses, was on a plane for Darwin, Australia.

# Chapter 12
## The Foxhole Circuit
## Soldiers in Greasepaint

NATHAN WAS SURE HE HAD NEVER SPENT SUCH A RESTLESS night. Throughout the evening, both at the USO and the Coconut Grove, Nathan would catch a quick glimpse of the back of a girl in a uniform with the same color hair as Lt. Salveson and he'd feel his heart begin to race thinking it might be her. He imagined scenarios in which she had brought her patients back to the hospital and taken a cab to come and see Nathan play. His mental wanderings cost him a reprimand from his bandleader for sloppy playing that night.

In anticipation of his lunch date with the Lieutenant, Nathan spent most of the morning trying on every shirt in his closet and most of his pants before deciding on an acceptable combination. He made a mental note to go shopping for clothes.

On his way to the bus stop, Nathan stopped by a pawn shop and found a used trumpet in good condition with a case for five dollars. The valves worked smoothly and the horn looked like it had been well cared for.

The Veterans Hospital was a short bus ride down Wilshire from Nathan's bungalow. He wasn't sure what time Lt. Salveson went to lunch so he got there well before noon. He wandered across the spacious hospital grounds and found the Visitor's Center.

"I'm sorry," the private at the front desk said. "Lieutenant Salveson is no longer at this duty station."

"But she was here last night. Where could she have gone?"

"I am not at liberty to give you any more information other than Lt. Salveson is no longer stationed here, sir."

"How about a Sergeant Petersen? Ken Petersen."

The private checked through his stack of records.

"Are you a relative, sir?"

"No, I'm a musician. Petersen and I used to play together. I've got his horn here. I'm returning it to him."

"I'll have to check the contents of the case, sir."

Nathan opened the case and showed the private the trumpet.

"Let's see, Sergeant Petersen is in Ward 10, building 14 Bravo, first floor. Three units to the West."

On his way out, Nathan stopped.

"You sure you're right about Lieutenant Joleen Salveson?"

"Yes, sir, she is definitely no longer stationed here."

Nathan finally located Building 14 and found Ward 10 at the end of a long, freshly waxed hallway. He combed his hair, neatened his clothes and walked through a set of double doors into a spacious day room with pool tables, card tables, a ping pong table and a small library. He spotted a few familiar faces from the bus the night before but no sign of Lt. Salveson.

Sgt. Petersen was playing ping pong on the far side of the room and was the first to notice Nathan.

"Hey, O'Shea, you come back for lessons? I'm a little busy right now," Petersen joked.

Nathan laughed as the patients from the bus gathered around him and gave him a friendly welcome.

Nathan shook hands with those men he recognized and introduced himself to the others in the ward. Sgt. Petersen worked his way through the crowd and stuck out his arm. Nathan shook his hand and they smiled at one another.

Nathan handed Petersen the trumpet case.

146

"I brought you a little present, Sergeant."

Petersen set the case on a nearby table and opened it. The bright rays of the sun coming through the day room windows ricocheted off the shiny brass of the horn nestled in the red velvet lining of its case.

"Wow, isn't that pretty," Petersen said as he stared at the glimmering gold instrument.

"Remember I told you about my friend Wingy in New Orleans?"

Petersen nodded, his eyes still on the horn.

"Wingy could just about outplay anybody with two arms. I'll bet you could figure it out pretty quick."

Petersen picked up the trumpet and inspected it closely.

"Wingy would put his little finger here and his thumb there so he had these three fingers free to work the valves. I found this book on how to play the trumpet in case if you're interested."

"Yea, I think I might be," Petersen said, leafing through the book. "How much do I owe you?"

"You know, a man gave me my first guitar," Nathan said quietly. "And I think I valued that guitar much more than if I'd paid for it because I thought very highly of the man who gave it to me. I would hope, Sergeant Petersen, that you would do me the honor of thinking kindly of me by accepting this as a gift."

Petersen smiled, "I get it, and maybe someday I'll get to do the same thing, eh?"

Nathan smiled and nodded.

"By the way," Nathan coughed trying to sound nonchalant, "How's Lieutenant Salveson? She recovered from our run-in last night? Is she around?"

"Nah, I heard she shipped out. Must have got orders last night. She was outta here at oh-dark-thirty. Didn't even have time to say good-bye to anyone. One of the nurses told me she was off to someplace in Australia."

"Australia? Wow, when did she know about this?" Nathan asked, trying to hide his disappointment.

"Apparently, she found her orders on her bunk last night. That's what the nurse said. These days, nobody's getting much advance warning. Security reasons, I guess. The man says "pack" and you're gone."

"Did she say where in Australia?"

"No, I don't think she even knows. They don't want any loose lips sinking anymore ships. Them Krauts and Japs got ears everywhere."

Nathan's spirits sunk as he thought to himself, "A girl runs me over me, the next day she disappears and I'm down in the dumps 'cause I can't find her. She must have knocked all the sense out of me last night..."

Nathan spent several hours in the day room. He wasn't any good at pool or ping pong and learned the hard way not to play penny-a-point gin rummy with these men. He left with a promise to come back when he had more money.

The next week, Nathan returned with Billy Montgomery, one of the trumpet players in Freddie Martin's band. Billy gave Petersen his first lesson.

Nathan continued to visit the wounded soldiers in Ward 10. In a way, his relationship with the men sustained a connection with Lieutenant Salveson, a memory, try as he might, he couldn't seem to get out of his mind. He continued to ask the doctors and nurses around the hospital if anyone had heard from her.

Sometimes he'd bring his guitar and sit in the day room and play for hours. His gin rummy game improved a little over time, but after months of talking with the men and gaining their trust, he discovered that his real gift was in helping the men write letters home.

Although postage for servicemen was free and there were stacks of paper and envelopes in the day room provided by the Red Cross, few letters came out of Ward 10.

Some of the men had lost the use of their writing hands due to amputations, burns or fractures. Others had darker reasons for their lack of correspondence.

They were ashamed that they were maimed and disfigured, less a man than when they left home. Somehow, they felt responsible for being a part of the worst defeat at the hands of a foreign power in the history of the American military. They had fallen to a surprise attack without virtually firing a shot at the enemy. In the midst of these kinds of feelings, words to family and friends were hard to find.

It was also fear that kept the men in Ward 10 from healing completely. They were afraid to go home and face the possibility of losing another battle in trying to fit back into society. Ward 10 was their safe place.

Nathan understood the soldiers' feelings that first night on the bus in front of the USO. He could imagine why they didn't want to go into the club. He himself had been self-conscious about his scoliosis. Playing in the band with E. Tim and Wingy on stage, or just having lunch together at a restaurant, he was way too familiar with pretending not to notice the stares and ignoring the whispers.

Nathan just wanted to help. He had gotten to know each of the men in Ward 10 and he genuinely liked them — they were good guys. He admired them for what they had gone through at Pearl Harbor and understood the obstacles they would have to overcome in the future. Nathan thought he could close some of the distance between the men and the world they used to know by encouraging them to write letters home.

Walking around the day room with a stack of envelopes in his shirt pocket, a pad of paper and a pencil in his hand, Nathan continually badgered the men to let him do the writing if they'd do the talking.

"All right, we don't have to tell them what's going on here," Nathan said to an 18-year-old private named Kenny Burnside from Ohio, whose fingers on both hands had been amputated after being critically burned aboard the U.S.S. Arizona. "But wouldn't you like to peek over a fence and see what's going on back home?"

The boy smiled, "Yep, there's a few fences in Ridgeville Corners I'd like to peek over."

"Then let's write your folks and ask them a bunch of questions about what's going on back home. You look like you played football."

"Yea, I did. Three years, varsity ball." The soldier looked down at his hands and said softly, "I was a quarterback."

"Well, let's find out how the football team did this season. How about your dog? I know you've got a dog back home. Let's find out what he's been up to."

Nathan adopted the theory that if the men weren't going to go home, then he was going to try and bring home to them.

Gradually the men began to let Nathan write letters for them. His comments were vague and non-nondescript about their physical condition, while mostly inquiring about things that used to be a part of their lives back home. The overall tone of Nathan's letter-writing style was upbeat and light and the men usually liked the way they sounded through his words.

At the same time Nathan became a regular visitor to Ward 10, he continued his off-night appearances at the Hollywood Canteen. He struck up acquaintances with some of the recording studio session players in Hollywood and got to know a number of sidemen who played in some of the big-name groups like Benny Goodman's and Les Brown's Band.

Nathan put together a pick-up house band to play at the Canteen on nights when there was no special entertainment planned and The Freddie Martin Band wasn't performing. Depending on who was working and who was in or out of town, the Canteen house band could have anywhere from six to twenty members. Plus, the bandstand was always open to servicemen who played an instrument or wanted to sit-in or sing.

It was during a break with the Canteen house band that Nathan heard about the USO's 'Foxhole Circuit'.

*In October of 1941, Abe Lastfogel, the king of the show business agents and Chairman of the Board of the William Morris Agency, had been made president of Camp Shows, Inc. and had put together four main entertainment circuits to tour and perform for American GI's.*

*The 'Victory Circuit' brought fully-staged Broadway shows to stateside military installations with large facilities. The 'Blue Circuit' was comprised of smaller companies of vaudeville entertainers and performed at smaller military bases. The 'Hospital Circuit' brought special entertainment units to military hospitals. The fourth unit was called 'Camp Shows' that toured the 'Foxhole Circuit'. By the end of the war, more than 7,000 entertainers would perform on the Foxhole Circuit.*

*These 'soldiers in greasepaint' as they became known, included Bing Crosby, Bob Hope, Ann Sheridan, the Andrews Sisters, James Cagney, Gary Cooper, Fred Astaire, Jimmy Stewart, Humphrey Bogart, Dinah Shore, Paulette Goddard, Al Jolson, Clark Gable, Carol Lombard, Jerry Colonna, Ed Gardner of the popular radio show, "Duffy's Tavern", Mickey Rooney, and Walt Disney.*

*Others included Edgar Bergan and Charlie McCarthy who were regulars on the Hospital Circuit as was Milton Berle. Brooklyn Dodger manager, Leo Durocher, Mel Ott and Carl Hubbell all toured with the 'Foxhole Circuit' entertainers.*

*Martha Raye would eventually entertain soldiers in every theater of war where American soldiers were stationed.*

*Joe E. Brown, who was to lose his son in the war, was the first Hollywood star to tour the front-line bases in 1942.*

*The very first overseas tour took off for the Caribbean on October 30, 1941 with Laurel and Hardy, John Garfield, Ray Bolger, Chico Marx and Mitzi Mayfair.*

*Marlene Dietrich's sister was a prisoner in a Belgian concentration camp and Deitrich herself was reported to be on Hitler's infamous 'death list'. Nevertheless, Dietrich performed at Utah Beach, only 28 days after D-Day.*

*Bing Crosby's European tour, done from the bed of a truck and put on wherever troops were gathered, became known as the 'Cow Pasture Circuit'.*

*Big bands like Benny Goodman, Les Brown and Sammy Kaye traveled the 'Foxhole Circuit'. Major Glenn Miller, whose band first recorded 'The White Cliffs of Dover' in 1941, was killed on December 16, 1944 when his plane went down en route from England to France. Bob Hope's radio show, sponsored by Pepsodent tooth paste, was broadcast live from military bases in Alaska and the Aleutian Islands. Spike Jones and Dinah Shore would perform before 16,000 GIs in Le Havre, France in 1944.*

*By the end of the war, 28 entertainers on the USO's Foxhole Circuit had lost their lives due to plane crashes, illness or diseases contracted while on tour.*

As soon as Nathan heard about the Foxhole Circuit, he contacted the director of the Hollywood USO and volunteered.

When he received notification that he had been selected for a Camp Show going to Panama with Bob Hope, Hedy Lamarr and Humphrey Bogart, Nathan knew he had to resign from The Freddie Martin Band.

"How many of these tours are you going to do, O'Shea?" the band-leader asked.

"As many as they'll have me, sir. I'm really sorry to have to quit the band but I feel like I've got to do something more to support our boys in the war. I'm 4-F on account of my back and I can't run a rivet gun. Playing guitar is about all I know how to do."

"And you do it pretty well, son. We're going to miss you. What will you do about money? Do these Camp Show people pay you?"

"I don't think so but I've got some money saved up, thanks to you. Do you want me to return my tuxedo?"

Martin laughed. "No, you can keep it. Who knows, you might need it in the trenches."

Nathan smiled.

"Listen, O'Shea, I admire what you're doing. I've got a son on a Navy destroyer. I'll tell you what, there will always be a chair waiting for you in the band whenever you come back from a tour. I'll put you next to your replacement and you can show him how we do things. I'll pay you full-time scale, too."

Nathan was deeply touched by Martin's kindness.

"Thank you, sir. That's very generous of you."

"My contribution to the war effort. Just make sure you come back safe, son. I hear they use live bullets over there, not just tomatoes. You remember how to duck."

Prior to taking off on the tour, Nathan was required to sign an Oath of Secrecy contained in the Espionage Act. Any entertainer convicted of violating the oath could be sentenced to a prison term of 30 years or more.

After signing the oath, Nathan boarded a C-47 and was handed a pamphlet given to all USO troupes entitled, 'The Guide to The Foxhole Circuit'.

> When you sign up for an overseas tour, you are giving yourself an opportunity to serve your country and your fellow Americans. In this great war for freedom, you are putting your name down on the list of those who have fought to win.
>
> When peace comes again to the world, it will be good to know that you found your place in the struggle.

Nathan re-read that paragraph in the pamphlet over and over until he had committed the words to memory. He leaned back against the rigid metal back of the C-47 seat and closed his eyes as the noisy engines started up, shaking and vibrating everything inside the plane. He was filled with an overwhelming feeling that he was exactly where he was meant to be. He was finally going to give something back to the soldiers who were sacrificing so much.

Nathan thought of the people who had guided and helped him to reach this moment. He thought about Big Ben, his mentor; Ednus Brooke at Hadley's; and the Dixieland All Stars who taught him how to be a musician. He thought of E. Tim and how even more wonderful it would have been if his friend were sitting in the seat next to him. The thought of E. Tim still brought a hollow emptiness in the pit of his stomach and always left him feeling lonely.

However, the pain eased a bit when he wondered if maybe, just maybe, he ever got to Australia, he might get a chance to make good on that promise of a lunch date with Lieutenant Joleen Salveson.

Nathan's first USO show in Panama was not exactly what he had expected, although he would learn that not a single one of the many Camp Shows he would play were ever close to what he expected.

In the Spring of 1942, following the attack on Pearl Harbor, thousands of soldiers were being shipped in transports through the Panama Canal, but the men were not permitted to leave their ships and go ashore, so the Camp Show units set up their stages on piers on the side of the canal playing to floating GI audiences. The ships moved slowly through the locks and the entertainers knew that their show may be the last taste of America these GIs would get for a long time. For some, it may even be their last.

It was easy to see how much the soldiers appreciated the shows by their response. They laughed and cheered at Bob Hope's jokes. Hedy Lamar was waving to the troops from the end of a pier and they threw their caps at her, begging for an autograph. She signed as many and as fast as she could. After she threw the first several caps into the murky water of the canal trying to return them, a young MP on shore who had mastered the art of 'cap sailing' took over the job of returning the autographed caps and was 100% accurate.

The eight-piece band played the hits of the time. The GI's sang mightily to "You Are My Sunshine" and many danced on the decks when they broke into the "Beer Barrel Polka".

As each boatload of men sailed past the pier and down the lock of the canal, the GIs would whistle and wave goodbye. Nathan, as did all of the members of the troupe, felt a sadness with the passing of each ship as though they had met, become friends with the men, and then had to say goodbye too quickly. As a ship moved away in the distance, an eerie silence would settle over the entertainers. A few members of the band would walk off by themselves and find an empty space of pier railing to smoke a cigarette and stare down into the slow-moving water. The stars would go back to their make-shift dressing rooms to get out of the heat. Nathan would watch every ship pass until it disappeared from sight.

Within twenty to thirty minutes, another ship would enter the lock and the laughter, singing and dancing would start up again. They did 12 shows the day after their arrival. By the time the last ship had passed, Nathan was physically and mentally exhausted. He skipped dinner in the mess hall and fell asleep on his bunk, still wearing his clothes.

Nathan spent the next three years on the Foxhole Circuit. He played Alaska and Hawaii with Benny Goodman's Orchestra. He traveled 13,000 miles in a B-18 transport plane on a tour ranging from Puerto Rico to British Guiana with Ray Bolger, Laurel and Hardy and the Andrews Sisters. He backed Frank Sinatra on a tour of Belgium and the Netherlands.

Nathan was true to his promise to his next-door neighbor back in Santa Monica whose audition had ultimately led him to a position with the Freddie Martin Band and, eventually, to performing for the troops. The female singer from Harry Lewis' Orchestra became ill at the last minute prior to a three-week tour of England and France. Based on Nathan's strong recommendation, Helen Gibson, the former Helen Schlosky, became her replacement. Helen remained in England where she enjoyed a popular singing career and eventually married a major in the RAF.

For the duration of the war, Nathan would return from one Foxhole Circuit tour, recover from whatever diseases he had contacted on the trip, gain back the five or ten pounds he had lost, and then take off on another tour. He never had to wait very long between trips, mainly because of Bob Hope.

Bob Hope wore out more musicians than any other entertainer during the war. He never stopped and Nathan was fortunate to land a spot in his band for five Hope tours.

Nathan had toured as part of the back-up band with a lot of big stars but there was no comparison in the responses of the GIs to Bob Hope. Hope's self-effacing style and occasional anti-army remarks made him a favorite with the GIs in every theater of the war.

Nathan would never forget a show with Hope, Francis Langford, Edgar Bergan and Charlie McCarthy in a hospital in Southern France.

Hope would open every show with a hilarious monologue. Nathan had sat through it thirty times but he still couldn't help laughing every time he heard it. The hospital show was no different. Men would slap their casts or crutches together to applaud, while soldiers with internal wounds would hold their stomachs trying to control their laughter.

Hope introduced Francis Langford and one of the soldiers in the audience called out for the song "As Time Goes By". Francis looked back at the band and Nathan counted it off and started up the introduction. Four measures into the song, the rest of the band came in on cue.

Francis had been working long and hard hours on the tour and her voice was hoarse and strained. She got through the first verse when she noticed a young soldier with a head wound in the front row sobbing. Suddenly she couldn't sing. She tried to continue, but she had lost her voice. She finished the song whispering the words into the microphone with only Nathan accompanying her quietly.

When the song was over, she broke down and ran off the stage. The room was silent — no applause, no whistles just an empty numbness.

Nathan watched carefully as Hope stepped off the stage and walked slowly down the center aisle of patients with his hands stuck deep in his pockets and a somber expression on his face. All eyes were cast upon Hope. Still wearing a serious look, Hope finally spoke to the audience.

"Fellows, the folks at home are having a terrible time about eggs. They can't get any powdered eggs at all. They've got to use the old-fashioned kind you break open."

The room full of GIs exploded with laughter and Bob Hope continued for another twenty minutes to the show's end.

Nathan got dengue fever in the Philippines, his skin turned yellow in the Dutch East Indies from taking the anti-malarial drug, Atabrine, and in Italy he suffered from both amoebic dysentery and its cure, a daily injection of Emetine with its side effects of nausea, vomiting and dizziness.

Whenever the band had some time off between shows on a tour, Nathan would visit the camp hospitals. He'd bring his guitar and play requests.

"I can play it if you if can sing it," was his standard line.

Nathan would also offer to help write letters home.

Among the wounded in France, Italy and the South Pacific, Nathan still came across the same reluctance to write home that he had encountered back in the States in Ward 10 of the Veteran's Hospital. Nathan would patiently walk from bed-to-bed, strumming a recognizable tune that was recorded before the war, and share stories about the celebrities and stars he traveled with on his many USO tours. Eventually, he would stop by a soldier with his arms or hands in a cast or a patient with his eyes covered with bandages, and ask if he could help write a letter to his folks back home.

At some point during each of his visits to hospitals, Nathan would casually ask the doctors and nurses if they had come across Lt. Joleen Salveson. Unfortunately, the answer was always the same.

"No. Sorry, nobody by that name. It's a big war, you know."

Nathan would pick up his guitar case, say goodbye to the doctors, nurses and patients, and head back to do the next show.

# Chapter 13
## The Battle of Corregidor
## Prisoner of War

WHEN JOLEEN RETURNED TO THE VETERAN'S HOSPITAL after her misadventure at the USO Hollywood Canteen, she found a note from her commanding officer ordering her to report to company headquarters as soon as possible. Initially, she thought this must have something to do with her taking her patients off the hospital grounds and out for the evening. She walked slowly in the darkness across the damp grass of the grounds towards headquarters. Joleen was wrung out emotionally to the point of not caring what happened to her. There was little in the way of punishment that her superiors could dish out that she hadn't already inflicted on herself.

"But, then again..." she thought to herself. "That nice, young man with the guitar, who I almost killed, turned everything around and it seemed like the men ended up having had a good time after all."

Wedged in her thoughts somewhere between her growing anxiety of what was in store for her at HQ and her shame at her own insensitivity by putting the men in an uncomfortable position, she felt a tiny flutter in her stomach, wondering if the guitar player would take her up on her invitation.

"Did I really invite him out to lunch?" she whispered to herself. "That was pretty bold, Joleen! I wonder if I'll ever see him again?"

As it turned out, Joleen would be leaving all her inner struggles and uncertainties behind. The following morning, March 8, 1942 at 0900 hours, without being able to say goodbye to any of her patients, Joleen boarded a C-47 along with 12 other nurses bound for the Royal Darwin Hospital in Darwin, Australia with a single stopover in Honolulu, Hawaii. The 6,000-mile continued flight from Hawaii to Australia took nearly 20 hours.

Immediately upon landing at an American airbase outside of Darwin, a lieutenant colonel escorted the exhausted nurses into a Quonset hut where there were basins filled with water.

While Joleen and the other nurses splashed the cool water on their faces, the officer returned, accompanied by three Filipino women in Army fatigues.

"May I have your attention, please. I'm not sure how many of you are aware of the current situation in the Pacific Theater, but I'd like to give you an update on what has occurred here since the Japanese attacked Pearl Harbor."

Joleen listened carefully while trying to fight off the effects of the long flight.

"To be perfectly honest, my objective, following this briefing, is to solicit volunteers among you to serve as the nursing staff in a field hospital located in the Malinta Tunnel on the island of Corregidor. Before you accept this assignment, you should be aware that this mission is quite dangerous. This is why I want you to pay close attention to this briefing so that your decision can be based upon my full disclosure of the situation and your best judgment. Is that understood?"

"Yes, sir," they all responded meekly.

The American nurses exchanged inquisitive glances. None of them had ever heard of the island of Corregidor and, at the moment, they all were convinced that nothing in the war could possibly be more dangerous than flying halfway around the world in a C-47.

"After their attack on Pearl, the Japs attacked the Philippines. On December 28, General MacArthur declared Manila an "open city", defined as demilitarized, open to occupation and not to be defended in order to spare its occupants, under military law, from bombardment or other military attack. On January 2, the Japs bombed the city and entered the capital unopposed."

"In the meantime, American and Philippine forces have re-grouped on the Bataan Peninsula and are currently waging a strong counter-attack against enemy troops while anticipating reinforcements. Any questions so far?"

"Where exactly is Corregidor, Colonel?" one of the nurses asked.

The colonel pulled out a large map and thumb-tacked it to the wall.

"Corregidor is a small island measuring three and one-half miles long, approximately 26 miles from Manila and four miles off the tip of the Bataan Peninsula. It was originally a lighthouse station. Due to a recent increase in its formidable defenses, it is regarded as the "American Gibraltar" of the Far East. Its guns prevent the Japanese from gaining entrance to Manila Bay, a highly strategic position in the battle for the Southwest Pacific."

The colonel took a sip of water and continued.

"The facilities on the island of Corregidor currently include an above-ground hospital, library, commissary, baseball diamond, four tennis courts, two swimming pools, a nine-hole golf course and two beaches, one for officers and one for enlisted men, both of which are protected by steel wire nets."

"The steel nets protect who from what?" one of the nurses asked.

"The steel nets are placed to protect swimmers from man-eating sharks as well as an especially voracious species of barracuda. In some cases, the nets protect the sharks and barracudas from the GI's."

The nurses laughed as the colonel pinned up another map.

"In 1938, the Army Corps of Engineers drove a shaft from a rock quarry directly through a hill, thereby creating the Malinta Tunnel System on Corregidor. Three interconnected systems were bored out of the island's bedrock to form an impenetrable fortress below. The main tunnel is 1,400 feet long and 30 feet wide."

"You mean we'd be working in a tunnel?" another nurse asked.

160

"Yes, ma'am. To the north of the main system, there is another series of tunnels which include a 1,000-bed hospital and surgical unit. Your accommodations would be adjacent to the hospital complex."

"Not for the claustrophobic, am I correct, sir?" one of the nurses joked.

"The tunnel containing the hospital is 850-feet long, 24-feet wide and almost 20-feet high. Fresh air is continually pumped throughout the entire system by an electrically powered ventilation system. The conditions are not unlike duty in a normal hospital."

"What's the casualty situation, sir?" Joline asked.

"Before the Japs attacked the Philippines, most of the casualties on the island were due to barracuda attacks, jeep accidents, sunburn and an occasional case of the clap. However, wounded personnel from Marivelas Hospital in Luzon, as well as casualties from the Bataan siege, have filled all available beds, which is why I'm looking for as many nurses as I can get. Any volunteers?"

Only the three Filipino nurses and Joleen raised their hands.

The rest of the nurses boarded a bus while Joleen and the other volunteers were taken to the officer's quarters next to the airfield. As the late summer sun set, Joleen took a cool shower, changed into her fatigues, and enjoyed a fresh fish and chips dinner in the officer's mess hall.

The four nurses sat together and introduced themselves. They tried to make small talk as best they could but Joleen didn't speak Tagalog and the other three nurses spoke only broken English. They were finishing their apple pie and coffee when the lieutenant colonel approached their table.

"You will be leaving at 2200 hours on a seaplane bound for the coast of Mindanao. You will then board a PT boat that will take you to Corregidor."

"You mean 2200 hours…tonight, Colonel?" Joleen asked.

"Yes. I apologize for the quick turnaround, but we are trying to accomplish two missions in one, including your landing and one important evacuation from Corregidor."

"Important evacuation, Colonel?" Joleen asked.

"Yes, but the mission is highly confidential and I'm not at liberty to discuss anything further. I suggest you try to get a little rest before your departure."

The seaplane broke from the water's grasp in Darwin Bay and whined into the inky black night air. Exhausted to the point of delirium, Joleen slept soundly through the drone of the engines and woke as the plane taxied to a stop.

She was suddenly nauseous as the plane rose and dropped in the heavy swells of the open ocean. Joleen staggered over to the door of the plane, struggled with the secured handle and finally flung it open. She felt the cold sting of salt water against her face as she vomited into the rough, choppy sea.

The lights of the plane were turned off. It seemed to Joleen that the stars and the moon were also extinguished. She had never experienced a night so dark.

For what seemed to be an eternity, the plane bobbed in the unmerciful sea. The other three nurses also fell ill to seasickness, some making it to the door, some not. The stench of vomit began to fill the inside of the plane.

Suddenly the sound of a powerful engine shook Joleen out of her sickly haze. The nurses were helped from the plane and onto the cold, wet, metal seats of a PT boat. As soon as the last nurse was aboard, the boat took off at full speed, cutting through the swells like a powerful locomotive punching its way through mountains of sea.

The PT boat followed a crazed and twisted trail through the spattered chain of islands between southernmost Mindanao and the main island of Luzon.

They arrived at Cavalry Point on Corregidor as the sun was coming up on March 10, 1942. Joleen and the Filipino nurses were met at the dock and transported by jeep to the Malinta Tunnel and driven to their quarters. Joleen stumbled drunkenly onto a bunk nearest to the door and fell into an exhausted sleep, deep within the hollow entrails of her new, underground home.

162

*The same PT boat that brought the badly-needed nurses to the island known as "The Rock" would refuel and make a secretive return journey that evening carrying a most prestigious dignitary. The passenger was the U.S. Military Commander in the Philippines, General Douglas MacArthur. The boat would smuggle the general through the closing fingers of the Japanese forces from his acting headquarters on Corregidor to a safer position in Australia. It would be nine days short of three years until MacArthur would return to the island of Corregidor.*

*Prior to Japan's attack on Pearl Harbor and the Philippines, there were 5,000 American and Filipino troops stationed on Corregidor. Evacuees from Manila and Bataan had swollen the population to over 15,000.*

Joleen awoke that evening to an army garrison that had been slowly starving on half-rations for the past two months and a hospital filled with sick, wounded and dying soldiers.

She was assigned two racks, each with three beds. Four of her first six patients died within minutes of each other during her first shift. The dead men were replaced by more wounded being brought in without time to even change the sheets on the beds. In some cases, intravenous fluid hook ups were removed from the arm of a recently deceased patient and immediately inserted into the arm of the new patient.

The fighting on the Bataan peninsula, four miles from Corregidor on the mainland, was in the process of becoming one of the fiercest battles in the history of World War II.

Based on faulty intelligence that the Japanese forces were twice their real strength, General MacArthur ordered his army of 43,000 American soldiers and advisers, along with Filipino scouts, into the Bataan Peninsula.

The Bataan Peninsula stuck out into Manila Bay like a stubby finger some 25 miles long and 20 miles wide. Protected from sea attack by the heavy guns on Corregidor and crisscrossed by ravines and mountain streams, Bataan seemed to be an ideal spot for a defensive stand.

The first week of January, 1942, the Japanese attacked with a frontal onslaught, flank actions, concentrated artillery bombardment, and seaborne infiltration. The American defenders bravely held their positions in the face of everything the Japanese forces threw at them.

Following the failure of their all-out assault, Japanese warships began sinking all supply ships to Luzon. By the end of January, rations for Americans on Bataan were cut in half. The besieged troops were stricken with malaria, dengue fever, scurvy, beriberi and amoebic dysentery, while the supply of drugs quickly ran out.

Gaunt, undernourished, and disease-ridden, the garrison still managed to continue the fight.

In early February, 1942, the Japanese had to suspend their operations on Bataan because their own men were struck down by malaria. At one point in March, the Japanese had only 3,000 troops in the Bataan campaign but the Americans, unaware of the lightened enemy forces and themselves suffering badly from disease, were in no shape to take the offensive.

On Corregidor, the soldiers listened helplessly to the desperate radio conversations of their comrades on Bataan as the Japanese troops and sickness took its toll on their fellow soldiers. The arrival of Joleen and the other nurses signaled a short-lived sign that the Pacific Command was going to draw the line of the Japanese encroachment across their island fortress. Unfortunately, later that evening when news spread that MacArthur had been smuggled off Corregidor via the same boat that brought in the nurses, morale plummeted.

Joleen's duty shift was twelve-hours on and twelve-hours off. During her time off, she wandered through the maze of tunnels and wings that branched out from the main tunnels. The wings were 400-feet long by 20-feet wide and contained ammunition, gasoline, aerial bombs, torpedoes, emergency command posts and living accommodations.

There were a pair of interconnecting tunnels known as the 'Quartermaster Area' and the 'Navy Tunnel' which contained wings filled with small arms, ammunition, combat uniforms and two carefully guarded vaults which housed cryptographers whose job it was to intercept and decode Japanese radio transmissions.

By the end of her third week on Corregidor, Joleen contracted malaria. Her fever hovered at 105 degrees for three days and brought with it an excruciating headache along with uncontrollable, bed-shaking chills. On the fourth day, large doses of quinine finally helped break the fever and the chills subsided.

On April 8, Lt. General Jonathan M. Wainwright, who had been assigned command of the American and Philippine forces upon MacArthur's departure to Australia, withdrew with a small force from Bataan to Corregidor leaving 35,000 men on Bataan to surrender unconditionally on April 9, 1942.

In conjunction with the arrival of General Wainwright's forces on Corregidor and the surrender of Bataan, there was a mandatory order for the evacuation of all female military and civilian personnel stationed on 'The Rock' on the evening of April 17.

At 2200 hours, Joleen and the other female nurses and civilians were standing on the beach gathered around six rubber, inflatable rafts. They were to row out in the rafts and board the submarine, *Spearfish*, waiting 1,000 yards off shore, and then were to be taken to Australia for further assignment.

Joleen had already become close to a number of her patients and was reluctant to leave them but she was also terrified of what would happen to her at the hands of Japanese captors following the eminent defeat of the American garrison on Corregidor.

Ironically, Joleen found herself sharing a raft with the same three Filipino nurses who had volunteered for the mission. They all shared a common sense of relief at getting off the island.

Each raft carried four people comfortably and was equipped with two oars. Each person was issued a pair of tennis shoes and a life jacket. A sailor who had rowed several of the rafts to shore from the submarine warned them of a shallow reef that lay 150 yards off shore and that they would have to walk the raft over the reef because of the low tide to prevent punctures.

"Keep your eyes on the horizon to the south...in this direction," the sailor announced as he pointed out to sea.

"The submarine will cast intermittent red flashes from the tower as a navigational aid for you. Paddle harder than you've ever paddled in your life, ladies, because if the position of the sub is compromised by the Japs, the mission will be aborted immediately. The red light will turn blue and within seconds the submarine will disappear beneath the surface and head out to sea. In other words, if you hear Jap artillery landing around you, turn around and head back for shore because we'll be getting the hell out of there."

Joleen was glad it was dark. She didn't want the others to see that she was shaking.

"On your way out to the sub," the sailor continued, "keep the rafts spread out. Maintain a good distance between you so in case the Jap observers see you, they'll think you're just a patch of seaweed. And again, make sure you get out of the rafts when you reach the reef. The coral is razor sharp and will slice up these rubber rafts like your Daddy carves a Thanksgiving turkey. Let's load 'em up and may God be with us all."

Growing up in Minnesota, Joleen had been paddling canoes since she was a child and was confident in her ability to reach the submarine as she shoved her raft off the sand and into the water. She handed the other paddle to one of the Filipino nurses, reminded the others to put on their life preservers as they climbed in, and began stroking earnestly toward the red light blinking on the dark and distant horizon.

The tide was going out and the rafts quickly separated from one another, despite the fact that they were all aiming toward the same objective.

Although still slightly weak from her bout with malaria, Joleen paddled with all her might, praying that the beacon would not change from red to blue before she reached the submarine.

After 15-minutes on the water, Joleen heard the sound of waves breaking against the shallow reef and could see their bluish-green phosphorescent crests just ahead. She ordered the others to jump out of the raft.

She noticed that the other nurses had not put on their life preservers.

"Put on your life preservers!" Joleen yelled above the pounding of the surf on the coral ridge. "You need to put on your life preservers or you will drown!" she screamed.

Joleen slid over the side over the side of the raft and landed in waist-deep water.

"Let's go, we've got to walk the boat over the reef!" she screamed. "Get out of the boat and put on your life jackets!"

The three Filipino nurses would not put on their life jackets and refused to get out of the raft.

The tide was dragging the raft towards the reef and despite Joleen's efforts to hold the boat off the reef, the weight of the three nurses and the slippery footing on the shallow bottom kept drawing it closer and closer to the razor-sharp coral.

"If you don't get out now, these chambers will pop and the boat will sink," Joleen said firmly while trying to keep her voice calm. Motioning with her hands she explained, "We all need to get out of the raft and push it over the reef."

The three terrified Filipino nurses ignored Joleen's pleas and clung desperately to the safety ropes strung along the sides inside the raft. They still hadn't put on their life jackets nor were they showing any signs of getting out of the raft.

"Come on, come on, get out, get out!" Joleen screamed, as the surging undertow pulled the raft toward the shallow ledge of the reef.

"No, no, many barracuda, many barracuda!" one of the Filipino nurses screamed.

Joleen did her best to negotiate the heavy raft and her passengers through the surf and over the coral stubble by herself. Just as she was about to give up, a huge wave broke on the raft nearly tipping it over. Joleen felt the coral bottom disappear from under her. They were suddenly in deep water and she realized that they had cleared the reef. She was angry and exhausted when she climbed back in the raft.

"Now paddle, god dammit!" Joleen growled. "Or I'll throw each one of you overboard to the barracudas!"

Joleen searched for the submarine's guiding light as she paddled away from the reef, praying that the reef had not torn a hole in the raft and that the light was still red.

At first Joleen thought that the current or tide had changed. The boat didn't seem to be moving as fast as it had been earlier. Perhaps they had taken on water going over the reef. She looked around the bottom of the boat for something to bail with. In her search, she discovered that the chambers on the right side and the rear were rapidly losing air. She stopped paddling and came to the bleak realization' that the raft, and her chances of getting off Corregidor, were both sinking fast.

As they all clung to the last remaining chamber that was still inflated, Joleen put her ear against the rubber tube and heard the distinctive hiss of another leak.

"The raft is sinking!" Joleen yelled at the Filipino nurses. "Put on your life jackets, we're going to have to swim back to shore! The boat is going down!"

Joleen tried to force a life jacket on one of the nurses but she tore it off and tossed it away.

"What's the matter with you? Do you want to drown?"

"Barracuda, many barracuda," the nurse answered. "Much better drown fast than eaten by barracuda slow."

The raft was completely deflated and was not much more than a black oil slick floating uselessly on the surface of the sea.

For a moment all four nurses bobbed together on the surface. Once again, Joleen swam over and tried to wrap a life jacket around one of the nurses but she shrugged her shoulders, let her arms slide out of the vest and slipped down into the darkness of the water without a sound.

Joleen frantically tried to grab her but she was gone. When Joleen turned to try and find the other two women in the water, they had disappeared as well. She found herself floating all alone in the water along with three empty life jackets.

When she realized that the raft was going to sink, she looked for the other rafts to try and get help, but Joleen had spent too much time getting over the reef and the other boats were well beyond her reach. When she was in the raft sitting on the pontoon paddling, she could see the red light of the submarine between swells. But floating in her life vest with her head barely above the surface of the water, she had no idea which direction to take. Even if she could somehow locate the beacon, she knew that she could never make it to the submarine.

Joleen looked at the three empty life vests still floating alongside of her and struggled trying to understand how these nurses, who had fought so bravely and desperately to save their patients' lives in the hospital, could have given up theirs so easily out of fear of a fish.

Joleen turned around in the water and looked back toward Corregidor. It looked like a monster rising out of the sea. She felt something brush against her leg and began to swim as fast as she could back toward the island.

When she reached the reef, she stood up in the shallow water and took one last look at the beacon from the submarine. It was still red. She imagined the rest of the nurses and civilians being helped out of their rafts and climbing aboard. Joleen fantasized that she was one of them and was being handed a blanket and a steaming mug of hot coffee before they submerged and headed back to the safety of Australia.

A cold, damp chill shook her out of her daydream. She stumbled over the coral mounds of the reef and fell back into the water for her swim back to the beach where she had started earlier that night.

Joleen rolled over on her back, unfastened her burdensome life vest and kicked off her tennis shoes. In her mind, it was summer and she was with her friends swimming from island to island on Lake Tamarac back in Thief River Falls.

She fought back against the outgoing tide. She fought back against the thoughts of being attacked by sharks or barracudas. She fought back the thoughts of making it to shore only to being taken prisoner by the Japanese. She stopped thinking and swam.

When Joleen finally reached the shore, she could barely crawl out of the water. She lay shivering on the coarse sand with her knees pulled tightly into her chest. She vomited the salt water she had swallowed and passed out.

An hour later, a soldier on guard duty found her unconscious on the beach and rushed her to the hospital.

The following morning, Joleen awoke as if from a terrible nightmare. Her heart and her head were pounding. She sat up groggily in her bed and slowly began to realize that the pounding she felt wasn't coming from within her body.

The Japanese had begun their siege on Corregidor with a massive barrage of artillery and bombs.

Six days after accepting the surrender of the American and Filipino troops on Bataan, Lt. General Masaharu Homma, commander of the Japanese troops, made preparations to march his captured prisoners from Marivale Islands in the south of the Bataan peninsula to railroad sidings at San Fernando. The prisoners, filthy, dazed, and nearly mad with thirst and hunger, were forced to march 60 miles in the excruciatingly hot tropical sun. The unspeakable brutality by the Japanese guards would eventually lead to General Homma's arrest, trial and execution by a firing squad in Manila in April, 1946. More than 10,000 lives would eventually be lost through summary executions, sickness, and starvation in what would be known as the infamous 'Bataan Death March'.

Following his victory at Bataan, Homma set his sights on Corregidor. He gathered more than 400 artillery pieces from all over Luzon plus six, super heavy, sixteen-inch siege guns from Japan, and wheeled them into position along the south shore of the Bataan peninsula. Each gun's site was trained on the tiny island of Corregidor some four miles away.

The pounding Joleen had awoken to the morning following her aborted attempt to escape from Corregidor, was the beginning of what would be a constant and massive bombardment of the island fortress by Japanese artillery and aerial bombing.

Over the following five weeks, Joleen would care for her patients, assist surgeons in the operating room and try to sleep and eat to the steady drumbeat of Japanese shells, sometimes as frequent as one every five seconds.

The entire underground garrison operated under constant nervous strain from the continual pounding and vibration. A dust cloud covered everything including medical instruments which made them nearly impossible to keep sterile. They had to work in stifling heat as landslides covered up the ventilation installations. They fought off swarms of voracious, biting green flies that would attack any open wound or exposed tissue. And they endured a constant numbing hunger from months of reduced rations. All this amid the bitter realization that their death or capture was ultimately inevitable.

The Japanese continued to cover Corregidor with literally tons of shells and bombs. Within a 24-hour period on May 4, 1942, following an attempted amphibious assault which was turned back by the Americans in hand-to-hand combat, the Japanese rained more than 16,000 shells on the island.

The constant pounding knocked out all American artillery emplacements, pillboxes, detonated their protective minefields, and created landslides which covered entrances to wings and tunnels.

On May 5, the Japanese attacked the island with battalion strength. Japanese Imperial Headquarters had assigned 200,000 of its best troops including its crack 4th Division, to take the island. General Wainwright had only 15,000 gaunt and weary soldiers at his command.

At 10 a.m. on May 6, 1942, while Joleen was in the operating room assisting the amputation of a gangrenous leg of a U.S. Marine, General Wainwright surrendered his entire garrison on Corregidor to General Homma to avoid certain mass slaughter.

Joleen and the doctor had just finished closing on the Marine when a squad of Japanese soldiers with bayonets drawn ordered Joleen, the doctors and the remainder of the make-shift medical staff out of the hospital wing where they fell in with the other American and Filipino prisoners who were being marched out of the Malinta Tunnel.

In the chaos of the evacuation, Joleen was surprised by the sound of gunfire coming from the depths of the tunnel behind her. The Allied soldiers had been ordered to lay down their arms and not to resist. The rounds she heard came as single shots, fired sporadically, and there didn't seem to be any return fire. She quickly realized that the Japanese were shooting all of the patients in the hospital.

"No!" she screamed, and tried to run back to the ward.

A Japanese guard rammed the butt of his rifle into Joleen's stomach. She collapsed and fell to her knees. Another soldier ran up and stuck the tip of his bayonet under her chin, screaming at her in Japanese and motioning for her to get up. Helped to her feet and carried by the American soldiers around her, she staggered out of the tunnel, a small bloodstain gathering on the front of her nurse's uniform.

Over the next two weeks, the Japanese interrogated the prisoners while sadistic guards robbed their weakened captives of their money, watches, fountain pens, glasses and any other personal belongings they could get their hands on. The guards would even taunt the starving prisoners by only eating half of their rations and throwing the rest of their food away in front of them. One American GI, suffering from malaria, accidentally stumbled into a Japanese officer. Over 100 prisoners watched helplessly as two Japanese soldiers took bayonet practice on the sick prisoner.

The Japanese grouped the prisoners in squads of ten. They were told that if one escaped, the other nine in the squad would be shot. Joleen discovered they were true to their word when a Filipino stole a boat and escaped during the night. The next morning upon discovering the prisoner's disappearance, the Japanese guards made the other nine members of the squad dig their own graves and then in front of all the prisoners who had been called to formation, shot each of the remaining members of the squad in the back of the head. They fell, face down, into their own freshly dug graves. A second squad of prisoners were selected to fill in the graves.

Of all the horrible sounds of war that this 20-year-old girl from a small town in northern Minnesota had been exposed to, from the heart-piercing screams of burn patients raging against the terrible pain, to week upon week of incessant artillery bombardment and all the rest of the horrifying sounds of a war up close, Joleen would never be able to escape associating the sound of a shovel piercing the earth with that horrible moment on Corregidor.

The Japanese organized the healthiest prisoners into work gangs, digging out the landslides and repairing the damage that their bombardment had caused. The bodies of the sick, wounded, and dying prisoners were strewn across canvas tarps outside of the main entrance to the tunnel. No one was allowed to either clean the prisoner's liquid excrement, caused by the dysentery, or protect their faces from the flies whose population had suddenly multiplied with the presence of so many rotting corpses on the island.

Joleen and the five naval medical officers were eventually returned to the hospital wing. The American and Filipino patients were gone and in their place were wounded and sick Japanese soldiers. Initially, Joleen and the doctors were assigned to cleaning bed pans, washing sheets and other menial tasks in the hospital. Their primary mission, however, was stealing drugs and medicine from the Japanese and smuggling it to the American prisoners.

Up to this point in the war, Joleen had never encountered the enemy. In fact, she had never met a person of Japanese descent in her life. She had heard terrible stories during her training and had seen the tragic effects of the Pearl Harbor attack on her patients in Los Angeles, but she didn't share the hatred for the Japanese that others in the Allied military forces seemed to harbor. To her it was the war that was evil.

As a prisoner on Corregidor, and a witness to the contemptible and criminal brutality of her Japanese captors, Joleen discovered within herself a cold, purposeful, and single-minded clarity that only hatred and repugnance could evoke in the human psyche.

The intense fear that Joleen faced every day as a prisoner of war became fuel for her hatred. Hatred made it easy for her to steal, even though she realized that she could be tortured or killed if caught. It was hatred that drove her to secretly slap the face of a dying Japanese soldier seeking a moment of forgiveness and compassion from her in the last few waning moments of his life.

Hatred enabled her to exist under the oppression of the continual fear and uncertainty that existed in the prison camp. Hatred enabled her to eat snakes and lizards instead of starving to death. If it was fear that saved her life during her swim back to Corregidor from the sunken life raft, it was hatred that built Joleen's overpowering resolve to survive as a prisoner.

In her first week as a captive, Joleen watched some American soldiers lie down and will themselves to die. Although she never considered herself brave, Joleen began to understand what her father meant when he preached to his players that giving up was the ultimate sin.

She recalled a note her father kept pinned over his desk. It read, "The great tragedy of life is not death but what dies inside of us while we live".

In moments of weakness, when she felt as though she could not endure another day, she found herself thinking of her father and wishing they could have been closer. In moments of strength, where she found incredible resolve within herself, she felt as though he was standing next to her.

Two weeks following his triumph on Corregidor, General Homma loaded his prisoners into amphibious landing crafts. There was a rumor among the men in the boats that the Japanese were taking them out to sea to be drowned instead of killing them all on land due to the mounting problem of flies and a sickening stench on the island from the many bodies already decomposing.

Joleen and the Navy doctors watched from shore as the boats pulled away. They were the only prisoners that remained on Corregidor.

Despite the growing fear of being slaughtered at sea, the prisoners were overwhelmed when they looked back at the island that was once their own.

Once covered with lush, tropical vegetation and dotted with white-painted buildings, manicured lawns and gardens, Corregidor was charred and blackened, cold and metallic like a piece of discarded coal. From the boats, the island looked void of life or greenery of any kind. The men were shocked at what they saw and amazed at what they had survived.

Members of the Corregidor force would not be drowned at sea. They would be held in a prison camp in Manila for nearly two and a half years.

Corregidor was an enormous victory for the Japanese. General Homma had defeated U.S. Sea and Air power. The Japanese now held one of the best harbors in the Pacific from which they could launch their offensives and supply their bases.

Equally important, the Philippines now presented a formidable obstacle to any American or Allied attempt to cut the line between Tokyo and the Japanese critical oil and tin supplies in the East Indies.

Conversely, the fall of Corregidor was a staggering loss for the American forces and at the time, plunged the Allied world into gloom.

Eventually, students of World War II and military historians would realize that the courageous stand made by soldiers who fought so desperately on Corregidor and Bataan had upset the Japanese timetable by denying them the use of Manila Bay for six months. In addition, the American forces had succeeded in holding a large force of Japanese troops, who could have been used elsewhere, and had immobilized a large proportion of the Japanese fleet for several months.

The stand at Corregidor also slowed the pace of Japanese operations in New Guinea and the Solomon Islands and helped the Americans take Guadalcanal. Tokyo had designated its 4th Division for the Solomons campaign but it was held up on Corregidor. Racked with malaria after the battle, the 4th Division had to be returned to Japan for demobilization.

For many reasons, the stand of the American-Filipino garrison at Corregidor was regarded as vital for the future course of the war and became a hallowed episode in U.S. military history.

Lt. Joleen Salveson spent the remainder of the war as a POW nurse, reluctantly serving the 5,000 officers and enlisted men of the Japanese Imperial Army permanently stationed on Corregidor.

While the majority of her medical attention was directed towards the soldiers and included suturing lacerations after fights or drunken falls down the rocky cliffs, severe sunburn, and a steady stream of patients suffering from jungle rot, malaria and dysentery, she also served as a medic and mother figure to two-dozen 'comfort girls', a collection of very young Korean, Chinese, Papuan and Filipino girls who had been brought to the island to satisfy the sexual needs of the Japanese soldiers stationed there.

There was a wing dedicated specifically to the activities between the soldiers and the comfort girls. The girls also had private quarters that they shared, under guard, with Joleen.

The comfort girls worked 12-hour shifts and would service as many as 50 men per day. They were beaten if a soldier they had been with came down with venereal disease. They were often beaten for no apparent reason at all after providing sexual pleasure to a soldier.

One girl was strangled by a Japanese officer who found that the throes of death from asphyxiation, which produced muscular contractions and convulsions, to be highly erotic and stimulating conclusion to normal intercourse.

For Joleen to exist, she learned that she had to function on a level numb of any feelings. She had to remain callous and remove herself from the world around her. Otherwise, she would have gone crazy. However, she did save her moments of compassion for the girls.

Four of the girls attempted suicide over a six-day period. Two were successful, but Joleen was able to save the other two. The Japanese commandant dealt with the rash of suicides among his comfort girls with a tried and successful method. He announced that for every girl who attempted suicide, successful or not, the guards would torture and kill five girls.

"After all," he added nonchalantly, "I can order as many girls as I want through Tokyo."

Suicide attempts among the comfort girls stopped completely following the commandant's announcement.

Despite being the only American woman on the island, Joleen was never attacked or molested during the two and a half years of the Japanese occupation of Corregidor. She was never physically harmed until the final minutes prior to her freedom.

The American's recapture of the Philippines began in October, 1944, with MacArthur's highly publicized return. American forces captured southernmost Leyte, the first island in the Philippines to be liberated, on October 20.

Although the tide of the war had shifted in favor of Allied and American forces, the Japanese troops were stubborn, and it took MacArthur until January, 1945, to work his way up the 1,500-mile archipelago to the main island of Luzon, and recapture the capital city of Manila.

On February 14, 1945, MacArthur's assault on Corregidor began with the 5th Air Force dropping more than 3,000 tons of bombs on the island, blowing away all the vegetation that had overrun the island during the three years of Japanese occupation.

The next morning, fourteen Navy destroyers and eight cruisers began plastering the island with continuous salvos from their big guns. Overhead, Liberator aircraft began saturation bombing using 500-pound fragmentation bombs. However, the onslaught of artillery had little effect, and resulted in few casualties on the Japanese soldiers who were well entrenched in the caves and crannies of the island.

Joleen and the American doctors were the only ones on the island who had lived through a bombardment from inside the tunnel. The tremendous explosions and vibrations that sent the Japanese soldiers scurrying for cover sounded like a symphony to her ears. Although the dust would choke her lungs and eyes, the heat would make her faint, and the lack of water made her tongue thick and her lips crack, every explosion that rocked the tunnel and sent landslides down the mountain covering entrances and ventilator shafts, released a tiny parcel of the anger Joleen had been storing and using as precious fuel for her survival. In its place she felt a flicker of hope rekindling her near-extinguished spirit.

On February 16, U.S. paratroopers surprised the Japanese garrison on Corregidor with a daring drop at the island's highest point despite dangerous high winds. An amphibious assault was launched simultaneously from Bataan.

The two weeks of fighting remain legendary in the history of the war in the Pacific. The Americans blasted the Japanese out of caves and tunnels. The Japanese countered with waves of screaming soldiers in suicidal *banzai* attacks.

The carnage from the massacre was staggering. The stench of decomposing bodies was carried out to sea by prevailing winds where PT boat and destroyer crews, sometimes several miles from the island, became nauseated.

The green fly population, already epidemic, exploded. Flies in the thousands covered open wounds. The flies were so terrible that twice during the battle American planes flew over the island shoveling DDT out of their side doors.

If conditions atop the island were dreadful, life inside the Malinta Tunnel was equally grim. All four water points had been destroyed during the American bombardment and there was a severe water shortage. The Japanese soldiers made every effort to carry their wounded and dead from the battlefield and into the tunnel so their enemy wouldn't know the casualties they had inflicted. The stench of the putrefying bodies was sickening and overpowering. American artillery had blocked the main entrance of the Malinta Tunnel and what little fresh air there was came from side tunnels, caves and emergency escape routes.

While the dusting of the island with DDT made the fly problem bearable up top, the flies in the tunnel were feasting on the stacks of corpses and covered the sides of the walls like thick, hanging draperies.

Joleen was alone in the hospital wing that was overflowing with wounded and dying Japanese soldiers. Bodies were strewn in piles, dragged into the hospital and left scattered among the dead.

There was nothing Joleen could do. Nothing she wanted to do but survive. Survive this last battle and get off the island alive. She stayed by herself in the hospital wing, figuring that if it was safe during the Japanese bombardment three years before, there was a good chance it would hold up again. She would learn later that the doctors with whom she had worked for three years were all killed when their quarters collapsed near the end of the American bombardment.

It was clear that the Japanese could not turn back the American assault but their *banzai* mentality would not allow them to surrender.

Near the end of the battle, there was an unnerving rumor that had spread to both sides that the Japanese were going to commit mass *hari kari* by setting off tons of explosives stored in the bowels of the tunnel, virtually leveling the island and taking most of the American forces with them.

A Japanese officer and two of his men entered the hospital wing where Joleen was hiding. The officer ordered her out into the main tunnel corridor.

For the first time as a captive, she directly disobeyed an order. She had broken nearly every rule, ignored orders and displayed her disrespect in innumerable subtle ways during her imprisonment, but always behind the back of the enemy.

Perhaps it was her frustration at the insane irony of possibly being blown up by her barbaric captors with her rescuers less than 50 yards away on the other side of a pile of dirt. Perhaps it was the flicker of hope she allowed herself to feel that had momentarily weakened her resolve to survive.

Joleen stared defiantly into the eyes of the officer. Her smile dripped with pent-up venom and was twisted in a derisive grin as she shook her head.

Enraged at this sign of disrespect, the officer ordered his men to seize her. She didn't try to run nor did she try to fight them off. Joleen stayed where she was, hands clamped defiantly on her hips, with a mocking smile snarling across her face.

The officer barked out another order but the men hesitated and cast questioning looks toward their superior. Infuriated at their insubordination, the officer slapped one of the men across the face and repeated the order even louder.

Joleen was suddenly bent over one of the hospital cots, her arms held down by the two soldiers, as the officer ripped off her ragged fatigue pants. She could feel his nakedness against the back of her thighs. He leaned over on top of her and pressed his pistol against her cheek.

The demonic inhumanity and unimaginable brutality that Joleen had witnessed on Corregidor suddenly came crashing down upon her.

"How can I live the rest of my life with memories so horrifying?" she thought to herself. "Will death not be a more welcome fate?"

The metal of the gun felt cool against her face. She had seen enough. She stopped struggling.

Although the officer had taken down her pants and was thrusting his hips wildly against her while the other two soldiers held her down, Joleen realized that she was not actually being penetrated. He had not entered her nor, from what she could tell, was he even erect. It was his last opportunity for a display of superiority and domination.

Joleen lifted her head and opened her eyes. She found she was staring directly into the saddened eyes of a patient who was occupying the cot she was pinned upon. She recognized the soldier. His name was Tamaki. He was much older than the rest of the Japanese soldiers and had thanked Joleen for her attention to his wounds and always managed a smile and a slight nod whenever she walked by his bed. In broken English, he had told Joleen that he grew orchids before the war and that he wished he could see one more flower before he died.

Instead of a flower, the last thing orchid-growing Private Tamaki would witness before he died was a violent assault by the Japanese officer on the kind American nurse. When Joleen's eyes met his and he realized what was happening, he looked back at Joleen with an expression of such sorrow that she began to cry for the first time since the early days of her capture.

It was over in less than a minute. When he had finished, the officer pushed Joleen to the floor and barked orders to his men as he buttoned his trousers.

180

Acknowledging his orders, the two soldiers reluctantly removed their weapons from their shoulders. The officer screamed at them again and jerked the rifles out of their hands. He kept the rifles and handed the men their bayonets.

He repeated his order angrily, made a sweeping gesture across all of the beds in the hospital, stopping to point directly at Joleen, and then stomped out of the hospital.

The soldiers looked hesitantly at one another and then down at the glistening bayonets in their hands. Joleen watched in horror from the floor as the two soldiers slit the throat of every patient in the hospital, under orders, apparently, to save their bullets for a final *banzai* attack on the approaching Americans outside the tunnel.

When the two men had finished murdering their own fellow soldiers, they began to argue. They were both drenched in blood and the green flies were already beginning to swarm all over them. One of the soldiers vomited and staggered out of the ward while the other approached Joleen and yanked her to her feet.

"No talk!" he said in broken English, his eyes wild and bloodshot, his face covered with blood and crawling with flies.

"No talk!"

Joleen shook her head and looked down at the floor.

"No talk," she repeated earnestly.

"No talk!" the soldier frantically screamed as he reached into her mouth and grabbed her by the tongue. In a single flash of silver, the soldier cut off her tongue.

"No talk, no talk," the soldier repeated as he raced out of the hospital.

Outside the ward in the main corridor of the tunnel, the Japanese were preparing to blast open the main entrance that had been blocked by American artillery and make a final *banzai* attack.

The explosion backfired killing more than half of the Japanese soldiers in the blast. The remaining troops poured out of an opening and were annihilated by the waiting machine guns of the Americans.

At the conclusion of the battle, of the 5,000 Japanese soldiers who had been stationed on Corregidor, only 29 were taken prisoner. The rest were killed or committed suicide.

Joleen was discovered by an American GI who stopped to empty the vomit from his gas mask after discovering the patients in the hospital ward with their throats cut.

She had the presence of mind to stuff her mouth with gauze to try and stop the bleeding. She knew she was losing a lot of blood and could feel herself slipping away into shock and unconsciousness.

"You're an American?" the astonished soldier asked.

Joleen looked up at the young face. She could see the boy's lips moving but she couldn't hear what he was saying. The explosion in the tunnel had temporarily deafened her.

"Jesus Christ All Mighty! Medic! Medic! We've got an American girl in here!"

# Chapter 14
# Molly Carolina
# Veterinarian Not Vegetarian

*U*NIVERSITY OF ARIZONA GRADUATION COMMENCEMENTS were a week away and Molly Carolina was looking forward to the ceremony. This was a time when most graduating seniors were stocking up for bacchanalian celebrations and thumbing through travel brochures to exotic destinations, courtesy of grateful parents who had written their final tuition check. It was a time to send out resumes, plan for the future and finally cut the educational cord.

"Got my degree, I'm free at last!"

Not so the case with Molly Carolina. True to a commitment she had made to her father when she was six years old after playing with a three-legged Labrador on a camping trip, she was going to be, as she put it at the time, a vegetarian…a doctor who takes care of sick and injured animals.

Molly will graduate from the University of Arizona, Magna Cum Laude in her class, having attained a 3.89 cumulative grade point average. She scored in the 97th percentile of the Graduate Record Exam and was accepted by every school she applied to and chose the University of California at Davis, the number one ranked veterinary school in the nation.

For Molly, and others in the medical and sciences field, a bachelor's degree was just the first slippery rung on a ladder that descended into an abyss lined with grey, 8' x 8' graduate student cubicles.

After starving, groveling and surviving a mole-like existence for six to eight years through grad school, med school, vet school, postdocs, residencies and internships, they would eventually emerge from their musty caverns, reeking of pork-flavored Top Ramen and rubbing their eyes in the bright sunlight, while boasting an impressive collection of letters, coupled like railroad cars, dangling from the end of their last name. Each letter representing tens of thousands of dollars in outstanding student loans.

It was her last night in the dorm. Molly smiled at the small duffle bag in the middle of her room that held all of her life's belongings. She had worked as a 'Resident Advisor' in her dormitory for all four years of college. Free room, free food, free parking, discounted tuition, $600 a month and a short walk to most classes. Plus, she was an attentive and caring advisor for students, many whom were a long way from friends and family.

There were only a few students left in the dorm. Tomorrow she would have to inspect their rooms, accessing any damage or breakage. It was an unusually quiet night and with no tests to study for and no papers to write, Molly turned off her phone and fell asleep before midnight, for the first time in her college career.

Molly slept late into the morning. When she awoke, she checked her messages on her phone.

"Molly, it's your mother. Your father is in serious condition at St. Mary's Hospital. Oh, God, I'm so sorry!"

# Chapter 15
## Eleanor Carolina
## The Consequences of Suicide

AFTER THE TRAGIC SUICIDE OF 16-YEAR-OLD ETHAN, THE remaining members of the shattered Carolina family each limped off in different directions to try and come to terms with, and at the same time, find their own hiding places from the guilt, shame, and grief that haunted them.

Molly Carolina completely immersed herself in her studies at college.

Bobby Carolina, unable to face the ghosts that possessed his home, found his penitence in the demands of the farm. He was in the fields from the first hint of daylight to the last dying embers of sunset. When night fell, he was in the barn repairing equipment and performing maintenance on his vehicles.

There was neither time nor joy left in the day for Bobby Carolina's prized garden. Once his pride and passion, now untended and abandoned, Bobby's garden became a dusty graveyard of dried stalks and trellis skeletons. Weeds launched an overwhelming assault on the once carefully tended furrows. Corpses of melons and squash lay rotting in the sun. The blood orange trees from Jerusalem had turned into mere sticks in the brittle ground now serving as reminders when times were better. Even his catfish ponds were empty and dry.

Eleanor Carolina had neither a grade point average nor a farm to maintain. There was no escaping the dungeon of depression in which Eleanor was forced to spend her days and nights. She was a prisoner in an unbearable hell, exclusive to mothers whose young children take their own lives.

Her demons would not let Davis' tragic suicide go away. They demanded a life for a life and would not rest until they held her firmly in their grasp and had convinced her that she was fully to blame. Eleanor was an easy target. She was quick to confess her guilt and eager to accept her punishment.

Eleanor Carolina had always been an extraordinarily gentle person. She walked as though she were gliding across a wet, tile floor. Everything she did had a natural grace to it. When she laid out place settings on the oak table in the dining room there wasn't a sound, not even the clatter of a plate bouncing against the bare wood, not even the chink of a spoon ricocheting off a knife. She scrambled eggs in silence, not even scraping the sides of the bowl with the fork when she beat the eggs. When she poured a glass of milk, she held the glass at such an angle that there wasn't a splash or gurgle. Eleanor was even gentle in her sleep. In the morning when she woke, her side of the bed hardly looked as though it had been slept in. Eleanor could walk in or out of a room without anyone noticing, like a subtle change in humidity.

Eleanor was personable and well-liked by everyone. She shared Molly's propensity for being interested in others. She could sit and talk with friends for hours without ever mentioning anything about herself. When a specific issue came up in the conversation, Eleanor usually had a thoughtful and respectful response for both sides. Her buoyancy enabled her to float above most of the problems that seemed to stir up her friends and neighbors.

But the night that Eleanor discovered the body of her son dangling from a rope above the washer and drier in her garage, the ice that she had once skated over so effortlessly began to crack and give out from underneath her.

Her usual glass of wine with dinner evolved into a glass before, one during, one after, plus a nightcap. Eleanor eventually graduated to vodka and orange juice during the day when she was alone in the house. Vodka didn't seem to linger on her breath and there weren't so many empty wine bottles to try and hide in the trash. Soon the orange juice became unnecessary.

Due to her quiet and gentle nature, she was able to interact normally with friends while in a near alcoholic stupor without any perceptible change in her personality. It was easy for her to hide her drinking from Bobby because he was in the fields all day and into the night. She would fix him supper, put it in the oven to keep warm, and then go upstairs and sleep off her day of drinking.

Eleanor began shopping at grocery stores outside of town so no one she knew could notice the half-gallon bottles of vodka in her cart. She stopped meeting friends for lunch and would turn away neighbors who came to visit her at the house with excuses that she wasn't feeling well. The only social obligations she kept were her lunch dates with her daughter.

Twice a month, Eleanor would drive to Tucson, pick up Molly at her dorm, and take her to lunch. Molly generally did most of the talking and eating. They behaved like two people who shared a terrible secret they couldn't speak about, both pretending that the elephant sitting at their table didn't exist.

After their lunch date, Eleanor would drop Molly off at her dorm, both of them relieved and anxious to get back into their own private worlds. Molly back to the books, papers, and tests. Eleanor back to the bottle.

Eleanor never drank before, nor during, her lunches with Molly. However, driving back home on the interstate after one of their lunches, Eleanor would begin to feel the cold, steely angst for the need of a drink.

She suddenly realized that she was driving way over the speed limit. When she glanced at the speedometer, she also noticed that her gas gauge needle was on empty.

Eleanor figured she was only 10 miles from home and that she probably could make it but the thought of possibly running out of gas, miles from home and a drink that she needed rather badly, convinced her to turn off at the exit for the town of Pina Blanca.

As she filled her tank at a Shell station, Eleanor noticed a sign on the opposite side of the street that read:

The River's End
Bar
Restaurant
Packaged Liquor
Pool

Although Eleanor's drinking habits had escalated from 'occasional' to 'heavy', she had never been in a real bar. She married Bobby after her senior year in high school and was busy running a house and a farm when she turned legal drinking age. Then the kids came along. Bobby was never much of a drinker and when they got the rare chance to be together, going to a bar and having a couple of drinks had never been a part of their social agenda.

On their honeymoon in Rocky Point, Mexico, Eleanor and Bobby had sat out on the veranda of the restaurant at their hotel and drank margaritas while they watched the sun set in the Sea of Cortez. That hotel veranda had been as close to a bar as Eleanor had ever come.

She paid for her gas with a credit card without ever taking her eyes off the sign across the street. It was three o'clock in the afternoon and the streets were empty.

After filling her tank, Eleanor pulled out of the station and slowly drove past the front entrance of The River's End. It didn't look too scary from the front and the idea of having a drink away from her home seemed inviting. On her third pass around the block, she discovered an alleyway leading to a dirt parking lot behind the bar. She felt confident that no one would be able to recognize her car from the street and noticed that there was a rear entrance to the bar. She parked

188

her car and walked through the back door of the first real bar she had ever been in.

Coming from the bright sunlight outside, Eleanor was immediately blinded by the darkness of the room. It seemed so dark inside that she thought the bar must be closed. While her eyes were adapting, her nose was being assaulted by the acrid smell of stale beer and cigarette smoke. She could hear a George Jones song she remembered from a high school dance.

When her eyes finally became accustomed to the dim light, she gazed upon a world she had never known existed.

The River's End was a typical Arizona bar. It had two pool tables, a couple of booths covered in red vinyl, a small stage with a dance floor in front of it, and a long wooden bar with stainless steel bar stools padded with black Naugahyde seats. Lighting was provided by a juke box in one corner casting a pink and yellow glow into the room; six, neon beer signs hung on the wall behind the bar; and two swag lamps dangling above each of the pool tables.

There were no windows or skylights in the bar. Except for patrons opening the door to enter or leave during daylight hours, not a single ray of sunlight had ever been invited to The River's End in the 15 years it had been open.

Eleanor glided towards the bar without crushing any of the peanut shells that littered the floor and stood behind one of the bar stools. Ed Rivers, owner, manager, bartender, bouncer, and, at the moment, dishwasher for The River's End, deftly moved his two-hundred and-something pounds away from the sink and gave Eleanor a friendly smile

"What can I do for you little lady?"

Eleanor's throat nervously fidgeted with her words and they came out as though she was talking under water.

"I'm sorry, what did you want?" Ed asked, cocking his head to the side and leaning over the bar towards Eleanor.

"May I have a glass of vodka, please?"

"Vodka? Rocks, neat, tonic, OJ... how would you like it?"

"Just a plain glass of vodka, please."

Eleanor glanced at the murky water in the sink and wondered if she should add the word 'clean' to her order.

"I'm sorry, can you make it with orange juice?"

"One vodka with orange juice coming up. Have a seat, ma'am."

Eleanor was fascinated. She stared at a large jar on the bar labeled, 'Spicy Pickled Eggs'. The eggs, floating in a briny bouillon, appeared to be colored a muted green. Their color came from the light cast by a beer sign behind the bar. They reminded Eleanor of the pig embryos floating in formaldehyde she had dissected in her high school biology class.

Behind the jar of floating pig embryos, Eleanor's attention was captured by a vast collection of bottles lining the shelf behind the bar. She had no idea there were that many different kinds of liquor. She strained her eyes trying to read the labels on each of the bottles and wondered what each of them must taste like.

She was more than halfway through her second vodka, still reading bottle labels and watching Ed wash his dishes, when she felt the presence of someone standing next to her. She'd assumed she was the only customer in the bar and hadn't noticed a group of three men sitting at a booth in a back corner.

"Can I buy you another one ma'am?" Jimmy Ray Bragg, part-time well-digger and tow truck driver, asked in a hybrid Arizona cowboy/southern Georgia accent. "We don't get too many women as attractive as you in here and I'd like to celebrate the occasion."

Jimmy Ray's lips curled into a sideways smile, still holding a cigarette in the corner of his mouth.

The first two drinks had successfully dulled the sharp edge of her craving and Eleanor began to recognize the familiar onset of the vodka's fuzzy glow.

The man standing beside her brought with him an exotic aroma. He smelled of beer, cigarettes, perspiration, and a brand of cologne she recognized from junior high. His hair was blond, long and stringy, and the muscles of his upper arms and chest bulged against his tight, white T-shirt.

190

Eleanor was startled when she looked down and noticed that his arms were covered with tattoos. She couldn't take her eyes off them.

"Where did you get these?" she asked innocently with just the slightest slur to her words.

Jimmy Ray Bragg picked up on the slur immediately, like a piranha tasting a fresh molecule of hemoglobin from somewhere up river.

"Hey, Ed, how about bringing us one more of these," Jimmy smiled, pointing at her near-empty glass.

"And give me another Bud, huh?"

Jimmy slithered onto the bar stool next to Eleanor. She noticed that his worn and faded jeans fit tightly across his thighs. Jimmy laid his arm on the bar in front of her.

"Where'd I get these? Well, I got almost all of these in Vietnam, except for this one." Jimmy pointed at a snake wrapped around a heart on his forearm. "I got this one in Juarez, I think," he coughed up a smoker's laugh.

"Did they hurt?" Eleanor asked looking closely at the tattoos beneath the sun-bleached hair on his arm.

"Well, I can honestly tell you that I didn't feel a thing from the one in Juarez and the others, hell, they didn't hurt too much worse in comparison."

"In comparison? In comparison to what?" Eleanor asked.

"In comparison to having a bamboo punji stick covered with Gook shit shoved up the back of my leg. Or sleeping twenty-six nights straight in the bush serving as target practice for Charlie and an appetizer course for every tick, leech, spider, and blood sucking, flesh-eating insect in the jungle."

"Oh, my goodness!" Eleanor exclaimed.

"Sorry, ma'am, I didn't mean to startle you. Sometimes I get going on these war stories and they just get away from me."

Ed Rivers arrived with their drinks. He flashed Jimmy a wrinkled brow and shook his head as he set Eleanor's vodka and orange juice and Jimmy's beer on the bar. Jimmy volleyed back with a threatening stare so icy cold that Ed had to turn his head away. Eleanor was looking at Jimmy's tattoos and didn't notice the brief, non-verbal interaction between the two men.

"That's eight dollars and fifty-cents, Jimmy."

Eleanor looked at the pile of bills in front of her from her initial twenty.

"No, I'll buy these. If you were in the war, I'd be happy to buy you a drink. Here, is this enough?" she asked pushing the money towards the bartender.

Ed picked out the correct amount and gave Jimmy a parting dirty look.

Eleanor was still busy staring at Jimmy's tattoos.

"You can touch 'em if you'd like." Jimmy said, sliding his stool closer and pulling his t-shirt sleeve up over his bulging biceps.

Eleanor gingerly ran her fingers over the tattoos on his arm. Tracing the injected stains of erotic art simmering beneath the surface of Jimmy's skin and inhaling his pungent, foreign scent made her lightheaded.

After Eleanor's fourth vodka and orange juice, she slurred, "I think I've had enough. I need to get home."

"Here, let me help you." Jimmy offered.

He took her arm and helped her off the bar stool.

"You parked out back?" he asked.

"Yes, I think so," she slurred as she wobbled in the opposite direction of the back door.

"It's this way, ma'am."

Jimmy Ray Bragg helped guide her out through the back door of the darkened bar and into the blinding sunlight of the parking lot. Her legs felt numb and wobbly and the sun stung her eyes so painfully that she kept them closed and held tightly on Jimmy's arm.

"Do you see a white Buick out here somewhere?" Eleanor asked drunkenly. "It's so bright I can't even open my eyes."

"Here it is," Jimmy answered in a comforting voice. "Can't miss it, it's the only car in the lot."

Jimmy pushed her back against the side of the car and pressed his body against her. He ran his hand across her chest and cupped her breast. Her eyes were still squinted, barely open. Everything seemed blurred and unreal. This man's body so close, almost suffocating, and his hand on her breast, seemed to be a part of a hazy dream.

Jimmy dug through her purse and found her car keys, along with all of the cash in her wallet, and her checkbook. He opened the door, reached in, and unlocked the rear door.

"You sure you should drive?" he asked while forcing her into the back seat. "Maybe you ought to just lay down back here for a while."

The car was cool and dark, the deeply tinted windows had effectively fought off the afternoon sun but still, Eleanor kept her eyes tightly closed. Her senses told her that she was in trouble but the alcohol had blocked out her instincts to fight or escape.

Jimmy slid in the back seat beside her and closed the door. Eleanor felt his mouth against the nape of her neck, his teeth nipping at the soft folds of her skin. Slowly, his hand left her breast, and his fingers began to trace their way down the front of her blouse, stopping between buttons to draw circles on the damp skin of her stomach. Eleanor felt as though someone was chasing her in her dream but she couldn't move her legs.

Suddenly his hand was under her skirt and between her legs, moving slowly up her thigh.

Eleanor never opened her eyes throughout the ordeal. She kept them clenched shut, even after Jimmy had finished with her and was getting out of the car.

"Any time, baby, you know where to reach me," he laughed.

Jimmy threw her keys on the seat, closed the door and walked away.

Eleanor lay on the back seat, blouse open, bra pulled above her breasts and her skirt gathered up around her waist. She slowly opened her eyes, hoping that what had just happened was a dream and that when her eyes were fully open, she would find herself somewhere other than in the back seat of her car.

Eleanor looked down at her disheveled clothes. She had not cried much at all throughout the aftermath of Ethan's suicide. Even during the funeral, she sat quietly staring at the coffin, watching stoically as they lowered her son into the ground. Her feelings of shame and guilt were so powerful that they had overwhelmed any other emotions that may have tried to come to the surface.

In the back seat of her car in the parking lot behind The River's End, Eleanor Carolina finally began to cry. She cried tears for the pain and suffering of her poor child. She cried tears over the joy, the pride and the promise she had felt when the nurse handed Eleanor her newborn son. She cried tears for what had just happened in the parking lot and the hopelessly bleak future that lay ahead of her.

When she could find no more tears, she put her clothes back together and began to think about what had just happened. Somewhere in the twisted and irrational mire of self-loathing and despondence, being raped by a loathsome creature in the parking lot of a bar simply reaffirmed her sense of self-reproach and provided even further evidence that she was a hideous and repulsive person, deserving to be stained by evil. In the midst of that confirmation, Eleanor felt a bizarre sense of contentment, as though what had just happened to her was a fair and deserved punishment for the sins she had committed.

Several times over the following months, Eleanor Carolina would try and atone for the sins of her son's death by seeking out the punishment she felt she deserved by meeting Jimmy Bragg at The River's End. She couldn't have picked a better executioner.

After a sufficient period of abuse and humiliation, Eleanor finally stopped seeking out her punishment from Jimmy Bragg. A friend of hers had found her throwing away empty vodka bottles in the trash bin of a local Circle K and convinced her to attend a meeting of Alcoholics Anonymous. It had been over a month since Eleanor had been to the River's End and she had been sober for 22 days.

Bobby Carolina came in through the back door of the house and looked up at the kitchen clock. It was almost midnight. He had just finished rotating the brake drums on the tractor and stood there trying to figure out how many hours he'd been working that day but stopped when he realized that there was no point in doing the math.

His hands stung in the hot water from a collection of cuts, burns and blisters as he washed them in the kitchen sink. Bobby walked into the living room drying his hands and looked down at his wife asleep on the sofa. In the glow from the TV, she looked as though she had aged 10 years since they had lost their son.

Bobby pulled the blanket up over Eleanor's shoulders, turned off the TV and went back into the kitchen. As usual, his supper was on a plate kept warm in the oven. He poured a glass of milk and sat down at the kitchen table to eat another meal alone.

He scratched at his meat loaf with the tip of his fork while he toyed with the thought that perhaps he had been feeling sorry for himself long enough.

He had recently begun to question why, since his son's suicide, he had distanced himself from the things that he cared the most about, like his marriage and his daughter, Molly. He realized that he had pushed them away at a time when they had probably needed him most. Bobby felt his eyes sting as they began to fill with tears. He had let his family go like he had let his vegetable garden.

Bobby knew he could revive the garden. He had come to the realization that there was nothing he could do to bring his son back and that it was time for him to try and revive what was left of his family.

The summer monsoons were approaching, which meant fewer hours in the fields. He decided to hire a couple of hands to help out after the rains and spend more time trying to re-connect with his family and some of the other things in his life that he cared about.

Bobby scraped his unfinished dinner into the trash and washed his dishes in the sink. He stared out of the kitchen window towards his garden. It was too dark to see outside, but he made a mental note for the following day to spend a couple of hours weeding. He would call Molly at school, see how her classes were going, and take a long walk with Eleanor in the evening right after they ate supper... together. He could feel the grip of his son's death gradually loosening its hold on him and he could tell that it was time for him to start letting Ethan go, as well.

While Bobby was drying his plate, he heard a banging on the front door. Visitors past seven o'clock in the evening were a rarity in the farming community. A caller at midnight meant somebody was probably lost or that there was an accident or some other emergency. Bobby turned on the porch light and opened the door.

A man with long, stringy blond hair and tattoos covering his arms swayed drunkenly on the front porch.

"Can I help you?" Bobby asked still drying his plate with a dish towel.

"I've come to get your wife," Jimmy Bragg announced menacingly.

"My wife? What do you want with my wife?"

"Same thing I been getting from her. That's what I want."

"I'm afraid you must have the wrong address, my friend. I don't think it's my wife you're looking for."

Bobby tried to shut the door but Jimmy stuck his boot in the jam.

"Her name, Eleanor by any chance?" Jimmy snarled sarcastically as he looked down at a deposit slip he had stolen out of Eleanor's check book.

"Of the Robert and Eleanor Carolinas?"

Eleanor was awakened by the knocking and came to the door. She gently pulled Bobby back away.

"I'll take care of this," she said calmly. "You go on back in the house, Bobby."

Eleanor stepped out on the porch and closed the door behind her. She grabbed Jimmy by the arm and walked him out into the middle of the front yard.

"Listen, I don't ever want to see you again. You come here again, I will call the police and have you arrested for rape, you slimy..."

Before Eleanor had a chance to finish her sentence, Bobby burst out of the door, across the grass and grabbed Jimmy by the shoulders.

"What the hell do you have to do with my wife!"

Bobby was a full six-inches taller than Jimmy and had to stoop over to put his face in Jimmy's.

"Same thing you should have, buddy. Hell, I been doing your job."

Jimmy reached down and grabbed Bobby by the crotch.

"What's the matter, you ain't got it in you anymore?"

Bobby backed away giving him enough distance to deliver a round-house punch on the side of Jimmy's face. His fist landed squarely on Jimmy's cheek, spinning him completely around. Jimmy licked at the slight trickle of blood dripping from the corner of his mouth, seemingly unfazed from the blow.

"Well, I take it back. Maybe you still got a little fight in you yet, old man."

Jimmy struck back with insane ferocity. Bobby was attacked with a savage onslaught of blows to the face and head. Jimmy drove his fist into Bobby's mid-section and when Bobby doubled over from the blow, Jimmy rammed his knee into Bobby's face. Blood spewed from Bobby's nose and mouth as he fell back onto the grass. Bobby tried to cover up and protect himself, but there was no defense against the wild animal, now set loose, that was caged inside Jimmy Bragg.

Brutal kicks to the head left Bobby unconscious but Jimmy continued his assault on the lifeless body.

Eleanor tried to pull Jimmy off. He slammed his fist into her stomach and she stumbled backwards, collapsing in the wet grass, gasping for air.

Jimmy's mind had crossed over into a violent rage and he continued to pummel Bobby's limp body.

"Guess you won't need these anymore, asshole." Jimmy growled, as he delivered a vicious kick to Bobby's testicles.

Finally exhausted from pulverizing Bobby's helpless lump of bloody flesh, Jimmy staggered over to Eleanor and kicked her in the middle of her back.

"Bitch! I'll be back for you!" he spit, as he got into his truck and drove away.

Eleanor crawled into the house and called the operator for help. When the ambulance arrived, Eleanor had covered Bobby with a blanket and was sitting next to him on the grass. Bobby was still unconscious and Eleanor thought he might be dead.

"Is he alive?" she whispered to one of the attendants as they loaded Bobby into the back of the ambulance.

"He's hurt bad, ma'am. We got a pulse, but it's weak and it looks like he may have some internal bleeding. We're going to have to take him to Tucson."

"Which hospital?"

"Saint Mary's is the only one equipped to handle something like this. You want to ride with us?"

"No," she answered still holding her stomach. "I'll follow in my own car."

"You sure? Are you OK, ma'am?"

"Yes, I'm all right. Please hurry and get my husband to the hospital."

The ambulance sped out of the graveled driveway, siren screaming and flashing lights piercing the heavy darkness. This was not the first time Eleanor had stood and watched an ambulance race down her driveway and off into the night carrying a member of her family.

Eleanor stood on the front lawn and listened to the eerie wail of the siren until she wasn't sure if what she heard was the distant faintness of the siren or its lingering echo in her head. Even after she was sure the ambulance was well beyond her ability to hear it, she thought she could still hear something faintly resembling a siren ringing in her ears.

Eleanor turned and staggered back into the house. Her stomach ached but she could tell that nothing was broken. She walked through the kitchen and opened the door that led into the garage. She turned on the light and stared up at the rafter where she had discovered her son dangling with a rope around his neck. She stood without moving, barely breathing, mesmerized by the bare wooden rafter with the frightening moment of discovering her son re-playing in her mind. It was as though Ethan was still hanging from the rope in front of her. Then the scene in her mind went out of focus and dissolved back into a new scene. In this one, it was Eleanor hanging from the rope instead of Ethan.

Eleanor looked curiously at the imagined vision of her own lifeless body dangling from the rafter. It didn't look all that frightening. Almost calming. She stared at the faint blue tinge of her skin and at the curious crooked angle of her head. The expression on her face seemed peaceful. Her body hung gently in mid-air as though she were finally at rest.

"Not yet," she whispered to the vision. "Not now."

Eleanor turned around and went back into the house. She called Molly and left a message to meet her at the hospital. She grabbed her keys and took off after the ambulance.

Molly arrived at St. Mary's the next morning and took the elevator up to the intensive care unit. She approached a group of nurses who were huddled around the reception desk.

"I believe my father is in here. His name is Robert Carolina."

A nurse wearing a blue, paper scrub gown gave Molly a slow, serious nod.

"Let me get Doctor Martinez. He's been with your father since he was brought in last night. Please have a seat in the waiting room. I'll let the doctor know you're here and I'm sure he'll be out as soon as he can."

Molly looked around the waiting room. She was alone.

The bitter, antiseptic smell of the hospital was completely foreign to the smells she had always associated with her father. Her father smelled of rich earth and piles of leaves. He smelled of clay and mud and dirt, not anything like the sterile, medicated air of the hospital.

A young doctor came into the waiting room.

"I'm Doctor Martinez. You are Mr. Carolina's daughter?"

"Yes, Molly Carolina. What happened to my father? Is he all right?"

"Here, let's sit down," Dr. Martinez said calmly.

"Your father was brutally beaten and sustained some very serious injuries. I don't believe his life is in danger now, but in addition to his other injuries, he's had some head trauma that we are watching very carefully."

"What kind of injuries?"

The doctor let out a long, exasperated breath lifting several dark hairs off his forehead.

"I'm afraid he has several cracked ribs. His spleen was ruptured and we had to remove it last night during emergency surgery along with one of his testicles which was also ruptured and damaged beyond repair. One of his lungs also collapsed. There was blood in his urine which may mean his kidneys could be damaged. We don't know the extent of the injury but the kidneys seem to be stabilizing."

"In addition to those internal injuries, his nose was broken in several places. His orbit, the bone around the eye, was fractured and his face was cut up pretty badly. To be honest, Ms. Carolina, I don't think I've ever seen a man take a beating this badly at the hands of another man."

"Who was this man? Why did he attack my father?"

"I'm sorry, I don't know many details about how or why it happened. The police were here last night and spoke with your mother. They would know more."

"What about his head injuries?"

"Apparently he was kicked in the head a number of times and his attacker must have been wearing steel-toed boots. Remarkably, there are no fractures of the skull, although there are several major hematomas, uh bruises, which have caused some pockets of fluid on his brain. We drained some of the fluid last night and, as of the last CAT scan about two hours ago, that condition seems to be stabilizing as well."

"Can I see him?"

"In case there may possibly be some injury to the brain, as a precaution, we are keeping him in an MIC, a medically induced coma. Your father is still unconscious and we put him on an artificial respirator."

"I'd still like to see him."

The doctor exhaled heavily again, raising the same hairs on his forehead.

It may be difficult for you, Miss Carolina," he said softly. "Right now, he may not look too much like your father."

"I want to see my dad!" Molly yelled as she began to cry. "I want to see my dad, god dammit!"

"Very well, please come with me. I must warn you, he has been badly beaten."

Molly followed the doctor into a room filled with flashing, multicolored monitors, their lights reflecting off shiny steel machines that surrounded the bed. The room was buzzing with electronic beeps and tones. A nurse was checking monitors. The doctor motioned toward a tangle of tubes, wires and bandages as Molly gazed at a face she did not recognize.

"Is that my father?" she gasped.

"Yes. The swelling in his face will eventually recede and plastic surgery should be able to repair most of the damage."

Dr, Martinez pointed to a monitor.

"As you can see, despite his injuries, his vital signs are all very strong."

Molly stared at what was supposed to be her father and felt her knees give way. She tried to grab onto the bed railing but her hands weren't functioning. The last thing she remembered was the beep… beep…beep of her father's heart monitor. She awoke in a chair in the hallway, choking on the fumes of ammonia.

Dr. Martinez handed her a paper cup filled with water.

"Are you back with us, Molly? Here, take a sip."

"Yes, I guess so. Thank you, doctor. Did I…?"

"Out cold. When was the last time you ate?"

Molly tried to think but there were still a few clouds in her head.

"I'm not sure. Maybe sometime yesterday."

"You need to eat, Miss Carolina."

"Doctor, what's the prognosis for my father?"

"Well, it's difficult to tell at this stage. It's still very early."

"Give me your best guess," Molly pressed.

"If I had to make a prediction, I would say that his kidneys are only bruised. He will probably be urinating blood for a short time and we will need to leave a catheter in until the bleeding stops, but this is an injury he can get through, I would think, without any complications."

Molly took a long sip of the water.

"As far as the head injuries, it's difficult to say. If there is no more fluid build-up, he may only suffer from a concussion, which still can be serious. I have him on anti-seizure medications. It's a possibility that trauma to the head such as this can lead to a form of epilepsy."

Dr. Martinez massaged the back of his neck with both hands.

"If it's only a concussion, his prognosis would be headaches and some dizziness for a while. Possibly some nausea and perhaps a temporary loss of short-term memory. He may not even remember what happened to him. Or he may have some post-traumatic injury problems with depression and flashbacks. These conditions could completely disappear in a short period of time or they may take months, maybe years, to resolve. If they can be resolved at all."

Molly squeezed the armrests of her chair so tightly that her hands were shaking.

"But like I said, based on his most recent CAT scan, there doesn't appear to be any more buildup of fluid pressing against his brain which is a very good sign. The ribs will take a while to mend and the chest tubes should come out in a day or so. You may not be able to hug your father quite as tightly as you wish for some time. The cuts will heal and the broken nose will leave him looking like a handsome, tough guy in the movies."

"Is my mother here?" Molly asked.

"She arrived shortly after your father was brought in last night. Your mother was here all night. She had some minor injuries but we sent her home. There wasn't anything she could do here. I suggested she come back later this afternoon."

"What happened? Were they in a car accident?"

"I believe your mother said something about a fight."

"A fight?"

The doctor nodded.

"Are you feeling alright? When is the last time you had something to eat?"

"I can't remember. Some doctor I'm going to make."

"You are a medical student?"

"Pre-vet."

"I passed out the first time I drew blood from a patient," Martinez smiled.

He turned around and parted his hair on the back off his head.

"I think I still have the scar from where I hit the side of the bed. You'll get used to it."

202

"Yeah, maybe."

"Are you feeling better?"

"I'm OK. I guess I'll just wait out here."

"Molly, may I make a suggestion? There is nothing you can do here for your father. He is in the best of hands. Let us watch him carefully over the next 24-hours. We will know a whole lot more tomorrow. Go home and be with your mother. I promise, he'll still be here."

Molly looked down the hall towards her father's room and then turned back towards Dr. Martinez.

The doctor nodded and gave her a kind smile.

"I'll take good care of him. I promise."

Molly got up from the chair and walked down the hall towards the elevator. Dr. Martinez kept his hand firmly locked around her arm.

"Are you feeling all right to drive?" he asked as they walked towards the elevator. "I don't want you getting in an accident. We'd have to put you in the North Wing and your father in the South Wing. That way we would have a North Carolina and a South Carolina."

The doctor leaned over and looked at Molly to check her reaction to his stupid joke.

Molly faked a laugh.

"Is this part of your bedside manner?" she asked.

"I'm sorry, it's not my best stuff."

"Well let's hope…"

"You hope I'm a better doctor than I am a comedian? Is that what you were going to say, Molly?"

"Something like that."

Dr. Martinez took her hand. He pushed the tip of his thumb gently against one of her fingernails and watched for the blood to return, checking to see if she was anemic.

"I'd prescribe a spinach salad and maybe some iron supplements."

The elevator doors opened to the ICU reception room. Molly and Dr. Martinez both turned to look at the occupants in the car. A young woman in a wheelchair glanced up at them and then smiled as she looked down at her newborn baby cradled in her arm. A young man, gripping the handles of the wheelchair, burst into a wide, proud grin.

Instead of getting in the elevator car, Molly remained outside. She managed to return their smiles along with a nod of congratulations. As the doors began to close, Molly turned around and burst into tears.

## *Chapter Epilogue*

*Over the next six months, Bobby Carolina would eventually recover from all of his physical injuries and, as Dr. Martinez predicted, would, indeed, end up looking like a handsome tough guy in the movies.*

*However, for several years following the beating, Bobby would suffer periodic epileptic seizures. He would never, on his own, be able to recall the events of that night.*

*Eleanor Carolina would stay active in the Alcoholic Anonymous program and never take another drink. She would confront her demons one-by-one and spend the rest of her life learning how to let go of those things that she had no control over.*

*And when she felt her husband was strong enough, Eleanor would tell Bobby the whole account of her disgraceful experience with Jimmy Bragg and what happened that terrible night. Recognizing Eleanor's confession as an essential part of her own healing and recovery process, Bobby listened bravely, all the while fighting to subdue his own anger and repugnance. At the end of the telling, Bobby took Eleanor in his arms. At first their embrace was stiff and brittle but they managed to clumsily hang on to one another until they both began to cry. And as they wept, their separate, individual tears flowed down each of their cheeks and into a single stream.*

*Perhaps, because of the miraculous courage and kindness within the human spirit and its remarkable capacity to find a tiny grain of hope among a mountain of grief and despair, Bobby and Eleanor were able to rebuild their relationship. Starting with a foundation of forgiveness and absolution, they discovered a love and devotion for one another far deeper and purer than they could have ever expected.*

*They sold the farm in Arizona and moved to Carlsbad, California, just 30 miles north of San Diego, where they bought a house overlooking the healing blue waters of the Pacific Ocean.*

*Bobby would take a job as a greenkeeper on the golf course at La Costa Resort and Spa where he worked no more than thirty-hours a week. Every day at noon, he would leave the course to go home and have lunch with the woman he had married long ago, in what seemed like a different lifetime and a different place. In the evenings, Bobby would tend to his vegetable garden in their small backyard.*

*Eleanor Carolina would enroll at the University of California at San Diego and eventually receive her Master's degree in psychology. She would open her own practice as a family crisis counselor, specializing in helping families through teenage suicides as well as continuing her work with Alcoholics Anonymous. She, too, would leave her office every day at noon to have lunch with the man she seemed to keep falling in love with throughout every stage of her life*

*Jimmy Bragg would be sentenced to six years in the Arizona State Penitentiary at Florence after being found guilty of aggravated assault and battery. In prison, Jimmy would fall in with other white prisoners who were members of the Aryan Nation.*

*With one year remaining on his sentence, Jimmy would kill a fellow white prisoner in an argument over a magazine. Although there were supposedly no witnesses, the leaders of the white power gang would expel Jimmy from their ranks.*

*Without any protection or threat of retribution by the other white inmates, Jimmy became an easy target for repeated beatings and brutal rapes by Black and Mexican gang members. With less than four months to go before his release, half crazy, paranoid, living in constant fear of the next attack and physically broken by the beatings and assaults, Jimmy would stab one of his tormentors during breakfast in plain sight of three guards.*

*He would be tried for first degree murder, found guilty, and executed, under the laws of the state of Arizona, by lethal injection six years later.*

# Chapter 16

## "Jesus, Get Me a Flamethrower!"

AVY NURSE, LIEUTENANT JOLEEN SALVESON'S LIFE WAS saved by the quick thinking of a 22-year-old medic named, Taylor Hutchinson. The soldier who first discovered Joleen slumped against the wall of the hospital with blood pouring out of her mouth, grabbed Hutchinson out of the rushing phalanx of American soldiers charging into the main corridor of the Malinta tunnel and pulled him into the hospital ward. Even after witnessing three years of gruesome and horrid casualties as a medic attached to an infantry unit fighting in the Pacific, Corporal Hutchinson was not prepared for what awaited him in the ward.

The throats of every Japanese patient lay agape where they had been slit. Many of the heads were nearly severed by the razor-sharp bayonets. The floor of the hospital was slick and covered with fresh blood. The smell in the nearly airless room was suffocating. The ravenous swarms of green flies clung like woolen scarves around the necks of the dead.

"Get your ass over here, Hutch," the soldier yelled, startling the young medic out of his stunned trance. "It's an American girl and she's bleeding like hell!"

Corporal Hutchinson ran towards the soldier where Joleen was propped up in the sitting position against the wall, her body limp and lifeless, her face an opaque white. Blood poured out from between her lips. As the medic pried open her mouth, the other soldier asked, "What's wrong with her?"

"Jesus, they cut off her tongue!"

"They what?"

"The Japs must have cut off her tongue just before we broke through. Son of a bitch!"

"She's hemorrhaging. If we don't stop this bleeding, she's gonna die. Go get me a flame thrower."

"A what?"

"Get me a god damned flame thrower! I've got to cauterize this wound before she bleeds to death. You've got about ninety-seconds to get that lighter or she's going home in a bag!"

The soldier raced out of the wing and was back with a flame thrower in less than a minute. Corporal Hutchinson took his spoon out of his mess kit and bent the handle at a ninety-degree angle. He quickly wrapped the handle of the spoon with gauze bandaging.

The medic held the end of the spoon up to the pilot flame of the weapon until it turned bright red. The heat slithered up the handle of the spoon and smoke began to swirl upwards from the gauze insulation.

Hutchinson hissed through his tightly clenched teeth as the hot metal seared the skin on his fingers. He stubbornly fought off the pain to hold onto the spoon.

"Hold her head back!" Hutchinson ordered.

As the soldier held Joleen's head, Hutchinson plunged the red-hot spoon into her mouth and held it against the gaping wound. The smell of the burning flesh and blood was sickening. The soldier holding Joleen turned his head and vomited.

"Again!" the medic screamed, forcing the soldier to hold the flame thrower upright in his other hand. Despite seriously scalding his hand and fingers, Hutchinson endured the agony from another heating of the spoon.

The second cauterization seemed to stop the bleeding. It was difficult to tell with her mouth full of blood.

"I've just barely got a pulse. Let's get her out of here now!"

Corporal Hutchinson carried Joleen out of the tunnel in his arms and loaded her onto a jeep that was carrying several other wounded soldiers.

The driver of the jeep looked curiously at the thin, limp body with blood-streaked, blond hair that Hutchinson was carrying.

"Is that a woman?"

"Uh huh, American, I think. The gooks cut out her tongue. She's lost a lot of blood. Better haul ass, soldier."

The driver nodded, jumped into his jeep, and sped off in a shower of dust, veering around and narrowly avoiding a flag garnished jeep coming from the opposite direction. The approaching jeep was carrying General Douglas MacArthur on his return to Corregidor. It was the second time Joleen and General MacArthur had crossed paths during the war.

Joleen was carried out of Malinta Tunnel on March 2, 1945. She had been a prisoner of war since May 6, 1942, when Lieutenant General Wainwright surrendered the garrison on Corregidor to Japan's General Homma.

General Wainwright would also be held as a prisoner with many of his troops from Bataan and Corregidor in a POW camp in Manchuria in Northeast China. Those that survived the horrifying conditions of the Manchurian prison camp would not be released until August 16, 1945.

Approximately two weeks after his release from the prison camp in Manchuria, General Wainwright would be a gaunt witness to the formal Japanese surrender aboard the *USS Missouri* on September 2, 1945. The war in the Pacific lasted nine months. The surrender ceremony lasted only 20 minutes.

Joleen never got a final glimpse of the Rock. The next piece of land she would open her eyes upon were the gentle, green carpeted slopes on the island of Oahu from her bed in the Pearl Harbor Naval Hospital. Joleen would spend the next six weeks at Pearl Harbor before being shipped to the Naval Hospital in San Diego.

As a prisoner on Corregidor, Joleen lived under the constant and oppressive anxiety of not knowing what her captors might do to her at any moment. However, her darkest moments came when she was alone at night knowing that whether she died as a prisoner at the hand of the Japanese on that god-forsaken island, or somehow managed to survive, she had no one who would either mourn her death or celebrate her return. There was really no real person to come home to. She knew, of course, that the people of Thief River Falls cared dear for her, but there was no real closeness or intimacy to be found in a relationship with a whole town.

Joleen's mother and father were dead. She had no brothers or sisters and there was no one even close to being the boy back home that the other nurses at the Naval Training Station had talked so much about.

She survived each day as a POW because she was born and raised of stubborn Norwegian stock. She feared and despised her captors, but her greatest enemy was a voice from within her that asked rhetorically, "Who do you have to live for?"

By comparison, almost every one of the soldiers Joleen had cared for, both American and Japanese, had a wife, children, a girlfriend, or family that was waiting for them. The soldiers clung to worn and ragged photos and letters as though they were good-luck charms. Upon waking in the morning or coming out of anesthesia after surgery, the very first thing a soldier did was to reach for his reason for living and his connection to home. On more than one occasion, Joleen had witnessed seemingly mortally wounded soldiers miraculously will themselves to stay alive by staring at a frayed photo of a girl back home.

Joleen had no pictures or letters to comfort her as she lay in the darkness on her cot, all alone in the Malinta tunnel's empty nurse's quarters on Corregidor. She had no token of remembrance to link her with the safety and sanctuary of life back home. Even her memory was unable to escape from her island prison.

During the eternal nights, when the harsh and foreign cries of the Japanese soldiers echoed through the cavernous maze of tunnels and into her quarters where she lay sleepless and frightened, Joleen would try and force herself to recall high school friends and the kindly people of Thief River Falls, but nothing would come into clear focus.

The weight of her perilous day-to-day existence and the uncertainty of her future had severed her connection with her past. Thief River Falls was too far away and too obscure to reach out and hold onto. The present was so dire that her past didn't seem to exist. Joleen's life, growing up surrounded by the gentle beauty of northern Minnesota's lakes and forests, seemed like an anachronism — a distant, unreal and forgotten part of her past.

Ironically, the only people that Joleen felt close to in her loneliest moments as a prisoner of war, were her former patients from the Veterans Hospital in Los Angeles. Although she had only been with the men who had been wounded on Pearl Harbor for a few weeks before she was shipped overseas, she felt a certain kinship.

Aside from their injuries, Joleen began to understand their reluctance to be with others in the outside world. She could relate to the shame and sense of failure the men must have felt. Certainly, none of them were in a position of command, nor could they assume any responsibility for an alleged letdown of American defenses in Hawaii, but they were still a part of the most devastating loss in the history of the United States' military. Even worse, their wounds prevented them from being a part of their country's ultimate victory.

Joleen felt a similar sense of failure. She had studied and trained to become a nurse and an officer. And though in no way accountable for the defeat of General MacArthur's forces in the Philippines, she had been captured and had spent the war tending to the needs of the enemy.

Now that she understood how the men must have felt, she regretted even more taking them to the USO in Hollywood. She hoped, if she survived, that she could make amends.

Dealing with the psychological trauma of three years as a prisoner of war, as well as trying to confront the humiliation of trying to start her life again as a young woman with half a tongue, Joleen succumbed to waves of depression while she was in the hospital in Hawaii. In addition to struggling with learning how to speak, eat and drink with half a tongue, Joleen found that, although she was thousands of miles from the terrors of Corregidor, she was still held prisoner by the despair that haunted her in the Malinta Tunnel.

Joleen had lost over 30 pounds during her captivity. She hadn't had a period in over two years and still suffered occasional relapses of malaria. The depression took away her appetite, but even when she tried to eat, every meal was punctuated with fits of choking and gagging.

In addition to her many struggles, Joleen was subjected to an annoying distraction during her hospitalization, almost maddening on those occasions when she was deeply engrossed in a period of feeling sorry for herself.

"Joleen Salveson, now where have I heard that name before?" a doctor or nurse, stopping at the foot of her bed and staring curiously at her chart, would ask her.

Too self-conscious to speak freely to anyone other than her doctor and her speech therapist, Joleen would shrug her shoulders, smile apologetically and shake her head as if to say, "I don't know."

These flickers of recollection from the doctors and nurses eventually became a source of aggravation to Joleen. There she was in the hospital trying to convince herself that no one in the world cared a damn about her, while at the same time, there were people walking by her bed who thought they recognized her name.

Finally, a patient in her ward, another Navy nurse who was recovering from a severe case of dengue fever while stationed in Burma, solved the mystery.

Walking by Joleen's bed on her way to the bathroom, the nurse stopped suddenly, snapped her fingers, and broke into a huge smile.

"Ah hah, I got it!" she exclaimed. "It was a musician in a USO show in Burma. He came into the hospital and asked every doctor and nurse on staff if they had heard of a Navy nurse named, Joleen Salveson.

Joleen cast her a skeptical frown.

"Oh, yea, I remember him 'cause I thought it was kinda cute, him searching all over the world for his sweetheart…"

"Sweetheart?" Joleen sputtered which sounded more like "eee ark".

"Well, I'm not sure he used that exact word but that was how I wanted to believe it. I remember he would play his guitar and then help write letters for the wounded men in the hospital. Most of those 'fly in and fly out' show boys were scratching around the nurses' tents between shows looking for a little, well, you know. But this guy was only interested in cheering up the boys a little and trying to find this Joleen Salveson. That's why I remembered him and that's why I recognized your name. I remember thinking, what a lucky girl!"

Joleen desperately tried to think back. She had no recollection of ever meeting anyone in a USO show. In fact, she had never seen a USO show. She remembered the Hollywood Canteen and vaguely recalled dancing with a boy from Georgia in what seemed like a long, long time ago. The only other people she had spoken to were Linda Darnell and Jimmy Stewart and she doubted that Jimmy Stewart was searching for her.

"Must be somebody else," Joleen protested, surprising herself by using more than one word in a spoken sentence.

"Somebody else? You are a lieutenant in the Navy Nursing Corps, is that right?

"Uh huh."

"And your name is Joleen Salveson?"

Joleen nodded.

"Honey, how many nurses named Joleen Salveson do you think there are in this woman's Navy?"

Joleen was positive that there was no man in her life. Certainly, there was no one who would go searching for her but the thought did snag a little bit of her curiosity enough to sidetrack her momentarily from fully focusing on her own problems.

After six weeks at Pearl, Joleen was transferred to the Naval Hospital in San Diego. On her second day in the new hospital, a doctor stopped by her bed and stared at her chart.

"Now why does the name Salveson sound familiar?" the doctor asked.

"A musician with the USO...?" Joleen answered sarcastically.

"No, where are you from?" the doctor asked.

"Minnesota," Joleen answered.

"Wasn't there a great high school football coach in Minnesota named Salveson?"

Joleen smiled.

"Yes, he was my father."

"Was?"

"He died in a car accident just before the war."

"Oh, I'm so sorry. He must have been a terrific coach. I'm from Wisconsin and I heard a lot about him."

Joleen nodded to the doctor, "Yes, he was."

There were several doctors and nurses at the Naval Hospital who had served in the European and Pacific theaters who recognized her name and associated it with a young man who had visited their field hospitals, thus, continuing the legend of Joleen Salveson's mysterious pursuer.

Although her bouts with depression seemed to be lessening, a sign of her stubbornness reasserting itself, during lonely moments before she fell asleep, Joleen found herself envying this other Joleen Salveson whose lover had searched for her to the farthest corners of the war.

The loss of over half of her tongue left Joleen with some frustrating challenges. In the beginning of her therapy, her speech was greatly affected. Consonants were particularly hard for her to enunciate. Joleen spoke like someone who had just taken a bite of a hot baked potato and, while waving their hand in front of their mouth, was trying to explain that, "ith ith ott!"

She had difficulty swallowing liquids and would have to throw her head back to get food down her throat. She felt that she drank like a porpoise eating a fish. Even the simplest of meals turned into an exhausting ordeal. Occasionally she would have to push her food down her throat with her finger.

What was equally disheartening for Joleen, when her appetite returned, was the discovery that she had lost her sweet, salty, spicy and bitter taste buds that had been located on the surface of her tongue. A Norwegian from Minnesota raised on the finest cinnamon rolls in the state and where a good cup of coffee started with two rounded spoonsful of sugar and three-quarters of an inch of sweet cream, Joleen had lost the ability to satisfy the cravings of her sweet tooth.

In a relatively short period of time, much to Joleen's surprise and delight, her sense of smell, which ultimately comprises the majority of one's sense of taste, actually became more acute and she was eventually able to taste both the tartness and the sweetness in an apple pie as well as smell what the hospital was serving for dinner even before the menus were delivered to the patients.

After a month in the San Diego Naval Hospital, Joleen began to grow restless. Her wound had healed and she felt she had progressed as far as she could with her speech therapy. She received a check for a substantial amount in back pay while she was a prisoner of war and was entitled to monthly disability for her war wounds. Joleen was also presented with the Purple Heart.

Joleen quietly processed out of the service. She opened a savings account at the Bank of San Diego and rented a furnished studio apartment on Coronado Island.

The first day she moved in, Joleen bought five bouquets of flowers and filled her apartment with fresh, bright colors. She also bought one orchid for the Japanese soldier she had met on Corregidor.

The first letter she wrote was addressed to Thief River Falls, Minnesota.

> *To all my friends in Thief River,*
>
> *Hi everybody, I'm alive! Sorry it's been so long between letters but I got stuck on some island in the Pacific for a couple of years.*
>
> *I'm fine but I think I'll be staying in California for a while. I think of you all often and I will never be able to thank you enough for taking such good care of me after my parents died.*
>
> *Love,*
>
> *Joleen Salveson*
>
> *p.s. Please write and let me know how the boys from Thief River fared in the war.*

The second letter she wrote was to the Director of Nursing at Balboa Hospital, a ferry ride across the bay from her apartment on Coronado Island. Her letter stated that she was seeking a position on the hospital's nursing staff and listed her qualifications.

The third letter she wrote was addressed to Ken Petersen in Manhattan Beach, California.

Prior to her discharge from the Navy, Joleen had managed to find the whereabouts of the men in her ward at the Veterans Hospital in Los Angeles. It took a touch of deception but she had gotten the current addresses of each.

The only man that was still residing in California was Ken Petersen, the sergeant that had lost his arm in the attack on Pearl Harbor.

From her sunny apartment, brightly adorned with fresh flowers, Joleen sat down to write a letter she had composed many times in the dank, musty caverns of the Malinta Tunnel.

> *Dear Sgt. Petersen:*
>
> *I'm sure you probably don't remember me but I was your nurse while you were recovering in Ward 10 at the Veterans Hospital in Los Angeles. I was the one who thought it would be a good idea to take you all to the USO in Hollywood.*
>
> *I spent several years as a prisoner of war on Corregidor and a day didn't go by that I didn't think about how insensitive I was.*
>
> *I never got the opportunity to say I was sorry since I was shipped out the following morning.*
>
> *Please accept this belated but heartfelt apology along with my hopes that you are well.*
>
> *Sincerely,*
>
> *Joleen Salveson*
>
> *p.s. If you have a moment to write, I would like to know how you're doing.*

# Chapter 17
## Molly Carolina
## Doctor of Veterinary Medicine

$\mathcal{M}$ OLLY CAROLINA WAS IN THE LAST SEMESTER OF HER final year of vet school at the University of California at Davis. Located 70 miles northeast of San Francisco, U.C. Davis is considered one of the most prestigious schools of veterinary medicine in the world. U.C. Davis only accepts the top undergraduate candidates. Those students who make it through the four grueling years, are vigorously courted by high profile employers throughout the world.

During her father's recovery in the hospital, Molly became close friends with his doctor, Carlos Martinez. Dr. Martinez was easy to talk to and Molly was able to confess her feelings about her brother's death as well as her concern and self-doubt over the motives behind her academic zeal.

"Molly, I can still remember some scary moments in medical school where I could not, for the life of me, find a single valid or convincing answer to the question, "Why am I doing this?" Martinez admitted.

Molly nodded in agreement over a cup of coffee in the hospital cafeteria.

"You know that cliche about the journey being more important than the destination? I think sometimes the road you're traveling on is so rough and treacherous that you can't even remember where it was you were going."

"So how did you get through those moments? What made you decide to keep going?" she asked.

"Honestly? I think I kept going because I was good at it."

"You mean you were a good student?"

"Yes, I was good at being a student. I studied hard and I got top grades like you, Molly. I know I'm never going to win a Nobel Prize for any scientific breakthrough but I think that how you do something deserves as much credit as why you are doing it. If I'm playing in a basketball game and I've made ten out of ten from three-point range, I'm not going to ask why I'm playing so well. I'm just going to keep shooting."

"You're suggesting I should stop the introspection and brooding self-analysis?"

"Yes, unless you want to study Russian literature. Then brooding and self-analysis is a good thing," Dr. Martinez laughed and continued.

"But I honestly think that the true answers to your questions about your motives and why you are doing what you are doing will only come in the future when you are able to look backward at this difficult period in your life."

After four years, Molly was in her last semester before graduating as a Doctor of Veterinary Medicine. Her grades put her at the top of her class and she had a file full of letters of recommendations, acknowledgments and accolades. She had co-authored a paper published in the Journal of International Equine Science and a second article was scheduled to be published in the American Journal of Veterinary Medicine later that year.

Academically, Molly could not have possibly accomplished any more. Socially, however, she regarded herself as a dropout and a complete failure.

She referred to herself, as did many of her friends at school, as "DVM", which stood for Doctor of Veterinary Medicine. However, in Molly's case, DVM also stood for Davis' Virgin Mary. She received invitations to classmate functions and birthday parties addressed to 'The Last Virgin on Campus'.

"Molly, this is a college, not a convent," her roommate, Debbie Winston, would say when Molly turned down invitations to parties or to go bar hopping.

Her chastity was hard to comprehend. It certainly wasn't intentional. She was pretty, popular, hormonally well-balanced and had a good sense of humor. Molly wasn't a total hermit but when she did go out with friends, instead of "seeking out prey", as Debbie put it, Molly found herself thinking about other things she should be doing. She wasn't much on drinking and always seemed to have an early class the next morning so she generally had to leave before the feeding frenzy occurred near closing time.

Her anti-social behavior was really just an odd, accidental combination of bad luck and inexperience along with her being a little shy, a little too tall, and way too busy that prevented her from participating in any college courtship and mating rituals. She had dates with several of her classmates but they always seemed to end up in a friendship rather than in a bed.

The first two years of vet school were all classwork. In her third year, Molly spent about half of her time in the classroom and the other half in the clinic on campus. She elected to work with large animals rather than cats and dogs and made the equine clinic her second residence.

By the last year of vet school all class work was completed. Fourth-year students spent their time working with live animals in the clinic as well as studying for the National Veterinary Board Certification Exam.

Molly was flirting with the idea of accepting a one-year post-doctorate internship followed by a two or three-year residency specializing in the field of oncological research and treatment, primarily with horses.

One Saturday afternoon in April, Debbie and two other vet students, raided the equine clinic and kidnapped Molly. They were taking her to a concert in San Francisco. Debbie had dated one of the members of the band that was playing when she was an undergraduate at UCLA. He had called and promised her group backstage passes.

They drove into the city, had burgers and beers at a bar around the corner from the club and picked up their passes, as promised, from Will Call. There was a long line out front and when they entered the club it was almost full. A security guard checked their passes and escorted them through a heavily guarded side door and up a dark, rickety staircase. Their escort pointed to a closed door with a sign that read,' Impaired Vision'.

"They're in the green room," the guard grunted.

"Impaired Vision?" Molly whispered to Debbie.

"Yeah. Brad was going to be an optometrist before he quit school to be a rock star. He sat next to me in a calculus class and copied all my answers on tests. I finally told him if he was going cheat off me, he'd better buy me dinner after every test. We ended up dating for about a year."

"Why didn't I think of using that approach?" Molly wondered aloud.

"Because you finished your tests so quickly," Debbie answered. "Nobody could copy off you."

Debbie swung open the door and led the vet students inside.

They walked into what could have been a steam bath except, what might have been water vapor and eucalyptus oil, in this case, was a combination of cigarette smoke, marijuana, beer, whiskey and pheromone-laced, teenage perfume.

It was easy for Molly to identify the members of the band. They all had hair down to their shoulders, wore tight leather pants, and were surrounded by a swarm of half-dressed, young, beautiful girls — all of them sharing a bottle of Jack Daniels and passing joints to one another.

All except for one of the members of the band who was sitting by himself in the corner of the room, fingering the strings of his bass guitar with his left hand while reading a copy of *The Adventures of Huckleberry Finn* in his right hand.

The four vet students suddenly felt old and not very hip.

"Deb, what's happening!" Debbie's old boyfriend, Brad, squealed when he spotted her from across the room. He parted a sea of teenage groupies, walked over and gave Debbie a big hug.

"Hey, listen up, everybody. I want you to meet the person who made me everything I am today."

The room quieted down as Brad kept his arm around Debbie.

"This is Debbie, the girl I write all my songs about. Well, most of them, anyway."

Brad flashed a tender smile to one of the groupies, a girl no older than seventeen.

"If Debbie hadn't dumped me, I'd be an optometrist fitting near-sighted old ladies with glasses."

The room erupted in laughter.

Molly noticed that the bass player who was reading Huck Finn didn't laugh at Brad's announcement. He looked up from his book with a reflective expression and studied Debbie and the other students one by one. When his gaze fell on Molly, he smiled. Molly caught the smile in her peripheral vision and felt her face prickle with the onset of a blush. She tried to return his smile but hers came out so clumsy and dorky that it could have appeared as though she was suffering from gas pains at the moment.

"Debbie and her friends are down from U.C. Davis," Brad continued. "They're all going to be veterinarians. Pretty soon, huh?"

There was a sharp knock at the door of the green room and an older man with an eye patch stuck his head in the door.

"Whenever you're ready, guys. They're about ready to go Vesuvius down there."

With the exception of the bass player, the members of Impaired Vision each took one last look at themselves in the mirror and downed a quick swig of Jack Daniels. The musicians and their entourage paraded out of the room in a storm of raging adrenaline. The band members swaggered down the stairs like Mongol invaders approaching a help-less, unarmed village. The thunderous chanting and stomping of the crowd inside the club was shaking the dust off the rafters. The tiny particles were ignited by the lighting from the stage and it looked as though they were walking through a psychedelic snowstorm.

The vet students were at the end of the procession with Molly in the rear. The bass player was the last to leave the green room. He calmly got out of his chair and fastened his strap onto the body of his guitar. Molly noticed that he was much taller than the other members of the band.

He walked over to Molly.

"You can't pray a lie," he said softly.

Molly was startled by his voice.

"I'm sorry, you can't what?"

"You can't pray a lie. That's the title of Chapter 31 in *The Adventures of Huckleberry Finn*. It's probably one of the most revealing and honest descriptions of how our innate sense of goodness and humanity is in direct conflict with the conventions and mores established within our society by the present religious and political attitudes."

"All that's in 'Huck Finn'?" Molly asked.

"Oh, yes, and a lot more. Hemingway said that all modern American literature comes from one book, 'Huckleberry Finn. Hi, I'm Greg."

"I'm Molly. Nice to meet you."

"Molly, that's a little girl's name. That's cool. You'll always have that little girl image. Do you feel that way?"

"Sometimes. Like right now for instance," Molly answered self-consciously.

The bass player laughed. "You gonna be here after the show?"

"I don't know. I came with my friends and I'm not sure what they're going to do afterward."

"OK. Here, read Chapter 31," he said handing his book to Molly. "It's a lot more substantive than our show. Come on downstairs if you want when you're done reading. It's only ten or eleven pages. If your friends are going to stay maybe we can talk about it after the show."

"OK, thanks," Molly stammered, somewhat taken aback by his "un-rock star" behavior.

"See ya," Greg smiled.

He turned around and walked out of the room. Molly watched him as he strode down the ramp, his guitar in one hand. He looked like a muscular Roman gladiator, weapon drawn, dutifully marching into the bright sunlight of the Coliseum.

Molly found herself alone in the room surrounded by beer cans and half-empty bottles of bourbon. One wall of the room was a continuous mirror with dressing tables and make-up lights. The other walls were covered with autographs and names of the bands that had played there along with their personal comments, artwork and graffiti scribbled in felt tip marker.

The green room, when it was filled with the exotic looking musicians and their young and attractive following, had seemed so electric and glamorous when she first walked in. Empty, it seemed dingy, seedy and smelly.

Molly heard a roar from the crowd downstairs as the band took the stage. A throbbing base riff rumbled through the wooden walls like an approaching earthquake followed by a machine gun volley from the drums. The guitars exploded like waves crashing on a rocky shore and she heard a high-pitched scream from the lead singer.

Molly stood there thinking about the bass player.

"What a strange guy," she said to the empty room.

She wanted to go downstairs and watch the band perform on stage in front of the crowd but she felt obligated to read the assignment she had been given.

"Always the good student, huh Molly?" she mumbled to herself as she stretched out on the leather sofa and scanned the book's table of contents for Chapter 31.

"Ew," she hissed as she thought about what sort of activities may have occurred on the couch in the past.

Molly jumped up, grabbed several clean towels that were stacked on the dressing table and spread them out on the couch before she sat back down.

The chapter entitled, 'You Can't Pray a Lie', is about the King and the Duke, a couple of frauds claiming to be royalty, that Huck and Jim had picked up in their raft. Desperate for money, the King turns in Jim, Huck's friend and Miss Watson's slave, for the reward money and leaves Huck faced with a dilemma.

Huck is miserable when he learns about the King turning in Jim. Alone on the raft, Huck comes to the self-incriminating conclusion, as Twain writes, *"The hand of Providence had slapped him in the face for stealing a poor old woman's slave and trying to help him to get his freedom."*

*"The more I studied about this the more my conscience went to grinding me, and the more wicked and low down and ornery I got to feeling."*

Molly felt a pang of familiarity about the way she felt after her brother's death. She wondered if she, like Huck, had blamed herself for the irrationality of others. The issue of slavery for Huck, the act of taking responsibility for her brother's life for Molly.

Huck knows that the proper thing to do is to write Miss Watson and tell her that her slave can be reclaimed from the King and the Duke. Huck writes the letter and prays over it to see if he feels any better after writing the letter.

*"I took it up (the letter) and held it in my hand. I was a-trembling, because I got to decide, forever, betwixt two things, and I knowed it. I studied a minute, sort of holding my breath, and then I says to myself: "All right, then, I'll go to hell"—and tore it up."*

The chapter ended in the middle of Huck's scheme to steal Jim back from the man the King and the Duke had sold him to and to help Jim escape to freedom.

It was a moving and entertaining read, especially through the words of young Huckleberry. Twain's dialect was hypnotic, capable of transporting the reader to the overgrown banks of the muddy Mississippi. Molly was tempted to continue reading to see how Huck was going to pull it off but it made her even more curious about the bass player and she wanted to see him on stage in his other persona.

The music grew louder as she walked down the back stairs. The dimly lit passageway led to a sign that read, "Back Stage—Entertainers Only". Two huge security guards stood on each side of the entrance looking like matching refrigerators.

As Molly approached, the guards inflated themselves to even larger proportions. She showed them her badge, which deflated the guards back to their original size, and they politely opened the door for her.

The sheer volume of the music literally pushed her back a step. It was as though she had been walloped in the stomach during a pillow fight.

She found her friends standing off to the side of the stage.

When Debbie spotted her, she yelled something at Molly. There was no way Molly could hear her but judging from her body language and the look of consternation on Debbie's face, Molly figured it was something like, "Where have you been?"

Molly smiled sheepishly, put her hands around Debbie's ear and shouted, "Reading."

Debbie's eyes widened in disbelief. "Reading?" she shouted. "You're impossible!"

Molly laughed, nodded in agreement, and then turned her attention to the audience.

The crowd was crammed in together like a new box of Q-Tips. A platoon of muscular and intimidating security guards in yellow windbreakers leaned into and against the front row of the crowd. Perspiration on the guards' faces glistened from the lights on the stage.

The bodies in the audience were packed together so tightly that the only free space unoccupied was directly above them. Arms raised over their heads and above their swaying bodies, the crowd looked like a bed of eel grass dancing to the surge of a powerful underwater current. Either that or a scene from an old movie where the mob was screaming, "Burn her, burn her! She's a witch!" In any case, it looked frightening and terribly claustrophobic to Molly.

On stage, lead singer Brad and the two guitarists were teasing the audience. Dripping with sweat, they would run towards the throng and lean over the front of the stage. The crowd would swell forward, nearly crushing the burly security guards, reaching out to touch their idols or hoping to grab a souvenir droplet of perspiration.

Brad and the two guitarists would then back off, shake their long, wet hair at one another, and the crowd would flex back to their original position.

Behind the three front-men were the drummer and Greg, the bass player. The drummer was on a six-foot high riser, incarcerated by a metal bulwark of cymbals and surrounded by a wall of drums.

The drummer's eyes were tightly closed and his head was cocked to the side. He shouted the cadence to himself and grunted through drum fills that encompassed 180 degrees of floor and rack toms.

Directly to the drummer's left, on a smaller riser, Greg stood calmly in front of a mountain of stacked amplifiers and speakers. Other than his hands, which seemed to be flying all over his guitar, the only other movement of his body was the slight bobbing of his head to the beat of the music.

Molly looked back at the crowd and noticed that there were sections near the front of the stage that were comprised primarily of young girls, each focusing on and screaming for the attention of their particular favorite member of the band. It was like footage of a Beatles concert Molly had seen where the camera panned the crowd showing some girls screaming for Paul and others screaming for John, George or Ringo.

Molly followed the eyes of the girls screaming at Greg and saw that he was not paying any attention to his adoring admirers. His attention was on the movement of his left hand up and down the neck of his guitar.

At the beginning and end of each song, Greg and the drummer would look over at one another to lock into the opening groove or match licks at the end.

The song they were playing came to an end with a piercing howl of feedback from the guitars, a driving and punishing bass riff, and a thunderous drum fill. The music stopped abruptly the instant Brad landed on the stage after leaping from the drum riser.

The crowd went berserk. Brad and the two guitarists raised their arms in the air with their fists clenched, like prize fighters who had just knocked out their opponents. The drummer grabbed a towel and took a long drink of water from a plastic bottle. Greg looked over at Molly and smiled at her.

Molly felt a slight wobble in her knees and a tingling in her stomach. She smiled back and applauded.

Greg rolled his eyes in a self-effacing manner. He pressed the sides of his flattened hands together, in the sign language gesture of a book, and gave her a questioning look.

Molly guessed he was asking her if she had read the chapter in *Huck Finn*. She nodded and placed her hand over her heart, nodded and smiled.

Greg smiled back and put his hand over his heart. Their eyes locked for a brief moment until the drummer banged his sticks against one another counting out the tempo to the next song.

The next song sounded a lot like the previous one to Molly. She had a hard time trying to understand the words and was amazed that most of the people in the audience were singing along.

Greg had disappeared back into a world of his own. Seemingly unaware of the other band members or the crowd, his eyes were closed, opening only occasionally to look at the drummer or at his fingers on the neck of his guitar.

Near the end of the song, two roadies on each side of the stage turned the fog machines up to full blast. In seconds the entire stage and the front rows of the crowd were engulfed in a thick cloud of gray smoke.

The song changed abruptly from hard, driving rock to a single acoustic guitar and Brad's vocal. The crowd grew quiet as the guitar faded out and only the singer's voice ended the song.

The crowd erupted, their screams louder than at any time during the concert. The roadies turned off the fog machines and switched on the large fans on the sides of the stage.

When the fog cleared, the stage was empty.

Molly felt someone beside her.

"So, you liked it, huh?" Greg shouted above the roar of the crowd.

"You guys were great!"

226

"No, not the band. The chapter in Huck Finn."

"Oh," Molly paused to alter her character from animated rock groupie to American literature critic.

"I remember it was my favorite chapter when I read it in high school," she shouted back. "It made me want to start reading fiction again."

The level of the noise from the crowd was near deafening. They were stomping on the floor, chanting and holding cigarette lighters above their heads, demanding an encore.

Brad ran over to Greg and screamed something Molly couldn't make out. Greg smiled at Molly, grabbed his bass guitar from a roadie who had tuned it, and sauntered back on stage.

Molly would have thought that it was impossible for the crowd to be any louder, but when the band came back on stage, she had to plug her ears with her fingers. The noise sent shooting pains down her ear canals.

The band and their sound man responded to the roar of the crowd by turning up their amps and the main speakers.

Debbie grabbed Molly's arm and signaled for her to follow her. The four vet students moved off to the side of the stage.

"Let's get out of here! I'm gonna be deaf for a week!" one of the students yelled.

Molly felt her spirits fall. Normally, she would be the one who always wanted to leave early but she didn't want to leave without seeing Greg once more.

"I've got to thank Brad," Debbie said. "Let's go up to their dressing room and wait for them to finish. I'll thank him and then we can leave."

Molly felt her mood improve instantly and led the way up the stairs to the green room.

When the encore ended, Greg was the first musician to enter the dressing room.

"Oh, great, you're still here," he said directly to Molly.

Debbie and the other students stared at Molly. Everyone seemed to be staring at Molly as though they were expecting her to do something. She did. Molly stood there and turned a bright, crimson red.

Greg kept his eyes focused on Molly as though there was no one else in the room.

"Would you like to have dinner with me tonight?" he asked politely.

Generally self-conscious in situations where she was the target of attention, Molly found it strangely easy to turn all her attention to Greg.

"I'd love to but my friends that drove me here from Davis are leaving."

"We've got a couple of limos at our disposal. I can take you back. Where's Davis?"

"It's pretty far. It's up by Sacramento. About 70 miles from here."

"No problem. In fact, I could use a quiet and peaceful drive."

Greg turned to Debbie and the students who were gawking at the scene they were witnessing.

"Is it all right with you all if I take Molly to dinner?" he asked. "I promise I'll get her home safely."

"Sure, but I want her home before the sun comes up," Debbie snapped in a motherly tone.

"I promise," Greg laughed.

Greg took hold of Molly's arm.

"Let's go out the back way and grab one of the limos. I've got to go back to the hotel and take a shower and then let's go get something to eat."

Molly waved to her friends as Greg whisked her out the door of the dressing room.

"It's after one in the morning. What's open at this time of night?" she asked.

"Chinatown. Chinatown's always open. You like Chinese?"

"Sure, I love Chinese," Molly lied after having lived on Top Ramen Chicken-flavored Noodles for most of the last eight years of her life.

Greg put his hand on Molly's shoulder.

"I feel very fortunate."

"Why?" Molly asked.

"I'm bringing a veterinarian to a Chinese restaurant!"

"What's so great about that?

"Well, you'll be able to tell if the meat is either dog or cat, right?"
"Yuck!"

Molly walked into her apartment as the sun was about to summit the east face of the Sierra Nevada Mountains. She threw her purse on the coffee table and plunked down on the sofa.

Debbie suddenly appeared in the doorway of her bedroom.

"Well?"

Molly looked over at Debbie but didn't say anything.

"Well…" Debbie repeated, louder and more emphatically, this time adding a tapping, impatient foot.

"Do I look any different to you, Deb?" Molly asked in a quiet voice.

"Do you look any different? Why, are you on drugs or something?"

Molly got up from the couch and turned around in a circle.

"No, I'm not on any drugs. Do I appear to be any different to you? That's all I'm asking."

Debbie looked her up and down.

"No, you look like the same Molly I used to know, as far as I can tell."

"Then I'm the same person I was yesterday?"

"Well, basically yes, but you're acting a little weird right now."

Molly sat back down on the sofa. Debbie plopped down next to her.

"Okay, tell me everything that happened," Debbie asked. "Did you go back to his hotel room?"

"Yes," Molly nodded.

"And ….?"

"He had a suite at the St. Francis Hotel so I watched TV for a little while and then looked out the window at the lights of the city while he showered and changed clothes. You know he looks really different in normal clothes, really handsome."

"And then…?" Debbie prodded.

"We went to dinner at this hole-in-the-wall Chinese restaurant in Chinatown. We were the only people in the whole place. It was like a movie or something. It was so romantic. We ate and talked for hours and none of the help seemed to mind. It was like the restaurant existed just for us."

229

"Ummm, and then…?"

Molly closed her eyes and took a deep breath. Debbie put her hand on Molly's shoulder and leaned closer.

"And then I did it with a rock musician in the back of a limousine!" Molly giggled.

"In the back of the limousine?" Debbie shrieked and threw her arms around Molly. Molly fell backwards and they both rolled off the couch onto the floor where they lay laughing hysterically.

Debbie sat on top of Molly and pinned her arms to the floor. They were both laughing so hard tears were streaming down their faces.

"All right, Molly Carolina. You look me in the eyes and swear to me that you lost your virginity to a guitar player in the back of a limousine! You swear to God?"

Molly couldn't stop laughing and could only nod her head.

"A rock star in the back of a limo!" Debbie exclaimed and rolled off of Molly back onto the floor. "It's so…so…un-Mollyish!"

"But he's a nice rock star," Molly said semi-seriously.

"Tell me, where did it happen? Debbie asked.

"I told you, in the back of the limo."

"No, I mean, where?"

"Oh, on the drive back from San Francisco."

"Well, where exactly? In the parking lot of the restaurant? Oakland? Vacaville? Out in front of our apartment…? I want to know precisely where it happened."

"Well, pretty much the whole way," Molly confessed with a shy smile.

"The whole way!" Debbie screamed.

"Well, it seemed like it went on all the way from the time we left the Chinese restaurant to here on campus."

"Through the city, over the Bay Bridge and seventy miles of I-80?" Debbie shrieked and doubled up laughing. "Oh, my God!"

"Deb, I've got to get some sleep," Molly sighed.

"Oh, no, I want to hear every detail. Speaking metaphorically, Molly, most people start out with a 5-K or a 10-K for their first, uh, race—not a marathon!"

"I've got to be at the clinic to assist a surgery at seven in the morning. That's less than three hours from now."

Molly curled up on the couch and wrapped an afghan around her.

"Can you wake me at eight-thirty, Deb?"

"Sure, but I want to hear everything tonight. My God, the last virgin has lost her thorny crown. Wait until the villagers hear of this. There may be panic in the streets."

Molly never heard the end of Debbie's commentary. She was fast asleep before the smile drifted from her lips.

"Are you going to see him again?" Debbie asked during their dinner that same night.

"I don't know. He told me the band is just starting a three-month tour on the West Coast. It didn't sound like they were going to get much time off between performances."

"Did he ask you for your phone number?"

"Yep."

"Did you get his?"

"Nuh uh."

"Do you think you'll…you know. I mean, do you wanna…?"

Molly laughed and shrugged.

"I don't know. No, I'm not being honest. Of course, I'd like to see him again. I had an unbelievable time and he made me feel…he made me feel like I was pretty and attractive and desirable, you know? He was funny and kind and intelligent and…cute. Did I mention he was cute?"

Both girls laughed.

"I guess it's up to him," Molly said. "Think about his life. He's on the road in a different city every night with, jeez, did you see all those girls screaming for him at the show?"

"Yea, but he picked you, Molly."

"Yes, he picked me…last night. But who knows who he's going to pick tonight?"

Fortunately for Molly, the National Veterinary Board Certification Exam was fast approaching. Between hours devoted to studying for the upcoming Boards and time spent in the equine clinic, Molly was able to rein in her attention whenever it started to wander back to Greg. It had been three weeks and there had been no phone call from him.

"Well, maybe you can just sit there and pretend that it doesn't matter to you, Molly," Debbie blurted out in the middle of a late-night study session. "But I can't!"

"What are you talking about?" Molly asked from behind a textbook.

"You know what I'm talking about."

Molly put down the book and tried to rub out a kink in the back of her neck.

"Deb, I was a one-night stand, okay? But I'm not sorry about what happened. He couldn't have been nicer and it was a…it was a memorable night. Why don't we just let it go at that?"

"I'm calling Brad."

"Why?"

"I don't know. Maybe he can give me some information on this guy."

Debbie walked into the kitchen, picked up the phone and dialed Brad's number.

"Aren't they on the road?" Molly asked.

"Yea, but I'm sure Brad checks his messages. I'm just going to ask him to call me."

"What are you going to say?"

"What, when he calls me back?"

"Yes."

"I'm going to ask him how the tour is going and why his sleaze ball bass player broke my best friend's heart."

"That may be a bit of an exaggeration, Deb."

"OK, I'll tone it down some."

"Hello…" a raspy voice answered.

"Brad?"

"Yeah, who is this? What time is it?"

"Brad, what are you doing at home?"

"I'm answering the fucking telephone. Who is this?"

"Brad, its Deb. I'm sorry. I was just going to leave you a message to call me. I thought the band was still on the road."

"Oh, hi, Deb."

"Are you drunk or did I wake you up?"

"A little bit of both I guess."

"What are you doing back in LA? I thought your band was on the road?"

"We had to cancel the tour."

"Why?"

"Our bass player OD'd in Portland. We couldn't find a replacement so we had to scrap the whole tour."

Debbie's face turned ashen. "He what?"

"Yeah, Greg overdosed on heroin. I found him in the bathroom of his hotel room. It was really fucked up, Deb. He was a good guy and an amazing bass player."

Debbie fell back into a kitchen chair.

Molly sprang up from the sofa when she saw the color disappear from Debbie's face.

"What's the matter?" Molly asked. "Are you OK?"

Debbie nodded.

"You still there, Deb?"

"Yea, I'm here. I'm just shocked."

"Yeah, it was bizarre. He'd been using for like ten years. He was pretty straight up with everybody in the band about it. He never got out of hand, just kind of maintained. He was always on time, always played great, and he never tried to turn anybody else on to it. He just had this little private habit."

"A heroin addict?" Debbie sighed.

"Uh huh."

"Heroin?" Molly repeated.

"When did it happen?" Debbie asked.

"Couple of weeks ago. Like a week after I saw you in San Francisco. We played this club in Portland and somebody stole one of his guitars out of our dressing room. Apparently, Greg kept his kit in his guitar case, so he took one of the limos to try and find someplace to score. Maybe it was cheap stuff or maybe it was purer than what he was used to, I don't know. All I know is, the next day he was late for the bus so I went up to his room to get him. He didn't answer when I pounded on the door so the desk clerk had security let me in his room. Man, it was gruesome."

"Could it have been…intentional?" Debbie asked.

"No, I don't think so. He was feeling pretty good. He really liked your friend. In fact, he couldn't stop talking about her. We all laughed like hell every time he told the story about taking a veterinarian to a Chinese restaurant. Nah, the cops said there was no sign of anyone else in the room and the autopsy said the cause of death was an accidental overdose of heroin."

Debbie tried to keep Molly from seeing the tear that slipped down the side of her face.

"Oh, Brad, I'm so sorry."

"Yeah, me, too. So, we had to cancel the rest of the tour and the assholes at the label canceled our record deal. Can you believe that? A guy in the band dies and the first thing the record company does is tear up our contract. Everything's pretty much fucked up…including me."

"You holding it together, Brad?"

"Yea, barely. Hell, I'll be all right. I think I'm gonna get my hair cut off and then re-enroll at UCLA. Jesus, I guess I'm going to be an optometrist after all!"

"Brad, I'm coming home after graduation. I should be back in L.A. in a couple of months. You think you'd be up for dinner at Tito's?"

"Tito's Taco's in Culver City? Yeah, my treat."

"It's a date. Take care of yourself, Brad. You're going to be fine."

"Yea, I'll be okay. Looking forward to seeing you at Tito's, Deb. Bye."

Debbie hung up the phone. She stood frozen with her hand in a tightly clenched fist and pressed it against her mouth. She took a long thoughtful breath

"I heard you say a heroin addict." Molly gasped. "Who?"

Debbie walked over to the couch and sat down next to Molly.

"Greg," Debbie whispered.

"Greg? Greg who? My one-night stand Greg?

Debbie nodded.

"Oh my God! He's a heroin addict?"

234

"Was, honey," Debbie said softly.

"Was?" Molly could barely get the word out.

Neither girl spoke for several minutes until Molly broke the silence.

"What did Brad say when you asked him if he thought it was intentional?"

"He didn't think so. Brad said Greg was feeling good."

Debbie suddenly burst out in tears.

"That's when Brad said that Greg really had a good time with you. He kept telling this story over and over about taking a veterinarian to dinner at a Chinese restaurant…"

The two friends collapsed into one another's' arms.

Molly explained the veterinarian in the Chinese restaurant joke and Debbie, whose older brother had gotten into heroin and eventually cleaned up, tried to answer Molly's questions about the addiction.

"When you and Greg…in the limousine…did he use a…?" Debbie asked.

"No, I don't think so," Molly answered.

"You don't think so?"

"It was dark and…I guess I should get a blood test, eh? HIV, hepatitis, venereal disease, jeez, the whole works."

"Yeah, you probably should. I'm sure everything's fine but just to be safe…"

"Oh, sure, everything's fine. I mean what are the odds of getting anything contagious from a one-night stand with a rock musician who happened to be a heroin junkie?"

"Molly, we did a full blood workup on venereal disease, HIV and hepatitis. They all came up negative," the doctor at the University Student Health Center told Molly in his office.

"However, just to be perfectly safe, I recommend that you get another HIV/AIDS test in three months."

"Thank you, doctor," Molly said in the midst of a long exhale of relief.

"There was one test that showed positive, however. It's standard procedure when we do a workup like this."

"Was it a test for a low IQ?"

"Uh, no," the doctor chuckled and then paused for a second. "Molly, you're pregnant."

Molly felt the sting of ammonia vapors as they burned the tender membranes in her nose. The cool tiles of the floor pressing against her cheek felt soothing until she felt someone lifting her into a chair.

There were sounds around her and the doctor seemed to be speaking but everything was garbled except for the words, "You're pregnant" which kept echoing loudly and clearly in her head.

The first words Molly was able to speak were, "I'm... I'm...are you sure?"

"We ran it three times and got three positives. Here, take a sip of this water."

Molly took the long way on her bike to the equine clinic. It was a beautiful spring day and the grassy areas between buildings were filled with students throwing Frisbees, laying out in the sun and sitting around in circles with friends. Despite being on a campus with over 30,000 students, Molly suddenly felt absolutely isolated.

During the first half of her ride, Molly tried to deal at her recent news from both a logical and an emotional perspective. She was single, pregnant, had $562 dollars in her checking account and had amassed student loans amounting close to the Department of Defense's budget.

She would be receiving her Doctorate of Veterinary Medicine in two months. However, a baby on the way meant no post-doctoral work and no residency.

Logically, emotionally, scientifically, or empirically, it all ended up in the same place... about a block and a half short of the end of the world. When she looked at how a baby would affect her at this stage of her life, there seemed to be only one obvious choice.

Nearing the equine clinic, Molly's thoughts turned to what she meant to the life of the baby. She felt a twinge in her stomach and thought about the embryo inside her that was growing by mitotic leaps and bounds. She sat down on a bench under a tree and shut her eyes. Her father had taught her to close her eyes and listen to the songs of the birds when she was a little girl. It was a farmer's form of meditation, without exotic music and incense, and it always seemed to help Molly see her problems from a different perspective. She sat under the tree for almost fifteen minutes listening to the mantras from the starlings, mockingbirds, scrub jays and finches.

When Molly got up from the bench, instead of riding towards the clinic where she was already late for morning rounds, Molly rode over to the School of Veterinary Medicine administration building and walked into the career guidance office.

"Do you have the DVM job listings in San Diego?" Molly asked.

An elderly woman behind a desk pointed to a stack of thick catalogs on a nearby table.

"DVM positions are in the green notebook — alpha by state, alpha by city."

She found a listing for an Assistant Veterinarian with the Del Mar Thoroughbred Racing Association and took down the information. The pay was one-fourth what she could have made in private practice. The deadline for applicants was three weeks away.

Molly caught the end of rounds and rode her bicycle home, carefully avoiding pot holes and other bumps in the road. She left her bike unlocked and ran up the stairs to her apartment where she put together a package which included her resume, letters of recommendations, an unofficial copy of her undergraduate and vet school transcripts, a copy of her paper which had been published in the Journal of Equine Medicine and a copy of her upcoming paper along with its accepted for publication notice.

She cautiously walked back down the stairs and rode off to the post office.

Had Debbie not been so busy studying for the National Boards Exam, along with everything else on the platter of a vet student preparing to graduate, she would have noticed that Molly was spending more time in the bathroom than normal and that she had changed her breakfast *carte du jour* from Pop Tarts to soda crackers. She would have noticed that Molly had actually stocked their refrigerator with fresh fruits and vegetables. Debbie would have also wondered why

Molly was spending an inordinate amount of time outside on their balcony with her eyes closed listening to the birds.

The call from the head veterinarian representing the Del Mar Thoroughbred Club came two weeks before graduation. He had reviewed Molly's credentials, was highly impressed and was willing to set up an appointment for an interview after graduation.

However, Molly was anxious to begin her job search and begged the doctor to schedule an interview that weekend if it was at all possible. The doctor, surprised and impressed with Molly's perseverance, scheduled an hour on Saturday afternoon for their interview.

Molly's next phone call was to her parents to tell them that she was taking the train from Jack London Square Station in Oakland and would be arriving at the Solana Beach Depot tomorrow around noon. She also told them about the interview with the Del Mar Thoroughbred Club. They were thrilled, both at her spur-of-the-moment visit as well as the possibility of her working one-mile away from their home in Del Mar.

Early Friday morning, Molly packed her pickup truck with a suitcase and four boxes of soda crackers and headed south on Interstate 80.

As she entered the city of Oakland, she spoke to the speck of life that was growing inside her.

"Well, little one, this is where you were conceived. You'll probably have a curious attraction to limos, long drives at night, rock music and Chinese food when you grow up."

Molly blinked to clear the salty sting from her eyes.

"I'm sorry I won't be able to tell you much about your father. I think he was a very nice person and...."

Molly wiped her eyes with the back of her hand so she could see the road ahead.

"...and I think he would have been a wonderful father and would have loved you very much."

Molly had to pull off at the next off ramp to compose herself. She blew her nose, got a cup of decaffeinated coffee from a service station, rolled down both windows and got back on the Interstate.

In Oakland, Molly bought a round-trip ticket to San Diego and boarded an Amtrak train at Jack London Square for the 14-hour trip south.

Bobby and Eleanor Carolina met their daughter at the Solana Beach Depot. It had been almost a year and a half since they had been together as a family and it was a warm and loving reunion.

"There it is," Bobby said as they took the Via de la Valle exit off Interstate 5.

"There's Del Mar Race Track right over there. 'Bout a 30-minute walk from our place. Bring your bike and you can come home every day and have lunch with your mom and me."

Molly had decided that she wasn't going to mention her 'condition' to her parents until the other part of her plan worked out first.

The next morning, they had breakfast at a beachfront café. Molly, using nerves over her upcoming interview as an excuse for an upset stomach, ordered only dry toast and tea.

They walked along the beach holding hands, Molly in the middle between her parents. Molly felt her hand in her father's. It was as though there was a river running between them and she wondered what her life would have been like if that hand had never been there to pick her up, to pat her on the shoulder and to rub her back to put her to sleep after she'd had a bad dream.

It was impossible for her to imagine her life without him. He was so much a part of her. She wondered if she had a right to bring a child into the world without a father.

Molly tried to fight back a surge of tears, broke away and ran towards the surf.

She reached down into an incoming wave and rinsed her face with a handful of cold, salty water.

Molly showed up at her interview with Dr. Richard Klein, Chief Veterinarian for Del Mar Thoroughbred Racing, Inc., thirty minutes early. The door was open but the office was empty when she arrived.

She was surprised by her sudden sense of determination as she anticipated the interview. Molly had always been strong-minded when it came to her own personal goals and achievements. With grades, tests, papers, research, and diagnoses, she had always been demanding of herself. But in her interactions with other people, Molly had always felt more comfortable being a team player.

Sitting in the empty reception area of the vet's office and pretending to read a past issue of *Blood-Horse Magazine,* Molly felt an almost Machiavellian sensation towards getting hired for the job. It was a novel feeling, an aggressive blend of confidence and cunning. She had no idea, even though she was less than a month and a half pregnant, that she was already behaving like a mother. According to her plan, getting this job was critical and she was going to do anything, including altering her personality, if necessary, for that child.

She had certainly altered her wardrobe. Molly was tall and always dressed for comfort, warmth and not to be noticed. For the interview, Molly had curled her hair and spent over twenty minutes doing her make-up. She found an expensive cream suit, cut two inches above her knees, at a designer consignment store, and wore it with a beige camisole and a single strand of pearls Debbie had loaned her. She couldn't remember the last time she had worn nylon stockings.

Molly got out of the chair and checked out her appearance a mirror on the empty receptionist's desk.

"Who is this gorgeous woman?" she whispered, striking a modeling pose.

The front door of the office swung open and a man in his mid-fifties walked into the waiting room.

"Molly Carolina? I'm Dick Klein. Thank you for coming, sorry I'm late."

The head veterinarian for the Del Mar Race Track was wearing untied, high top tennis shoes, red nylon shorts and a Dewey Weber Surf Boards t-shirt. His full head of long, dark hair, slightly graying around the ears, was mussed and damp. He held a surfboard under his right arm. He was slightly taller than Molly with the strong, muscular body of a man half his age.

Molly stuck out her hand.

"Nice to meet you Dr. Klein," Molly smiled, in part out of self-consciousness for being so overdressed and part at her misguided preconception of what she imagined this Dr. Klein was going to look like.

"Come on into my office," he said as he leaned his surfboard up against the wall of the reception room.

Molly followed him into a large office. The walls were covered with photos of famous racehorses and posters of surfers riding huge waves.

Molly quickly scanned the walls in search of his academic certificates although she had already done a background check on his credentials. There were no framed degrees or board certification papers. It was obvious that Dr. Klein was not terribly interested in impressing others.

She noted that her resume, transcripts and monograph from the Journal of International Equine Science were on the top of a ten-inch stack of similar looking folders.

"The competition…" she thought to herself.

"Please sit down, Ms. Carolina," he said as he picked up her file and flopped into a leather chair behind his desk.

"Your academic credentials are impeccable. Let's see, magna cum laude at Arizona; VET-CAT scores are on the moon; you're already published… and these letters of recommendation… are you sure you didn't write them yourself?"

He took her file and tossed it back onto the pile of other applicants. He stared at her with a stern expression.

"I'm, sorry, I can't possibly hire you for this position."

Molly felt her cheeks redden.

"May I ask why not?" she asked in a hoarse voice.

"I can't possibly have someone working around here that's a lot brighter than I am. How would that look?"

Molly didn't know how to respond until Dr. Klein burst into a smile.

"I'm just kidding. Well, I'm kidding about not hiring you but I'm dead serious about your being smarter than I am. You're a real gem. How come you're not going into private practice? You know what this job pays?"

Molly quickly regained her composure.

"Yes, I know exactly what the job pays and you should be ashamed."

Dr. Klein barked out a laugh.

"But I want to work with thoroughbreds and I'd like to work here."

"Could be a bad career move, Molly. Can I call you Molly?"

"I don't think so...I mean about the career move. Yes, of course, you can call me Molly."

"What do you need to know about this job?" he asked.

"When do I start?" she answered.

Dr. Klein laughed again.

"Well, I've got this stack of other applicants..."

"Dr. Klein, I'm usually not this frank or forward but I really want this job and I think I'd be pretty good at it. I worked with horses from Golden Gate and Bay Meadows at Davis. I'm a good student and a hard worker. Plus, I fit right in with the dress code."

They both laughed at themselves.

"You know you're over qualified for this job, Molly?"

"Yes, sir, perhaps. With all due respect, Dr. Klein, so are you. I've read your work and I'm aware of your academic background.

"Touché," he smiled. "So, you want me to hire you right now without interviewing any other candidates?"

"Yes. Hire me today and go back surfing."

Dr. Klein got up from his chair and walked out of his office without saying a word leaving Molly alone in her chair.

Molly panicked. Thoughts raced through her head like, "I was probably too aggressive. I should never have suggested that he not interview the other candidates. I can't believe I told him he was overqualified!"

This new Molly, she feared, had blown her chance at the job.

She put her hand over her tummy as if to console the tiny clump of replicating cells inside her.

Molly heard Dr. Klein's voice from the reception room. She got up, tried to shake the disappointment from her face, and walked out of the office. Dr. Klein was standing in the reception room holding his surfboard.

"Okay, you're hired. I'm going surfing. When do you get out of school?"

She was so happy, the old Molly slipped back into her persona and she leaped in the air, forgetting that she was wearing high heels. Molly winced as her right ankle turned and rolled off her shoe when she landed.

"June twelfth," she said, wincing through the pain.

"Great. Get down here as soon as you can. Start studying for the California State Boards and…"

Dr. Klein pointed at her as he opened the door of his pickup truck, "You're going to have to lower your standard of dress around here."

Dr. Klein drove off, his surfboard dangling over the end of the tailgate of his truck.

Molly took off her shoes and limped across the parking lot. She climbed into her father's truck, made sure that the windows were up and that there was no one around and screamed, "Yes! We got the job!"

Somehow, she had pulled off the first part of her plan. She started the truck and began to go over the second half of the plan as she drove back to her parent's home.

Molly limped into the living room, high heels in her hand.

Her mom looked up from her magazine, "Looks like that was a tough interview."

"How come you never taught me how to walk in high heels?"

"I don't think you ever owned a pair of high heels. How did it go?"

Molly stared up at the ceiling, feigning deep contemplation for dramatic effect.

"I got the job!" she yelled. "I got the job and I start right after graduation!"

"That's great, Molly! Good for you! Heck, good for us all, huh, Bobby?" her mom crowed.

Wearing a big smile, her dad got out of his chair, walked over and gave her a kiss on the forehead.

"We're proud of you, Molly," he whispered. "You want some ice for that ankle?"

"And a couple of ibuprofens if you've got some. Uh, no, never mind the ibuprofen," Molly answered. "Just some ice, please, Dad."

Molly took a deep breath.

"Mom…Dad…I've got some more news."

"What's that, Molly?" her mother asked, straightening up the newspapers that were scattered over the top of the coffee table.

"I'm pregnant."

The first response to her latest news was the sound of an ice tray crashing on the kitchen floor.

"You're what?" both parents asked in unison.

"I'm pregnant," Molly repeated softly.

"How far…?" her mother whispered.

"Just about two months."

"Tell me about the father," her dad asked.

"Well, uh, he's a musician…he was a musician"

"Was a musician?" Bobby asked. "What's he do now?"

Molly took another long, deep breath knowing this was going to be the most difficult part of her plan.

"He died. It was an accident. But he was a wonderful guy.

"Wait a minute," her mom interrupted. "Let's start this over again, right from the beginning. Molly, you're pregnant?"

Eleanor stopped and let her words hover over the room like the pelicans soaring over the ocean outside their window.

"Are you absolutely sure?" Eleanor asked in a calm manner.

"Oh, yes. I'm positive," Molly sighed.

"Okay," Eleanor paused. "So how do you feel about being pregnant, Molly?"

"Well, at first I thought it was the end of the world. But lately I've been getting these feelings that, I don't know, that it might be the beginning of a different kind of world."

What had begun as a thin smile on Eleanor Carolina's face burst into a broad grin.

"You're going to have a baby! I think it's wonderful!"

244

Her mom clapped her hands together and sailed across the room. Tears streamed down her face as she hugged Molly.

"Of course, it's the beginning, honey. It's the beginning of an incredibly wonderful world!"

Eleanor squeezed Molly's hand in hers and they both looked expectantly over at Bobby.

Bobby Carolina's head was still buzzing with the part about the father of his grandchild being a dead musician. His thoughts came to him like a chain reaction of cars rear-ending one another after an interstate accident. Bobby knew Molly had set lofty goals for herself. Those goals included post-graduate work. He knew that trying to continue her education as a single mom would be extremely difficult. He thought about how hard she had worked in school and now, because of the baby, she was settling for a position with a race track instead of private practice. His last thought was how do you raise a baby without a father?

Bobby stared at his daughter's face and recognized a look in her eyes he had seen before. As a child, Molly had always been frank and forthright. When she would come upon a situation that she didn't understand or if she had done something and the consequences of her actions weren't clear, she would come to him, explain her problem or dilemma openly and honestly, and then wait patiently for his answer.

Her delicate innocence and absolute trust had always touched him deeply and so deserved more than a simple, knee-jerk, flippant answer. He had always made it a practice to honor her trust with a sincere and well-thought-out response.

Molly was now looking at him with that same innocent expression.

As Bobby sifted through his thoughts, he realized that the only absolute fact that existed in the whole mess of fears, worries, loss and sacrifice, was that his daughter is having a baby. When he thought only about Molly having a baby and eliminated the 'would haves' and 'could haves', he discovered a warm, resonant feeling deep within himself.

Bobby smiled at his daughter.

"Honey, if that child is anything like you, you're the luckiest person in the world. I think it's wonderful, Molly."

Molly started to cry, which set off her mother's tears and when her father joined them in a three-way hug, every cheek in the huddle was drenched and every kiss tasted wet and salty.

When all the noses had been blown and the cheeks dried, a small mountain of rumpled tissues rose atop the coffee table.

"Would it be all right if I moved in with you guys until I had the baby and got my feet on the ground?"

"Of course!" Eleanor exclaimed. "You can have the second bedroom and we can make the office into a nursery. Bobby, we're going to have a baby in our lives!"

"Thank you, but Mom, I'm not even out of my first trimester. Let's make sure it's going to take before you renovate the whole house. But, thank you, thank you…". Molly started to cry again and reached for the tissue box.

"God, I'm so emotional!" Molly laughed through her tears. "Thank you for loving me."

She looked down at her stomach, "For loving us."

Molly took the train to Oakland and drove back to Davis.

"I got the job!" Molly yelled as she walked into the apartment.

Debbie was vacuuming the living room and jumped when she heard Molly's voice. She turned off the vacuum.

"You scared the crap out of me! What did you say?"

"I got the job."

"The job at the race track? The Assistant Vet position at Del Mar?"

"Yep," Molly beamed.

"Uh, that's great. What about your post-doc? What about your oncology research?"

"I can always do that later."

"Right. Wait a minute, you're going be a Vet at a race track, right? Hmmm, do you realize that all you have to do is juice one horse. You and I bet the ranch on him and all our student loans are paid off. Okay, I see where you're going with this."

They both smiled.

"Where are you going to live down there?"

"I'm going to stay with my parents for a while. They live less than a mile from the race track. And... I'm going to have my baby there."

Debbie cocked her head sideways.

"You're going to have your what?"

"My baby."

"Your baby? Aren't you skipping a few things like meeting a guy, getting married, buying a house, getting divorced, getting the house, meeting another guy...you know, those kinds of things?"

"Well, yes. At least most of them."

Molly grinned as she walked into the kitchen to pour herself a glass of juice.

Debbie stood frozen in the center of the living room; her hand locked in a death grip around the handle of the vacuum. Her eyes narrowed into a suspicious gaze and she stomped after Molly into the kitchen.

"No!" Debbie screamed.

"Yes," Molly answered in a nonchalant voice.

"No!"

"Yes."

"Oh my God! Greg, the bass player?"

"One for one. I'm batting a thousand as they say in baseball," Molly laughed. She couldn't believe that she was actually laughing about being pregnant.

Debbie staggered backwards, tripped over the vacuum cleaner and landed on the sofa.

"Oh my God, Molly! You're going have a baby! I'm gonna be an aunt!"

The last six weeks before graduation flew by quickly with Debbie doting on Molly like an overprotective mother. Debbie wouldn't let Molly lift anything heavy, cooked healthy meals and gained six, 'sympathetic pregnancy' pounds.

Following commencement exercises, the graduating Doctors of Veterinary Medicine held their traditional 'Woodsy Celebration' up in the foothills overlooking the campus. There were two kegs of beer, a case of Jose Cuervo tequila, a local band, a few tears and a lot of promises to stay in touch.

After Molly had said her goodbyes at the party, she walked over to Debbie and put her arm around her.

"Would you mind being a godmother?"

Debbie burst into tears and the two best friends hugged and cried.

"L.A's only 100 miles from Del Mar," Debbie blubbered. "Tell your parents to put a roll-away in your room."

Molly drove back to her apartment and finished packing. She looked at the small stack of clothes, keepsakes and books. With the exception of what she was carrying inside her, everything she had accumulated over the past four years fit easily on the passenger seat of her truck.

Debbie eventually took a position with an animal hospital in Brentwood, not far from the UCLA campus where Brad was continuing his studies in Optometry. True to her promise, Debbie visited Molly on her days off and became a second daughter to the Carolinas.

On her first day of work at Del Mar, Molly informed Dr. Klein that she was three-months pregnant and asked him if her condition jeopardized her ability to perform the job.

"Is it mine?" he asked feigning alarm.

"No, you were acquitted by the DNA test,"

"Well then, I have no problems. Just don't lift any horses until after you have the baby. Congratulations, by the way."

On December 12, 1989, Molly gave birth to a seven-pound, nine-ounce, twenty-one-inch-long, healthy baby girl whom she named, Sarah Twain Carolina.

Molly would work with Dr. Klein at the Del Mar Race Track for five years until offered a lucrative position as Head Veterinarian for an owner/breeder of a large stable in nearby Rancho Santa Fe.

She continued her studies and research in equine lameness, became a board-certified equine practitioner and eventually opened one of the most successful and respected, large animal orthopedic treatment centers on the West Coast.

True to form, Molly was busy with her work and spent all her free time with her daughter. When Sarah turned five years old, Molly bought a house in Carlsbad, three blocks from the beach, and around the corner from Pine Elementary School.

# *Chapter 18*
# The War Is Over!

WHEN GENERAL DOUGLAS MACARTHUR ENTERED TOKYO on September 8, 1945, one month after a pair of atomic bombs had incinerated 150,000 people and obliterated the cities of Hiroshima and Nagasaki, the deadliest war in history was over. The United States and its allies had re-righted the world and crushed the verminous enemies of freedom and democracy.

Nathan's last scheduled show with the Foxhole Circuit was on the Fourth of July, 1945, on Okinawa, site of the final amphibious landing of the war. The island had been captured only twelve days earlier and the show was canceled at the last minute due to the presence of Japanese snipers stubbornly defending their lost cause to the death.

The transport plane carrying the movie stars, singers, dancers, musicians and stagehands, along with their equipment, turned around on Saipan and headed back to the States stopping to fuel in Wake Island and once more at Pearl Harbor.

By the end of 1945, the war was over. The troops were coming home and America was ready to dance and... (more babies were born in 1946 than ever before: 3.4 million).

Nathan had gained a reputation as an accomplished guitar player among the band leaders and other musicians he had played with on his many USO tours and had no trouble finding work when he got back home.

Freddie Martin offered Nathan his full-time job back and several other big band leaders had offered him a seat, but big bands toured and Nathan was done traveling. After the aborted Okinawa show, Nathan took his worn and tattered suitcase and set it out with the Monday morning trash. He had logged well over 100,000 miles in every type of transportation imaginable and that was enough of the road for Nathan.

The Swing Era was coming to an end. Bebop, a new jazz genre featuring small ensembles led by the likes of Dizzy Gillespie and Charlie Parker, blossomed on the music scene. While there were fewer musicians in each of the groups, the number of bands and the opportunities to play had greatly increased. Nathan's versatility and ability to adapt to all kinds of music kept his date book full.

The work was steady and the pay was union scale. Travel to the dates was short and there was no one shooting at anybody. Nathan felt he had given the best he could to the soldiers who fought during the war. Now he had the good fortune to help them celebrate. Nathan couldn't have been more content.

Nathan also found himself in the center of a sort of musical renaissance. People from all over the United States had migrated to California to find work in the defense plants. Soldiers, fresh from being mustered out of the service up and down the West Coast, also decided to make California their home.

These transplants and their families brought their music from home with them. On a warm evening you could take a long walk through any neighborhood and hear country and western, gospel, bebop, blues, boogie woogie, folk music, mountain music, jazz, Latin, ragtime, bluegrass, and Dixieland music drifting through the curtains of open windows.

The music in and around Los Angeles was as varied and eclectic as the growing population of immigrants putting down payments on houses and nailing their old, out-of-state license plates on the cross beams of their garages.

Small clubs and juke joints sprouted up like dandelions. On Tuesday night, Nathan would be playing bebop in four-four time. On Wednesday night, he'd be playing mambos and sambas in six-eight.

The only night that stayed blank in Nathan's date book was Thursday. Every Thursday night, Nathan appeared at 'Lefty's', a small club in Santa Monica on Wilshire Boulevard, owned by Ken 'Pete' Petersen.

Petersen was the soldier who had lost his left arm in the attack on Pearl Harbor and whom Nathan had strummed guitar with on the bus parked outside the Hollywood Canteen the night Nathan and Lieutenant Joleen Salveson collided on the sidewalk.

Nathan brought Petersen a trumpet the day he came to the Veterans Hospital anticipating a luncheon engagement with the young nurse that had torn his tuxedo, skinned his elbows and left a deep and lasting bruise on his heart.

Despite Lieutenant Salveson's disappearance somewhere in Australia, Nathan and Petersen continued their relationship and eventually became best of friends. Nathan encouraged Petersen to continue practicing on the trumpet by telling him stories of his old friend and bandmate, Wingy Mignon, the one-armed trumpet player. Between his travels with the USO tours, Nathan would bring some of the best trumpet players in the Los Angeles music business to the VA Hospital to give Petersen lessons.

After each lesson, Nathan would spend the day losing money to Petersen in gin rummy and talking about the war and Nathan's experiences with the Foxhole Circuit.

Although the incisions on the stump of Petersen's amputated left arm had long healed, his struggle to walk away from the safety and security of the hospital and face the world with an empty sleeve, was difficult for the proud, young man.

Fun-loving, friendly and sharp-witted with the doctors, nurses and other patients, Petersen was one person in the hospital and another in public. His outgoing personality would shrink whenever Nathan lured him out of the hospital for a cold beer and lunch at a nearby restaurant or bar. Nathan had witnessed E. Tim and Wingy become withdrawn in public places, even though they had lived with their disabilities almost all their lives. He wondered how long, if ever, it would take Petersen to overcome his self-consciousness and summon the courage to leave the hospital.

Petersen shied from people outside of the hospital but he loved to ride around in Nathan's car. Petersen would roll down the window and whistle at all the girls and wave at people on the street, so Nathan always made it a point to pick a spot for their lunches that was located some distance from the hospital.

On one of Nathan's breaks between tours during the war, he and Petersen visited a little greasy spoon in Santa Monica called 'Harry and Mickey's'. It had been highly recommended by the drummer in Freddie Martin's Band who had sworn to Nathan that they served the best cheeseburgers in all of Southern California.

Harry and Mickey's was small, dark, and completely empty when Nathan and Petersen walked in at twelve-thirty in the afternoon. There was a bar with six stools that faced into an open kitchen. Six, wooden tables filled up the rest of the place. They looked around at the empty room and sat down at a table near the back. Alone and in the dim light of the bar, Petersen relaxed.

"Anybody home?" Petersen called out.

A thin, tired-looking woman in her mid-thirties wearing a dirty, white apron approached their table.

"What can I get you boys?" she asked in a rich, syrupy, hillbilly accent.

Petersen spoke right up. "We'd like a couple of cheeseburgers and two cold beers, please ma'am."

"Got no meat and alls we got is Brew 102 on tap," the woman said dryly.

Petersen looked over at Nathan, "I thought you said this place served the best cheeseburger in town?"

"Not any more, hon," she answered.

"You sure this is the right place, Nathan?"

Nathan looked up at the waitress, "This is Harry and Mickey's right?"

"Well, sort of..."

"Sort of?" Petersen asked. "Is Harry here?"

"Nope, Harry was my husband. He got drafted into the Army and was killed somewhere I can't even pronounce in France."

"I'm sorry for your loss, ma'am," Petersen said softly.

"Me, too," Nathan added.

"How about Mickey?" Peterson asked.

"You're looking at what's left of her."

She noticed Petersen's empty sleeve, "How'd you lose that arm?"

"Uh, Pearl Harbor."

"Well, God bless you. You boys got ambushed for sure but I hear you put up a helluva fight."

Petersen winced.

"Would you like to sit down, Mickey?" Nathan asked pulling out a chair and subconsciously slipping back into his southern accent.

"You look a might tired."

"Well, what'll I do with all the rest of the customers?" she asked, sarcastically looking around at the empty room.

"Things tough since your husband went off?" Petersen asked.

Mickey pinched a cigarette out of a pack of Lucky Strikes in her apron pocket. When she struck the match to light the cigarette, Nathan and Petersen both noticed that her fingernails were bitten down almost to the quick. Through the cloud of exhaled smoke, she nodded.

"Tough? Yep, pretty damn tough."

Mickey put the cigarette down in an ashtray on the table and walked over to the bar. She returned to the table with three beers and sat down.

"I usually don't start drinking 'til after closing but being as I'm with a genuine war hero here, I reckon I can make an exception today."

"You mind if I ask what happened to your business?" Petersen asked.

"Why not? I asked what happened to your arm didn't I?" she smiled.

Petersen smiled back at her.

"Well, we were doing pretty good with this little place. Harry sold the farm back in Paducah, Kentucky and we come out here and opened this little cafe. Harry worked the bar and I did the cookin'.

There wasn't much call for crawdads and collard greens, so we started cooking hamburgers."

"So, you did serve the best burgers in town at one time?" Nathan asked.

"Well, I don't know if they were the best, but folks sure seemed to like 'em. The secret was in my mama's roadkill sauce. Squirrel, possum, coon, rabbit, hell, even a neighborhood dog would get run over, you cook it up with my mama's sauce and it's pretty damn tasty. 'Course we only used ground beef here, not a lot of road kill on Wilshire Boulevard, but I'd mix it with mama's road kill sauce. Gave the meat a particular flavor that people seemed to favor."

"Then your husband got drafted?" Nathan asked.

"Well, the war was coming like a nasty old bear crawling out of hibernation and Harry happened to be walkin' right by the front door of the cave. I think I'd a made it without Harry if it weren't for that damned Beaudrow."

"Beaudrow?" Nathan and Petersen both asked at the same time.

"Yea, Harry's good-for-nothin' cousin came out to help run the bar and do the paper work when Harry got called. While I was in the kitchen cookin', Beaudrow was drinking up the inventory and using his pockets as the cash register."

"He was stealing from his own cousin?" Peterson asked.

"Beaudrow'd steal from his blind mama begging on the corner if she only had a nickel left in her tin cup."

"Is Beaudrow still around?" Nathan asked.

"Hell, no. He dropped out of sight when them buzzard bill collectors started circling. It's my own fault. I never should've trusted him."

"So, what's going to happen to you?" Petersen asked.

She carefully brushed the ashes off the tip of her cigarette on the edge of the ashtray.

"Well, someday, two nice young boys are going to walk in here and offer me a train ticket back to Kentucky, a ride to the station, and two hundred dollars cash money. I'm gonna go upstairs, there's a nice apartment up there that comes with the place, pack my suitcase, and I'll leave them with mama's roadkill sauce recipe along with five months back rent, a stack of bills and everything else that goes along with this place."

She leaned back, took a long drag from her cigarette and chased it with a swig of beer.

"And you know what I'd name it if I were those guys?"

"What?" Nathan asked.

She stared directly at Petersen.

"I'd call it Lefty's."

Two months later following their lunch that day, minority investor, Nathan O'Shea, owner and proprietor, Ken 'Pete' Petersen, and Mr. Charles Wonderlick from the Santa Monica Bank watched from the sidewalk on Wilshire Boulevard as a sign painter whitewashed over the name 'Harry and Mickey's' and replaced it with 'Lefty's'.

With his savings, monthly disability checks, and an occasional transfusion of cash from Nathan along with a growing customer base comprised of locals and patients from the Veterans Hospital, 'Pete' Petersen, or 'Lefty' as he soon became known, managed to keep the doors open and his head above water during the waning war years.

When the war finally came to an end, 'Lefty's' business boomed. When a sewing machine repair shop next door went out of business, Nathan and Pete knocked down the wall between the two spaces and expanded their business. They added a stage and a dance floor surrounded by tables and booths.

Friday and Saturday nights were always crowded but on Thursday nights, there was a line outside the door and halfway down the block. Thursday night was 'Jam Session Night' and the band was always a surprise. Lefty's Director of Entertainment was Nathan O'Shea who recruited and invited all the musicians not working that night to sit in.

The food was good and booze for the band was free so Nathan had little trouble attracting some of the best players in Los Angeles to jam with him at Lefty's on Thursday nights. The musicians liked the casual and friendly atmosphere. They could interact with the crowd, play whatever they felt like playing, try out new songs and eat and drink all night for free. The only house rule established by Nathan was that during the last set of the night, owner/proprietor, 'Lefty' Petersen, was summoned to report to the stage with his trumpet. The musicians had a great deal of respect for the wounded veteran and the crowd loved it when he got up on stage in his apron, cracked a few 'one-armed man jokes', and played his heart out when it was his turn to solo with the band.

Late one Thursday night, after chasing the customers out and locking the doors, Nathan and Pete were having a cup of coffee and talking about baseball when Nathan happened to glance at a bundle of mail that was jammed in Peterson's shirt pocket. Nathan cocked his head sideways. Suddenly his eyes opened wide and his jaw dropped.

"What?" Petersen asked, startled by Nathan's expression. "You okay, Nathan? What the hell's the matter with you? "

Dumbfounded, Nathan could barely speak. He could only point at Petersen's pocket.

"That's her…that's her," Nathan muttered.

Petersen turned around in his chair and looked behind him thinking Nathan was pointing towards someone who may still be in the club.

"Come on, Nathan, you're starting to give me the heebie jeebies. Who are you talking about?"

A plain, white envelope happened to be at the front of the stack of bills, notices and other mail that Petersen had stuffed into his pocket earlier in the afternoon and had forgotten to put in the office. Nathan stared at the return address on the front envelope. It read, 'Joleen Salveson, 364 Emerald Street, Apt. 2, Coronado Island, California'.

Petersen, finally realizing what Nathan was looking at, pulled the stack of mail out of his pocket and looked curiously at the top envelope.

"Joleen Salveson…Joleen Salveson… Hey, wasn't she the nurse…" Petersen stopped.

His face swelled up into a wide grin.

"Wasn't that the girl you used to have it bad for O'Shea?"

"That's her! And she's here in California, down in San Diego! I can't believe it. What's she writing you about, Pete?"

"Got me. This is the first I've heard from her since the VA. Let's open it up and find out."

"Don't tear the address on the envelope!" Nathan blurted. "Here, let me open it with my pocket knife."

"It's my letter," Pete teased, holding it away from Nathan.

"Give me that!"

Nathan grabbed the letter and stared at the return address. He ran his fingers over the ink as if trying to feel Joleen's hand through her script. He slit open the envelope with the care and precision of a surgeon and handed the neatly folded letter to Pete.

While Pete read the letter, Nathan turned the envelope over and over in his hands like a prospector who had just uncovered a monstrous, gold nugget. He brought the empty envelope up to his nose when he was confident Petersen wasn't looking and tried to see if there was a trace of the perfume he had smelled and never forgotten when they collided on the sidewalk.

"What's the letter say, Pete?"

"Whoa…" Petersen whistled out a breathy exhale as he read the letter to himself.

"What?" Nathan demanded.

"She says she was taken prisoner by the Japs on Corregidor."

"You're kidding."

"No, for a couple of years, she says."

"Oh, my God!"

"And listen to this, she wants to apologize for taking us to the USO that night. Boy oh boy."

"Can I read it?" Nathan pleaded.

"Yea, sure," Pete answered and drifted off to the distant memories of that night in the bus outside the Hollywood Canteen and a vague recollection of himself, a person he had left behind what seemed like a long time ago.

Before he even read a word, Nathan looked at the letter as though the stationary were a canvas and Joleen's handwriting the work of a revered artist. Past memories of their brief but lasting encounter suddenly became clear and vivid, brought into the present by the curves and swirls of her delicate handwriting.

After his devout moment of grace, Nathan read the letter.

"Looks like you better write her back, Pete," Nathan spoke quietly as he handed him back the letter. "I'll go get a pen and some paper."

"Nate, it's two o'clock in the morning!"

"Perfect time to write important letters," Nathan called from the office.

Nathan returned with a pad of paper and a pen and dropped them on the table in front of Petersen. Nathan sat down, folded his arms across his chest, leaned forward, and stared across the table.

"Start writing."

"I suppose you're planning on hand delivering my response to her letter?" Peterson smiled

"That's absolutely correct, Mr. Petersen. Special delivery. Very special delivery. Now, if you would begin writing, please."

After a near sleepless night, Nathan got an early start for San Diego the next morning. It had been almost five years since he had made the drive from Los Angeles to San Diego and he marveled at the vast difference in circumstances. The morning sun lit a bright path down the Pacific Coast Highway as opposed to his harrowing trips hauling gasoline in the dark of night on bald, skin-thin tires and battling fog with only the weak glow of his 'dim-out lights' to show him the narrow ribbon that lay between the pavement and the possibility of a fiery crash.

But it was difficult for Nathan to dwell too long on the perils of his past when his present journey held such promise. If his vision was once impaired from the cab of a gasoline tanker truck at the beginning of the war, on that clear Southern California day behind the wheel of his shiny, black 1938 Ford coupe, he was a helpless romantic, this time blinded and smitten by a single, chance encounter.

Nathan arrived in San Diego just before noon and drove onto the ferry bound for Coronado. He spent the entire time sitting in his car during the short crossing re-combing his hair and straightening out the wrinkles in his suit. The crisp ocean breeze evaporated the beads of nervous perspiration that kept sprouting up on his forehead.

The envelope with Joleen's address rested on the seat next to Nathan. He had memorized it the second he'd first seen it sticking out of Pete's pocket in Lefty's but he kept glancing over at it to make sure the numbers had not mysteriously changed during his voyage across San Diego Bay.

Nathan drove off the ferry onto the Coronado Ferry Landing and parked his car in front of a clothing store on First Street. He purchased a new shirt, his own damp with nervous perspiration, and got directions from the clerk to Joleen's apartment.

It turned out that Joleen's apartment building was less than a mile away from the ferry landing. But he needed a little more time for his *'hope for the best'* to overcome his *'fear of the worst'* so he drove around the neighborhood several times until he felt that he was ready.

Three-sixty-four Emerald Street was a neatly kept, two-story, four-unit apartment building. A dark green lawn of well-tended dichondra grass spread from the sidewalk to a small border at the edge of the building where spindly stemmed rose bushes gushed with gaudy, colorful flowers.

The cement walkway that bisected the lawn was painted a deep, brick red. The sidewalk was so shiny and polished that Nathan had to check the bottom of his shoes to make sure he had not walked over wet paint.

Joleen's apartment was upstairs. Nathan counted each of the sixteen, carpeted steps to himself and straightened his coat and tie for the last time as he stood facing the door.

Nathan had even deliberated on the appropriate number of knocks he should make on Joleen's door. He had decided that three knocks would be proper. One or two, he argued with himself, might seem too familiar or may not even be heard. Any more knocks than four might be alarming or seem too aggressive. He was confident that three knocks would be just right.

As he raised his hand to knock, suddenly his memory replayed the scene of the last time he saw her. Nathan was waving to the men on the VA bus from the sidewalk when Joleen stuck her head out of the door as the bus.

"Maybe we could have lunch tomorrow," she said as the driver started the engine. "At the Veterans Hospital on Wilshire."

"That would be swell!" he yelled back. "That would be swell!

Nathan shook his head to bring himself back from the past and his task at hand. He knocked three times and immediately looked down at his feet. He had come up with the head down position because he was afraid that if Joleen opened the door and he first looked into her eyes, his mind could go blank and he might forget his carefully rehearsed introductory remarks. Looking down at the door sill would also give him a moment to deal with the possibility of crushing disappointment should a man in his underwear come to the door instead of Joleen.

He gingerly held Peterson's letter in both of his trembling, perspiring hands.

Nathan heard the door unlock and watched the door knob turn. As the door opened, he whistled a subtle sigh of relief when his eyes captured the sight of two fuzzy, pink bedroom slippers with two, definitely feminine, legs protruding from each.

Joleen opened the door wider and stared at the top of Nathan's head which was still facing down at his shoes.

"Yes? Can I help you?"

As Nathan glanced up at her, he felt as though he might lose his balance and tip over.

He looked into her face. It had changed some from what his memory had been clinging to all these years, but it was as breathtaking and strikingly beautiful as he had remembered. The sunlight flooding through a large bay window behind her outlined her blond hair with a radiant aura. Her eyes were the color of the blue waters of the Pacific Ocean that danced in the distance.

Before Nathan could deliver his much-practiced opening lines, something remarkable and completely unexpected happened.

Standing there on Joleen's doorstep and staring into her face, Nathan began to weep. He was shocked and embarrassed as he stood there helpless while tears leaked down his cheeks.

Thoughts and visions of E. Tim falling off the stage, the many wounded and dying soldiers he spent time with in the hospitals he had visited with the USO tours during the war and the horrors he had imagined of Joleen's imprisonment by the Japanese flashed across his mind. The more he tried to stop the tears the more he wept.

"Are you okay, young man?" she asked bending over to look up into Nathan's contorted face. He noticed that her words were delivered in a slow, deliberate manner.

Aside to the reader: *Joline spent months undergoing speech therapy during her stay at the Balboa Naval Hospital in San Diego. She continued to practice her enunciation when she was released. D's and T's were particularly difficult for her. "Thank you" came out as "haink you" and the word "dear" as "ear". Words with the letter 'L', which required a tip of the tongue to the roof of the mouth, could also be challenging.*

*However, being the only daughter and witness to the State of Minnesota's most successful husband and wife, high school football coaching brain trust, Joleen learned that if the opponent took away their outside running attack, call plays that attacked the middle of the defense. Also, having lived through barracuda attacks, drowning and torture at the hands of the Japanese army, struggling with a few consonants wasn't going to be too difficult for Joleen.*

*Her game plan started with introducing herself to others as Jo. That took care of one 'L'.*

*Her next play was to store a Thesaurus of synonyms in her memory to replace words that she struggled with like "dinner" which would come out as "inner". "Supper" just required a hiss through her front teeth and a pucker of her lips.*

*"Merci" replaced "thank you" in her vocabulary and even added a sort of international mystique to her persona along with the possibility, in the listener's mind, that English may not be her first language.*

*In other cases, she could just throw away a tongue-tying 'T' like the word "breakfuss". Even people with full-length tongues didn't bother to pronounce the 't' in "breakfast".*

*With the combination of her slower cadenced speech (giving her time to search through her library of synonyms) and her native Scandinavian inflection, her accent took on an almost southern regional drawl.*

Nathan took a deep breath and cleared his throat.

"I'm so sorry. I always get these terrible allergies this time of year. Hay fever, you know?"

Joleen stared at Nathan curiously as he wiped his eyes with his handkerchief.

"I have a letter addressed to 364 Emerald Street for a Miss…"

Nathan paused, waiting for the dreaded man in his underwear to appear behind her in doorway.

Joleen gave him an encouraging nod.

"…Joleen Salvesen. Is that you?"

"Uh huh," she answered, her curiosity rising around this strange man.

"He doesn't seem very threatening," she thought to herself.

Nathan wiped the sweat off his forehead with his handkerchief.

"Could I have a glass of water, Miss Salvesen?"

"Of course."

Joleen opened the door and motioned for Nathan to come inside.

Nathan heard her odd pronunciation but it didn't capture his attention. He was too concerned with regaining his own composure after his embarrassing performance in the doorway.

"Thank you," he stammered.

Nathan walked into her apartment and was immediately taken by the number of vases filled with fresh cut flowers. The walls of her living room were painted bright yellow and the flowers were of every color imaginable. He had never been in a cheerier room.

"How about a glass of lemonade?" she called from the kitchen.

"That would be terrific," Nathan answered, thinking that something cold might help prevent another tearful outburst.

Joleen came back into the living room carrying two glasses.

"Maybe you have hay fever," she said handing the glass to Nathan.

"Probably. I think I'm better now. I get these sudden attacks every once in a while, then they disappear.

"Maybe I should move…," Joleen said picking up one of the vases.

No, no! These flowers are beautiful. I've never seen a flower like this one. Is it real?"

"It's an orchid… for an old friend…from the war."

Nathan took a sip of the most bitter lemonade he had ever tasted. He turned his head so that Joleen wouldn't see his eyes watering again.

He wiped his eyes with his handkerchief and cleared his throat.

"I have a letter for you. It's from Ken Petersen. He was one of your patients at the VA."

Nathan handed Joleen the letter and felt his pulse race briefly as their fingers brushed against one another.

Joleen looked at the damp, tear-stained envelope. She noticed that there was no postage affixed to the letter and looked up curiously at Nathan.

"No, I'm not with the Post Office. I'm a friend of Pete's and I happened to be coming down here on business anyway so I promised him that I'd deliver it to you in person."

"Very nice of you, Mister …?"

"O'Shea. Nathan, er, Nate O'Shea, ma'am."

"I'm Jo. Please sit down, Nate O'Shea."

Nathan noticed that she had omitted the 't' in her pronunciation of his first name.

Joleen looked thoughtfully at Nathan for several seconds. He sat down on the sofa and almost slid off from the plastic slipcover covering the sofa, hitting his shins against the sharp edge of the coffee table.

"This lemonade is very, very… refreshing," he spoke up, nervously trying to break the silence of her stare and rubbing his bruised shins.

"Good," Joleen answered. "You, okay?"

"It's just a nick," Nathan winced while rubbing his shin.

Joleen sat down at the dining room table and opened the letter.

Nathan allowed himself to cast his full attention upon her while she read Petersen's letter but after a few moments he was forced to look away. His whole body seemed to ache and his chest felt as though it was being crushed by his pounding heart.

He got up from the sofa and walked over to the window

"She doesn't know me from Adam," he silently lamented to the unsympathetic ocean in the distance.

Joleen finished reading the letter and smiled. "Sounds like he's doing well. I'm so happy for him."

"Yes, he's doing great."

"You are friends?" she asked folding the letter and putting it back into the envelope.

"Yes, we are. Pete's been out of the service for quite a while now. Most of us just call him 'Lefty'. We own a business together."

Joleen shrugged her shoulders and giggled. "Lefty, that's funny."

"He lost his right arm in the war…Pearl Harbor."

"Yes, I remember. I was his nurse for a while at the Veterans Hospital."

"I know, he told me a lot about you."

"Oh? I remember he was having some struggles in the hospital," Joleen said softly. "I was concerned."

"Me, too," Nathan answered. "But he managed to work his way through most of them."

"How?" Joleen asked.

"How?"

"Yes, how did he heal? How did get over his handicap? Do you know?"

"Well, like a lot of the guys, he had a lot of ghosts he had to clear out of his attic from Pearl Harbor and he had to learn how to live with only one arm. He also had a hard time with people staring and feeling sorry for him, as I guess anybody would, huh?"

Joleen nodded and seemed to be looking right through Nathan.

"How did he get over his handicap?" she asked.

"Well, he once told me that humility was the greatest healer in the world. First, he said, he came to the realization that one man couldn't have won or lost the war all by himself. That sounds pretty simple but I think it's a lot more complicated than most of us think. For a long while, he said he was seeing everything through that morning in December. Every day he woke up he was being attacked by the Japs again."

"Then one day he was listening to a World Series game on the radio between the Yankees and the Dodgers. Pete is a fierce Yankee fan. Well, the Dodgers beat up on the Yanks pretty bad that day and Pete was down in the dumps and grousing around when it hit him that a person can't connect who they are with things that happened to them that they couldn't necessarily do anything about. I think he realized that there was nothing he could've done that could have changed the outcome of that ballgame and somehow that same train of thought carried through to his feelings about Pearl Harbor."

Joleen got up from the sofa and walked over to the bay window. She stared through the glass and then turned to Nathan and smiled.

"Good for him," Joleen said as she walked back into the living room and sat down. "How about his arm?"

She was close enough for him to smell her subtle, clean scent. He wasn't sure whether it was perfume, soap, shampoo, or lotion but whatever the fragrance was, it stirred his senses and muddled his concentration. He took a sip of the bitter lemonade to shock his attention back to the conversation at hand.

"I'm sorry, what about Pete?"

"His amputated arm. How is he doing with that?"

"Oh, his arm. It sure doesn't seem to bother him much. He never complains, although once in a while he gets these strange sensations that make him feel as though the arm is still there. It certainly hasn't slowed him down any. You're probably not going to believe this, I'm not sure that I can believe it, but Lefty, I mean Pete, swears that losing his arm was the best thing that ever happened to him."

"Hmmm..." Joleen pondered aloud, wondering about her own war wounds.

"Honest to goodness," Nathan said shaking his head. "That's what he said."

Joleen leaned back in the chair and smiled contentedly. She turned her head and looked at Nathan.

"Were you friends in the Army?"

"No, I met him when he was in the hospital in Los Angeles."

"VA?"

"Uh huh."

"Were you wounded?"

"Oh, no. Not exactly. Actually..."

At that moment Nathan decided to go for broke. He leaned towards Joleen and smiled directly into her bright blue eyes.

"Petersen and I met on a bus. A bus from the VA that was parked in front of the USO Canteen in Hollywood."

Joleen stared intently at Nathan. Her eyes widened and she covered her mouth with her hand.

"You played music for my patients!" she cried out in a muffled shout.

Nathan smiled sheepishly and leaned back against the sofa. As he did, he slid down the slick slipcover, banging his shins again against the coffee table.

Nathan's winced from the pain and wondered if he was going to suffer some sort of injury every time he was with this woman.

Joleen cupped her hand over her mouth.

"I ran into you and knocked you over! You were the guitar player!"

"Well, I'm not sure who ran into who, but we did have a minor collision several years back," Nathan laughed.

"I was so upset. I hoped the USO would help cheer them up but it just made them feel worse. But when I came back, I remember you all were singing and laughing."

"And you promised me a lunch date the next day," he scolded her playfully. "Do you remember that? Just as you were leaving on the bus to go back to the hospital you said that maybe we could have lunch the next day at the VA."

"I did? Oh, but I shipped out next morning."

"I know, I checked. I missed out on a lunch date with a beautiful girl but ended up gaining a terrific friend in your patient, Pete Petersen."

Joleen suddenly became aware that she was still in her slippers and housecoat.

"Will you excuse me for a minute?"

"Sure. But how about that lunch you promised me? Do you have to be at work or anything?"

Joleen stopped and thought for a moment.

"If not, how about dinner?" Nathan asked. "You know you owe me one."

As had been her habit since she got out of the hospital, Joleen tried to come up with a reason not to go out. A few of her standard excuses came to mind but none could outweigh her obligatory feelings toward the guitar player who had cheered up a whole busload of wounded soldiers that she had placed in a terribly insensitive position.

"Lunch at Hotel Del Coronado!" Joleen beamed. "Much better food than the VA"

"It's a deal. I've played there several times with an orchestra but I've never eaten there."

"It's not far."

"Great," Nathan answered with a broad smile.

"I'll get dressed. Would you like some more lemonade?"

"Uh, no, no thanks, I'm fine, thank you."

They ate lunch beneath the sugar-pine ceiling of the Crown-Coronet Room in the beautiful and luxurious grand Victorian Hotel Del Coronado.

Joleen ordered a bowl of clam chowder and Nathan had the same. They talked around themselves as they waited for their meal. They talked about the hotel and Coronado Island, which wasn't an island at all but a peninsula connected to the mainland by a neck of land named the Silver Strand.

Joleen wanted to know more about Petersen so Nathan told her the whole story behind 'Lefty's'.

When their food arrived, Joleen looked down as she stirred her chowder with her spoon.

"I was captured and held prisoner by the Japanese for three years," she said quietly, keeping her eyes cast down as she crumbled crackers into her bowl.

Nathan swallowed hard.

A full minute of silence stretched like a rubber band between them until Joleen spoke up again. She was still looking down, haphazardly playing with her chowder.

"They cut off my tongue," she said quietly. "That's why I talk like this. I also lost most of my taste buds."

Nathan felt his eyes burn and soon his tears began to flow. This time he didn't question their origin.

When Nathan looked over at Joleen, she raised her head and looked up at him. There were tears in her eyes which made Nathan feel even sadder. He wanted to get up and take her in his arms, but before he could figure out what to do or say, their waiter approached their table.

Noticing that both his customers were crying, the waiter asked if there was anything wrong with their food.

Joleen glanced over at Nathan's wet cheeks, smiled at him and then looked up at the waiter and shook her head.

"Allergies," Nathan explained. "We both have hay fever. The food is just fine."

Nathan reached across the table and took Joleen's hands in his and they both let out a long sigh that seemed to stop the tears.

Nathan and Joleen finished the rest of their meal without ever saying a word. Remarkably, their silence was not uncomfortable for either in the slightest. Joleen began to feel the icy wall she had built up inside her begin to melt, while Nathan tumbled head over heels, as though weightless, into a cavernous abyss reserved only for those few fortunate souls who find themselves in the presence of their true love.

When they got up to leave, Joleen put her arm in Nathan's and they walked out of the hotel towards the beach. They stopped and sat on a low wall to take off their shoes. Still, they had not exchanged a word.

When they reached the edge of the wet sand, still arm in arm, Nathan broke the silence.

"How was your lunch?"

A voice inside his head spoke, "Now that's a pretty dumb question!"

She looked over at him and felt an expression appear on her face that seemed foreign to her facial muscles. She couldn't remember when she had looked at another human being with what, she guessed and hoped, was a loving expression.

"Wonderful," she smiled.

Nathan courageously took her hand, holding his breath and hoping that Joleen wouldn't contest his advances. She didn't and they turned and walked up the beach without saying another word, letting the waves, the sea gulls and the wind do all the talking.

On their way back to the hotel, they walked along the main street and looked in the windows of the shops and cafes. A double-feature with *National Velvet* starring Mickey Rooney and twelve-year-old, Elizabeth Taylor, along with Elia Kazan's, *A Tree Grows in Brooklyn*, was playing at the Village Theater.

"How about a movie?" Nathan asked as they looked at the posters in their glass cases lining the outside of the theater. "Have you seen these pictures?"

"Yes, I saw them last week. Wonderful movies. I'll see them again if you'd like to go," Joleen answered.

"I've seen them, too. You're right, terrific movies. In fact, I played with Gene Krupa's band for the stage show before the Hollywood premier of *National Velvet* at the Paramount Theater."

"Was it exciting to see all the stars?"

"There were plenty of them in the audience. I met a lot of famous stars during the war. How about an ice cream cone?"

They ate their ice cream and walked back to the hotel and Nathan's car. Nathan drove to Joleen's apartment, silently wishing that she lived a lot further away.

When he pulled up in front of her apartment, he got out and opened her door.

"Do you have time for a cup of coffee before you go?" Joleen asked. "You said you have some business down here?"

"I took care of it earlier this morning. I'd love a cup of coffee."

The front of Joleen's apartment building looked vastly different to Nathan than it had when he first arrived. He remembered thinking it was a citadel, a castle that was almost insurmountable and fortified with impossible obstacles. Four hours later, walking with Joleen up the shiny red walkway, Nathan felt at ease.

They sat near one another on the sofa drinking their coffee. Nathan had to take two sugars and three helpings of cream to make her strong and bitter coffee drinkable.

"What did you do during the war?" Joleen asked.

"I came out to Los Angeles from New Orleans. I tried to join up but, as I'm sure you noticed, I have scoliosis, curvature of the spine, and they wouldn't take me. I drove a gasoline truck between Los Angeles and San Diego in the beginning of the war, then I got a steady job with Freddie Martin's Orchestra. I played with them for a while and then joined the USO's Foxhole Circuit and played shows for the soldiers."

"Where did you go with the USO?"

Nathan smiled.

"Just about wherever we could find malaria, dengue fever and dysentery. Panama, Europe, the Pacific. We sort of followed the war around."

Joleen set her cup of coffee down on the coffee table, tucked her left leg under her right and turned towards Nathan.

"This may sound funny, but did you ever meet a musician in the USO that may have mentioned my name?" she asked.

Scrunched up on the sofa beside him, she looked so pretty that Nathan casually placed his hand over his heart so she couldn't see it beating so fast.

"Everywhere I went," Nathan answered proudly. "Everywhere I went."

Joleen untangled her legs and flew off the couch. She stretched her arms towards the ceiling and screamed, "It was you!"

Nathan's immediate reaction was that she was furious and about to throw something at him. He braced himself for the worst.

"There really was somebody looking for me!" Joleen began to laugh uncontrollably, so hard that she fell to her knees on the living room floor.

"It was you!" she managed to squeal between fits of laughing.

Suddenly Joleen leaped around the coffee table over to Nathan's side of the couch, bent down and kissed him fully on the lips.

Joleen drew back quickly.

"I'm sorry, please forgive me. It's just that..." Joleen stopped and started laughing again.

Nathan was speechless. He had gone from anticipating a man in his underwear answering her door to receiving a big smooch on the mouth by Joleen in a matter of a few hours.

Nathan had to clear his throat several times before any words would come out of his mouth.

"Uh, no...no apology necessary. Maybe an explanation would be in order though."

Joleen sat down in the chair next to the sofa and told Nathan the story of her rehabilitation in the hospitals at Pearl Harbor and in San Diego along with her experiences with doctors and nurses who swore to her that there was a man, a musician, who was looking for Lt. Joleen Salveson.

"I thought they were mistaken and was certain there must be another Navy nurse with my name. It was you!"

She reached over and pried his folded hands apart and held them in both of hers.

"You kept me from..." Joleen paused.

Nathan cocked his head curiously.

"I was very sad in the hospital. Like Sgt. Petersen, but I think maybe even worse. There were times I thought it would be better not to be alive than to be so sad. The things I saw, the things that happened to me... I'm ashamed of those feelings now, but then, I don't know, back then they were very, very powerful.

Joleen drew in a long breath and let it seep out between her pressed lips.

"But it seemed like whenever those feelings were strongest and they began to overwhelm me, this thought, a fantasy, would pop into my head that maybe there was someone who was really searching for me. Then I would get angry with myself for being foolish and then I'd get angry at the doctors and nurses who were telling me that there was someone looking for me and then suddenly I wasn't feeling so sorry for myself anymore. I was fighting, with myself, but I was fighting. And somehow I'd manage to make it through another day."

Nathan didn't exactly know if he had just received a compliment or a complaint.

"Can I ask you a question?" Joleen asked.

"Sure," Nathan answered quietly.

"Why did you keep asking about me when you hardly knew me?"

Nathan tried to think of a glib answer or some kind of witty line that Cary Grant or Humphrey Bogart would have come up with in a movie, something less obvious than his sappy feelings, but he came up empty-handed.

"That's a good question. I'm not sure I completely understand it myself. I can tell you that I've never done anything like that before. Of course, I've never been plowed into and knocked tea kettle over keister by an officer in the U.S. Navy either."

Joleen chuckled and Nathan bought a little time to figure out whether or not he should risk laying all of his cards on the table. In gin rummy, laying all his cards on the table would signify the end of the game and he knew he wasn't a very good card player. Then again, he and Joleen had seemed to have skipped over game playing. After what she had gone through, she deserved an honest answer.

"I'm sorry, I wish I had a more reasonable answer but somehow you came out of nowhere and, well, you just knocked me off my feet... literally and figuratively.

"When you got back on the bus, I could hardly take my eyes off you. I couldn't wait to see you the next day and even though you were gone, I couldn't seem to forget about you. If it sounds strange to you, I can tell you it sounds even crazier to me. I don't know, maybe it's like music."

Nathan paused and stared into Joleen's blue eyes.

"Like music?" she asked. "What do you mean?"

"Sometimes you hear a song just once and you never forget it. Sometimes you meet someone and you never forget them."

Nathan squirmed nervously as he waited for Joleen's response to his heartfelt confession.

After a long, contemplative pause, Joleen spoke quietly.

"I'm a lot different person now than that girl who knocked you off your feet years ago."

"Maybe to you. I hardly knew her, remember?" Nathan countered.

"She didn't know how mean people could be and she was easier to understand when she spoke."

Nathan smiled knowingly.

"Joleen Salveson, I was born and raised in Ballard, Mississippi where some folks speak their whole lives without ever moving their lips. I also lived in New Orleans where some of the accents are as thick and murky as Old Man River himself. I can understand every word you say perfectly. Besides, it's what you say that's important… not how you say it."

There was another lengthy pause in their conversation.

Nathan glanced out the window and noticed that it was getting dark. He pulled out his watch, it was almost five o'clock. He hated to leave but he knew he had to get going if he was going to be on time for his show that night.

"You have to go?"

"Yes, I have a show tonight."

"Will you come visit again, Nathan O'Shea?"

"If it would be all right with you, I sure will."

"I think I'd like that. Maybe I could make you a home-cooked meal."

Nathan paused for a moment thinking about her sour lemonade and bitter coffee.

"How about I take you out to dinner. How about next week? Do you always get Friday's off?"

"Not always, but I'll make sure to get next Friday off."

Nathan got up from the couch and walked towards the door. Joleen followed right behind him.

"I've had a wonderful day," she said. "Thank you for coming."

Joleen put her hands on his shoulders and kissed him on the cheek.

"Thank you so much," she whispered in his ear.

Standing at the rail of the ferry, looking back towards Coronado Island outlined in a faint hangover of colors left over from a wild binge of a long past sunset, Nathan struggled to translate his emotions into manageable and meaningful thoughts but they were too unwieldy and intoxicating to be sorted out, identified and analyzed. In a way, he felt like a pirate who had sailed for years in search of a legendary treasure chest and when he had finally dug it up, overflowing with jewels and riches he had only dreamed of, he had to sail away, leaving his treasure behind. Nathan just stood there, as numb to the turmoil inside him as he was to the cold, salty spray off the white caps that splashed against his face.

Nathan was an old hand at auditions and was experienced enough to know that he was no judge of what other people were thinking about him. He had played poorly in auditions and been offered the job on the spot. He had played over his head and never even got a call back.

Had he made a good impression on Joleen? It wasn't until he was half way home that he allowed himself to entertain the idea that he may have sparked a little bit of interest in her.

"Of course," Nathan thought to himself. "It might have just been gratitude from that night on the bus or possibly from making her angry during her rehabilitation and taking her out of her melancholia."

Gratitude wasn't exactly the impression that Nathan was hoping for but if that's what got him an invitation back to see Joleen again, he'd take it gladly.

And just when his own self-effacing humility was looking the other way, three blocks from his home, Nathan let out a whoop, honked his horn, and pounded his hands on the steering wheel. He'd found Joleen at last!

Prior to Nathan's surprise visit, discovering romance was about the last thing on Joleen's list of things to accomplish. The current item on top of the list was trying to pronounce her 'D's' so that they didn't come out like 'E's'.

She had never had a real boyfriend. Although she was aware that men on the street occasionally turned their heads when she walked by, she was resigned to the fact that no man would be interested in a woman with a speech impediment.

Then all of a sudden, this kind and gentle man appears at her door who admits that he has been carrying a torch for her for almost four years and isn't repulsed by the fact that she was missing most of her tongue. For a moment that night, over her re-heated dinner of meat-loaf and tomato soup, Joleen's self-protective defense mechanisms, built on expecting the worst, presented the idea that maybe Nathan wasn't coming back and that he had stayed only because he felt sorry for her. But similar to what had happened to Nathan on his drive home, when Joleen's guard was down, the young girl in her broke through the barricades and bubbled up as she turned out the light near her bed.

"He is kind of cute," she giggled into her pillow.

Every Friday for the next several months, Nathan visited Joleen in Coronado. Sometimes he'd drive his car. Other times he'd take the train to San Diego and hop the 'nickel snatcher', a passenger-only shuttle between San Diego and Coronado Island, and walk the few blocks to Joleen's apartment.

Their relationship had started somewhat backwards. Instead of the more conventional order of romance, beginning with an intro-duction, dating, courtship, intrigue, infatuation, captivation and the eventual vows of allegiance, Nathan had pledged his troth from the very beginning.

Although it only took Nathan a matter of minutes to plunge through most of the preliminary stages, which gave him a substantial head start in the development of their relationship, Joleen had yet to put even a single, pearly pink toe in the murky, swirling waters where Nathan was swimming.

She still struggled with the painful memories of her captivity on Corregidor and felt disfigured when she had to speak to others so it was difficult for her to fully comprehend Nathan's seemingly unconditional acceptance and affection for her.

Nathan, however, had learned to play music by heart instead of by chart and so he was happy to let Joleen set the tempo while he just followed along.

They went to movie matinees, avoiding war pictures which were very popular in the theaters. They walked on the beach and exchanged knowing smiles with other couples as they passed one another. They visited the flower fields in San Diego's North County and filled Joleen's apartment with fresh-picked flowers.

Joleen explained to Nathan the story behind the orchid she always kept in her house and their armloads of bouquets always included a mutually agreed upon orchid in honor of the old Japanese soldier who died on Corregidor. The end of the story of the old Japanese soldier lay buried in a dark and distant place that seemed to be getting further and further away from Joleen's memories.

It was difficult for Joleen to completely let go of her darker side. Her past was a tragedy she could not give up easily, if for no other reason than out of respect for the torture she had endured. As dire as conditions were on Corregidor, she had lived. That was something worth holding onto in her mind. But her heart had begun to grow disinterested with her embittered past when the present offered a fresh breath of promise and hope.

Joleen wanted to watch Nathan perform and see Sgt. Petersen again so she arranged her schedule at the hospital so that she could get a Thursday and Friday off.

She rode the 'Nickel Snatcher', a five-cent boat ride from Coronado to North Island, and took the train to Los Angeles where Nathan picked her up at Union Station.

He brought her to Lefty's and then left, saying he had an important errand, allowing Joleen and Pete some time alone to share and compare their lives since they had last seen one another. An instant friendship blossomed between them and Joleen found Petersen's irreverent sense of humor and his cultivated appreciation for irony to be both healthy and healing. They were drawn together by both their wartime experiences as well as their mutual feelings for Nathan.

When Nathan returned to Lefty's, Joleen and Pete were laughing and giggling. When he walked up to their booth, they both covered their mouths in an attempt to stifle their laughter. Nathan smiled at their friendly camaraderie and felt it a compliment that they were comfortable enough to make fun of him.

"All right, what's so funny, you two?" Nathan demanded.

The expressions turned innocent. "Oh, nothing," they chimed, before bursting into laughter again.

Nathan slid into the booth next to Joleen.

"I've got a room for you at the Wilshire Hotel just down the street and dinner reservations at Lawry's in Beverly Hills for seven o'clock tonight."

"Phew," Pete whistled. "Looks like Casanova here is getting ready to make his move!"

Joleen blushed and gave Petersen an elbow in the rib cage.

"We can have dinner and then come back here in time for the show," Nathan said, ignoring Petersen's remark.

"You're welcome to join us, Pete, if you'd like."

"Oh, I'd love to chaperone you two," Peterson faked a cough. "But I think I'd better stay here and keep an eye on the store."

The maître d' at Lawry's showed Joleen and Nathan to a spacious booth located along the side wall of the restaurant. The booths on the side were raised above the rest of the tables on the main floor and the red upholstered seat backs extended more than two feet above their heads. As they scooted towards the back of the booth, it was as though they had crawled into their own private nook overlooking the rest of the diners. They each ordered Lawry's famous prime rib and Yorkshire pudding, along with an expensive bottle of wine recommended by their waiter.

There were several Hollywood stars eating in the restaurant and when Bob Hope and his party walked by their booth, Hope recognized Nathan from their Foxhole Circuit tours together and stopped to say hello to Nathan.

"Can you believe it? We get to eat on top of the tables instead of under them," Hope joked. "Nice to see you again Nathan. I think we helped a little...over there, huh?"

"You were remarkable. I think the smiles you brought to those boy's faces were as good as a letter from home. Oh, Mr. Hope, this is Joleen Salveson."

"Nice to meet you, Joleen," Hope smiled. "Be nice to this guy, he's a hell of a guitar player."

As Hope walked away, Nathan was amazed that Bob Hope had remembered his name.

"I just met Bob Hope!" Joleen swooned. "He's so funny and he seems so nice!"

"I think he was about the hardest working USO entertainer of them all," Nathan said. "On stage or just horsing around with a couple of GIs in the mud, he never missed a chance to cheer the guys up."

Neither Joleen nor Nathan had much experience with drinking wine so they both assumed that that the giddy, light-headed feelings they experienced as they left the restaurant were entirely due to their being in one another's company.

When they returned to Lefty's after dinner, there was a long line outside the door.

"Gee, all these people are here to watch you play?" Joleen asked, impressed by the size of the crowd.

"Oh, not me. There are some very good musicians playing in the band tonight and a singer you're not going to believe. No, they're not here to see me, I'm just the guitar player."

Nathan never felt prouder in his life as he walked past the line with his arm around Joleen.

Joleen was surprised at the number of heads in the crowd that turned to stare at Nathan as they walked past. A few people even called out his name and whistled. Nathan only noticed the feel of Joleen's narrow waist in his right arm and her shoulder gently rubbing against his. His guitar case swung casually back and forth in his left hand.

Lefty's was nearly full when Joleen and Nathan walked into the club. They were greeted by a thick haze laced with the pungent smells of whiskey, perfume, and cigarette smoke—a severe contrast to the fresh, invigorating winds off the Santa Monica Bay outside.

Pete met them and spoke in a fairly convincing French accent.

"Madam…monsieur, may I show you to your table?"

Joleen was stunned at the transformation Lefty's had undergone since her reunion with Pete that afternoon. The quiet little tavern was now packed with people laughing and talking. There was a buzz in the room born of anticipation and excitement that made every movement and expression seem more animated than normal. Although Joleen had never been in a real nightclub before, she assumed that "the joint was jumping".

The men all seemed to be dashing and handsome and the women striking and exotic. In her plain, cream-colored, poplin dress, Joleen felt a little intimidated, surrounded by so many young, beautiful girls wearing the latest fashions of the day. Many of the dresses were short, tight, and designed to be revealing and provocative.

Pete led them to a table directly in front of the bandstand at the edge of the dance floor. There was a pretty girl sitting alone at their table.

"Mary Martinez, this is Joleen Salveson. Joleen, this is Mary," Pete announced.

Mary Martinez had long, coal black hair, almond-colored skin with wide, brown eyes, and a smile that revealed the whitest teeth Joleen had ever seen.

Nathan walked over to Mary and they exchanged kisses on the cheek.

280

"You look lovely tonight, Mary. You know, you could do a lot better than a one-armed bartender," Nathan said.

"You mean like a musician?" Mary teased.

"No, honey," Pete laughed. "He said a lot better than. What can I get you girls?"

"I'll have a Coca-Cola, please," Joleen answered.

"I'll have the same," Mary replied.

"Two Coca-Colas coming right up."

The members of the band were starting to mingle on the bandstand, laughing and talking with one another. A few were warming up their instruments and a wispy, thin black girl was testing the microphone at the front of the stage.

"Come on up and meet the guys in the band," Nathan whispered to Joleen.

Joleen again felt the eyes of the audience on her as she walked across the empty dance floor. She squeezed Nathan's hand tightly and he noticed her arm stiffen slightly. He put his arm around her and when she looked up into his face he smiled at her as though there were no one else in the world. Suddenly the stares disappeared and the room seemed empty. She felt Nathan's arm pulling her close to him, supporting her as they walked toward the bandstand.

Nathan helped Joleen up onto the stage and introduced her to all of the members of the band.

Almost all of the musicians had nicknames that either related to their physical appearance or the instrument they played. A chorus of friendly and polite, "nice to meet you, ma'am", "my pleasure" and "how do you do" echoed from the likes of 'Fat Boy', 'Cheeks', 'Red', 'Skeeter', 'Slide' and 'Tiny' who was anything but.

Nathan introduced Joleen to Sugar Brown, the female vocalist. Sugar had skin the color of cinnamon, was barely five-feet tall, and was straight razor thin. Her bright red and white striped dress was cut short, at mid-thigh. The sheer material clung so tightly to her body that Joleen could clearly see the outlines of her ribs and her small breasts. Sugar acknowledged Joleen with a warm but shy smile and then disappeared back into her own world and a song that was playing in her head.

Nathan walked Joleen back to the table and she sat down next to Mary.

"Have you heard him play yet?" Mary asked Joleen when Nathan walked back to the stage to join the band.

Joleen shook her head.

"He's really good."

"How long have you known Pete?" Joleen asked.

"We've been dating for about a year. Pete told me you two go back a ways."

Joleen smiled and nodded. "We met a long time ago."

Mary leaned over close to Joleen, "If you don't mind me saying so, Nathan seems like he's pretty twitterpated over you."

"Twitterpated?"

"You know, head over heels, mad about…twitterpated!"

Joleen blushed.

"Hmmm," Mary smiled. "Looks like you might be coming down with the same bug, huh?"

Before Joleen could come up with a reply, Pete's voice boomed out of the speakers, "Ladies and gentlemen, welcome to Lefty's."

Many of the regulars in the audience responded by calling out, "Who's Lefty?"

Pete smiled and shook his head at the band, "Looks like we've got a dangerous crowd tonight, boys. Ya'll are gonna have to watch my back." He spoke into the microphone so that the audience could hear him. "Because, as you can see, I'm unarmed."

The audience roared.

Pete turned around to the band and asked, "How do you get a one-armed man out of a tree?"

"Wave", came from a chorus of musicians

Over the din of laughter and applause, Pete continued.

"Ladies and gentlemen, how about a warm welcome for tonight's Thursday Night Jam Session All Star band featuring Miss Sugar Brown."

Joleen heard Nathan count, "One, two, three, four" and the band broke out into an up-tempo, blues number. A throng of couples jumped out of their chairs and in seconds the dance floor was packed.

Joleen stood up and peered over the tangle of gyrating bodies. She could see that Nathan and the rest of the members of the band were paying little attention to the pandemonium on the dance floor. The musicians were tuned into themselves, smiling at one another as though they were sharing a private joke and bobbing their heads to the music. They seemed to be enjoying themselves as much or even more than anybody else in the club. Joleen noticed that Nathan's slightly curved posture seemed more relaxed.

Joleen could see Sugar Brown sitting off to the side of the stage while each of the members of the band traded instrumental leads with one another. Sugar held a highball glass in one hand and a cigarette in the other. Her eyes were almost closed, as though she was about to nod off to sleep. Her head swayed sideways with the music and she wore a tight-lipped, dreamy half-smile.

Joleen sat back down and sipped her Coca-Cola. She noticed that Mary was gone and eventually spotted her on the dance floor with a young man.

Just then the band backed off to only drums and the bass fiddle.

The sudden change in the music turned the crowd's attention to the band stand where Sugar Brown now stood behind a microphone that almost obscured her thin face. Nathan gave Sugar a smile and a subtle nod of encouragement.

The drummer and the bass player paused for a moment and out of that tiny-framed, whisper of a girl, rose a voice so mean and raw-boned that the couples on the dance floor took a step backward. All conversation in the club stopped.

"Baby...you gotta stop!" she wailed as the horn section punched out a solitary one-count hit behind her and then stopped abruptly.

"Baby...you gotta stop!" she cried out again raising her voice a full octave, stretching the single word, 'baby' into a whole paragraph. Once again, the band punched out another one-count hit.

"I said baby, baby, baby, my sweet baby…" she pleaded, bent over at the waist and straddling the microphone stand between her legs, her eyes clenched tight and her free hand waving in the air.

"You better stop!"

The crowd cheered enthusiastically back at Sugar.

"You…" she sang and then cupped her ear with one hand and motioned to the audience with her other. The crowd responded with another roomful of 'oh yeahs' and 'amens'.

"You better stop!" she snarled.

Sugar opened her eyes, casting a chilling, icy glare across the room. Her voice took on a bluesy/gospel tone.

"You better stop messin' 'round on me…"

On the word 'me', the band piled on in full force with the horn section nearly blasting the roof off the club.

Most of the popular female singers of the day who fronted the big bands wore formal dresses and stood behind their microphones with their hands folded demurely. Sugar Brown worked the stage like a Southern Baptist preacher — strutting and gesticulating, jumping and waving her hands as she sang, dragging the microphone stand behind her. Every eye in Lefty's was locked on the riveting performance by Sugar Brown. At a period in America when most young men didn't even know that women perspired, Sugar Brown was spraying the front rows of the audience with sweat off her forehead.

When the song finally ended, the audience fell silent for several seconds before a wave of applause and cheers began to build.

Nathan stepped forward and put his arm around Sugar who had instantly disappeared back into her own world, seemingly unaware of the response from the crowd.

"Sugar Brown, ladies and gentlemen," Nathan announced. "You're gonna hear a lot of that name pretty soon. Hey, why don't we slow it down a little …"

Sugar Brown sat back down on her stool, lit up a cigarette, and the band broke into 'Tenderly', a popular song performed by Sarah Vaughn.

Nathan appeared at the table and surprised Joleen.

"Shouldn't you be working?" Joleen asked.

"Nah, they can handle this without me. Would you care to dance, madam?"

"Oh, I don't think...I'm not a..."

"Me either, but it doesn't look all that hard. I think the trick is to forget about all the other people on the dance floor and just let the music lead you around."

Joleen gave him a blank stare.

"Come on, Joleen," Nathan said as he helped her out of her chair.

They walked out onto the crowded dance floor. At first, they were stiff and self-conscious.

"It might be easier if we danced closer together," Nathan whispered.

Joleen stepped up into Nathan's arms, put her head against his shoulder and closed her eyes. She felt his body against hers and the side of his face pressed against her hair. At that moment, Joleen felt as though she was standing on a ledge, faced with a decision to step back to safety or take a step forward and surrender to the unknown.

*Dexter Malone was fifty-seven-years-old and had played the saxophone since he was nine. He had played with almost every popular band and singer. Up to the age of fifty, Dexter was noted for his incredible speed. His riffs were legendary for the remarkable number of notes he could jam into a four-count measure. Audiences would cheer as his fingers flew up and down the shiny brass body of his alto sax, showering them with notes like midnight confetti on New Year's Eve. Dexter could also play two saxophones at the same time, one horn on the left side of his mouth playing the harmony part to the other horn on the right side of his mouth playing the melody line.*

*At the age of fifty, Dexter Malone completely disappeared from the music scene. His wife had died unexpectedly and after burying her, he put his horn away and sold door-to-door for the Fuller Brush Company during the day and drank himself into a stupor at night.*

*Late one night, after finishing the last of a bottle of bourbon and still desperate for a drink, Dexter thought he might have stashed a half-pint away in his saxophone case as many musicians did. When he opened the case and stared down at the beautiful instrument he began to cry.*

*After that night, Dexter Malone never took another drink and discovered that he had turned into a completely different type of musician when he began to play again.*

*Instead of his old style of playing music like a hail storm, Dexter discovered that he could take one note, as though it were a lump of clay, and mold it and shape it into a work of art. Every single note he played was sculpted with character and emotion, as though it might be the last note he would ever play again.*

At the moment Joleen was dancing in Nathan's arms to the song, 'Tenderly', and struggling with the decision whether to hold back or let go, Dexter Malone stepped to the front of the stage. His head was bowed reverently as he cradled the saxophone in his hands. His eyes were closed and he seemed to be breathing in the body and fragrance of the music, like a connoisseur might test a glass of fine wine. When he was ready, Dexter brought the instrument to his lips and began to play.

Joleen would forever remember the song, Dexter Malone's solo, and the feel of Nathan's arms around her at that euphoric moment of surrender when she relinquished the memories of her past along with her uncertainty about the future to the overwhelming rapture and power of that very moment.

Joleen wilted into Nathan's arms and it seemed to her as though she were caught in the eye of a hurricane. Despite the band playing, the other dancers on the floor and the overall din of the nightclub, she felt strangely peaceful and calm.

Nathan sensed a subtle change in the way Joleen felt in his arms as they danced. He didn't realize at the time that her heart had just reached out to touch his.

Throughout the rest of the evening, Joleen and Nathan danced every slow number together.

Sugar Brown continued to ignite the audience with her exotic blend of gospel and shantytown blues and the band kept the dancers in a frenzy until, by the end of the night, almost everyone in Lefty's was exhausted. Near the end of the last set, Pete got up on stage and played trumpet with the band but even Pete, known for his unlimited energy and bounce, seemed a little spent.

When the doors were finally closed behind the last customers, Pete, Mary, Joleen and Nathan sat at the bar drinking coffee and talking about the evening. They were all worn out to the point where just trying to make conversation was an effort.

"I'm going to take Joleen back to her hotel," Nathan announced when he saw her hide a yawn behind the back of her hand. "We've got a big day tomorrow before she catches her train back to San Diego."

The two couples exchanged goodbyes and Joleen and Nathan walked out of the smoky club into the cool, damp air. Nathan took off his coat and put it over Joleen's shoulders.

"Thank you," Joleen purred, and nuzzled up against Nathan.

She kissed him on the cheek and tucked her head against his shoulder. They walked to Nathan's car, cuddled together in a silence that spoke far more eloquently about how they felt for one another than any words could ever manage to convey.

Nathan promised to pick Joleen up at the hotel at ten the next morning and take her to breakfast. He told her that he had to stop by a recording studio on the way to the train station and that they would still have plenty of time to make her one-fifteen train.

As Joleen fell asleep in her hotel room after the magical evening at Lefty's, she wondered if her new found feelings would disappear by morning.

She was so anxious to know that she asked the front desk for an early wake-up call.

The next morning, a bell hop knocked on her door at six a.m. Joleen sat up in bed and put her hand over her heart. She closed her eyes and the first thought that came into her mind was of Nathan and she felt that same euphoric lightness along with a giddy twinge of excitement anticipating the morning together. She smiled, put her arms around her pillow, and fell back into a contented sleep.

Joleen was already in the lobby when Nathan came to pick her up. She was trying to read the morning paper but she couldn't seem to pay enough attention to make any sense out of the articles.

When Nathan walked through the revolving doors, Joleen surprised them both, and everyone else in the foyer, by dashing across the lobby and throwing her arms around him.

"Good morning, "she whispered in his ear as they hugged each other.

"Good morning," Nathan purred back. "How did you sleep?"

"Very well. I've never slept in such a big bed."

"Hungry?" he asked.

"Famished!"

Nathan picked up her suitcase from the Bell Captain and they walked out into the bright Santa Monica sunshine.

It was the most beautiful morning Joleen had ever seen. She turned back and took a last look at the hotel marquee. She wanted to remember it forever. It seemed to Joleen that the world had changed overnight. Everywhere she looked there were couples in love, hand in hand, walking down the sidewalk or staring into shop windows.

They had breakfast at a New York-style delicatessen in Beverly Hills that was known for wonderful food and rude, impertinent waitresses.

Joleen ordered soft boiled eggs. Nathan ordered bacon and eggs. The waitress, recognizing Nathan as a regular, shook her head.

"We've got one hundred and twenty-four items on the menu and the best you can come up with is bacon and eggs?"

Nathan smiled. "Yep, bacon and eggs, please."

The waitress dropped her head in disgust.

"You want toast or are you gonna just scoop 'em up with your thumb?"

The waitress leaned over to Joleen, "Is he always this dull, honey?"

288

At first, Joleen was put off by the waitresses' attitude but when she saw Nathan smiling, she figured out that it was all part of the show.

"Always," she confided to the waitress.

"Poor girl," the waitress said softly and then turned to Nathan. "How do you want those eggs?"

"Scrambled, please."

"Honey, we're too busy to beat 'em. I'll bring you whatever the cook has time for," she said as she walked away.

"Are they always like this?" Joleen asked.

"Oh, yes. She may bring me bagels and lox."

"What will you do if she does?"

"Eat 'em," Nathan laughed.

They ate breakfast (Nathan got his eggs scrambled) and talked about everything that had gone on at Lefty's.

The food tasted wonderful, even to Joleen's limited attendance of taste buds, but she noticed that Nathan only finished half of his breakfast and seemed slightly distracted.

As they were leaving the restaurant, their waitress yelled at them, "You know there are plenty of other restaurants in this town that serve eggs!"

"With more polite waitresses, too!" Nathan countered back.

Nathan seemed to be nervous as they drove up into Hollywood so Joleen stared out of the window, looking at the shops and the people bustling up and down the street.

Nathan turned right off La Cienega and onto Sunset Boulevard.

"When is your appointment, Nate?"

"Oh, there's no real particular time. I just have to stop and ask someone a question."

"Think any of these people walking around are movie stars? They all look so glamorous."

"They might be. If they're not, there's a good chance that they're trying to be."

They stopped at a red light and Nathan dug a small sheet of paper out of his pants pocket. He stared at it for a few seconds and then put it back. He was fidgety and Joleen assumed that he must be anxious about his appointment so she continued to search the sidewalks and passing cars for famous people.

Nathan found an open place on Sunset and parked the car.

"Come on with me," he said as he opened Joleen's door.

"Oh, I'm all right here. You go on. Will it take long?"

"Ummm…it might. Maybe you should come along. You might find it interesting and maybe you'll see some movie stars."

Joleen got out of the car and reached out for Nathan's hand. She noticed that his palm was damp.

"Wow, this must be a real important meeting," she thought to herself.

They walked up to Cahuenga and crossed with the light to the west side of the street. The sidewalk was crowded with shoppers, tourists and businessmen. There seemed to be an abundance of beautiful young girls in the stream of people as though they were cast in a scene from a movie.

They walked for about half a block when Nathan stopped suddenly and took both of Joleen's hands in his. Passersby cast sharp glances at them as they veered around Nathan and Joleen who were blocking the sidewalk.

Joleen looked curiously at Nathan as he took in a long, deep breath.

"Joleen, I don't know if you remember, but we are standing on the exact spot where we first, uh, ran into one another."

Joleen looked around and recognized the building that was once the USO's Hollywood Canteen and was now comedy club.

"Oh, my goodness! This is where the USO was!"

Joleen was beaming but when she looked back at Nathan, he wore a serious expression on his face.

"It's like I said before, sometimes you hear a song just once and you never forget it. Well, you've been in my heart from the first moment I saw you and I'm afraid you're going to stay there until … until it just stops beating."

A fat man with a black fedora and a huge cigar sticking out of his mouth bumped into Nathan.

"This ain't no bus stop, buddy," he grumbled as he passed.

Nathan paid no attention to the man as he held onto Joleen's hands and stared into her eyes.

"I realize that I've been in love with you a whole lot longer than you've even known I've been alive, but I have to let my intentions be known to you or I'm afraid I'm going to burst."

The earnest expression on Nathan's face and Joleen's rapt attention attracted the curiosity of some of the people passing by. Several couples stopped to listen, thinking there may be something juicy going on. Other people walking by stopped to see what the others were looking at and soon a small ring of concerned eavesdroppers had circled around the young couple standing in the middle of the sidewalk. Neither Nathan nor Joleen were aware of the crowd gathering around them.

"To come right out with it, I'm asking you to marry me, Joleen Salveson."

An "ahhh" rose from the crowd and a small dog yipped, annoyed that its walk had been interrupted.

"You don't have to give me a yes or a no right now because I know this comes as a surprise and it may be a little too sudden but I just had to ask."

Nathan fumbled in his coat pocket and all heads in the crowd followed his hand. Nathan pulled out a black velvet jeweler's box.

The crowd responded with a higher pitched chorus of "ohhh".

Joleen gasped.

"The day I bought this ring for you was the happiest day of my life and no matter what you say or do, today or tomorrow, it will always be the happiest day of my life until…until the day you take it out of the box and put it on your finger. Then today will be the second happiest day of my life."

Nathan held the box out to Joleen in his outstretched hand.

The onlookers shifted their attention from Nathan to Joleen whose mouth hung open in astonishment. Somehow sensing the importance of the moment, the small dog stopped barking.

Joleen stared at the box, then up at Nathan, and then at the circle of concerned strangers surrounding them.

Nathan followed her eyes and he, too, suddenly became aware of their audience.

Joleen's porcelain Scandinavian skin blushed red. She reached out with both hands and clasped them around Nathan's hand holding the box.

"Say yes, honey," a pretty, young starlet whispered.

Others shouted their agreement and the crowd began to applaud as Joleen and Nathan broke through the ring of people.

Joleen held Nathan's hand, the soft felt covering of the box separating their palms.

When they reached the car, Nathan opened the door and Joleen slid onto the seat, still holding Nathan's hand. For a moment they both shared an equal grasp on the tiny package until Nathan felt her fingers tighten around the box and release his hand.

Nathan walked around the car and got in while Joleen stared at the still unopened box in her hand.

Although they exchanged glances a number of times, neither spoke a word during the drive to the train station.

When they reached the station, Nathan got out and took her suitcase out of the trunk. When he went to open Joleen's door, he saw that she had opened the box and was staring at the ring nestled in the slot of the black felt liner.

"It's beautiful," she whispered, not taking her eyes off the ring.

Joleen snapped the box closed and got out of the car. They walked into the station holding hands, Joleen clutching the ring box in her free hand.

"We'd better hurry," Nathan said glancing at his watch.

When they reached the platform, the Red Caps were helping passengers board the train to San Diego. Nathan handed Joleen's suitcase to one of the porters. When he turned around to say goodbye to Joleen, she fell into his arms and they kissed, a long, passionate kiss.

The porter tapped Nathan on the shoulder, interrupting their embrace.

"All aboard," he said softly. "Train to San Diego 'bout to pull out."

Nathan and the porter helped Joleen up the steps of the car. Nathan kept pace with her while on the platform, following her through the windows of the train as she walked up the aisle of the car. Joleen found a seat next to the window on the platform side of the train and smiled down at Nathan. Nathan smiled back.

Joleen looked down at her lap as the train started to slowly move away from the station. Nathan walked along beside the train keeping pace with Joleen.

Joleen looked back at Nathan and began to write on the window with her lipstick. She wrote the letters Y-E-S in reverse so Nathan could read it in big, red letters.

Nathan beamed as she held the back of her left hand against the train window. His ring was on her finger. She smiled and mouthed a slightly slurred, "I love you."

Walking faster as the train pulled away, Nathan stumbled over a bench on the platform. He got up and jumped into the air to make sure she could see him and yelled as loud as he could.

"I love you, too!"

Nathan looked down at the rip in his trousers and his bloody knee.

"I've just got to be more careful around her."

Six months later, Joleen and Nathan were pronounced man and wife by the Honorable Robert Jackson in the Santa Monica Courthouse. The short ceremony was witnessed by Ken Petersen.

Joleen quit her job at the Balboa Hospital in San Diego and was hired as a pediatric nurse in the delivery room at Santa Monica Hospital. Pediatrics was becoming the busiest ward in the hospital following the return of the soldiers at the end of the war.

Nathan found a small, two-bedroom house with a brand-new coat of yellow paint only four blocks away from the hospital, and put down a $600 down payment.

They spent their honeymoon in Thief River Falls, Minnesota.

It was a joyful reunion between Joleen and the people of her home town. She proudly introduced Nathan to nearly every person in town and they all took him into their hearts. When he played "Beer Barrel Polka" on a borrowed guitar after a dinner party at the Lindqvist's, Nathan was instantly awarded 'native son' status.

Thief River Falls appeared to have changed very little since Joleen left. The streets, houses, stores and businesses looked the same. However, they had lost fourteen sons in the war, almost one-third of the men from Thief River who had volunteered to serve. It was a grievous loss that still hovered over the small town.

Blue banners with gold stars still hung in the windows of homes and businesses. The soldiers that survived and came back to Thief River, after living through the horrors of the war, had to deal with the painful loss of brothers, relatives, and friends they had grown up with.

Joleen's presence helped ease some of the pain. After all, she was the adopted child of everyone, and had made it home safely.

The loss of children, husbands, fathers, and friends in the war by the people of Thief River Falls, helped Joleen put her own war wounds into even greater perspective. When she visited a family, who had lost a son in battle, she saw their struggle with trying to justify their loss with a sense of pride in what their lost son had done for his country and the rest of the world. It was a difficult task to ask a medal to fill a boy's empty room.

Every gold star that Joleen noticed in the window of a family she had known since she was a child, reminded her that she was fortunate to have made it back.

From her perilous swim through shark-infested waters off Corregidor and surviving three years as a prisoner of war, to standing next to a man she loved with all her heart on a warm summer's evening in northern Minnesota was an almost unfathomable journey. That some people had trouble understanding her when she spoke was a small price to pay compared to what had happened to others and what very well could have happened to her.

Joleen and Nathan left Minnesota after their two-week honeymoon deeply committed to one another and ready to begin the rest of their lives.

Over the next few years, Joleen helped coax hundreds of babies into the world while Nathan re-directed his career from the bandstand into the recording studio.

Americans had become accustomed to listening to the radio for news about the war. Now this radio audience wanted to hear music. And, if they liked what they heard, they wanted to buy the record.

Far-reaching and rapid advances in the technology of magnetic tape recording, brought about by the war (and particularly the Germans), enabled small, maverick record companies to sprout up in the shadows of giants like Capitol and RCA.

*The first widespread application of magnetic tape recording occurred during WW II when speeches by Hitler and other prominent Nazi leaders were broadcast at times and from locations calculated to confuse Allied intelligence.*

*The clarity of these speeches was so good that those Allied intelligence sources monitoring German radio were convinced that they were live.*

*Ampex Corporation of California developed the first audio recorders patterned after the German machines.*

*The first magnetic tape recording in the United States was used for the delayed broadcast of the Bing Crosby Show.*

*Eventually, American record companies used the German-designed tape-recording machines to equip their recording studios to produce music that would be pressed into vinyl records.*

The recipe for a hit record was fairly straightforward. Sign an artist, record the song on tape, press the record, and get it to the radio stations and the record stores.

The most expensive stage, in both time and money, was the actual process of recording the song.

Producers, engineers and musicians were paid by the hour, whether or not they were actually recording or just sitting around waiting for the drummer to sober up. Tempers grew short during repeated takes as musicians would make mistakes and the whole band would have to start the song "at the top" again. Fights sometimes broke out and the time it took to break them up and cool down the combatants represented costly down time for the studio and the recording company.

Eventually, record companies and producers found 'session players', experienced studio musicians, to back the artist in the studio and replace the musicians that normally toured and performed for live shows with the artist.

Session players were local musicians who were highly skilled, could read music, had the ability to play and comprehend a wide range of musical styles and, most importantly, could play it right on the first take. The best studio musicians got first call for a recording session and some of them could play two or three sessions a day for different artists, musical styles and recording companies.

Nathan was a skilled guitar player, had learned to read music on the USO tours, and had a wide breadth of styles of music he could play, whether the session called for Dixieland, swing, gospel, country-western, jazz, or anything in between.

There was also a new type of music coming out of some of the sessions. It was an exotic concoction of blues and boogie woogie that, despite all efforts to categorize it in the current status of musical styles of the day, would eventually be heralded and argued as the precursor to rock and roll.

It was a fair bet that if a recording studio was cutting a record of this new type of music, whatever they called it, 'Nate O'Shea, Guitar' would be printed on the back side of the record cover, often with the title, 'Musical Director'.

At the start of a session, even excellent and experienced studio musicians struggled to find the beat or the groove the producer and artist were looking for behind this unfamiliar music.

But Nathan had heard the rhythm behind this new music years ago while sitting on Big Ben's porch on Sunday mornings in Jackson, Mississippi when he and Ben would play along with the tambourines and the voices coming out of the Pentecostal church just up the street.

"Is this what you want?" Nathan would ask at the start of a session, strumming the rhythm on his guitar, or sometimes even turning his guitar upside down and drumming out the beat on the wooden back.

"That's it!" the producer would shout from the engineer's booth. "That's it!"

Many times, Nathan would pick up a tambourine and guide the rest of the musicians at the session down that dusty street in Jackson, Mississippi.

Three years after Nathan and Joleen were married, Joleen gave birth to a baby boy they named, Hap E. Tim O'Shea.

The tragedies that Joleen had endured on Corregidor and the dark depression she had battled after the war, had hollowed out a deep and cavernous crevasse in her soul. Time, and Nathan's rock-steady love for her, helped heal the pain from her past, leaving Joleen with a capacity to love equal to the depth of her suffering in the past.

Her love for Nathan grew stronger and deeper as time went on and her work at the hospital, handing newborn babies to their mothers, was a daily source of joy.

When Hap was born, Joleen discovered a love within her that was even greater than she could have ever imagined. Any remnant particles of her painful past were cast out by the purity of her love for her son and the innocence of his love in return.

Hap E. Tim O'Shea grew up in a home governed by love and music—both territories that knew no bounds, that bore no limits and that allowed his spirit to flourish and grow strong, wild, and occasionally reckless.

# Chapter 19

# Lunch? That would be swell!

*H*AP WAS BALANCING THREE AWKWARDLY STACKED BOXES filled with his musical instruments on the way to his van when he noticed Sarah Carolina sitting dejectedly on a bench outside the administration office.

"Hi, Sarah with an H, Twain, like the author, Carolina like the states. What are you still doing here?"

"I'm waiting for my ..."

From around the corner of the building, a young woman, at full stride, ran smack into Hap and his precariously stacked boxes of instruments. Hap and the contents of his boxes went flying in different directions. Hap ended up on his back and the instruments lay scattered over the sidewalk in front of Pine Elementary School. The collision sounded like a head-on crash between two silverware trucks. Two cymbals, a tambourine and a tom-tom rolled toward the middle of the street.

"Oh, my goodness!" the woman cried. "I am so sorry. Are you OK? I'm late for an appointment with the principal and was looking at my watch instead of looking where I was going. I'm so sorry. Are you okay?"

At the same moment Hap realized that he was uninjured, he noticed that the person who had blindsided him happened to be a very attractive woman.

"I'm fine. Hey, it was probably my fault. I wasn't exactly looking where I was going either."

Hap smiled as he got to his feet. "Are you alright?"

"Yes, I'm fine," Molly Carolina answered, picking up a shattered maraca off the sidewalk. "But I think I owe you a shaker."

"It's a maraca, mom!" Sarah corrected her mother.

"Sarah, honey, can you help this gentleman with his things, please? I should do it but I'm really late for my appointment with Mr. Bender."

Sarah's mother rolled her eyes and leaned toward Hap.

"God, I'm 34-years-old and I'm still nervous about seeing the principal," she whispered and flashed Hap a sort of 'dumb me' smile that struck him as being so cute that he was momentarily stunned.

"Me, too. Sarah and I can take care of this. You go on to your meeting with Bender. By the way, I'd take the water boarding over the bamboo under the fingernails if I were you."

"OK, water torture, no bamboo…thank you, Mr. …"

"O'Shea. Hap O'Shea."

The expression on Molly Carolina's face softened when she heard his name.

"You're Mr. O'Shea? Sarah's told me wonderful things about you. You're her favorite teacher. Oh, God, I've gotta go. Nice meeting you, Mr. O'Shea," Molly yelled looking backwards at Hap as she ran towards the principal's office.

"Nice, uh, running into you, Mrs. Carolina," Hap said as he watched her disappear through the doors of the administration office.

Sarah returned with the runaway drum and cymbals and helped Hap gather up the rest of the instruments.

"You should marry my mom, Mr. O'Shea. She's funny like you and she's really nice and I think she could help you dress better."

"Your mom isn't married?"

"Nope, it's always been just the two of us. My father was a musician but he got sick and died before I was born."

"Oh, I'm sorry, Sarah. No wonder you were so good in my music class."

Sarah shrugged her shoulders.

After a long pause, Hap asked, "Do you know why Mr. Bender wants to see your mother, Sarah?"

"I think Mr. Bender and Mrs. Armstrong believe that I planted the balloons in the garden but it wasn't me! I didn't do it, honest!"

Hap stopped packing his instruments.

"They think you planted the balloons?"

"Yea, I wanted to but Mrs. Armstrong wouldn't let me. I thought it would be neat to grow balloons but, I promise, I didn't do it!"

"I know you didn't, Sarah," Hap yelled as he took off running towards the Administration building. "I did!"

Hap burst through the front door and sprinted past the secretary.

"Excuse me, Mr. O'Shea. Mr. Bender has someone in…"

"I did it!" Hap blurted out, throwing open the door to the principal's office and planting himself in front of Mr. Bender's desk.

"I was the one who planted the balloons in the garden! Sarah had absolutely nothing to do with it!"

"You?" Bender asked.

"You?" Molly asked.

Hap turned and locked eyes again with Molly Carolina who was sitting stiffly on Mr. Bender's wooden chair, the seat the students called the 'electric chair'.

"Yes," Hap answered sheepishly. "It was me."

"Why?" Molly asked.

At the sight of Molly, Hap was momentarily distracted from his quest for justice. When he finally looked away from her, he noticed that he was holding a tambourine in his hand which broke his concentration.

"Uh, could you repeat the question, please?" Hap asked.

Molly smiled at Hap as he self-consciously put his hands behind his back trying to hide the tambourine.

"Why did you plant balloons in the garden?" Molly repeated.

Mr. Bender sat at his desk with his mouth agape, trying to follow the conversation between Hap and Molly, his head turning side-to-side as though he were watching a game of ping pong.

"Why? Well, I've got Sarah, or I used to have Sarah, in my music class and…"

"What do you mean you used to have Sarah in your music class, Mr. O'Shea?" Molly interrupted.

"Call me Hap."

"Hap?"

"Yea, it's a long story."

"OK, Hap. Why isn't Sarah still in your music class?"

"Uh, I got fired today."

"Fired?"

"Yes, fired."

"Sarah loves your music class. Do you mind if I ask why you were fired?"

"Oh, it could have been anything. Excessive noise from my class-room, bad taste in clothes, the marching band incident…"

Mr. Bender cleared his throat, "There are also budgetary consider-ations, Mr. O'…"

"The marching band incident?" Molly interrupted, a stitch of a smile betraying the indignant tone of her voice.

"Yeah," Hap grinned. "Well, it seemed like a good idea at the time."

"So, what happens to your music class?" Molly asked.

Hap shrugged his shoulders and they both turned toward the principal."

"Well," Bender began, "due to …"

"Budgetary considerations…?" Molly and Hap chimed simultane-ously, surprising one another.

"Ok, we can get to that later. Mr. O'Shea, uh Hap, why did you plant the balloons?" Molly asked.

"Sarah is, or was, in my music class and it doesn't take a genius to see that she is obviously a bright, curious and imaginative kid. Of course, I'm sure I'm not telling you anything about your daughter that you don't already know, Mrs., uh Miss…"

"Molly."

"Molly? I love that name!" Hap gushed.

"Thanks," Molly smiled. "Please go on."

"Anyway, Molly, one day I'm in the Teacher's Lounge and happen to overhear Sarah's teacher, Mrs. Armstrong, talking to you on the phone about how difficult Sarah was and how she was disrupting her class and that she wanted to grow balloons, which, by the way, sounded like a really cool idea to me. By the way, Mrs. Armstrong is just an old, dried up, mean-spirited, vindictive..."

"Mr. O'Shea!" the principal shouted. "That's enough!"

"It's true, Bender. She's not a teacher. She's a cantankerous, ill-tempered disciplinarian who doesn't have a clue how to deal with an intelligent and imaginative student like Sarah. I know, I had a teacher just like her once who told me that I would never amount to anything..."

Hap paused, looked down at himself holding the tambourine behind his back. "OK, well maybe I'm not a good example."

Molly laughed out loud and felt herself starting to like this guy.

"So, you thought it would be a good idea to..." Molly continued.

"I don't know, maybe it was a dumb thing to do. I never would have done it if I ever thought anyone would get in trouble, especially Sarah," Hap said, casting a reproachful look towards Mr. Bender.

"I guess I just felt that I had to score one for the kids who believe in things beyond the ordinary."

Molly stared at Hap and sensed the genuineness that lay beneath his comedic front.

"Maybe I did it to give Armstrong a kick in the pants. Maybe I did it for all the kids she bullied. I don't know, maybe I did it for myself when I was Sarah's age."

There was a long pause as Molly, Hap and Mr. Bender exchanged glances.

"Dr. Carolina, in lieu of Mr. O'Shea's admission, I believe I owe you..."

"Doctor?" Hap interrupted, obviously impressed.

"I'm a veterinarian," Molly answered.

"Cool," Hap grinned.

"Mr. Bender, in lieu of an apology to me and my daughter..." Molly repeated his phrase in a sarcastic, sing-song voice. "I think three things need to happen here," quickly changing her tone into a more serious and business-like manner.

The principal cleared his throat and turned his attention to Molly. "Yes, Miss Carolina?"

"One, I want my daughter out of Mrs. Armstrong's class. Immediately!"

Bender began scribbling on a notepad in front of him.

"Do you have a problem with that, sir?" Molly asked.

"No, ma'am, Sarah will be transferred to Mr. Dierker's class in Room 8 beginning tomorrow."

Molly looked over at Hap.

"Mr. Dierker?"

Hap smiled and nodded approvingly. "He's cool."

"Thank you, Mr. Bender. The second thing that needs to happen is that you should seriously consider the reinstatement of Mr. O'Shea and his music class."

The principal dropped his pen, took off his glasses and rubbed his forehead.

"Dr. Carolina…" Bender groaned.

"Mr. Bender, I have a sense that Mr. O'Shea is probably the best teacher you have at this school and that reinstating him would save me a visit to the school board regarding this incident, including your false accusations toward my daughter, along with Mrs. Armstrong's obvious lack of compassion for her students."

Bender brought both hands up to his head and began to massage his temples. He let out a long exhale and picked up a folder off of his desk.

"This is your file, Mr. O'Shea, and these are your termination papers that I was going to forward to the district this afternoon. I can replace the termination papers with a reprimand, which would mean you still have your job here. Not because of Dr. Carolina's well-intentioned threat, it's evident to me that you do care a great deal about your students and I would imagine that you have the potential to be a good teacher one day but you must assure me…"

"No more planting balloons. No more marching bands, I promise!" Hap announced, raising his right hand in the air.

"Thank you, Mr. O'Shea," Bender said wearily.

"Now, Dr. Carolina, I believe you asked for three concessions. Did I miss something?"

"No, sir. My third request is that you excuse Mr. O'Shea at noon tomorrow afternoon so that I can take him to lunch."

Bender squinted over his glasses at Hap.

"That would be entirely up to Mr. O'Shea's discretion, Dr. Carolina."

Molly reflected Bender's expression toward Hap.

"Lunch?" Hap smiled so wide his lips almost disappeared. "That would be swell! That would be swell!"

# About The Author

ROBERT GARRETT SERVED AS A U.S. ARMY CORRESPONDENT covering East Asia as a stringer for Associated Press, United Press International and Stars and Stripes Newspaper. Following his term of active duty, he was a Copywriter for J. Walter Thompson Advertising Agency; Marketing Director for Sepia Magazine, a monthly magazine for the Black readership; and Program Director for the USA Olympic Volleyball Team.

Garrett's previous works include a screenplay entitled 'Scrum', a comedy about rugby and 'Wake Up', a musical stage play with 16 original songs about saving the environment that has been licensed to be performed in Europe. The stage play script is currently being adapted for an animated movie (see www.wakeupthemusical.com). He has also recorded three original albums.

Garrett received his BA in Zoology from UCLA and his MS in Fisheries Science and Aquatic Ecology from the University of Arizona. He is currently a Professor of Biology at Palomar College in San Marcos, California and a guitarist with the Fabulous Pelicans, a world traveled rock and roll band. (see www.pelicansband.com).

CPSIA information can be obtained
at www.ICGtesting.com
Printed in the USA
JSHW021718131122
33069JS00004B/15